FIRESTORM

I'm Your Man Series

Book Three

Blaine Kistler

Book and cover design by eBook Prep
www.ebookprep.com

February, 2018

www.blainekistler.com

DEDICATION

CHAPTER 1

The fire raged out of control. Puma knew it. O'Shea, the incident commander, knew it and the crew knew it. Once it jumped the fire line, the inferno would engulf the nearby settlement of summer homes and race toward the river, feeding on every tree, bush and animal in its path.

It shouldn't have happened.

Normally the smokejumpers would have contained the blaze quickly and been heloed back to base, but within minutes of landing Puma knew his men couldn't hold it. He'd radioed and asked for the dispatch of a hotshot crew and air tanker drops of fire retardant. Command had waited too long to act.

Five hours later, Puma's head lifted skyward at sound of the powerful engine of the air tanker coming in at two-hundred feet above tree level. Accompanied by the cheering of his besieged crew, the tanker made four drops, two at the head of the fire and one at each flank, dumping its cargo of red rain, a mixture of water, clay, fertilizer and red dye. The retardant coated the trees and brush and knocked back the flames.

His men worked feverishly to take advantage of the reprieve, but the wind never let up and the forest was a tinderbox of duff and drought-stricken vegetation. By the time the hotshot crew arrived, the smokejumpers had fought the blaze alone for eighteen hours, and the perimeter included several hundred acres. Four hours later it doubled.

"Can you hold her?"

Puma turned to the sound of Sheriff John Achenbach's anxious voice. "No. We'll pull back to the safety zone. I'm waiting to hear from the Command Post, but it'll burn now until the front hits the river. Pray for rain."

"Hasn't rained in four months. Don't know why it would today."

"It's the damned wind. Everything we throw at the perimeter isn't enough. The dragon's out of control."

The sheriff hacked a cough as a new blast of smoke engulfed them. "It sure enough is a bad one. Them tankers and helos been dumping retardant for hours. Over fifty men battling the blaze. You'd think that'd do the trick."

Too little, too late. Puma held his tongue. The system had failed, but it wasn't his place to say it publicly. A Type Two Incident order should have been issued when he first radioed in, but they sat on their hands at the Command Post and hoped the smokejumpers would take care of it. He'd put that in his report. There would be a review and a bland explanation offered to the public, placing the blame on his smokejumpers. It was infuriating. But for now, Puma's concern lay in getting his crew to safety before the situation turned deadly.

"My men and I are out of here," Puma said. "You're sure your deputies checked each cabin and trailer at the camp?"

"Knocked on every door. Everybody's been took to safety. Shame about the homes, though. Looks like everything will burn clean to the ground."

"We gave it our best, sheriff. My people worked themselves to the bone, with no rest and nothing but cold rations on the run for twenty-six hours. They're dirty, hungry and exhausted."

"I know that, son. Mother Nature done beat you is all. I'd pin a medal on every last one of you men."

"Men and women. The women firefighters held their own today."

The sheriff nodded in agreement. "I'd best round up my deputies."

Puma yelled at his number two man and gave the pullout signal, his voice swallowed by the furious roar of the dragon's fire. Jackson waved in understanding. The men were expecting it. Jackson's face was black behind his protective facemask, his helmet and yellow Nomex suit coated with ash. They all looked pretty much the same. The crew packed up and headed for the trucks. They'd regroup and start controlled backfires when the wind died, but command would have to send in fresh firefighters. These men were reamed out.

His radio squawked, and he flipped on the switch. "Ansari."

"Pull back. She's crowning on the east flank and the wind's shifted."

"Roger that." No need to mention he'd ordered the exodus five minutes ago.

He kept careful count as his men sprinted toward the trucks that would take them to the safety zone. It was his job to be sure everyone got out. Anyone left behind would be lucky to make it alive. The fire would move faster than a man could run. With the last crewmember and the equipment aboard, Puma took a final look around, squinting his eyes through the curtain of smoke. Everyone was accounted for, but he'd seen a slight movement in the surrounding brush.

The smoke cleared briefly. An animal crouched in the tall grass near the fire perimeter, his tawny fur matted and streaked with soot. Puma had a stab of pain and recognition. A cougar. The mountain lion was Puma's animal totem, foretold by his grandfather to bring his grandson a life of luck and prosperity. Superstitious nonsense. But whatever the reason, Puma supposed he'd had his share of luck in some tight situations.

The animal must be sick. All wildlife had moved toward the river long ago. Nothing he could do for the doomed beast, but he wished for a gun to end its misery fast.

The mountain lion rose with fluid grace. He nursed a gimpy back paw but looked healthy enough. Puma reached for a stone and threw it toward the animal, hoping it would take the hint and vacate the dangerous ground. The cougar halted and looked back to the summer settlement, his tail switching. His massive head swiveled toward Puma as if he expected him to follow.

Puma threw another stone. "You're on your own, boy! Vamoose!"

The huge cat responded with a snarl and sprang toward the cabins. Puma shrugged and trotted after the truck, the animal no longer his concern. The wind wailed a piercing lament and the flames roared an answer. Fire licked at his boots and his men shouted at him to hurry. The smell of burning pitch permeated the air. The head of the dragon crept toward them with the deadly intent of a fast-moving freight train. He hauled ass onto the truck bed and straddled the water tank and jumble of high-pressure hoses. Time to go.

A sharp crack of sound split the acrid, smoke-laden air.

What the hell? A gunshot? He swiveled toward the campground, questioning what he'd heard. The wind spat live coals ahead of the front and many of the roofs already smoldered. Within minutes the settlement would be consumed in a holocaust. The place appeared deserted but he'd heard a gunshot, he was sure of it.

Someone was still in there.

The cougar snarled and stood beside the manmade trench that separated the camp from the advancing flames. His amber eyes drilled a message. *Follow me!*

No mortal animal would behave like this. Puma's heart thudded heavily. One other time such a beast had appeared and lingered in a similar watchful fashion. That was the day Puma rode his stallion deep into his ancestral homeland and scattered his Ute grandfather's ashes from a sacred mountaintop, a view that few white men had ever seen.

Puma scrambled over the tangle of hoses, and hammered his fist on the truck roof. "Jackson! Turn it around! I'll drive."

Jackson and Tim Hardesty were the only two in the truck. The rest had departed for the safety zone. Obediently, Jackson spun the truck into reverse. Hardesty opened the driver's door, Jackson scooted over and Puma jumped into the driver's seat. Squinting to clear his blurred eyesight, he drove along the rutted pathway, their vehicle enveloped in a haze as thick as syrup and caustic as lye.

"Where to, boss?" Jackson croaked.

"Back to the campgrounds. I heard a gunshot."

Hardesty leaned forward, nose against the windshield. "Anybody at that camp'll be dead of smoke inhalation within minutes, boss. I can't see squat. How do you know where you're going?"

Puma knew where to go because he followed the trail of the big cat. He didn't know why, just that there wasn't an option. "Did you catch sight of the big mountain lion? Either of you?"

Both men shook their heads and frowned, clearly thinking he'd lost his mind. "Boss, you're seeing things. Any critter with sense is gone," Jackson said. "So what the hell are we doing here?"

"I know what I heard." Puma kept the cougar in his sights as the animal jumped puddles of smoldering grass and loped toward a cabin on the fringe of the grounds. The dwelling's front door stood open and the elusive cat bounded inside. Puma halted the truck and climbed out. "Turn it around, Jackson, and leave the motor running. Hardesty, come with me."

His men might think he was nuts, but they obeyed orders and both of them were fearless. His eyes streaming tears, Puma groped his way up the cabin steps, Hardesty at his heels. The smoke lessened inside the dwelling. An elderly woman sat in a chair by her kitchen table, holding a gun. A dead dog lay at her feet. She raised the gun to her temple.

"Don't!" both men shouted.

"We'll get you out, ma'am!" Puma said urgently. "Just put the gun down."

She looked at him with dull red eyes, the gun wobbling at

her temple. "I had to shoot Blarney. I couldn't let the fire get him. Burnin's no way to go. Guess I'll see him soon."

Her finger tightened on the trigger and she closed her swollen eyelids. Hardesty swore and lunged toward the woman. Puma held out an arm and stopped him. "What about the cat, ma'am? You going to let him suffer?"

She opened her eyes and her fingers went lax. "Cat?"

Both men leapt at the same time and grabbed the pistol. She looked at them in puzzlement. "What'd you go and do that for? I only got two bullets left."

She sagged against the chair, mumbling in protest. Puma and Hardesty exchanged glances. No time to argue. The woman was in shock; her faded blue eyes stared at them vacantly.

Hardesty tore off his Nomax jacket and wrapped it around her. "Can you walk, ma'am? We can carry you."

"I need my cane. It's back there somewhere." She waved in the general direction of the rear of the cabin.

"Not necessary, ma'am. We'll help you and you'll do fine," Puma soothed.

She struggled to her feet and stood docilely while the two firemen each took an arm and carried her to the truck. The second they piled in, Jackson hit the accelerator. Hardesty squeezed next to Jackson, the woman sprawled on his lap. Puma's hip jammed painfully against the door handle, but no one complained. To be out there on foot meant certain death.

The smoke cleared enough they could see the bare outline of the primitive road. A wall of flame lay ahead, behind, and flanked each side of the pickup. Jackson plunged through the inferno, his foot to the floorboard. Puma swore and pulled his bare hand from the metal doorframe. The interior panels were blistering to touch. The woman's unconscious head lolled against Hardesty.

The bitter smell of burning rubber filled the truck. "The tires are on fire!" Jackson shouted. "We're not making it!"

"Keep going!" Puma shouted back. "Another two miles we'll be below the fire line." The motor whined in agony as Jackson kept his foot to the floorboard.

The woman opened her eyes. "I don't have no cat."

She immediately went unconscious again. If the truck stalled, the men would have to carry her. Puma wasn't much for praying, but he sent a silent appeal to the spirit of his shaman grandfather. A plea that was denied as the truck shimmied to a halt, the engine blown. The firemen swore simultaneously. Either Puma's grandfather hadn't heard or wasn't listening.

All three men piled out. Glowing ashes seared the soles of their boots. Puma tossed the woman over his shoulder and they started down the trail at a run. When he lagged behind, Hardesty took over. Five minutes later Jackson took a turn. The woman passed between them like a lumpy sack of potatoes, moaning occasionally.

Still, none of them questioned that they'd make it. The air grew cleaner, and more breathable; the smoke wavered and became a thin, opaque veil. "The safety zone, brush monkeys!" Hardesty shouted. "Straight ahead, maybe a hundred yards. We made it."

"Damn," Jackson said, stopping to remove his helmet. He swabbed at his filthy, streaming forehead. "That was close. How the hell did you know the woman was in that cabin, Ansari? She going to be okay?"

"I figured the gunshot for a distress signal. Let's get her to the medical tent."

Puma eased the woman to the brittle grass. "Bring a stretcher, Hardesty. I think she'll be okay but she's in rough shape."

Grunting in agreement, Hardesty took off for the temporary medical facility. Puma elevated the woman's head on his bent knee and reached for his water bottle to moisten her white lips. Fright and the jarring run had wrecked her physically. She needed immediate treatment for shock.

"Outta a dozen cabins you drove right to hers," Jackson continued to argue.

"Blind luck. I knew the general direction and spotted the open cabin door. Get something to eat and catch some sleep, Jackson. We'll be on this bitchin' fire again in four hours."

Jackson refused to budge. "I'll wait and help with the stretcher. What was that about seeing a mountain lion?"

Puma shrugged. "Wasn't one. Big Ernie, playing tricks with my eyesight."

Big Ernie, the smokejumpers' capricious god. Like the coyote deity of Native American folklore, Big Ernie was a god with a bizarre sense of humor. A trickster who toyed with the fate of puny mortals and laughed while they twisted in the wind. Every smokejumper believed in him, whether admitted to or not.

Jackson snorted. "Big Ernie blows engines, cuts fire hose and jams ripcords. Don't know as he fools with our eyesight."

"Yeah, well, here's Hardesty. Lend a hand." The three men lifted the unconscious woman to the stretcher and carried her to the medical tent, Puma grateful for the reprieve from Jackson's probing questions.

The cougar had been close enough that Puma could smell his feral breath and see the corded muscle ripple beneath the tawny hide. Every civilized teaching ingrained in him struggled against what Puma knew deep in his bones. That the spirit of his grandfather watched his grandson through the eyes of the cat.

CHAPTER 2

———◆———

Eight months later

Puma stripped and stepped in the shower, grateful to ease his stiff muscles under the steaming water. The rugged workout had left him regretting the winter's excesses. Too much food and soft living. Fat season, the smokejumpers called it, and he had less than a month to get in shape. Failing the annual fitness test meant turning in your gear, and that wasn't an option.

The doorbell chimed over the drum of the sluicing water.

He shut it off and slid back the shower door, narrowed his eyes and listened. It was late. Almost midnight, and his ranch lay a mile from the nearest neighbor. Not that someone after his scalp would enter by the front door, but uninvited guests didn't venture near Sundance. If a snarled warning didn't suffice, the German Shepard could knock a two-hundred pound man flat and keep him there.

Why wasn't the dog barking?

Puma toweled off quickly and pulled on his jeans. His inner eye served him well, and instincts inherited from his shaman grandfather warned trouble lurked behind the door. He yanked it open, ready to take someone's head off. "Yeah?"

The woman stood in the shadows, her face concealed in the depths of his porch. Her tawny hair gleamed under the artificial light. Like the moonlight. No, not moonlight. The shaggy tumble over her shoulders was too warm for that. Not the coolness of moonlight, but the dappled bronze-gilt of sunlight streaming through an aspen grove. Her clothing blended into the night and added to the illusion of a faceless phantom. Black trousers, a black tee shirt under a jacket of muted tweed. She wore arrogance like perfume.

His heart thumped in his chest.

He'd had no warning, no premonition of this. Nothing to prepare him for the sexual reaction that sliced his gut. The sensuality emanating from the phantom woman who stood on his porch staggered him. He pitched his voice low, to a growl of menace.

"Who are you? Show yourself."

She stepped into the light. "Sorry. I know it's late. I'm Rachel Cortez."

Her face shimmered into focus and became a beautiful woman. Creamy skin, brilliant emerald eyes. Her light scent hovered just out of reach. Sweet clover, maybe. Again, he endured a clutch to his gut. He'd preferred the phantom to reality. It made no sense. She wasn't his type of woman at all.

She was tall and thin, almost bony. Only the luxuriant, amber hair softened the image. She wore boots with high heels and the two of them stood eye to eye. He favored small women, dark-haired and dark-eyed. Cuddly, submissive women. Women that he could tuck under his chin, who would follow his lead in bed. He'd never been emotionally unfaithful to Sadie. Even ten years after his wife's death, he had a woman only when his sexual appetite clawed so fiercely that he gave in to it or lost his sanity.

Always he took soft, Rubenesque women.

This woman was not soft.

He swept cold eyes in her direction. "State your business."

"Could I come in? It's personal. That is, it's business and personal."

"FBI business is never personal."

Her lips curved. "They told me you were good. What gave me away?"

"Other than the pistol holstered on your belt? The attitude, lady. I've dealt with you people before. Let's see your badge."

Still smiling, she palmed the badge from her jacket pocket. "Can I come in now, Mr. Ansari?"

"We weren't introduced. How do you know who I am?"

She looked him up and down, the smile replaced by a dispassionate stare. "Fletcher, aka Puma, Ansari. Thirty-four years old," she recited. "Ex-Delta, expert smokejumper. Five-foot ten and a half inches tall. That gives you a half-inch on me. Weighs in at one-seven-two. Dark hair. Bronze-skinned from one side of his family tree, blue-eyed from the other. Meaner looking than the file photo. Cheekbones that could cut ice. A sensual mouth—"

She bit her lip, shutting off the speech with an unladylike mutter.

He folded his arms over his bare chest, amused despite his distrust. "I doubt all of that is in my file. Why should I let you in?"

"Talk about attitude."

He laughed. Couldn't help it. "You nailed me."

"I brought an old friend who wants to talk."

Ah, now it made sense. "So, is Hooker lurking in the vicinity?"

The voice came from ten feet away, the man cloaked in the darkness of night. Puma knew the voice. Crisp, authoritative. "Here, Ansari. Let the lady in. She has a case to state, and it needs to be done in private."

Grudgingly, Puma opened the door. There weren't many men he respected enough to overlook his screaming instincts for self-preservation. Dan Hooker was one of them.

She stepped inside, bringing her female scent into his

house. Hooker followed. The hair rose on the back of Puma's neck as she brushed past his shoulder. He was crazy to let her get within ten feet. He'd listen politely, and then hustle them out the door.

He remembered his duties as host. "Could I get you something to drink? Coffee? Soda?"

"I'd take a beer." Hooker's deep voice rumbled as he shrugged out of a leather jacket and tossed it on a nearby armchair. Dan Hooker taking a drink? And out of his usual three-piece tailored suit? Puma's inner voice screamed again. Whatever the pair's business, it wasn't official.

"Nothing for me," Rachel said. "Shall we get down to it?"

The tone of a woman used to taking charge. If his instincts weren't so busy shouting at him, Puma would have found that an amusing challenge.

Puma glared at the long-legged woman prowling the perimeter of his living room, his temper at low boil. "Absolutely not. I won't even debate this. She'd never stand up under the physical demands."

He wasn't having much luck in getting his uninvited guests to leave. Hooker was settled into the most comfortable chair in the room and looked like he planned to grow roots there.

The FBI man took a deliberate swallow of his beer. "She's a quick study, Puma. And tougher than she looks. She'll do."

Puma jumped up from the couch and began his own pacing. "Dammit, Hooker, do you know what you're asking? It takes months of training to master the techniques of smokejumping and firefighting. And it never stops being dangerous."

The woman, Rachel, halted and faced him. "I'm not a doormat here. Include me in this discussion, please. I can perform any task necessary, Ansari."

Puma hadn't bothered to don a shirt to answer the door. Why should he? It was his house, and he was decently covered. Still, her scathing glare made him feel naked and he wished he'd taken time to pull on a shirt. And boots. She irritated him. She was too tall and too flinty for a woman. Too snippy. And her buddy-buddy way of referring to him by his last name annoyed him. Even more annoying was the fact that Sundance was crouched in the corner of the room, tail thumping expectantly. When Rachel bent to scratch his ear, Sundance quivered and whined, his brown eyes mooning over the sexy witch. Damn worthless dog was in love.

No question the woman radiated sensual heat. It made a man wonder if she'd take that same energy to bed. He fantasized tangling his fingers in that tawny mass of curls and shutting that lush, smart-alecky mouth with a thorough kiss. Of suckling those delicate breasts until she moaned with pleasure. There's a woman somewhere under that hard-ass exterior. Bet you wouldn't be so snarky flat on your back, baby. It would be fun to find out.

Dangerous thoughts. He had to get rid of her.

Puma turned his attention to the FBI man who watched them both with amusement he didn't bother to conceal. "Send me a man to train, Dan. I'll do it if you send me a man."

Hooker raised his eyebrows. "A woman is less likely to be suspected as a plant. Rachel's worked undercover before, and she's good at it. This is important, Puma, or I wouldn't ask. I need her to establish a credible cover in three weeks, and I can't go through regular channels."

"Why?"

"You figure it out." The FBI man's face darkened.

"You have a leak? Where? In the Denver office?"

Hooker waggled his beer bottle. A gesture that could mean yes or no, but he wasn't going to discuss it further. "Just take my word for it. Washington Okayed going off the books for this one, so we're covered. You know I wouldn't shag you, Puma. And you owe me a favor."

"You never proved a thing with that Hoover Dam business. I was a tourist tooling around the desert on my dirt bike. Nothing illegal about that."

Hooker barked the sound he called a laugh. "Caught on the bluff overlooking the dam, carrying a recently fired M40 rifle. The same caliber that took out the terrorists' pickup. Personally I'd have pinned a medal on you, but you know those boys in Washington. By-the-book types and starchy about civilians interfering with fed business. You and your Delta pal left a lot of bodies behind."

"Not all our work. Your people did their share," Puma said. "If the nuke had destroyed the dam, the body count would have been a lot higher."

"The Bureau took responsibility. We kept you out of it."

"Because you didn't want a panic. Charging Jake and me would have made it public."

"No need to give other crazies the wrong ideas," Hooker nodded. "We stopped them. You helped. That's what's important."

"A dead terrorist is better that a live one any day."

"No argument. That's why I'm here. We need to establish how deep this conspiracy goes and crush it."

"I know you're working with the FBI anti-terrorist task force, Dan. So whatever this is about, it isn't local."

"We think our old pals, the New Sons of Liberty, have reorganized. This time they're going after our forests, planning to burn and destroy as much property and as many lives as possible in the process."

Puma shook his head. There had been devastating fires earlier than normal this season, but the experts, and Puma was considered one of them, blamed it on the drought and unusual high winds. After two years of inadequate rainfall, much of the natural forest system was tinderbox dry.

"A small number of fires we deal with are arson, no question," Puma conceded. "But most are natural phenomena, lightning strikes, spontaneous combustion, and some are purely manmade carelessness. You have evidence there's a terrorist conspiracy to burn the forests in Colorado?"

"Not just here. California. Arizona. Oregon."

"Whoa! You're talking about something that widespread?"

"Yes," Hooker nodded. Hooker never used two words where one would do.

This was troubling. Dan Hooker was a good agent and a careful one who believed in solid evidence before he made an arrest. Given the proper motivation and weapon, Puma could knock a squirrel from a tree at 700 meters. Call it frontier justice, if terrorists were burning his forests, Puma would find them and bring them down.

He didn't need the woman for that.

He shifted his attention to her again. "What's her angle?"

"She's usually based in New York. No one around here knows her, which is a definite plus."

"I don't know her, Dan. I won't baby-sit a rookie who could get herself killed on my watch. Send me a man to train, give me six weeks to get it done, and I'll pay off that favor."

Baby-sit! Rachel's temper slipped into the red zone. She'd been letting the two males duke it out, but enough was enough. She hissed a protest. "If I might have a word, gentlemen?"

Hooker shot her a warning look, which Rachel ignored. So he was her superior and her boss. He was getting nowhere with the stubborn Mr. Ansari and this was too important. Her career was on the line. The FBI promotion system guaranteed equal treatment of the sexes, but if she were turned down for this assignment because she was a woman, there would be consequences. Subtle, but nonetheless damaging, and her personal ambitions would be scotched.

She walked toward Fletcher Ansari and pursed her lips, turning on the sugar, appealing to his reason. "Look, why don't you hear me out? I'll make you a deal."

The half-naked savage glared at her and stepped closer, threatening her by force of his personality. "What deal? The only deal I want is for you to leave."

Rachel swallowed. Damn, the man intimidated her. An aura of menace shimmered around him like body heat. She was used to working with dangerous men, but this one was in a class by himself. She'd read his records and knew he'd performed deeds that were legendary while in the service, that he'd volunteered for missions no one else would consider. He was a loner with his own code of honor and as far as anyone knew, incorruptible. Also, it seemed, unbendable.

She would have to be very careful.

Fear wasn't in this man's makeup, and he would have no patience with it in others. She had to keep her secret close. He would be contemptuous with her terror of fire, no matter the reason. Perhaps facing her old nightmare would conquer it.

"Hooker thinks if anyone can get me ready in three weeks, you can."

"I didn't say I couldn't. I said I wouldn't."

"Because I'm a woman."

He hesitated. "Yeah. Because you're a woman."

"There're women firefighters. There's one on your duty list." Thank God she'd done her homework. He'd have to find a better reason than her gender to refuse Hooker's request.

"Jeanette? She's a pro. You're not."

"But you could turn me into one."

"Not in that amount of time. Do you have any idea what's involved?"

Good, she had him talking. That was progress.

Out of her side vision she saw Dan Hooker lean back and relax. Her boss would let her run with the ball, at least for a while. She looked the firefighter in his Viking eyes, and felt a stir in her belly when his pupils warmed and darkened. Any woman breathing would've been attracted to him. The superb body, the sensual mouth, and the subtle bad boy mystique that presented an unspoken dare to a female. *Tame me if you can.* Wouldn't it be fun to try?

He smelled of freshly showered male and carnal knowledge. She itched to tangle her fingers in the damp hair, to soften that hard, whiskered jaw with a brush of her lips. No question it would be stimulating. She took a deep breath and shook off the thought. She wasn't here to play with the man, tempting as the idea was. Humility. She'd go with humility. "You're right, I don't know what's involved. So tell me."

"You need a valid red card to get a job with any firefighting unit."

"No problem. Hooker can get me one."

"Not a legit one. If you want me to sign off on your red card and place you on my team, you earn it."

"How?"

"Minimum three months of class work. A year in the field. That will qualify you for certain positions. Not smokejumper. That calls for more extensive training."

She brushed that aside. "I don't plan to do this fulltime. Just long enough to catch the psychos who're setting these fires. All I need is enough basic knowledge to carry off my cover story."

"Just enough to make you dangerous, you mean. I have my people to think of, and we're a team. One rotten link could endanger us all."

"I'll work hard. Do what it takes to pull my weight."

He stared at her like she was a lower life form. "You'd ruin your manicure, sweetheart. Wouldn't want that, would we?"

She looked down at her hands. Her hands were one of her few vanities and she kept them creamed and the nails polished. Her breasts were small, her legs too long and ugly, but she had pretty hands. "To hell with my manicure. All I'm asking is a week. If I can't cut it in a week, I'll back off and let Hooker recruit someone else. A man."

"A week? How about a day?"

"Try me."

His grin widened to the smirk of a winner. "Okay, it's a deal. You get a day. Drop and give me twenty."

She blinked. "Excuse me?"

"You heard me. If you can't do twenty pushups, no need to go any further. Actually, to pass the physical test, you need to do forty, but I'm taking into consideration you're not used to our altitude. So. Drop and give me twenty." He stepped back and gestured at the floor.

Panicked, she looked at Hooker. Her boss shrugged. She was on her own.

"Right here and now?"

"Good a place as any. And keep your knees off the floor, Cortez."

She could do this. Damn, she hoped she could do this. She did a few pushups as a part of her daily fitness regime, and she kept in shape. Agents were tested for physical fitness once a year, and she'd never had a problem passing. Clamping her jaw, she sat on the floor and pulled off her boots. A glance up through her lashes revealed a smug Fletcher Ansari with his hands on his straddled hips, triumph gleaming in his feral eyes. Her boss appeared to have dozed off in his easy chair. It would be no problem to hate them both.

She flopped over on her belly. Turn your mind off, Rachel. Suck it up.

She made it through ten. A little winded, but being a flatlander the altitude made a difference. Ansari, the bastard, leaned against the wall and counted out loud as if he expected her to cheat. The burn started. With every heave upward, fire shot through her biceps, her triceps. Her belly and thighs shook with effort. Muscles turned to jelly; her breath wheezed from tortured lungs. At fifteen count, she knew she wasn't going to make it. Sixteen. She collapsed and laid her face against the smooth grain of the wood floor, gasping, thinking death didn't sound too bad. Damned if she let him see her cry.

A strong forearm reached to help her up. Powerful, calloused fingers grasped her shoulder. Capable hands that knew hard work. She slapped him away. "Don't!" she said fiercely. "You didn't say the twenty had to be consecutive."

She zoned. Went out of body. And did five more.

Clap. Clap. Clap. Hooker applauded and chortled. "There're a lot of men who couldn't do that, Puma."

Rachel rolled over and sat up, struggled for breath and

knew she'd soon hurt in every muscle and bone. Sweat dripped from her face and trickled between her breasts. Her boss chuckled. Puma wore a strange look on his face. Bemused. Half admiring. And troubled.

"She's stubborn enough," Puma admitted. "But three weeks, Hooker? Not likely. She'll need a minimum of five practice jumps before I'd think of letting her chute into mountainous terrain to face a forest fire. I'd have to tandem jump with her. Who'd fly the plane? We can't use Forest Service facilities if you want this kept quiet. And help from your agency is out, if you suspect a security leak."

"You have private contacts, Puma. Use them and send me the bill. Anything within reason."

Puma turned his troubled gaze on her. "Look, Rachel. Are you prepared to jump out of an airplane with a parachute strapped to your back? Think about it."

It was the first time he'd used her given name. Why did that please her? She couldn't afford any personal feelings for the man. "I'm a qualified skydiver and've made over a hundred jumps. Never into mountainous terrain, but I can adjust."

"You're a skydiver?" He shook his head and frowned. Clearly he doubted what he heard.

"I belong to a skydiving club. We jump on weekends. Sometimes we entertain at local festivals and fairs. It's fun."

"You're a piece of work, lady."

"You don't have to like me. Just train me. I can do this, Ansari."

He nodded. "Maybe you can. I'll just be a minute."

He turned on his bare heel and left the room, heading for the back of the house. Rachel whooped and grinned at her boss. "He's going to do it, Dan!"

Dan Hooker stood and stretched his lanky body, sighing as if he'd been the one undergoing torture. "Looks like it. Don't make the mistake of thinking it'll be easy, Rachel. That's one hardnosed sonnova bitch. If you call in a week and tell me it's too much, I won't be surprised. Disappointed, but not surprised."

"We've worked together before, Dan. If you didn't think I could do it, you wouldn't have requested me for the job."

"You may not thank me before this is over. You'll have to live here while you train. Can you handle that?"

She nodded, mentally brushing aside her initial physical reaction to the smokejumper. "You said a couple served as his ranch caretakers. The LaCroixs? And a fulltime ranch hand lives here. It's not like the two of us will be alone."

"The LaCroixs have their own bungalow on the property. The ranch hand lives in a trailer nearby. Essentially, you'll be alone in the house with Puma."

Had her boss caught Rachel's temporary flash of sexual insanity? "I don't see a problem. He doesn't even like me."

Dan Hooker shook his head. "Hell, Rachel. You don't really believe that?"

"I'd say it's obvious. He not only doesn't like me, he doesn't care for women in general. Nothing will happen between us, believe me."

"Rachel—" Hooker threw up his arms in surrender. "Never mind. He'll keep his hands off you unless you say different. Check in with me once a day. Use your sat-phone. It's secure. Or plug in your laptop and send a coded message."

She nodded. The government spent a lot of money insuring no one could hack into its satellite system. "I'll do that."

"If you don't report every other day, I'll figure something's wrong and move in. These are dangerous men we're after, Rachel. Puma's training you is just the first step."

"I know. I'll do my job."

"If things go sour, get out. No arguments. Last agent who pulled a hotdog on me got dead."

She shrugged, and Hooker narrowed his eyes. "Really," she said smoothly. "I hear you. I'll be careful."

Now that the job was hers, she'd do her damndest to get it done right. She hated deskwork. She'd worked the organized crime scene undercover a few times, but this assignment was a step up. Hooker hadn't related the entire operation, but enough that she knew his terrorist task force was after a very big fish.

Rachel didn't intend to go back to a desk. Her job was to identify the flunkies carrying out the big man's orders and let Hooker take it from there. Rachel had her own agenda. If she could gain the arsonists' confidence, she could get them to lead her to the headman and earn a permanent assignment on the task force. She smiled at her boss and did her best to look guileless. He'd thank her when she delivered the big fish, gutted, smoked and on a platter.

CHAPTER 3

Fletch Ansari walked back into the room fully-dressed, wearing heavy work boots and a white tee shirt that rippled with underlying muscle. Large boots. He'd grown six inches and radiated power. This man had no tender spots. If she admitted to her fire phobia, he'd show her the door in a heartbeat. When the time came, she'd manage the fear alone. She had to.

He stopped short of invading her space. "Let's understand each other from the start, Ms. Cortez."

"Rachel, please." She stared into his chilly eyes and wondered what lay ahead. At least the sexual heat was gone. She could no more climb into bed with this man than with Attila the Hun.

"Okay, Rachel," he grunted. "I see you want this. That helps, but guts alone won't do it. I need to build you up physically and teach you in three weeks what normally takes months. There's more to smokejumping than bailing out of an airplane. For the next twenty-one days, your ass is mine. You follow orders without question. Understood?"

She nodded, shaking inside, and reminded herself that Dan Hooker trusted this man. "I accept that as necessary."

"Once we start, you can't quit. I won't let you quit. By this time tomorrow you're going to hate me. Within a week you'll want to kill me. You're not a woman to me; you're not even a person. You're a rookie. Got it?"

"Got it. You're not a man to me; you're not a person. You're the devil incarnate."

A grin tugged at his mouth, and for a nano-second he looked human. "Good answer, Rookie. Make sure you don't forget that. If we survive this, I'll sign off on your red card and bring you onto my team. She'll need a cover story, Dan."

Dan Hooker gave a thumb up. "In the works, Puma."

"Make it good. Smokejumpers are a mobile group and most of us know people on the other teams. There'll be questions. About her background. Where she got her training."

"I'm very good at lying," Rachel interjected.

"You better be. And thick-skinned. The humor gets rough in the field. I won't step in to stop the hazing. You'll have to handle it alone."

"After six years in the FBI? I think I can handle it."

"Good, you've been warned. Here's your first assignment." He removed a pair of manicure scissors from his back pocket. "Cut your hair to no more than two inches all over your scalp." He lifted the tangled mane from her neck. "It should be no longer than mine."

Horrified, she backed away, refusing to take the scissors. "You're joking!"

"Down the hall. There's a mirror in the bathroom. Do it, or I'll do it for you."

She clutched at her hair. She really, really liked her hair. She tamed the thick curls with cream rinse and wore it in a casual shoulder-length style. Men usually liked her hair, for god's sake. Maybe this one really was the devil incarnate. "Why?" she whispered. "What's wrong with it?"

Puma forced himself to shrug in disinterest. *Wrong with it?* Hell, he wanted to run barefoot through that hair. "Nothing's wrong with it, Rookie. I don't want you going up like a Roman candle when you get that mop near a raging fire. Or have it pulled out by the roots if you get tangled in a lodgepole pine during a jump."

Slowly she wrapped her fingers around the scissors, and nodded. "If it's necessary, I'll do it, but I don't like it."

"Lesson number two. You don't have to like it or agree with it, you do it because I say so. In an emergency situation there won't be time to explain. Every member of my team understands that, or they don't stay on the team."

She swung around and started for the bathroom.

"And don't leave any hair clogging the sink!" he hollered after her. She saluted him with her middle finger.

Dan Hooker gave a low whistle. "A bit rough on her, weren't you, hoss?"

"How do you deal with insubordination on your team, Dan?"

Hooker cleared his throat. "Generally, there isn't any."

"Exactly."

"In other words, you'll do your best to wash her out."

"For the first week. If she makes that, I'll do my damndest to keep her in."

Hooker shook his head. "Asking Rachel to crop her hair? Are you sure it's necessary? The other woman on your unit—"

"Wears her hair butch. Your female agent needs to realize there's no place for vanity when you're fighting a fire. It's rough, dirty and dangerous work. They're less than ten percent women smokejumpers in the country. Not many women want the job."

"Yes, I can see that," Hooker nodded. "Maybe I should have recruited a man, but I thought with Rachel's sky jumping experience, she'd be a natural."

"It's one less thing I have to worry about, that she'll freeze when the time comes to bail at three-thousand feet. We'll see if she's physically up to the job."

"She's tough and fearless, Puma, and you're the one man I know capable of getting her ready. With the main fire season ahead, we need to locate these fanatics before our western forests are devastated."

Hooker had boxed him in. First by calling in an old debt, then by appealing to Puma's personal commitment to keep his ancestors' forests safe. "I won't operate blind. I need to know everything you have on these people and who else is working for you. I'd bet Rachel won't be the only agent you send undercover."

"You know I can't divulge that. Rachel will fill you in on a need-to-know basis, but you're not involved other than training her. Once she locates the inside person, she notifies me and my team takes over."

"Unacceptable. You've handed her a risky assignment and made me responsible for her safety."

"She's qualified in what she does. You wouldn't do what you do if you weren't committed, nor would she. Mold her into a smokejumper, and Rachel will do her job."

"She'll have to stay here. I'll be in her face 24/7."

"She's prepared for that. Looking forward to the challenge, I think."

God help him. She'd be living in his house until he could get her trained and Hooker could establish her cover story. Puma wasn't a monk, dammit, and the woman appealed to him. A lot. Keeping his sexual instincts under control would be a constant aggravation. How much of this was his grandfather responsible for? If Joseph Red Feather were involved, he'd let his grandson know soon enough.

Puma shrugged, accepting the inevitable. "Where's her luggage?"

Groggily, Rachel reached to shut off the alarm that shattered her dreams. Pitch darkness surrounded her. She fumbled on the bedside table and the clock crashed to the floor, still clanging. She moaned, pulled a pillow over her head and burrowed deeper. Why was she getting up in the middle of the night? If she ignored the noise, it would go away. When quiet reigned again, she dove back into the dark velvet of sleep.

The second alarm sounded. This one came from across the room and wailed like a dyspeptic banshee. No question of going back to sleep now. Why had she set two alarms?

She rolled out, switched on the lamp and rubbed her

neck, missing the familiar weight of tangled curls, trying to orient herself. Her breath made steamy puffs in the air. Every muscle hurt. Her hair was gone. The bed wasn't hers. Ditto the second alarm clock.

Awareness crept in. Puma Ansari's guest bedroom.

Muttering phrases she reserved for dire situations, Rachel reached for her robe and pulled it over her nightgown. She really wanted to go back to bed. The mattress was comfortable and the down quilt kept her cozy. Given the room's subzero temperature, her host must not believe in turning on the furnace. He probably slept on a bed of spikes, or maybe hanging from his heels.

She shuffled barefoot across the cold wooden floor to silence the malevolent alarm clock. On her first trip to town she'd buy warm slippers. It was almost April for Pete's sake. Back in her New York apartment the days were balmy and a joy to wake up to, and her feet sunk luxuriously into wall-to-wall carpet.

She put her tweed jacket on top of the robe. Shivered and sniffed. Coffee. Maybe she'd live. She found her boots and pulled them on.

Her nose led to the kitchen. Puma stood looking out the backdoor, a steaming cup in his hand, a blast of icy air sweeping the room. The stars were still out. He stood barefoot and wore nothing but jeans, no sign of goose bumps on the smooth, tan skin. The man wasn't human.

She headed for the percolator bubbling on the stove, splashed black liquid into an empty cup, wrapped her fingers around the warmth and inhaled. The devil's spawn knew how to brew coffee; she'd give him that.

"Heaven," she sighed and slurped.

"Nice outfit," he commented, reaching for the pot to pour himself another. "Goes well with the bedhead. Luckily we're not much for high style around here."

He smelled of fresh air and crushed pine needles. She took another swallow. "Don't talk to me. Could we close the door and have some heat in the tepee, please? Winter's still here, in case you haven't noticed."

"Tough, Rookie. This is mountain weather. I turn the furnace off by April."

"You set that second alarm? The one that sounds like a Swiss yodeler in orgasm?"

"That'd be me," he confessed, grinning in enjoyment.

"You're pure evil, Ansari."

"On my good days. Finish your brew and get dressed."

"I'm taking a shower to warm up. Toast and juice will do fine for breakfast. Unless you have a bagel?"

He shrugged his sexy shoulders and raised an eyebrow. "My, my. You've mistaken me for your mother. You're lucky I made coffee. Your turn tomorrow."

"Fine. Get out the electric coffeepot and I'll manage. Wait! Don't tell me. No bagels. No electricity either?"

"No bagels. No breakfast. No shower. Get that lazy butt into some sweats. We have three miles to run and thirty minutes of workout time ahead of us. Afterward I'll feed what's left of you and the real day begins."

She smirked at him. She ran five miles every morning, but he didn't need to know that. "I don't believe in violent exercise before noon. Unless it's of a sexual nature."

"These are the times that try a woman's soul. You have five minutes. Whatever you have on is what you run in, if I have to drag you by the short hairs."

Damn, she wouldn't put it past him. "Are you aware it's four a.m.? This is genuine cruelty. Even your dog is still asleep."

"Sundance is out prowling. He'll run a ways with us. May I add his disposition is much sunnier than yours in the morning?"

"What do dogs know?" she grumped and grabbed her cup, heading for her bedroom to change.

"Ah, Cortez? One other thing," he called after her.

"Yes, Satan?"

"About that violent exercise of a sexual nature? It could be arranged."

Her knees turned to water. Damn. She'd thought that particular craving under control. She willed herself to turn around and glare at him. He had this habit of not buttoning the top button of his jeans. It really, really unnerved her. So did the prominent bulge between his legs. He slouched against the counter grinning like a male wolf about to pounce. No question he was edible. "Will it buy me two more hours in bed?"

He ran his forefinger around the rim of his cup and frowned, seeming to think it over. "An hour," he conceded. "But there wouldn't be much sleeping."

So much for verbal sparring. He was even better at it than she was. "I'll think about it," she said, in her best sultry voice. "Don't count on it."

Puma wasn't sure who'd won that round. He did know his morning erection pressed against his zipper to the point of pain. What was so compelling about this mouthy, skinny scarecrow of a woman? He'd been doing okay until she came scuffling into the kitchen wearing those ridiculous layers of clothes, all rumpled and sweetly smelling of dreams. He wanted her. Damned dangerous, if she ever decided she wanted him.

"*That's* where we run?"

"I'm being good to you. Starting tomorrow we use the county road and run five miles every morning." Puma squatted and began a series of leg stretches.

"That's straight uphill!"

"It's a private road that curves up to the north pasture, skirts my neighbor's land, and back around to the ranch house. Not all of it is uphill. It's a pussy run. Barely two miles."

She mirrored his warm-up routine, and touched the toes of her running shoes to stretch her calf muscles. A run sounded good. She'd spent yesterday in airplanes and skipped her daily exercise regimen. He was right. Two miles was a pussy run.

They started off in a rhythmic jog, easy enough she could scan her surroundings in the emerging dawn. Sundance tagged her heels for a bit, then loped ahead to keep up with Puma. Even the dog was a smart aleck.

A pink glow smudged the eastern sky, illuminating the ranch buildings hunkered against the mountain foothills. The house was a rambling affair of spilt logs with a green-shingled roof. An ancient trailer parked beside the barn. Other than an occasional birdcall she saw no sign of life.

The windmill by the corral turned idly, pumping water into a metal cistern. She'd thought windmills extinct long ago. Fir trees grew in abundance, smaller specimens alongside the road and larger ones clumped in masses on the rocky terrain. The scent of pine permeated the air as the morning mist burned off before the rising sun.

Running steadily, they rounded the first bend in the road and were engulfed in taller foliage. The buildings disappeared. She was grateful for the easy pace. A five-mile run was a cakewalk in Central Park. Two might be major here.

A jackrabbit dashed across their path in a furry blur. Sundance yipped in delight and gave chase across the wildflower-dotted meadow. The bunny disappeared, but it looked like joyous fun. Must be nice to have four legs.

Rachel glanced at her watch. They'd been running up an incline for fifteen minutes and while she wasn't nearly spent, she began to lag further behind. She resisted the impulse to put on a burst of speed. It was humiliating to be outpaced, but it would be worse to burn out and have to stop.

Her sweatshirt grew uncomfortably warm. She slowed down and yanked the garment off and tied it around her waist, which gave her running partner enough time to pull further ahead. He disappeared from sight, amid a copse of aspen. A steady pace finishes the race, she reminded herself.

Her feet stumbled as she saw the cougar.

A good seven-feet long, his lithe, buff-colored form lay hunkered among the brush. He rose in a lazy stretch of powerful haunches, his black-tipped tail swishing and ears upright. Rachel froze, her feet planted mid-stride. Other than a bear, he represented the finest killing machine the mountains offered. Her only chance was to appear non-threatening and unafraid. They faced each other, the primal beast and the puny human, the human fervently wishing she had her pistol thrust in her waistband.

He was magnificent.

"Nice kitty," Rachel croaked. *Don't turn and run, Rachel.* It would trigger his hunting instincts. He'd be on her in seconds.

He growled, stepped onto the trail and started toward her in an unhurried pace, placing his hind paws in the imprint made by the front ones. Very large paws that left a distinctive four-toed imprint in the dusty ground. The cougar walk. One hind foot dragged slightly, but it didn't lessen his lethal potential. Molten amber eyes drilled into her, measuring her. Strange behavior for a wild animal. She knew better, but it seemed as if he wanted to talk to her.

He halted a body's length away, tail moving side to side, a growl pulsing his throat, his teeth bared in a snarl. She could see the rising mist of his hot breath. One lurch of those powerful legs and he would have her by the throat.

"Ssst," she hissed. "Stop right there, buster."

She loosened the sweatshirt from her waist and wrapped it around her left forearm. It would provide some protection if the animal attacked. She squatted, her eyes glued to the cougar's snarling muzzle, and grasped a fist-sized rock from the trail. If he sprang, she would throw up her padded arm and go for the animal's eyes and tender snout.

"Rachel!" Puma's impatient shout sounded a distance away. "Get in gear! You can rest at the top of the trail." The cougar halted, his paw poised for another step, and cocked his tawny head toward the direction of Puma's voice.

"Hear that, kitty?" Rachel crooned, not daring to shout back. "If you've got any ideas about inviting me for lunch, there's another guy involved here. And he's got a prior claim on my ass."

The growl rumbled as the cat backed slowly into the brush. Rachel held her breath. The amber eyes gave her a last sweep. Intelligence. She saw intelligence there. Only the slight rustling movement of the grass marked his departure.

Rachel slumped to the ground, her heart beating triple time. That was fun.

"Rachel, are you all right?" Puma stood over her, legs straddled, hands on his hips.

She took a jagged breath, the view of his corded thighs distracting the paralysis. "Give me a minute. It isn't everyday I'm featured as the lunch entree."

"What the hell does that mean?"

"I met one of your native predators. A large mountain lion. We retired to neutral corners. Good thing. I have a feeling I would have lost the fight."

He gave a hissed curse and knelt, searching the trail. Strange, Rachel thought. The cat's paw prints were no longer visible. Puma sat back on his haunches.

"There are no signs. Tell me exactly what you saw."

She'd been trained to be observant. She closed her eyes, recollecting. "He hid in the brush. I didn't see him at first. Seven feet long if he was an inch. He started toward me deliberately, in no hurry. Snarling. God, I was petrified, but he was gorgeous. Primal, you know?"

"Rachel, are you sure?"

She opened her eyes. Puma crouched in front of her; skepticism etched his face. "He left tracks," she insisted. "I don't know why they disappeared. Maybe the wind blew them away."

"There's scarcely a breeze. An animal that size would have left some sign. Where did you first see him?"

She scrambled to her feet. "There." She pointed. "Behind that scrubby brush, waiting in the tall grass."

She followed him to the spot in the trail where she'd seen the cougar emerge. Carefully Puma parted the vegetation, searching, shaking his head. "No sign an animal had been lying here. No flattened grass, no scuffed earth."

She gnawed her lip. "He was there. He walked with a limp. Like his hind leg might have been injured once."

Puma's head snapped up and his eyes narrowed. He gave her his full attention. "A limp? You're sure?"

She knew what she'd seen, and as much as he tried to hide it, Fletcher Ansari was on full alert. "Look," Rachel said. "I don't care if you believe me or not, but an animal that big could be a threat to your livestock. Don't mountain lions usually roam further away from human habitation?"

"Usually, but this is mating season and the Front Range is prime mountain lion country. If you really saw a cat that size, could be he's on the prowl for easy pickings. It won't hurt to corral the colts and calves at night. And if he really came at you aggressively, I should warn the neighbors."

"Then, warn them!"

"No need to get snappy. Let's get on with our business here. We've wasted more time than we can afford."

He started off at a fast trot, and she followed, fuming. She'd damn near been the cougar's next meal, and Ansari had brushed her off. Obviously he didn't believe her. She glanced warily from one side of the road to the other, but saw no further sign of the feline predator. Her anger soon dissipated. With the pace Puma set, she struggled to keep on his heels. He swung around, jogging backwards, his frown saying he was displeased with her performance. "When we reach the top, we'll stop for a drink."

"Not on my account." Despite her best effort, the words came out as panting grunts. She knew as well as he did that if she couldn't cut the physical requirements, he'd drop her from the program. Training would be over.

"I need a drink and so do you. It's easy to get dehydrated in these mountains. The air is bone dry."

They passed another clump of fir and came to an open space. Here the vegetation was chopped back from the road and the ground was littered with rocks and boulders, but nature had found a way. Scrubby bushes interspersed with tufts of grass stubbornly hugged the shallow soil.

She stepped to the ledge and took a breath, wiped perspiration from her face with her sleeve and reached for her water bottle. "Wow. How much of this is yours?"

Puma's ranch nestled in the valley like a monopoly board. The sun rose on the horizon, a burning orb that swathed the countryside in gold. Talk about a Kodak moment.

He stood beside her and pointed. "Everything you see north and south from this side of the county road and to the tip of the bluff behind us."

"You own a mountain!"

He laughed. "Part of a small one. On the eastern side of it. That's not as impressive as it sounds. Not much of it's good for commercial use. The pastures support about forty head of horses and a small herd of cattle. We grow a few acres of alfalfa and bale it for our own use."

"I hear a stream somewhere. Rushing fast."

"Spring fed, swollen with snowmelt. We'll run alongside it on the way down. There's a tarn further up. Good fishing, but you have to go in by jeep or horseback."

"It's the forest primeval, other than this access road. Do you harvest the trees?"

"Not on my watch. I cull and do controlled burns during the rainy season. I've seen what fire can do to old forests that harbor dead trees and a thick layer of litter." He unscrewed the cap of his water bottle and swigged.

She followed suit, drinking gratefully, still fascinated by the scene below. "The airfield and hanger? Yours?"

"Uh-huh. We better get started again or you'll cramp up."

He was right. She replaced her water bottle to its belt holder. "What do you mean, your watch?"

"My grandfather left it to me. It came to us by way of Gram's family. They struck it rich in the 1890s gold fields and were smart enough to put the profits in land. But the land belongs to no one. We're just caretakers, and for now this is my piece to tend."

The run back went faster. They cooled down with five minutes of tone-down stretching. A sheen of perspiration beaded her skin, and an elephant crushed her chest. How long would it take her oxygen-starved body to get acclimated to the altitude? Desperately thirsty, she chugged from her water bottle until it was empty.

"Go easy," Puma said. "Too much water too fast and

you'll get nauseated. You can refill your bottle at the windmill spigot. I have the well tested twice a year. The water's safe and tastes fine. Rich in minerals."

She held her bottle under the pipe and let the icy cold stream run over her fingers, then splashed some on her face. She drank a swallow and it wasn't bad, only a slight iron taste.

"Is the water behind your hard attitude?"

He cocked an eyebrow at her. "Possibly. Head for the barn, Rookie, and the workout room. Lindy's fixing breakfast, but you haven't earned it yet."

Naturally he'd have a workout room. They entered a fair-sized room, probably fourteen-by-twenty, with high-beamed ceilings, the walls constructed of silvered cedar padded to shoulder height, and the floor layered with a spongy composition material. Nautilus equipment, a weight bench and a treadmill stood in the center. No television to ease the tedium of working out. It was a serious room built for serious workouts. A chinning bar and a steel-runged ladder were bolted to one wall, and a thick, knotted rope hung from a sturdy beam twenty feet overhead. A rappelling rope. She'd never been any good at rappelling.

"This must have cost more than my apartment."

"An apartment in New York? I wouldn't think so. But as much as a good stallion, and that's a buck or two."

She wrinkled her nose at the locker room smell. The room saw hard use. "Do you bring women here often?"

"You're the first." He clamored ten feet up the ladder and pulled open a wooden trapdoor. Outdoor air gusted in. "Better?"

Her skin responded with a rash of goosebumps. "Swell. Where do I start?"

He grabbed the rope, rappelled down in seconds and walked her way. The goosebumps melted as her internal heat revved. It wasn't only the muscled arms and shoulders, or the hard, masculine legs finely dusted with hair that turned her on. He moved like his namesake. Like the cat on the mountainside. Smoothly, with oiled efficiency, and deadly purpose. He would know his way around in bed, would move just as skillfully. Her tongue stuck to the roof of her mouth.

"Pushups, Rookie. And pull-ups."

She cleared her throat. "How many?"

"I'll do two to your one. Are you up for that?"

"Whatever you say, hotshot."

A rolled exercise mat leaned against one corner of the room. He snorted and unrolled it and dropped to the floor. He cadence counted to fifty, moved to the chinning bar and did a quick twenty.

"Twenty-five push-ups, Cortez. Ten pull-ups. I'm hitting the shower. Come in for breakfast when you're done. Before you leave, shut the trapdoor and rappel down." He grabbed a towel from a nearby shelf and started for the door, wiping his face and neck.

"You're not going to monitor me?"

"I figure you can count."

She figured herself lucky he'd stopped at fifty. Three weeks stretched ahead like three years.

CHAPTER 4

Puma left the barn and walked toward the house, teetering on the edge of a vile temper. No one had ever seen the phantom cougar, his personal curse, and yet Rachel described the animal exactly. It couldn't be coincidence. His grandfather had something to do with this. It scared the hell out of Puma. The old shaman had run some kind of crazy-ass test on the woman. *Rachel Cortez, if you can see my grandson's totem, then you're the woman for him.*

Joseph would show himself eventually, and words would be exchanged. "Stay out of my business" words. Puma believed in respecting your elders, but had a right to live without interference from his grandfather's ghost.

He stepped inside the kitchen, swearing under his breath. The smell of frying sausage and baking biscuits welcomed him. Comfort food, as only Lindy could prepare. His mother's cousin and her husband were a part of Puma's life since he'd been a kid. After his mother and father dumped Puma and his sister on their grandfather, Uncle Frank and Aunt Lindy came to live with them. Frank and Lindy were both in their fifties, but to Puma they were ageless.

Lindy looked up from the stove. "Such language. You're in a mood."

He reined in his temper and took an appreciative sniff. "I hope you made plenty, my lovely Kaguchin."

"I'm too young to be your grandmother in any language, but I appreciate the lovely. Wash up for breakfast and explain yourself."

"I'm being respectful so you'll feed me. Explain what?" Puma snatched a sausage patty, barely missing the smack of Lindy's spatula. Years of practice made him quick. Lindy wielded a mean spatula.

"The woman's clothes in the guest room. Who and where is she?"

"Working out in the gym. We have a business arrangement."

"Size eight. Long legs, from the look of her jeans. I like her perfume. French. Expensive. I found an FBI badge in her jacket pocket."

Puma laughed. "The feds should hire you. You didn't notice her perfume in my bedroom, did you?"

"If I had I'd be smacking this spatula on your butt. This one's a lady."

Puma shrugged. "A lady with a sharp tongue who carries a gun."

"Missed that. Probably under her pillow. Sounds like you'd best be careful about any late night excursions."

"I'd sooner bed a barracuda. What makes you think she's a lady? I'm not sure I agree." Puma tweaked the thick braid that hung down his aunt's back.

She snorted and patted his hand. "She's tidy. Made her own bed and left the bathroom clean."

"Well, of course that proves it. What was I thinking? Where's Frank?"

"Hauling Sully out of bed to help with feeding the livestock. I swear that hand's so lazy he's near worthless. Dratted ski bum." Lindy opened the oven door and checked her biscuits.

"Give him time," Puma said. "He's young and only been here a month. He'll learn. Besides, you know how tough it is to find someone willing to work for these wages." A twenty-year-old high school dropout, Brent Sullivan worked just hard enough in the summer to support his skiing habit during the winter months. That made him suspect in the ambition department in Lindy's scheme of things.

"He eats enough for two. I say you pay him more than he's worth in food." She pulled a pan from the oven and slammed it down with enough force that the biscuits jumped. "Breakfast in ten minutes. Get a shower before your lady friend appears. You smell like a horse."

Puma raised his eyebrows. She turned her rigid back toward him as she dished sausages onto a plate and slid them in the oven to keep warm. Something ate at his aunt that had nothing to do with Rachel or Sully. He nuzzled her cheek with his nose and wrapped his arms around her. Her small frame settled against him, her heart fluttering like a hatchling bird. She's scared, Puma thought.

"What is it, Aunt Lindy? Can I do anything?"

"Can you convince your stubborn uncle to go back to the doctor? He's having heart palpitations again."

Damn, the old coot was secretive about his health. And stubborn. And his uncle worked too hard despite Lindy's and Puma's scolding him to slow down. "I'll talk to him. Is he taking his medicine?"

"The pills are by his plate. He'll swallow 'em all right."

They hugged each other. He kissed her withered cheek. "I'll keep an eye on him. You're right, Sully needs to shoulder more of the workload. I'll talk to the kid and warn him to quit dogging it."

Boots stomped into the kitchen and the backdoor slammed. "Bring the food on, woman! We've got a full day's work ahead of us."

Frank's voice sounded strong, if a bit wheezy. Lindy put a warning finger to her lips and shook her head at Puma. She might be worried about her husband, but would never let Frank know it.

"Take off your boots, old grouch. You too, Sully. This is a clean floor." Lindy shook a warning spatula at them.

Sully shook off his boots and ambled to the table. "Hey, Puma! Who's that hot piece of—ah, that woman working out in the barn? With the mile-long legs?"

Lindy sniffed in disapproval, and Puma frowned. Sully sported a mouth on him as well as being a slacker. It wasn't Lindy's job to put the spurs to the kid. That was up to Puma, and he'd let it slide too long. "The lady is Ms. Cortez, Sully, unless she says otherwise. I need to talk to you after breakfast. Plan on it."

The ranch hand's doe-soft brown eyes shifted and worry lines appeared. "Yeah, sure. Anything wrong?"

"Later. I'm grabbing a shower. You all go ahead and eat."

Showered and shaved, Puma reentered the kitchen. Sully and Frank sat with polished plates, nursing cups of coffee while they ogled the tall, amber-haired woman who stood by the stove with Aunt Lindy. Rachel held a mug in her perfectly manicured hands, and the women were both laughing and having a grand time together.

Rachel's newly cropped hairdo framed her animated face and focused attention on her emerald eyes. Her knockout legs were encased in baggy sweats, but the skimpy top left little of the rest of her to the imagination. She wore one of those body-hugging, midriff-baring garments designed to drive the male sex crazy. Sully looked close to drooling. Puma's loins stirred and he gritted his teeth. It promised to be a miserable three weeks. He walked to the stove, mumbled a hello to both women and filled his plate with sausage, biscuits and gravy.

"Are you eating?" he growled, fixing a glare on Rachel. "You better. We'll be in the field until late afternoon."

"I scarfed a biscuit. It just melted in my mouth. Lindy is a fab cook."

"Eat more. Where's your sweatshirt? You're half-naked."

Aunt Lindy's spatula went at the ready. "Fletcher Ansari, you be nice. Rachel's dressed just fine. Have another biscuit, dear."

Rachel bit into the honey-laden biscuit his aunt handed

her and sighed in pleasure. "Your aunt told me about the time you got snagged in a tree, stealing honey from a beehive, with your butt hung out like Pooh bear. She says you've been off honey ever since the bees rear-ended you en-masse. Personally, I'm fond of honey. Bees too, after that story." She chuckled and the sweetener dribbled down her chin. Puma reconsidered his taste for the gooey stuff. If he could lick it off of those pouty lips—damn it.

"Cut me a break. I was six." He stomped over to the table and attacked his food. Frank and Sully shifted in their chairs, Frank grinning, Sully looking worried. The kid should be worried. Puma planned to ream his ass.

"Been a long time since Lindy had another woman to talk to," Frank whispered. "Nice for her, don't you think?"

Puma supposed so. It was a male-dominated household for years, even more so when his grandfather still lived. "Yeah," he said, shoveling in food. The women were off in a corner, heads together and nattering. From the expression on Rachel's face, Aunt Lindy was telling tales again. "Nice."

"Pretty gal, too. Whadda you think, Sully?"

"She's a real hottie."

Puma cowed the kid with a look. "She's pretty enough. Are you done eating? Don't you have work to do?"

"Sure," Sully said. "Did you want to talk to me?"

"We'll make it later. Rachel and I have a full schedule today."

Sully disappeared out the door, his too-handsome face expressing gratitude at the reprieve. Frank rose and kissed his wife. "Best work on that disposition, son," he said, exiting behind Sully. "You're gonna give yourself terrible indigestion."

Too late. Puma's gut churned.

"I like your aunt and uncle." Rachel said. "They're good people."

Puma grunted agreement and shifted his pack from his shoulder to the ground. She eyed the pack, curious as to its contents, and surveyed the meadow they'd driven to. The clearing encompassed maybe five acres, and was surrounded by fir trees and dotted with yellow and blue wildflowers. Sparse new growth pushed up through brush and dried debris. It didn't look like ideal pastureland. Scrub trees were taking over the native grasses. As little as she knew about ranching, she figured that couldn't be good.

They were a long way from the house. In the typical rancher's disregard for roads, Puma drove straight up the side of the mountain, breaking trail with his wide-track SUV. The sun hung in the eastern sky and Rachel looked at her watch. Eight a.m. No exotic animals visible. She didn't mention it, but along with sandwiches and a water bottle, she carried her 9mm in her backpack. The mountain lion had spooked her. She didn't plan to be caught unarmed again.

"What torture do you have in mind for the rest of the morning?"

He nudged the gear with his booted foot. "Unload. I'll be right back."

She laid out the tools from his backpack as he walked to the edge of the clearing and used his pocketknife to cut two needle-laden boughs from a small spruce tree. He returned and dropped the boughs beside the tools. "Are you familiar with these tools and their uses?"

"A shovel? To dig up dirt?"

"Very good. Fire won't burn dirt." He hefted a peculiar looking tool, half-hoe and half-axe. "This is a Pulaski. The forest firefighters' best friend. You'll grow to hate it. Where're your gloves? Get 'em on."

"Yessir." She removed a pair of leather gloves from her jeans pocket and put them on, along with the hardhat and attached wire facemask he insisted she wear during training. He handed her the Pulaski and picked up its twin.

"We're going to dig a scratch line around the perimeter of this clearing. A scratch line is made quickly, to hold a fire until a permanent line can be constructed. It doesn't have to be pretty, just effective. Got it?"

"I guess." She frowned as she hefted the heavy, clumsy tool, and chopped at a bunch of dried grass with the hoe part. The stuff barely budged. She chopped again more vigorously, and the thatch of grass went flying.

He raised his eyebrows. "Not bad. Use the axe side to chop out brush and small trees and toss them in the center of the clearing. The shovel works best if you come to a stretch of ground with light vegetation. Cut a line two-feet across, and get down to the bare dirt. You start here, I'll begin across the way and we'll work around the perimeter until we hook up."

"What are the spruce branches for?"

"We use them to beat out small flare-ups. I'll show you later."

That apparently was the extent of his directions. He strode to the far side of the meadow, carrying a shovel, the Pulaski and a water bottle. No hardhat or facemask. She scowled, grateful for the gloves, but the hardhat kept slipping over her nose and was annoying and sized for Ansari's big head. If she still had hair to stuff under it, the pesky thing would have fit better.

Straight across from her, Puma hacked at the earth. He dug and threw dirt northward, which meant she should head south. She estimated her half would amount to nine-hundred meters of sweat labor. She pulled off the hardhat and her sweatshirt and began digging.

Moving dirt with the shovel and hoeing grass tufts came easily, but she quickly learned the little scrub trees were tougher than they looked. It took a lot of chopping to eradicate the stubborn devils. The Pulaski was sharp. If it slipped she could end up missing a few digits. She needed better boots, the kind with lug soles and steel-reinforced toes. Her bare arms were soon bloodied with ugly scratches from encounters with the scrub and thorny brush. She'd sloughed the sweatshirt, and needed long sleeves like the work shirt that Puma wore. Hell, she needed the muscled arms that were inside the shirt. No wonder the regimen of pull-ups and pushups.

She stuck to the task doggedly, stopping occasionally to swig at her water bottle and mop away the sweat. Her arm and back muscles screamed. It would be even worse, burdened with the clumsy Nomax gear the smokejumpers wore while fighting a blaze. She shook aside the scary thought of facing an actual forest fire. Time enough to deal with that fear later.

She'd done maybe half her share when Puma met up with the point where she'd started digging. He gave a shout and trotted to the side of the meadow, found a soft spot under a tree and stretched out, using his knapsack as a pillow. Humiliating. She gnashed her teeth at his friendly wave. Snores soon followed. She tried to decide. Would bashing his head in with the Pulaski be worth a jail term?

Burning. There would be a burning.

Zeb licked his lips and ached with anticipation. It had been too long. Without the bright flames to warm his gut, he was barely alive. No one had died in the last several fires and that disappointed him. The damned firefighters were too good, too skilled, no matter how hot and deadly the blaze. The ecstasy increased tenfold when someone died. Soon. He would have that thrill again, soon.

The last one to die was the derelict that burned up in the coffee warehouse. The memory comforted. A wonderful burning. Crimson reds. Sulfur yellows. Blue death. The roar of flames and the fiery fingers reaching to the heavens, the shouts of fear as the building went down. Unfortunately, the fire crew escaped before the inner walls tumbled and the roof caved. It was true rapture when a fireman died.

In the backseat of his car, Zebedee clutched himself, his ecstasy growing. He could taste the ashes, could feel the inferno searing naked flesh. The heady aroma of roasting coffee mingled with the scent of charred wood and brick. He imagined the tramp screaming in his death throes as bags of coffee beans exploded around him. The glorious image sang through Zeb's body, and erupted from his loins.

He gasped for breath, his heart slamming against his chest as the vision ebbed. A poor substitute for a real burning. Slowly, he came back to reality. He climbed out of the car and straightened his disarranged clothing. He'd watched his employer enter the bar half-an-hour before. He was a big man who walked with a cocky stride, wore a black leather jacket and matching pants, his blonde hair tied back in a ponytail. A muscled pretty boy who thought himself God's gift to the ladies. Chic Fillmore. Arson for hire was a dangerous business, and Zeb kept safe by being a cautious man. When he was sure no one had followed Chic, he entered the front door and headed for the back booth where they agreed to meet.

"Sorry I'm late, Mr. Fillmore. Traffic, y'know."

"This is getting to be a habit, Zebedee," Chic Fillmore snarled.

Playing hard, Zeb thought contemptuously. I can show you hard. He shrugged. "Sorry."

"I'm a busy man. Plan better next time."

Zebedee slid into the booth, sticking to the plastic upholstery. Someone had spilled a drink and no one bothered to clean it up. Globs of someone's lunch smeared the table. It was that kind of bar. Zeb had chosen it deliberately.

"I'm good at planning, Mr. Fillmore."

His voice held a warning. Noting that, Chic Fillmore nodded and plastered on a smile. When the time came he would squash this creep like a worm. "I appreciate your talents, Zebedee. Sorry for the temper, but I'm under heavy pressure from the boss. What'll you have? My treat."

"Shot of whiskey. Beer chaser."

Chic waved at a waitress and the two men did no further talking until after she served his cohort. Zebedee tossed back the booze in one motion, sipped at the beer, and belched. "Good stuff. Let's do business."

Zebedee's basic nastiness set Chic's nerves on edge. In certain things the firebug was a genius. And like all geniuses, was volatile. Chic detested everything about the weasel, from his yellow teeth and rodent face, to the sly way he continually smirked as if he enjoyed a private joke. The filthy khakis and shirt the man wore were right at home in the skuzzy bar. Chic glanced around in distaste. Ordinarily he wouldn't put a foot in the dive, but the location was ideal, located in the seamiest part of Denver. The surrounding streets were peppered with topless joints and back alleys where drug deals went down twenty-four/seven. An ideal place to meet with a stone killer.

Chic had killed. But they'd been righteous kills, done quickly and efficiently. To enjoy watching someone burn to death, that took a special breed. A crazy not to be trusted, even when you owned him. Give Chic a clean kill with his K-bar or 357 magnum anytime, but for now, Zeb was a useful tool. Fletcher Ansari? Now, that was a different case. Chic would enjoy seeing Ansari burn. Chic sipped at his own beer.

"You've been watching the ranch house? Getting Ansari's routine down?"

"With binoculars. From a bluff overlooking the grounds. I ain't getting nowhere near that German Shepard of his. I know an attack dog when I see it."

"See anything unusual? Any visitors?" Chic winced at the scratching sound as Zebedee dug at his crotch.

"Dunno what you think's unusual. He's got a woman living with him, but I didn't get much of a look at her. I could use another shot, partner."

"Sure. When the waitress comes back. You mean his aunt? She keeps house."

"Huh-uh." Zebedee shook his head. "This un's young. Tall drink of water. Way she moves her hips makes a man slobber."

Chic sat back and took a swig of his beer. He would have to look into this. Their source hadn't mentioned a woman, and supposedly the mole possessed access to the latest FBI data. "Too bad for her, then. Can you burn the place?"

"Sure. Anytime that dog ain't around. But it wouldn't surprise me none if Ansari has other security. Hidden cameras maybe, and a silent alarm. If he goes anywhere on horseback or in his SUV, he carries a rifle. There's a look to him."

"You're right to be cautious, he's dangerous. I can see to it the electricity's cut and take out the dog," Chic said.

"The old lady and her husband live in a cabin on the other side of the barn. Ranch hand sleeps in the trailer. They're all in the main house during meals."

"I want the house to burn with Ansari inside. When he's asleep. Set fire to the barn, burn all the outbuildings, the hanger. Scorch everything to the ground, animals included. The place is pretty isolated, so the rural fire department won't get there in time if you do it right."

"Setting all them fires the same night? I dunno. Not that I couldn't do it. I could set timed fuses to go off all at once." The arsonist licked his lips and drummed his fingers on the filthy table. "It'd be sweet. Snuff his family at the same time. I'd almost do it free."

"Enjoy it all you want, but don't get caught and do the job. If you get caught, shut your mouth and we'll see you get a lawyer, the best money can buy. But if you talk or let Ansari get away, your life won't be worth rat piss."

The arsonist nodded. "Like I said. I'm good at planning. Seems you got a real hard-on for this guy."

"Let's just say I enjoy the irony of him burning in hell."

Zebedee frowned, obviously puzzled, and Chic realized he wasted his breath. The arsonist wouldn't have the slightest idea about irony. Zebedee was a simple man. He lived for one thing, to kill by fire. His tunnel vision was useful. But it was fueled by madness and could just as easily turn on his employer. Right now Zebedee was necessary. When this was over Chic would personally dump the weirdo's body on the FBI's doorstep. "Forget it. You'll be well paid."

"Seems you've made this personal."

For a minute, Chic let the hate take him. Personal? Oh, yeah. This part of the op was Chic's own baby, and the boss had gone along with it. They wanted the FBI to think an arsonist was at work in the area. That way when the forests started burning, it would be laid on one man's insane obsession. Zebedee was the perfect fall guy. A nutcase who loved to burn. Chic smiled, savoring the sweetness of revenge.

"It's personal all right. He killed my brother."

Puma woke with a start and smelled burning tobacco. His grandfather sat cross legged under the tree. The old man wore his favorite plaid shirt and old jeans, a cigarette dangled from his mouth. Puma sat up and waved the smoke away. "Those things'll kill you, Joseph."

His grandfather cackled in appreciation. "Too late."

"Okay, am I dreaming again? Is this a vision, or what?"

"What do you want it to be, Fletcher?"

Puma sighed. When his grandfather called him Fletcher, it meant a lecture. "What I would appreciate is for your spirit to settle down. Find a nice tree to occupy instead of that gimpy-legged cougar, and leave me be."

Joseph Red Feather contemplated his cigarette. "What makes you think I have anything to do with the cougar? Your animal totem appears when you need him. It's up to you to decide why he's there."

"Don't give me that shaman bull. Rachel saw him."

"Really?" Joseph's eyebrows rose. "Interesting. It appears your totem thinks she has importance. Have you slept with her?"

Puma gnashed his teeth and stifled a curse. "You don't know first-hand?"

His grandfather looked surprised, then offended. "Of course not. I don't spy on you, Fletcher, but I am concerned. Perhaps when you settle down, my spirit will also. Perhaps this Rachel is the woman for you and the cougar knows this."

"Joseph, my woman died. I'm not interested in another."

"That's the guilt talking."

Puma hissed in a breath. His grandfather still knew what buttons to push. Even after ten years Puma carried plenty of guilt. If he'd been a proper husband, Sadie would still be alive.

His grandfather took a last puff of his cigarette and flicked it away. The smoldering butt landed in a bunch of dried grass. A curl of smoke rose in the air. Ordinarily, Puma would have jumped up and stamped out the glowing ashes, but of course it wasn't real. Nothing about this was real. "Call off your totem, old man."

"It isn't my totem." The old man leaned against the nearby stump of a tree and watched in silence as Rachel hacked away at scrub pine. "She's a woman of power. An ideal mate for you."

Puma rubbed his eyes in resignation. Joseph would have more to say. "It's a business deal, Grandfather. I'm doing a favor for a friend. A month, six weeks tops, she'll be gone. She has no interest in me as a man."

"Ah." The old man nodded and clicked his tongue. His grandfather could say more with a tongue click than anyone Puma had ever known. "I think there is a log in your eye, Fletcher."

There it was again. His German grandmother had been a devout Christian, and Joseph Red Feather thought nothing of intertwining Christian symbolism with the beliefs of his Ute ancestors. A strange mixture of two powerful religions that Puma often thought had a lot going for it.

"My eyes are wide open, Joseph. I know what I'm talking about here."

"You want the woman. I can see this."

"Yes." No need to deny the obvious, but anything that happened between him and Rachel would be strictly physical. "But that is not going to happen, Joseph."

His grandfather rose with the agile grace of a much younger man. It appeared death had cured his arthritis and lame knee. "We'll talk again, Fletcher."

"Yeah, I figured. Thanks for dropping by."

His grandfather clicked his tongue and Puma winced. It was the old man's shame-on-your-rudeness click. Already his image was fading, but Joseph's dark eyes were alive.

"There is danger ahead, and great challenge. For you both. The cougar can only do so much. The rest is up to you." The shaman tuned and looked across the clearing to the female figure till chopping away.

Puma's skin chilled. "Danger? Not to Rachel?"

"Yes." Joseph's voice whispered as the vision faded. "And to all you love."

CHAPTER 5

"You've been sitting on that tree stump and staring into space for five minutes." Rachel dropped the Pulaski at Puma's feet. "And talking to yourself."

He started out of his reverie and looked at his watch. "It took you four hours and twenty-five minutes. You need to work faster."

"I'm too tired to argue. And I have blisters on my blisters." She stripped off her gloves and winced.

"Let me see." He took her hands and examined the palms. "You'll toughen up. I'll get the first aid kit." Gripping her wrist, he started for the pickup. She trotted beside him.

"Did you have a nice nap while I did all the work?" she asked.

"Just dandy." He retrieved the kit and lifted her onto the hood of the truck. "Didn't I tell you to wear long sleeves? Your arms are a mess."

"I got too hot."

"No excuse." He cracked open a brown bottle and doused a gauze pad with its contents. "This may sting a little," She screeched as he swabbed at the scratches. "Hold still and don't be a baby."

She bit her tongue and bore up under his ministrations.

Not that he was rough. His hands were gentle as he cleaned the abrasions and applied antibiotic ointment and wrapped her blistered fingers in gauze. "You're enjoying this too much, Ansari."

His mouth twitched. "Maybe you'll listen next time. Put fresh antiseptic cream on tonight and by tomorrow you'll be fine. Feel better?"

Actually it did. She flexed her fingers. "Will there be more hard labor right away? I'm starving."

"We'll have lunch. Then take a three-mile hike carrying a pack. You'll have ninety minutes to complete the task. Think you can manage that?"

"Piece of cake."

He laughed and that made her uneasy. Still, a three-mile hike in ninety minutes? Even over rough terrain that couldn't be much of a challenge. She reached into her backpack and handed him one of the ham sandwiches Lindy packed. He unwrapped his while she bit into her own and moaned in pleasure. She didn't know when food tasted so good.

He hauled a sleeping bag out of the back of the truck, unzipped it and spread it under the tree. "Bring the food over here in the shade. We'll talk and eat at the same time."

She sat cross-legged beside him. "You talk," she said through a mouthful of sandwich. "I'm concentrating on what's important. Do you want your pickle?"

"Yes. My, such manners. Are you trying to kill that food or eat it?"

She reached in the pack for another sandwich. "Fortunately it's already dead. There're chocolate chip cookies. And apples. Oh, bliss, I love you, Lindy."

"Keep your hands off my share."

"I don't know what's the matter with me. I never eat this much."

"Your body is telling you to replenish. You'll lose weight this week. Minimum weight for a smokejumper is a hundred-twenty pounds. I'll bet you don't weigh much over that now."

"One twenty-seven. Does that mean I get your cookies?"

"Not on your life."

They finished the food and she stretched out on the sleeping bag, sighing as the fatigue hit her. "I need a nap."

"A ten-minute break. That's it, Rookie."

Two seconds later he was shaking her awake. "Time to get cracking."

"Go away," she grumbled. "You said ten minutes."

"Which out of the goodness of my heart, I let stretch into forty. Let's go."

Still grumbling she rolled to her feet. The nap had refreshed her. "If I do the hike in sixty minutes, what's it worth?"

"If you do it sixty minutes, I'll eat my boots."

"Really?" She grinned in delight. "You're on. I'll even let you use catsup."

He knelt, rolled up the sleeping bag and stowed it in the back of the vehicle. "So you want a wager?"

"Yep. I'll do your lil' ole three-mile trek in under sixty. Guaranteed."

He cocked his head up. "Carrying your pack?"

"Well, sure. That's part of it, right?"

"What if I win?"

"You want me to eat your boots?"

"Huh-uh, not my boots." He chuckled, leered wickedly and did the Groucho Marx eyebrows bit. Heat rushed to her face.

"In your dreams, Ansari! And it's not funny! You're warped!"

Still laughing, he grabbed her by the knees and toppled her to the ground. "Okay, I'll settle for a kiss."

He pinned her arms back, his weight holding her down, his mouth hovering inches from hers. His scent was earthy, that of a healthy male animal in his prime. Intoxicating. Heat swarmed to her abdomen and thighs and her heart rate went into rapid-time. "A kiss?"

"Yeah. If it takes you over sixty, I get a kiss."

He released her and pushed himself up with feline grace,

taking his heat with him. Her pulse rate slowed to normal. She considered. A kiss wouldn't be so bad. Much tastier than digesting boots, which gave her the best of the bargain. And she rather liked the idea of kissing him. One kiss wouldn't alter their relationship that much. "Agreed. One kiss."

"And I choose the time and place."

She shrugged. "Okay. One kiss anytime, anyplace. And because I'm a gracious winner, you can boil the boots first."

"Done." He reached in the truck again and hauled out a leather strapped canvas bag. "Here's your pack."

She frowned and the first uneasiness hit her. "I thought you meant I'd carry my own backpack."

He hefted the canvas sack one-handed. "Standard training issue. I'll carry one just like it. You want to back out?"

How heavy could it be if he lifted it one-handed? "Ha! A bet's a bet."

"Then let's go." He hauled another pack out of the truck bed and slung it over his shoulders, slipping into the leather straps. He checked his watch. "Sixty minutes, Rookie. I'll lead the way."

"Where're we going?"

"Up the mountain a short hike. Then across a narrow gulch and through a stand of birch, reverse and trek back here to the clearing. Some of the ground is rocky and rough. I paced it off and set out red flags along the course. It's a little under three miles roundtrip."

"When did you do that?"

"While you were napping."

Which meant it took him less than an hour. It would be no problem to duplicate that even carrying a pack. She reached and yanked at the leather straps. And fell on her butt. "Sheez, Ansari! How much does this puppy weigh?"

He started out without looking back. "A hundred-ten pounds. You're wasting time, Rookie."

The damn thing weighed almost as much as she did.

She'd been had. What did Hooker like to say? Screwed without being kissed. First problem. How to hoist it to her shoulders? She solved that by spreading the pack on the ground, rolling on her back, slipping her arms into the straps and buckling the belt around her waist. She turned over on her belly and went to her knees and pulled herself up. With the weight distributed evenly she could manage the load. She looked at her watch.

Okay, Ansari. I'll show you.

Rachel peered out of the window as their airplane circled the fake fire zone she and Puma would be jumping. The plane had been modified for jumpers by the removal of the regular seats. Mike, the pilot and owner of the plane, was an ex-Delta buddy of Puma's and an expert jumper himself.

A thousand feet below, a clearing lay amid the endless stretch of green forest and rocky terrain. When she'd undergone skydiving instruction, she was taught to steer away from hazards like power lines, buildings and trees. Today she would be chuting directly into a dense forest where some of the pines reached two-hundred feet, the dreaded timber jump required of all rookies toward the end of training.

Rachel loved skydiving. She wasn't afraid of the jump, but the thought of hanging helpless high above ground made her stomach churn. As standard issue, she packed a hundred-fifty feet of rappelling rope in the leg pocket of her Nomex coverall. Hopefully she wouldn't need it.

She'd survived the past two weeks, though there'd been times when she'd wondered. Mentally she reviewed the regimen Puma had laid out. Up at 4:30 to run five miles, followed by thirty minutes of calisthenics before breakfast. Mastering a devilish obstacle training O-course, that included scaling and rappelling down a twenty-foot rope, bar pull-ups, landing falls, climbing ladders to crawl across log bridges and pummeling at sandbags. It took agility as well as strength.

Mid-week, they strapped spurs on their boots and

climbed trees. Fortunately, heights didn't get to her. One morning he drove her into the mountains and dumped her with a compass and a water bottle. Completely disoriented, it took her half a day to find her way back. When she walked into the ranch yard, rather proud she'd made it so quickly, he nodded an acknowledgement, obviously unimpressed.

"That took long enough. Two rounds on the O-course, rookie. Then half an hour with the weights. Tomorrow I introduce you to fire shelter deployment."

God, she hated him.

Hauling the heavy pack, she'd tramped the rugged three-mile hike he'd laid out until she managed it in the allotted time. When nothing else was going on she hacked at the ground with the Pulaski, often for four-hour stretches, while Puma attended to ranch work. She'd gone through several tubes of muscle relaxant. If he called a break, she studied one of the half-dozen manuals he assigned her on different aspects of firefighting.

Give the man credit; he trained beside her and worked as hard as she did. A smokejumper never quit training, Puma said. When they reported to base camp all candidates were required to requalify, and anyone who didn't make it was out. No exceptions, even for the old-timers with twenty seasons under their belt.

She'd lost weight and was down to the minimum one-twenty, despite packing in the tasty meals Lindy prepared. If she lost any more, she'd have to load her pockets with buckshot when she weighed in. And water? She was always thirsty and drank two gallons a day. Surprisingly, she'd never felt better in her life.

The plane lurched and nosed downward, a reminder the jump was only minutes away. Rachel stared at her hands. The knuckles were raw, nails broken and palms blistered. Hands that were no longer pretty, but at least the calluses made them tougher. Her feet looked just as bad.

"You ready, rookie?"

Puma's husky voice jarred her back on track. He grinned down at her and her gut clenched. They'd be spending two days alone in the wilderness. She had mixed feelings about that. She knew he desired her sexually. The signals he gave off weren't subtle, but he never touched her unless it was necessary. The problem was she wanted his hands on her, for him to kiss her. Yes, dammit, she wanted his sleek, muscled body entwined with hers.

Rachel always kept her sensuality under control. Loss of control made you vulnerable, made you do stupid things, and something an ambitious FBI agent couldn't afford. She'd never been in love, and that would be the biggest stupidity of all. She wasn't in love with Fletch Ansari, but it seemed she was in lust.

"Rachel, are you ready?" Puma repeated the question as he pulled on his helmet. His yellow Nomex coverall gave him the appearance of an astronaut ready for a moonwalk. Even under the bulky suit he radiated confidence and power.

"Let's do it." She stood and reached for her own helmet, moving clumsily under the eighty pounds of gear she wore. Except for her outfit being goldenrod in color, she was a ringer for the Staypuft Marshmallow Man.

"Buddy check. You know the drill." His ice-blue eyes raked over her, missing nothing.

She tugged at her parachute. "Chute buckled and secure. Line release clear."

"Check."

"Reserve chute attached through harness loops and buckled."

"Check."

"Helmet fastened. Face mask and gloves in place."

"Check." They went through the litany of examining each other's equipment until he was satisfied.

"Guard your reserve," he said. "I'll open the cargo door to let the drift streamers loose."

She crossed her arms to prevent her reserve chute's accidental release. Puma attached an anchor line to his harness and to the metal bolt inside the door. The restraining device was to protect the spotter from being swept off his feet. They were flying too low to give his chute time to deploy. He thrust the door open and an icy blast pierced the cabin.

"Circle while I let the streamers loose to judge the wind drift," Puma shouted at the pilot, who turned the plane into a three-sixty swath. Puma released the first wind gauge, its colorful red and yellow streamers a sharp contrast against the clear blue sky. The twenty-foot streamers, weighted to drift at the same speed of a jumper, unfurled and sailed toward the designated jump spot. As it approached the ground the vivid wind gauge swerved, drifted south and lit in some jack pine.

So, you just had to be a smokejumper, Rachel baby?

She'd made over a hundred jumps, nice easy jumps well away from trees and dangerous high wires, landing in mall parking lots, fairgrounds or open fields. For pleasure and showmanship. Adrenalin junkies, her mother called Rachel and her skydiving buddies, unable to comprehend her daughter's love of the sport.

This time she'd be jumping into solid timber, some of the trees over a hundred-feet tall. Maybe her mother had a point.

Puma frowned. "Turbulence. Four-hundred yards of drift. Got that, rookie?"

Rachel nodded, and Puma yelled at the pilot to take another pass. Mike circled the jump spot again and Puma released the second streamer. It hung suspended for a minute before it dove to earth and sailed off course. The men discussed the necessary adjustments, and on the third pass the streamer settled in a tree on the edge of the target.

"That looks good, Mike! Make a low flyover and we'll drop the supplies. Then take her up to jump altitude."

"Got it," the pilot sang back.

The plane swooped over the clearing, skimming the treetops, and Puma shoved their supplies out the door. The canvas bundle fell end-over-end until its red and white cargo chute snapped open. Rachel watched the supply pack settle near the designated site. They would need the sleeping bags, food, and water to survive the two-day, thirty-mile hike back to the road where Mike would meet them with his jeep.

The idea behind the exercise was to give her experience in a timber jump and offer a quick course in map and compass skills. Looking down at the vast sea of solid forest and craggy rock, she could see how easy it would be to get lost. Tall buildings and crowded streets were her usual environment.

The plane gained altitude and she settled into the jump seat. Crunch time.

When they leveled out, Puma gestured and Rachel took her position on the edge of the cargo door, her feet and hands braced against the metal frame. She was dry-mouthed and endorphins pumped through her bloodstream. If you weren't edgy before bailing, you were an idiot. Too many glitches were possible, and a jumper stayed fully alert or ended up like Humpty-Dumpty.

She was conscious of Puma's stance, rock-steady behind her as the pilot made his last approach. The sky was the transparent blue of water under glass. The snow-capped Rocky Mountains loomed below and stretched west and north and south. Their site was a U-shaped valley at approximately six-thousand feet elevation, with rugged cliffs surrounding it on three sides. Colorado Springs lay somewhere behind them to the east. Sunlight sifted through the clouds, but provided no warmth. She breathed deeply and did her final mental check. Static line, cutaway clutch, emergency chute handle, all ready and in plain view.

"Watch for wind gusts," shouted Puma. "Those are dangerous rock formations near the northern cliff. Hold upwind and steer for the clearing. I'll be right behind you."

She braced herself. The signal slap came down on her shoulder and she pushed hard into space, cleared the tail and tumbled away. The shadow of the plane passed overhead, the engine a steady thrum through her helmet.

The static line streamed behind her as she fell at ninety-miles per hour.

Jump one thousand, look two thousand. On the fifth count the canopy billowed open and halted her free-fall with a jerk.

The rush hit. Better even than sex. She rolled to one side and watched Puma's chute bloom above her. They floated two-thousand feet over the earth. He whooped and laughed with sheer joy and she whooped back, sharing his delight. It was the kind of day skydivers live for. Clear and almost cloudless with little wind to disturb the rocking motion of their chutes. The air was fresh and sharp. She closed her eyes and savored the freedom of slipping the bonds of earth, cushioned in the hands of God. This was as close as she could come to flying.

She spread her arms and legs wide, embraced the sky, and dipped her head toward the forest below. The wind picked up and she sailed faster, her Nomex coverall pressed forcefully against her body. She began to glide away from the drop zone.

Watch it, Rachel.

She pulled on the left toggle, adjusted into the wind and her forward drift slowed. Good, she was still on target for the clearing, and approached at a manageable speed. She would land a few seconds before Puma. Suddenly the crosscurrent hit; the chute waffled and spun her away from the jump site. Now she was running with the wind. The landscape rushed underfoot at top speed.

The steep escarpment that loomed underneath was peppered with rock outcroppings and scrub trees. A landing there meant abrasions, broken bones or worse. Frantically she pulled her toggles to reverse direction and turn against the wind. The crosswind died as suddenly as it came up. Back in control, her pulse slowed as she shifted toward a stand of cedar. Gravity would have its way and she'd overshot the target. The best thing she could do now was aim for a small open space she spied in the midst of the timber. The earth flew beneath her feet.

She settled downward and steered for the open spot.

She almost made it.

In the last seconds her chute caught in a tall cedar near the edge of the clearing. She crashed through the top branches and dangled eighty-feet above the ground, almost peeing her pants. With raucous cries, a clatter of birds winged away from their perch on the treetop, a reminder that the sky was not man's natural milieu. If she'd ever made a worse landing she couldn't remember when. She swallowed and waited for her heartbeat to calm. She looked down, instantly regretting it. Oh, yeah, this was turning out to be a real good time.

Think it through, Rachel.

She'd practiced the correct procedure the day before, suspended on a steel cable stretched between the windmill and the barn on Puma's property. She yanked cautiously on her risers. She was perched securely enough she could tie off to her chute and avoid a climb back up after it. Puma would have a fit if she left the chute behind. She undid her reserve chute, loosed her personal gear bag, and winced at the dull thuds when they hit below. It was a hellova long way down.

"Rachel!"

She craned her neck around as Puma entered the clearing, his parachute over one arm. Naturally he'd seen her clumsy landing. He stood straddle-legged, hands on his hips and stared up at her. If he laughed, she'd murder him when her feet were on the ground again.

"Are you okay?" he shouted.

"Fine," she hollered back and reached into her leg pocket for her letdown rope. "I meant to do this."

He did laugh then. "It happens to everyone sooner or later. I'll talk you through it."

No way. She could do this herself. She was thoroughly versed on the procedure. "I'll talk it through. You check me."

"Take it nice and slow."

"No lines around my neck," she muttered to herself. "Facemask in place."

"Pass the rope through your D rings first," Puma shouted.

"I am, I am!" She pulled the rope right to left through the rings at the belt of her jumpsuit, mentally reviewing the steps. "Unwind six-feet of rope," she whispered. "Leave the rest stowed in your leg pocket until needed."

"When you tie off—damn it, Rachel! Holler out the steps so I can hear you."

"All right! I'm reaching for the tight riser!" She pulled the rope through her left riser and tied it off, unwound the coils and dropped the other end to the ground. Now for the fun part. She grabbed the right riser and pulled herself up one-handed.

"Careful, Rachel! The chute is slipping!"

"It's secure, I swear!" The tree branch she dangled from gave a sharp crack and bowed. Yep, secured all right.

"Rachel, don't move!"

He dropped his chute and sprinted toward the cedar, jumped and caught the lowest limb. He intended to climb up after her! Her pulse pounded. The tree was ancient and her weight was already a strain on the brittle branches. Add his extra weight—

"Stay back, Puma! I'll be okay!"

She gripped the letdown cable in her right hand and released the cutaway clutch with her left, made a final check that she was clear of any lines, wrapped the rope around one leg and began to descend slowly. Again the tree creaked ominously, and she dropped ten-feet fast, stopping with a jolt. Puma shouted instructions, swearing a blue streak. She'd left her stomach back there somewhere.

"It's holding! I'm okay!"

She reached the halfway point. Sweat poured off her body. Heavy pollen drifted from the tree and clung to her clothing. The spicy scent of cedar clogged her nostrils. She sniffled and sneezed violently. Of all times for her allergies to kick up. Branches whipped across her protective helmet, hampering her vision. She really hated rappelling.

He caught her as her legs kicked against his chest. "Okay. Let loose now."

More relieved than she cared to admit, her feet wobbled

to the ground. She brushed the tree residue from her suit and wrinkled her nose. Puma pulled off her helmet and facemask, and stroked her cheek with his knuckles.

She allowed herself to enjoy the caress. "Does this mean I flunk out, Prince-of-Darkness?"

"You scared me spitless," he said. "What happened?"

"Crosswind. You must've missed it. Or you're better at this than I am."

She shivered and went lightheaded as his caressing fingers slid over her lower lip. For two weeks he'd avoided touching her. She liked his tender stroke on her face a lot. His hands cupped her face and his head bent down, his pupils dilated with male intent. "You did fine for your first timber jump, honey. I was the one who panicked, not you."

Honey? What happened to Rookie?

Pollen from the tree wafted up, tickling her nostrils. She jerked her head away from his descending mouth. "Don'd!"

"You owe me a kiss, remember? You might like it. And after the scare you gave me, I know I need it."

"Dough, id's dot dat—I'mb—I'mb—" Her sneeze exploded all over him.

He wiped his face. "Bless you. I think."

"Dank you. Baybe we better boastbone the giss."

"Definitely. Don't tell me. You're allergic to tree pollen?"

"Uh-huh. I hab somb andy-histabean bills ind by leg bocket."

He collapsed on the ground, clutched his gut and howled.

She glared at him. "Id's dot dat fuddy!"

Still chuckling, he swept his arm across the back of her legs and pulled her down into his lap. "How in the hell a woman so tall and bony and contrary can be so damn cute is beyond me."

"Id's by sbarkling bersondality."

"Must be. I intend to kiss you properly, Sparkle, and soon. Can you breathe through your nose at all?"

"Dough."

"Then let's find those damn pills."

CHAPTER 6

Clearly the man sitting across the desk was more than annoyed. Dan Hooker stayed silent, waiting for Ash Calloway, the SAC, Special Agent in Charge, of the Denver office, to explode and get it over with. Hooker was grateful Calloway didn't have a saber hanging from his belt.

Ash took the lead. "Washington realizes we have our own Joint Terrorism Task Force in place? That the unit includes our top agents and reps from various law enforcement agencies throughout the state?"

Calloway drummed his pen on his desktop with the rat-a-tat-tat of a Confederate cavalry charge, his southern accent more pronounced than usual.

"C'mon, Ash. I'm not here to step on your toes, and I'm not here to displace the local task force. When the Rapid Deployment Team has done its clean-up job, we're out of here. You'll be the one to talk to reporters and CNN, not me."

The SAC perked up at that. Ash Calloway was a thirty-year career man not far from retirement. Going out in a blaze of favorable publicity would suit him fine. A special commendation would be even better.

Calloway threw down his pen. "Okay, I'm listening.

Would've been nice of Washington to warn me before you arrived."

"It was decided a discreet face-to-face would be best under the circumstances."

"And the circumstances are?"

Hooker decided to dispense with diplomacy. Calloway could be hardheaded, at times self-serving, but his loyalty to the Bureau and to his country was unblemished. "Your office leaks like a sieve, Ash. No one is to have access to our records or our plans. No faxes, no email, no communication about my team is to go out of here without my okay."

Coldness settled over Callaway's face, his ruffled feathers replaced with a dispassionate stare. "Is my fidelity in question here, or simply my competence?"

"Washington has no doubts on either, Ash. I'm instructed to brief you fully."

Callaway flicked on the intercom. "Grace, hold any calls and set my voicemail. Take a coffee break."

"But sir, I just took a break. I have reports to type."

"They can wait. Check back with me in half an hour." He terminated the connection.

"Grace is as devoted as ever, I see."

"I have a great support staff." Ash tilted his leather chair and steepled his fingers. "What have you got for me, Dan?" he drawled. "Some damn strong evidence to back this up, I hope."

Silently Hooker shoved a file folder across the desk. "Records from payphones made the last month within a mile radius of this office. Calls to a suspected terrorist, Chic Fillmore. We've been trying to locate Fillmore since the Hoover Dam incident where his brother was killed, and he's surfaced in the Denver area. We obtained his cell phone number from our singing canary, Sammy Cedardahl, who's in lockdown at Langley."

"Cedardahl. The New Sons of Liberty crackpot you took into custody after the Hoover takedown. How reliable a source is he?"

"He's not the sharpest pencil in the box, but his info has been good. The asshole has his vices, women, booze, cigarettes and television, in that order. We furnish cigs and a television with access to the Playboy channel, which seems to take care of his basic needs. He's a pretty blonde boy, and understandably anxious to stay out of the general prison pop."

"That would be good leverage."

"Yeah. The snag is he doesn't know much about the terrorists' future plans, and he never set eyes on the Sons' leader. Cedardahl refers to him as Four Star."

Ash swore in shock. "This Four Star bozo isn't one of our acting generals?"

"Huh-uh. The Sons fancy themselves a patriotic militia group. They all take military handles."

"Okay, so this Chic Fillmore is in the Denver area. Tell me where, and we'll pick him up. Sweat out what he knows."

Hooker shook his head. "No precise location. He moves around. Last call was made from the Colorado Springs area."

Ash grunted and flipped through the file. "I hope you have more. Unless the calls came directly from this office, that's damn flimsy stuff. Oh, ho!" He looked up at Dan. "You're monitoring him on Narus Insight?"

"Fillmore swaps cell phones frequently, but we have a tracker on his vehicle, and Insight records every message he receives or sends. We have a federal warrant."

"And you think he has a contact in this office? Bullshit, Dan. I can vouch for every one of my people."

Hooker winced in sympathy. He knew how he'd feel if he was on the hot seat. "Fillmore has been hacking into the FBI mainframe. When we change the password and install a new firewall, he gets around it within days. There's no doubt someone from this office passes high clearance information on to the Sons, Ash. We just not sure who yet."

Ash Callaway snapped his jaw as if he'd taken a physical blow. "Who do you suspect?"

"Everybody. We know the Sons plan an all-out attack on our national forests, based from the Denver area. You either have a bad apple in your support staff, or a rogue agent."

Calloway was probably envisioning the rest of his career assigned to the Buffalo office as a lowly field agent. A security leak of this magnitude was disgraceful, and the buck stopped on the desk of the Special Agent in Charge. Unless the leak was plugged quickly and the terrorists caught, Calloway's career was in the toilet, and he knew it.

But the man hadn't gotten where he was without being made of strong stuff. The SAC lifted his head and looked Dan in the eye. "This is my responsibility. What can I do to help?"

"We're working another angle on the terrorists, and putting an agent in the field, training with a local smokejumper, Fletcher Ansari. Our agent should be in place within the month."

"This smokejumper. He's a qualified agent? Or freelance?"

"He's doing me a favor. He's the guy who took out Fillmore's brother during the Hoover Dam incident. If Fillmore knew that, Ansari's life wouldn't be worth ten pesos."

Puma stepped to the edge of the cliff and surveyed the valley below. The Ute Sleeping Warrior God had changed his blanket from white to the light green of spring. He and Rachel were camped halfway up an unnamed mountain located a few miles east of the Florissant Fossil beds. The Place of Many Bones, Puma's ancestors had named the lowlands that lay at his feet.

The only way to approach their campsite was by horseback, on foot, or 4-wheel drive. There wasn't another human within miles, which was fine with Puma. Once the training was complete and they reported to base camp, his gnawing worry about Rachel's safety would slam into high gear. He'd worked her hard, but she wasn't ready to face an actual forest fire. A somewhere out there a beast in human form was prowling, looking for blood.

He'd gotten to know Rachel fairly well the past two weeks. She was cool, tough, and very competent. But too damn ambitious. Ambitious enough she could ignore the danger, and go after the arsonists without waiting for Hooker's team. Past experience with the New Sons of Liberty had shown Puma what ruthless bastards they were. Fanatics willing to use a nuclear weapon to further their cause wouldn't hesitate to kill an FBI agent, no matter that she was a woman.

So when they got to base camp, he would watch her. Watch her and notify Hooker when the time came. Tonight he wanted to concentrate on the woman and forget Rachel was a federal cop. The Milky Way painted a swath of brilliance against a canvas of deep purple, and the moon hung over Ute Pass, clothing the trees in shimmering gowns of silver lace. A soft breeze rustled in the crisp, clean air. The peace and beauty soothed him. Nearby a glacial spring swollen with spring melt sang a lullaby on its journey to the lake in the valley below.

He always slept better in the mountains.

A Great Horned Owl called from the branches of nearby pine, a signal that the nocturnal hunters were out. The scratching night sounds hushed, and frightened, furry creatures burrowed deep in their nests. He watched the hooting bird rise in flight, its dark silhouette and huge wingspan gliding noiselessly across the moon's path. Even in its haunting beauty, there was no mercy in nature. You were the hunter or the hunted.

Puma had never enjoyed being hunted.

He retrieved his boonie cap from his gear and pulled it over his eyes. From his experience, women went nuts over a boonie cap. He fished two cans of fruit from their stash of supplies, dropped beside Rachel and stretched his legs, planning his next move. She sat propped against her pack and stared into the fire, seemingly mesmerized by the flames.

"How're the allergies?"

"What?" She blinked and came back to the world. "Oh, fine. Under control."

"Lucky you came prepared."

"I always pack allergy meds in the spring. My nose goes crazy when the trees mate."

"You suppose they get a kick out of it? Dusting themselves with their own effluvia and calling it sex."

"They seem to know what they're doing. There're lots of little tree babies sprouting around us. By the way, not a bad supper, Ranger Rick."

"Canned hash and powdered eggs are my specialty." And it was traditional to feed a woman before bedding her. Puma believed in tradition. He handed her a small can of peaches and a plastic spoon. "Dessert."

"Thanks." She snapped open the can and dug in. "A culinary delight."

"Nothing's too good for the rookie."

"Remember, you didn't want me around. You were sure I couldn't cut it."

"So I was wrong. You got yourself out of a tight situation today, like a pro. And physically—"

"Uh-huh?"

She tipped the can back and sucked out the last of the peach juice. He watched the slender column of her throat work as she swallowed, and mentally stroked the sensitive area between her shoulder and neck. The firelight flickered over her features like sheet lightning, flushing her skin with heat. Her green eyes slanted toward him, sleepy and heavy-lidded. Eternal woman. Eve, the temptress.

He was plenty tempted, and didn't intend to wait any longer. His mouth and hands would soon know every inch of her. And she would know him. Because his need throbbed painfully, he'd take her hard and fast. The second time would be slow, and very thorough.

"What physically?" she repeated, licking her lips.

He cleared his throat and hoped her night vision was impaired enough from staring into the fire that she wouldn't notice the bulge in his jeans. If she sensed what he was thinking, she'd run like a rabbit from a coyote. He knew she was attracted to him, she zinged vibes whenever he came in touching distance. But she was strangely wary of intimacy, and kept a protective shield firmly in place.

"Physically, you're ready for jumping fire. Which doesn't mean I'll let up this last week. There's still a lot to learn, and you've yet to master the textbooks. I can get you there, but I can't take the tests for you."

"Perish the thought that you'd let up. Especially since we have sixteen-miles of rough terrain to cover tomorrow. I swear that pack weighs three-hundred pounds. And if I have to pick up that Pulaski again soon, I'll bury it in your skull." She reached for his empty can, stood and carried both tins to the plastic sack they used to stow trash.

"This is what we do, Rachel. It's hard, physical labor and dangerous. Sometimes it's boring. You knew that going in."

She shrugged and dumped the cans. "I'm tired and grumpy. Sorry."

"You need to relax, enjoy yourself a bit. It's a great night and the sky is so clear you can see the Pleiades."

"Where? You made that up."

"There," he rolled on his back and pointed. "Almost invisible in the northern hemisphere, next to Orion. No stars like that in New York City, I'll bet."

"No," she admitted. "Too many tall buildings and exhaust fumes. Where did you learn about the stars?"

"Most of the Middle East is monotonous, harsh land with few landmarks. Sometimes the stars and a compass were all I had to find my way back."

She looked at him thoughtfully. "You don't talk about it much, do you? Delta Force. Your time over there."

And a mistake to bring it up. Duty in the 'Stans had been so brutal, so exhausting and frustrating that jumping fire was a Sunday school picnic in comparison. "It's over and done. This is my home, the home of my people. I plan to stay put. To the modern world, the stars are faraway, burning gasbags. To the Utes, the stars are our ancestors, watching over us."

She gave him a measuring stare. "You're right. It's one of the prettiest spots I've ever seen. Primitive and unspoiled." She stretched her long arms skyward and leaned over to touch her toes. "I need to get out the liniment again."

Propped on one elbow, Puma admired the tight buttocks and heart-stopping legs outlined by her jeans. Her long-sleeved tee top was the amber color of her tousled hair, and clung to delicate, shapely breasts. Not large breasts, but high and proud. When she bent over, her shirt hiked up to expose a patch of creamy skin.

The need to have her had grown from a nagging itch to the point of pain. He'd kept his distance. Tried to concentrate on the training rather than the woman. It hadn't worked. She filled his days with torment and his nights with erotic dreams. The obsession went beyond anything he'd ever felt for a woman. If he didn't slake himself inside of her soon, he'd go loco.

She straightened up and caught his intent stare. "What?"

"You look good."

"Oh." She ran her fingers through her hair. "You mean for a tall, skinny woman with butch hair? You go for the androgynous look? Think I'll fit in with the guys?"

"You don't faintly resemble a guy, Rookie. You're as androgynous as I am."

She grinned. "Now there's a paradox. Puma Ansari and androgynous. Are you making a move on me, boss?"

"Sexy and smart. A scary combination." He patted the blanket that covered the spongy cushion of pine needles. "Sit by the fire where it's warm. I'll rub the kinks out of your back."

She kept her distance. "I'm not sure that's a good idea."

"I can control myself, Rookie. Have I laid a hand on you? Except when it's a necessary part of your training?"

"I appreciate that. Saves me having to break your nose."

He snorted a laugh and shook his head.

"You don't think I could?"

"You could try. Depends on how lucky you feel."

"Ha!" She took a step toward him. "I aced my Martial Arts class. I've taken down bigger guys than you, no problem."

"Really?" He didn't doubt she was well schooled in the martial arts. She was lithe, quick and fearless. But it was dangerous to underestimate an opponent and she was no physical match for him. He raised his eyebrows, intrigued with the idea of a little rough foreplay. He'd let her deck him, pull her over his knee and lay a swat on that luscious ass to make his point, then roll her on her back and kiss her senseless. From there it would be a simple move to them sharing his sleeping bag.

"You sure you want to try me?"

She took another step. "Only in self-defense. Will I need to?"

"Look." He raised his arms. "No dirty moves, I swear. Are you going to sit down here or not? I give great backrubs." She gave an ungracious sniff, sat and turned her back to him. A good thing because his physical problem was growing by the second. Damn, was it growing. He could use his cock for a fencepost.

She sighed as his fingers worked her shoulders. "Who told you that?"

"Hmmm?" He concentrated on the knot of nerves down the back of her neck. She quivered, but didn't jerk away. He'd have to lift her sweater to get to her back muscles. And unhook her bra. He shifted his legs to ease his physical discomfort. "Told me what?"

"That you give great backrubs? A woman, no doubt."

Was she jealous? His hands stilled while he thought out the answer, and figured he was in trouble no matter what he said. He dodged the bullet. "What do you think?"

Deftly he lifted her sweater, laid his hand on the soft warm skin of her back and stroked his thumb down the indentation of her spinal column. There was plenty of muscle tone there, but she felt fragile beneath his touch and it triggered his protective male instincts. He'd been useless when she hung up in that cedar, with nothing he could do except yell directions. Not that she'd needed them.

"Oh, it was a woman," she said. "And more than one."

He couldn't deny that. "I don't see any woman here but you, Rookie."

She craned her head around and looked at him, her forehead creased in a frown, the green eyes unreadable. "And we're just friends, right?"

"Is that what you want?"

Over the past few days he'd undergone a major attitude adjustment. At first Rachel Cortez was an irritation, an amusement, a nagging temptation, and now he found he wanted to protect her. Which was crazy, because he'd never met a woman more capable of taking care of herself.

She was the opposite of Sadie, who'd been a helpless creature, sweet and clinging, passive-aggressive and controlling. Strange, but he could no longer picture Sadie's face or hear her voice. Rachel walked her own path and asked quarter from no one. He pressed his thumbs on each side of her spine, working out the tightness in her muscles.

"Is it?" he repeated. "Do you want us to be nothing but friends?"

She wondered. Did she? She'd never felt anything more soothing than his hands, or more rousing. "I think anything else and it could get—complicated."

"Ah. Complicated. Lie down on your stomach."

She complied without thinking, stretched out on the blanket and cradled her cheek on her arm. For days she'd obeyed him without question, and it seemed natural to respond to the command in his voice. She sunk into the fragrant bed, her bones melting to mush under his skillful hands. His touch felt wonderful. He straddled her legs and began work on her buttocks.

She froze, all lethargy vanished. She might be relaxed, but he sure as hell wasn't. There was no mistaking the hard length prodding against her thighs. "Ansari, you stop that!"

"Can't," he chuckled. "Damn thing has a mind of its own."

"Am I supposed to be flattered? Because I'm the only woman within fifty-miles and you're horny? Get off me, lech!"

"Whatever you say, Rookie." He rolled her over and captured her wrists in one hand, his weight pinning her to the ground. "Time for that kiss you owe me."

He didn't hurt her, but she was effectively immobilized. His eyes were in shadow under the bill of his cap but there was no mistaking the set of his jaw, the slight parting of his sensual mouth and the rapid breathing. Or the erection nestled comfortably between her thighs. She wet her lips. "All right," she whispered. "But let go of my hands."

He released her, gathered her into his arms and pulled her up into his lap. God, he was strong. His biceps bulged with roped muscle and his chest was like a rock wall. Even though his arousal prodded against her bottom in explicit demand, she knew she was safe with him. Obviously he planned a seduction and was doing a really good job of it, but he wouldn't force himself on her.

His scent was hot and male, mixed with the spicy aroma of the pine needles they rested on. Her own juices were running liquid and warm between her thighs. Why fight something she wanted so badly?

She reached, pulled off his cap and ran her fingertips around its bill. The khaki material was shabby and had seen many washings. He'd probably worn it while on the peacekeeping force in Bosnia, and later to hunt down the Taliban in the wilds of Afghanistan. In a way it was symbolic of his military career.

"Nice cap."

"You like it?" He retrieved the boonie cap from her hand, pulled it over her head and tucked stray curls under its edge. "Looks better on you. Keep it."

He bent and kissed her forehead, his mouth sliding to her temple, down her jaw line to the exquisitely sensitive area at the side of her neck. He had her full attention. She quivered and squirmed against him and he tightened his grip, murmuring soothing sounds in her ear. She had seen him do the same to quiet a skittish colt. She dug her fingers into his thick hair and pulled his head closer. Her tongue was too thick to speak; she could only make incoherent sounds in her throat. Not that what he was doing wasn't wonderful, but she craved more.

Then his mouth was on hers, softly coaxing, hot and wet. All thought, all the night sounds vanished. She spun upward into the sky and flew with the stars, his scent and taste mingling with hers until they were one being, one column of aching need. He lifted her flat onto the ground, fitting his body to hers, lips, chest and sex pressed together. His guttural gasps enflamed every nerve cell, his kiss no longer coaxing but hard, searing and demanding.

"I'm going to make love to you until we both pass out," he growled. "Tonight you wear my brand."

His mouth went to her throat and he drew the soft flesh into his mouth, using his teeth. She sobbed and wrapped her legs around his waist as he ground his erection against her soft mound. She edged close to climax with the erotic sensations racking her body. "Say it," he demanded. "You want me."

She shook her head wildly, afire inside but afraid of his intensity. She was her own person and belonged to no one.

"No!" she said, even as she tightened her grip around him with her legs and arms.

"By God, you will," he promised, and his mouth came down in another soul-searing kiss. His hand crept under her sweater and unsnapped and tugged at her jeans until they were down to mid-thigh.

"Puma, wait!" She rolled out of reach.

"I'll wait long enough to get us naked. Maybe."

"No, please! I have to tell you something. You might change your mind."

He took a deep breath. "You have some kind of exotic disease?"

"Of course not! But—"

"Neither do I. And nothing short of being swallowed up in a number ten earthquake will change my mind." He pulled her sweater over her head and tossed it aside. "I brought a dozen condoms. I hope that's enough."

Despite her fears she laughed. "A dozen? Damned arrogant aren't you? And full of yourself."

"Cocky, even," he grinned. "You have two seconds to get out of those jeans, Rookie."

He reached.

She scrambled to her feet and clutched at her disheveled clothing.

"There are some things I haven't—Oh, damn, this is so— you need to see my legs. I'm used to them, but some people are shocked. So look and decide if you still want me." She wasn't embarrassed to undress in front of him, which was strange. Usually she insisted on disrobing and crawling under a sheet before she let any of her lovers near. She sighed and peeled off her jeans.

He stared in shocked silence and withdrew his hands. Tears filled her eyes. It wasn't the first time a man found the sight of her ruined legs disgusting. But this time it mattered. This time her heart would crack. She reached for her jeans in slow motion, her arms heavy with pain.

"Don't," he said, pulled her back into his lap and wrapped his arms around her. "You were burned. When did it happen?"

"A long time ago. They took skin grafts from my thighs and repaired the damage, but the scars are ugly. I don't blame you for being repulsed."

He stroked her face. "I'm not repulsed, baby. I want you more than ever. Tell me about it."

"I was ten, young enough I still played with Barbie dolls. We lived in an old two-story house, and my brother Doug had his own pad in the attic."

"There was a fire?"

"Yes. It was late at night. Maybe the smoke alarm went off and we didn't hear it. Or maybe it just didn't go off. My dad shook me awake and yelled at my mother to get me out, then he started up the attic stairs for Doug."

She shuddered and caught her breath. She'd never talked

about this to anyone except the child shrink they sent her to afterward.

He brushed the tears from her cheeks. "Go on," he said quietly.

She couldn't stop now. She had to let it out. "My mother dragged me outside and told me to stay there while she ran next door to call the fire department." She caught her breath. "It's stupid but I don't remember being frightened for myself. But I loved my dad and brother and I was terrified for them."

"You went back in after them," he said, enclosing her nakedness under his jacket and hugging her closer. "You were a brave little girl."

"No, just irrational. By this time the downstairs was full of smoke. The hem of my nightgown caught on fire and I ran screaming out the door, in total panic. We'd had the Stop, Drop, and Roll technique drummed into us at school. I'd even practiced it, but I forgot everything and all I could do was run."

"You were a child. I've seen grown men panic in less dangerous situations."

"My mother—she heard me screaming. She threw me on the ground and beat the flames out with her bare hands. I had third degree burns from my ankles to my knees. It hurt, oh, God, how it hurt. I screamed until I lost my voice. Until the medics came and gave me a shot to knock me out." Rachel rubbed her face, the memory still vivid after all these years.

He rocked her in his arms, comforting her. She sagged against him, desperately needing his warmth as the chilly mountain air seeped into her bones.

"What happened to your father and brother?"

"There was a double funeral. Closed coffins."

"Jesus."

They didn't say anything for a long time. Just sat and held each other and thought their own thoughts. Finally he sighed and pulled her to her feet and she shivered at the loss of his warmth. He wrapped her in the blanket they'd been sitting on.

"You're freezing and we both need some rest. We'll zip our sleeping bags together and share the tent. I want you next to me. Just to sleep."

She nodded, her head against his strong chest. He was right. Emotion and old memories had exhausted her to the point of numbness. Right now she needed him far more than he needed her.

CHAPTER 7

Puma shook himself from twilight sleep, wakened by a bred-in-the-bone instinct for danger. It was predawn, the time of shadows, the dream stage between slumber and consciousness. He lifted his arm from under Rachel's shoulder, tense and fully alert. The air reeked with the scent of musk. A soft, guttural sound droned in his ear. A sound from within their tent.

Rachel sighed in protest and snuggled closer.

Cautiously, Puma edged his hand toward his pack and reached into the side pocket, feeling for his 9mm S&W. The smack of the automatic in his hand was like shaking hands with an old friend. He slid back the safety, rolled away from Rachel and aimed toward the menacing sound.

Two yellow, elliptical eyes stared at him, unblinking.

The cougar crouched in the corner of the tent, regal as the Sphinx and totally calm, disdaining the deadly weapon pointed his way. He stared at Puma and continued to lick his enormous paws and wash his face. Puma held the gun rock-steady and waited. If the cat sprung, those powerful jaws could clamp around Puma's throat in seconds. But not before he emptied a full clip directly between the amber eyes. The cougar halted his grooming activity and blinked.

"Impasse, boy?" Puma whispered.

The cougar yawned, pushed to his feet and stretched his sleek body, and ambled toward the tent entrance. He walked with a slight limp. This was no shadowy phantom, it was a living, breathing beast of prey, and very dangerous. And familiar.

The flap of the canvas shelter hung agape, and pale dawn seeped through the opening. Puma knew damn well he'd zipped it securely before he'd crawled into the sleeping bag next to Rachel. The cougar paused and looked back, as if he expected to be followed. Hair rose on Puma's scalp. Christ! He'd never been this close to the animal before, but there was no question what it was.

It was always a bad omen when his totem appeared.

Rachel stirred, rubbing her eyes.

He removed one hand from the pistol and placed it on her shoulder. "Don't move, Rookie."

"What is it?" she asked sleepily.

"We have a visitor. Stay calm."

The cougar snarled softly and swished his black-tipped tail; his magnificent head moved from side to side, watching them. He was eight feet in length if he was an inch. Close to two-hundred pounds. Thick cinnamon fur ruffled along his back, tapering to a pale cream at his chest and belly. His feral breath steamed in the icy mountain air.

"Oh, God," Rachel breathed. "You wouldn't shoot him!" Her eyes were wide with amazement. There was no doubt she saw the mountain lion clearly.

He shook his head. He'd have to deal with that knowledge later. For now his worry was their safety. "Not if he behaves himself. They rarely attack humans."

"What is that sweet smell? Sort of metallic."

"He made a kill recently. A deer, probably."

The cougar growled, leapt through the breach and into the dawn. The tent flap swung behind him.

"You mean he ate Bambi?" she raised an eyebrow, and Puma grinned despite himself.

"A wild deer is no more Bambi than this guy is Disney's Lion King. Stay here." He stepped into his jeans and shoved his gun at the waistband. Although he wasn't clear on how he could shoot a ghost.

"Wait! I'll go with you." She scrambled to locate her clothes, rooting in her backpack. She didn't intend to be left out. Something very strange was happening. "Just because he isn't hungry doesn't mean he's not dangerous."

"I'll follow him to be sure he leaves our campsite. Stay out of the way." He squatted by the tent opening, and his jean-clad legs and bare feet disappeared from view. He moved as silently as the big cat.

Stay out of the way? How typical.

Rachel pulled on her pants and sweatshirt and gave brief thought to digging her own gun out of her backpack. Probably not a good idea. She wasn't sure if she could tell man from beast once they were swallowed up in dense foliage. She yanked on her boots, not bothering with socks. Pine needles were painful to walk on with unprotected toes.

It was very cold outside the tent. She shivered, grateful for the warmth of her sweatshirt, and looked around for a stout stick to use as a club. If you shouted and threw stones at a mountain cougar he likely would back away, but if Puma planned to track the animal into the brush, that was risky.

The lion stood at the edge of the clearing, with the half-naked man crouched only yards away. The rising sun winked through the tall pines and bathed both figures in a frozen tableau, one that might have happened two-hundred years before, the Indian warrior stalking the beast, bent on proving his manhood. It was mystical, eerie. Rachel shook her head in wonder and the big cat turned toward her, the ancient eyes steady and unnerving.

Follow me.

She'd seen that intelligence before, felt the cutting urgency of the stare. Known this same psychic connection.

Her heartbeat went into triple time. It couldn't be! Puma's ranch lay forty miles southeast, through dense forest and mountainous terrain. And the odds of the same animal leaving his territory and appearing in their camp? In their tent? Astronomical. From what she knew about mountain lions, they stayed away from people.

What do you want? Her lips formed the silent words. The cougar snarled and leapt from the clearing into the dense pinion forest.

Follow me.

A back paw dragged and looked slightly deformed, as if it had once been caught in a trap. Rachel rediscovered her legs, pivoted and sprinted after the tawny beast as he disappeared into the underbrush.

"Rachel!" Puma's harsh shout halted her in her tracks.

"I have to follow him! He wants—"

"I know what he wants. It won't do any good to follow him. He's gone."

"Fletcher Ansari, what is this about?"

"We have to pack up and leave, Rachel. There's a ranger cabin and lookout tower an hour's hike from here and they'll have a radio. I need to contact Mike and have him copter in to pick us up as soon as possible."

"I'm not moving a step until you explain! What's the connection between you and that wild creature?" She planted her feet astride, folded her arms and glared. Unless he picked her up bodily, she wasn't budging.

He rubbed his face wearily. "We'll break camp and I'll explain on the way. Not that you'll believe me. I'm not sure I believe it myself."

Rachel narrowed her eyes. "This is weird. And I swear that cougar—okay, maybe I'm crazy. It was like he spoke to me, and you feel it too. I never saw a wild animal behave like that."

"It isn't an ordinary animal. Not quite."

"You're saying I'm hallucinating? That we both are!"

"That may be as good an explanation as any. He's an animal, and he isn't. You and my grandfather are the only humans other than me to see him."

"Dammit, Ansari! You're talking in riddles."

"Rachel, please. We have to hurry." His face was strained and lined with worry. "I have to get home. Something terrible has happened. Or is about to."

* * *

The sun beat down from a cloudless sky, and despite the coolness of the spring day, the man hunkered in the brush was sweating. There was damned little natural protection on the lookout spot he'd chosen, but it had the advantage of a clear view of Ansari's ranch house.

The ledge jutted out a bit and hung over a steep slope covered with oak brush and scrub pine. Zebedee's clothing blended into the landscape——khaki pants, brown shirt, socks and boots. The cap he wore was a camouflage mix of green and tan, an army surplus purchase. Bought at the same time, the binoculars were dull green metal, non-reflective and high quality. Properly adjusted, the high-powered binocs offered a clean view of the house, the barn and all the outbuildings.

He'd spent too many days doing this. His arms and face were sunburned and the effing mosquitoes were driving him nuts. Fillmore was sure as hell going to pay him extra for the pain and aggravation. Zeb spat in disgust as another swarm of mosquitoes attacked his neck, and he reached for the bug spray. Not that it did much good. The little suckers lapped the stuff up like cotton candy.

He'd done his homework and it was time to get on with the job. He had timers, ignition devices and his special fuel mixture stowed in his jeep. Enough to burn down a dozen city blocks. But the smokejumper and his bitch girlfriend weren't around, hadn't been for two days, and Fillmore had made it plain Ansari went up in the flames, or no payment.

The harsh sound of a revving engine caught his attention and he swung the binoculars to his face. Something was happening below.

Zeb adjusted the field glasses for a clearer view. The lenses blurred as he found the proper setting. The ranch hand cowboy, the one who lived in the trailer and didn't do squat work as far as Zeb could tell, gunned the SUV out of the garage and came to a jolting stop in the driveway, left the car door ajar and motor running, and sprinted for the house.

Cowboy emerged five minutes later, his arm around the old guy Fillmore said was a shirttail relation of Ansari's, and half-dragged the geezer to the car. The Indian woman trotted behind them, jabbering and waving her arms. Couple of monkeys for sure.

This was interesting.

Zeb guessed the old fart took sick. Maybe had a heart attack or stroke. The three piled into the SUV and cowboy took off in a cloud of dust. Headed east at the turnoff. To the hospital in Colorado Springs, maybe. The ranch was deserted except for the dog tearing up and down in a fenced area next to the barn, howling his head off. Loud enough the eerie sound carried to the cliff where Zeb lay hidden.

The boss was not going to like this.

Depending on what was wrong with grandpa, part of Ansari's family might be away for a while. Which would royally screw up Fillmore's plans.

And Zeb's. He'd never incinerated a whole family before, and the anticipation had been giving him wet dreams for a week. He'd have to find a payphone, call Fillmore and leave one of those stupid code messages. The man was paranoid. Thought the feds were listening in on his calls. Well, if they were, they wouldn't learn much. Far as Zebedee could tell, Fillmore never called from the same number twice or let one incriminating word drop.

He gathered up his gear. No use sticking around, and he had to get to a phone ASAP. He thrust his water bottle and bug spray in his personal gear bag, fit the binoculars into their leather case and slung the sack over his shoulder.

The dog howled again and Zeb's bones shivered. Sounded like a damn wolf was loose. Someday he'd kill that stupid animal.

The dog.

Slowly Zeb lowered his pack to the ground. The watchdog was the only thing Zeb was worried about in the setup. Not only did the animal have acute hearing, he had the look of a killer.

It was too good a chance to miss.

No one was around. No witnesses except a few horses and cows. He could slip into the back of the barn and take care of the mutt for good. He reached for the knife he kept in his belt, and paused. A knife was no good. The wolfhound would chew him to pieces if he got too close, and Zeb didn't have a gun.

He'd have to hike a mile back to where he'd hidden his jeep and drive to the nearest shopping center, buy a pound of hamburger and some rat killer. No dog alive could resist raw meat. The mutt would gobble the treat down and never notice that Zeb had loaded it with enough poison to kill a cow.

CHAPTER 8

The copter hovered over the small airstrip that edged his ranch property, and settled down as gracefully as a plump goose on a nest. There was no movement, no sign of life except for the horses corralled by the barn. An air of desertion hung over the place, and Puma's nerves stretched beyond bearing. He ducked under the rotating copter blades and took off in a flat-out run for the house, Rachel at his heels.

The front door stood ajar, and Puma's fears heightened. They seldom locked the door during the day, but Lindy wouldn't leave it standing open. He called her name sharply as he entered. No answer. Soiled breakfast dishes were scattered on the kitchen table and the odor of bacon and stale coffee hung in the air. Leaving a mess wasn't something Lindy would do without drastic motivation.

Rachel entered the kitchen, gasping for breath. "Where're Lindy and Frank?"

"I don't know. Can you check their place? I'll try to locate Sully."

"I hope Frank isn't sick again," she said.

"Yeah," Puma said. "But it's possible."

He forced his heartbeat to slow as he cursed his own

neglect. His family had left in a hurry. Maybe the cause was Frank's shaky health, maybe an emergency at a neighboring ranch, or possibly with Puma's sister. Whatever it was they couldn't get a hold of him. Not deep in the mountains where a cell phone didn't work. Damn, he should have taken a two-way with them. And insisted that Frank go to the doctor for another checkup. He'd known Lindy was worried sick.

The barn and corrals were empty except for the horses placidly chewing their breakfast hay. The stalls were raked out and layered with clean straw. No one answered his shout. He headed for Sully's trailer. Sometimes the kid holed up there when the morning chores were done. After banging a warning, he opened the door and peered inside. Nothing but silence and empty space.

Something was very wrong.

Lifting the cumbersome garage door, Puma stepped inside. His pickup and Sully's motorcycle were parked in their usual places. The SUV was gone. Where should he start looking? He turned at the sound of Rachel's pounding feet and her voice.

She thrust a note in his hand. "I found this note by the telephone. From Lindy. Frank got sick and they took him to the ER in Colorado Springs."

He snatched the paper from her fingers. "The copter can have us there in thirty minutes. Mike knows people; maybe he can get permission to land on the hospital helo pad."

"We should call. Check to see if Frank was admitted."

"Yeah, I'll do that. Would you find Mike and tell him what's going on?"

"I'm here, Puma. What's up?" Their pilot stood in the garage doorway. Twirling his sunglasses with one hand, the other thrust in the pocket of his leather jacket.

"My uncle had an attack of some kind and my aunt and ranch hand took him to the emergency room. Can you wait around 'til I check with the hospitals? Then fly us into the Springs?"

"No problem. I'll call in that I'll be tied up a while." He

pulled his cellular from his pocket, had a quick conversation and hung up. "Taken care of. What else can I do?"

"I need to locate my family before we can do anything."

"I'll have a look around," Mike said, waving his hand. "Go make your call."

"Puma?" Rachel spoke. "Where do you suppose Sundance is?"

Puma frowned, thinking. "Maybe they took him with them."

"To the hospital?"

"Rachel and I will look for the dog," Mike interjected. "The ER unit at Memorial is the best, Puma. I've been there often enough on a case."

Puma nodded, somewhat relieved. Mike had a steady head and Puma would trust his judgment in any situation. "Good to know, Mike. Sundance comes to Rachel's whistle as fast as he does to mine. He's probably off hunting a rabbit."

They watched Puma sprint toward the house. Rachel's sense of foreboding deepened. The memory of the phantom cougar's amber eyes haunted her.

"The dog run is on the other side of the barn, Mike." Rachel put her fingers to her mouth and gave a piercing whistle. Usually Sundance appeared within minutes, no matter what he was up to. She whistled again and called his name.

"Maybe he's taking a nap somewhere," Mike said.

"Not Sundance. He should be racing to greet us by now."

"We'll find him."

They walked toward the barn, Rachel periodically whistling and calling. When they approached the corral, Dragon snorted and trotted to the fence, along with Wind Song, the stallion's favorite mare. The other horses were at the far end of the meadow, small blobs in the landscape. No sign of the dog.

"If he was within earshot, he'd be here by now," Rachel said, patting Wind Song's velvet nose.

"I'd guess it's like Puma said. The dog's off chasing rabbits."

Rachel wished she could be sure of that. They walked around the barn to the dog run. It was empty. No Sundance. "I'll check inside his house," Rachel said.

She unlatched the wire gate, and both of them stepped inside the pen. The bowls that contained water and food for the dog were both brimming full. Sundance hated to be caged, but sometimes he was shut in for his own safety, if Sully or Frank were operating heavy machinery, or if stock was being moved.

Mike placed his hand on her arm. "Rachel, what's that noise?"

She heard it then. A low, moaning sound.

"Oh, my God," she whispered and sprang toward the sound, Mike right behind her.

Sundance lay whimpering in the shadow of his house, his tongue lolling. The bitter odor of vomit hung in the air. Mike's hand stayed her from jumping to the dog's side. "Wait, Rachel. Let me take a look, he may bite you."

"Sundance would never bite me!"

"Could be rabies. Animals go out of their heads and do bizarre things if they get infected."

She brushed his arm away. "No! Sundance had all his shots. Puma takes care of him like he was his own son."

Mike picked her up bodily and set her away from the doghouse. "Maybe, but stand back. I'll look at him."

He knelt by the dog. Sundance opened his eyes and feebly wagged his tail. The thump, thump broke Rachel's heart. "We have to get him to the vet right away," she whispered. "He's terribly sick, maybe dying."

Mike leaned over and sniffed the pile of vomit, and gave the dog a gentle pat. He stood, blocking her progress. "I think he's been poisoned. A vet won't do much good, Rachel."

She shook her head wildly. Not Sundance! "We have to try, Mike! We can't let him die without trying to save him."

"Get Puma." Mike removed his jacket and covered the

shaking, hapless dog. Sundance feebly licked his hand. "Good boy," Mike whispered, his voice thick. "We're going to help you, old fella. Make you feel better."

The import of Mike's words finally registered with her. "My God! Who would do such a hateful, wicked thing?"

"Get Puma, Rachel, and I'll look around. Could be someone was careless. Left a footprint or something behind."

She spun and raced toward the bungalow.

Puma waved and grinned as he stepped out the door. "Frank's been admitted for observation. The doctor is pretty sure it's appendicitis and they'll probably operate today. Thank God it wasn't his heart."

She flung herself at him and hugged, tears running down her face, her voice frozen in her throat. How could she tell him?

He hugged her back. "What, Rachel? Calm down. Frank will be fine."

"S-Sundance. He's——he's really sick."

Puma's smile died and his grip tightened. "Where?"

"In his pen. Someone—God, Puma, I'm so sorry."

He took her hand and raced toward the dog run. Mike was standing by the gate, holding a crumpled plastic wrapper.

"Where is he?" Puma rasped the question.

"Next to the doghouse," Mike answered, jerking his head in that direction. "It's not good, buddy. I'm guessing someone bears a grudge and took it out by poisoning the dog."

Puma knelt by his pet. Sundance wagged his tail and tried to get up. Gently, Puma took the dog in his lap and made soothing sounds. The dog whimpered and shivered, hunkering into his master's arms. Rachel could barely see for her flow of tears. The sheer cruelty of the act made her nauseous and furious at the same time.

Puma raised his eyes to Mike, his face a mask of pain. "Poisoned? You're sure?"

Mike extended the plastic wrap, filthy with dirt and what

looked like dried blood. Rachel noticed that he wore gloves and was careful the way he held it. "I found this stomped into the ground in plain sight. Traces left of something mixed with hamburger residue. From the dog's symptoms, I'd guess strychnine."

Puma's Viking eyes flashed like lightning on a gun barrel. "You think someone loaded the meat with poison, threw it to the dog and didn't care if I found the wrapper? Maybe wanted me to?"

Mike nodded. "We'll have it analyzed. Find out if the store clerk remembers who purchased it."

"What's your best guess for his chances, Mike?"

The two men exchanged steady glances, Mike's face full of pity. "I'm no expert."

"Dammit, Mike! What are his chances?"

Mike winced. "The poison's deep in his system. He vomited some of the stuff up, but it's too late."

The pilot turned away, his body language and expression telling Rachel what he couldn't bring himself to say. Rachel knew Mike had been a Special Forces medic before he started his own security business. He had dealt with murder, and that's what this was. Pure and simple murder.

Puma nodded slowly, in acceptance. "How long?"

"It could be a while," Mike said reluctantly. "Strychnine isn't a fast or easy way to die. Hopefully he'll lapse into a coma and slip away."

Sundance opened his eyes and whimpered.

Puma stroked him, crooning softly. "It's all right, boy. I'm here."

Sundance tried to lick Puma's hand, his body shaking with the effort. He fell back and stiffened, spasms racked his body; foam poured from his mouth, but no sounds. Puma held him tightly until the convulsions stopped and the dog lay still. The air grew silent except for Rachel's quiet sobs.

Puma looked up at Mike. "Give me your gun," he said, his voice rough with grief. "Take Rachel back to the house."

Mike shook his head. "Let me do this for you, buddy."

"I raised him from a pup and we've been together for three years," Puma said stonily. "I'll send him on his way."

Without another word, Mike removed his pistol from the back of his waistband and handed it over.

Rachel protested, her heart breaking. "Please, Puma. Let me stay. I love him, too."

"Leave us, Rookie, so I can say goodbye. Will you go in the house and find me a clean sheet to wrap him in? Give him a pat before you leave."

She knelt and gave Sundance a lingering stroke and last kiss. "I love you, boy," she whispered, now weeping uncontrollably. "There're lots of rabbits in heaven."

Mike lifted her to her feet, as if he knew her legs couldn't manage it on their own. "Come, Rachel," he said gently. "Give them some time alone."

They were almost to the doorstep of the house when they heard the gunshot. Rachel staggered as if she'd been struck, a haze of hatred overpowering her grief. Sweet, loving Sundance was gone.

"When Puma finds who did this, God help him," Mike said. "The murdering bastard will be lucky if Puma kills him quick."

Rachel gritted her teeth. "Unless I find the murdering bastard first."

CHAPTER 9

Rachel limped into the kitchen nursing new blisters, one on each heel. "Yum," she said, sniffing the hearty aroma of browning meat and garlic. "I'm starving. Your nephew doubled my afternoon training exercises."

She reached into the earthen bowl on the table and snagged an oatmeal cookie. A rich burst of cinnamon and butter exploded on her tongue. She hummed in enjoyment and reached for another. Lindy shook her spatula in warning. "Don't spoil your appetite filling up on cookies. Fletcher won't be here for supper. You'll have to fight Frank and Sully for his share."

She bit into a second cookie. "I'll take them both on for your beef stew. Frank looks ever so much better, Lindy. It's hard to believe that four days ago he went under the knife."

Lindy nodded in acknowledgment. "He'll land back in the hospital if he doesn't slow down."

"I wouldn't worry. Sully won't let him lift anything heavier than a coffee cup." She gazed longingly at the cookie bowl, calculating her chances of snatching another. Lindy could do serious damage with her spatula.

Lindy added chopped carrots and onions to her stew. "If you're that hungry, peel some more potatoes. Easy to stretch stew with a potato or two. Fletcher says you need to gain some weight before you check in at base."

"I'm at the minimum weight. Why won't Puma be here for supper?" Something was bothering Lindy. Her snappish tone was out of character.

"He didn't say." Lindy shrugged and covered the stew pot, lowering the stove temperature to simmer. "He loaded some supplies and took off on Dragon. Said he'd be back in time to report to base on Monday. For you to study your books. And to keep up the training so you'll be able to pass the PT test."

"He'll be gone the next two days? He didn't mention anything to me."

Puzzled and not understanding what she heard, Rachel frowned. An hour ago she'd been cursing the man's ancestry back to the Stone Age, but Lindy's news wasn't good. In fact, it was alarming. If she didn't have Ansari's support she'd never make the cut, and if she didn't qualify Hooker would drop her from his deployment team.

"Give the pot a stir when you're done peeling potatoes. I'm going to check on Frank." Lindy wiped her hands and whisked off her apron, avoiding Rachel's eyes.

Rachel had never seen Lindy look more Indian or more tight-lipped. She laid a hand on the older woman's arm. "Lindy, what's going on? Did I do something to make you angry? And Puma's been gruff with me for days. Ever since we lost Sundance."

"It's none of my business what goes on between you two."

"I don't understand."

"He's done this since he was a little boy, takes off when something gets to him. He was gone for two weeks when his Grandpa died. Came back and went on with life. Like he'd found some kind of peace in the mountains."

"You think he needed to get away and grieve? It's weird, but I thought I saw Sundance playing in the meadow this morning. My mind playing tricks and wishing he was there."

The little woman cocked her head back and gave her a

steady stare. "Maybe you did see him. Stranger things have happened around here. Sundance loved to romp in the meadow."

Rachel remembered the cougar's appearance in their tent and Puma's reaction to it. The animal's feral smell and haunting amber eyes, and the eerie way it seemed to communicate telepathically. And how Puma had been so sure something was wrong that he'd rushed home. Strange things did happen in these mountains.

"Lindy," she said, her voice carefully neutral. "Have you seen a wild cougar hanging around the ranch?"

"Last year a big cat took one of our calves, but the forest rangers hunted him down and killed him. I've never seen one near the house though."

"Just wondered," Rachel shrugged. "I guess I'm seeing things a lot lately." She would have to look elsewhere for answers. First Puma and now Lindy had resisted her probing questions. Maybe she'd talk to Frank.

He is an animal, and he isn't. You and my grandfather are the only humans other than me to see him.

"The dog dying was bad," Lindy said. "But the boy is worried more trouble is coming. He won't talk about it."

"It worries me, too." Suddenly Rachel understood why Lindy was upset with her. "You think I'm responsible? That my being here is causing trouble?"

"I don't know. But we never had this kind of goings on before, and Fletcher doesn't panic easily."

Rachel hated to air her fears aloud. "Is he planning to hang here at the ranch, and let me report to base on my own?"

"He'd rather stay to take care of his home, but he'll do his duty, Rachel. He always does."

"Okay." Rachel knew there was more. "What else?"

"He hired Mike Devlan's security service and one of Mike's men will move in with Sully tonight. They're bringing two trained Dobermans as watchdogs. We'll be safe enough. Likely the problem will go away when you leave."

Rachel slumped into a chair and waved her hand in protest. She had to clarify this. "Lindy, my assignment is top secret. No one outside of my immediate superior knows I'm here, let alone why."

"This boss of yours—you talk to him lately? Tell him what's going on? About Sundance being poisoned?" Lindy's reproachful dark eyes drilled into Rachel and stirred uneasy guilt.

"I check in daily to let him know everything is fine." Okay, she hadn't reported the dog's death to Hooker, and she should have. But her FBI boss was security conscious to the point of paranoia, and it wouldn't take much for him to pull her assignment. "Lindy, I had nothing to do with Sundance's death. I loved that dog. Isn't hiring Mike a bit overcautious?"

"Fletcher and Mike found evidence that someone's been spying on us."

The hair tingled on Rachel's scalp. "What evidence?"

"Tire tracks on our land and fencing cut. Trampled grass on a cliff overlooking the house and a couple of discarded whiskey bottles. And Sully noticed a strange SUV driving around the back roads the past two weeks."

"Oh, God. He didn't tell me!" Her stomach heaved and the cookies threatened to make a reappearance. She would be ass deep in alligators when Hooker heard this. "Why didn't he tell me?"

Lindy scowled. "He'd have to answer that."

Rachel knew why. Since she and Puma had spent the night together, almost but not quite making love, she avoided him when possible and sent silent back off messages if he got too close. He'd responded with a tight-lipped indifference.

God, she was such an idiot. What did she think he was going to do? Jump her bones and rape her? Never.

A physical fling with the man would be hot. Anything more was out of the question, for both of them. She loved her career too much to leave DC, and Puma's heart was entrenched in his mountains. *Are you afraid you'd like it too much, Rachel?* Afraid that you'd give him more than your body?

Right. No fling.

Slight problem. She wanted him with a bone-deep, painful ache. Wanted his hands and mouth on her, their bodies coupled. Just the sound of his voice melted her into a pool of butter. Fortunately after they reported to base, intimacy would be close to impossible and she'd be too busy to brood over Fletch Ansari, his perfect male body, those ice blue eyes that stirred fire in her belly. And there was the way he could kiss. God, could he kiss. Forget it Rachel. Don't lose sight of the goals you've set for yourself.

"Lindy, would you excuse me? I need to make a phone call and check this info out with my boss."

Ten minutes later she returned to the kitchen, her ears smarting and knees shaking. She'd never had a fiercer dressing down in her life, and she still hadn't told him about Sundance. To say Hooker was upset was conservative. He was livid that Puma had evidence someone was spying on the ranch, and had left carrying his rifle. She'd been lucky to survive with her skin. Her direct orders were to locate Ansari immediately. Her assignment would be aborted if she didn't follow orders. Dammit, she would find him.

"Where did Puma go, Lindy? I need to talk to him right away."

"I'm not sure he'd want that. He made it plain he wanted to be alone. He took Sundance's ashes with him."

"Please. It's important. Do you know where he is?"

"Maybe," Lindy admitted reluctantly. "There's a campsite up in the mountains he likes to visit. Frank and I used to camp there."

Rachel watched in amusement as the woman's cheeks flamed. "Lindy, you're turning red."

"Redder, you mean?" Lindy chuckled. "It's a special place, Rachel. I can tell you how to get there, but you better be sure of what you're after."

"What does that mean?"

"Puma needs you, Rachel, and I think he's done asking. If you follow him, he's likely to take that as an invitation."

As if she had a choice.

If it hadn't been for the pony, she never would have gotten this far. There was a path, almost invisible in the lengthening shadows of dusk. Probably a deer track. It meandered in the direction of the stream gurgling in the distance, a happy, peaceful sound. The path ran through a grove of aspen and was marked with fresh scat, proving that the deer that had originally broken the trail still used it.

Rachel shivered in the night air, wishing she'd worn a heavier jacket. She'd kill for a hot drink right now. Mountain air turned frigid after the sun went down. There was a blanket stowed in the saddlebags flung across Wind Song's rump. She'd have to dig it out soon.

She wondered again if she'd come on a fool's errand. She and the pinto had been trekking for two hours with no sign of their quarry. Even with Lindy's instructions, there was no guarantee they could find Puma. Hoping the filly would sense where Dragon had gone, Rachel let her have her head. Wind Song tossed her mane and picked up the pace.

They continued to follow the twisting path, ducking occasionally to avoid the branches that hung over the trail and whipped behind them as they passed. Foliage rustled in the breeze and the rising moon cast a shimmer on their surroundings. The slender white trunks of aspen trees marched beside them like ghostly sentinels, and the acrid scent of crushed leaves mingled with the heavy odor of conifer.

Despite the late afternoon shower they had ridden through earlier, the forest floor was dry. The pony's hooves made a soft, thudding sound on the thick underbrush. Freshly fallen twigs and leaves shrouded the duff underfoot, a layer of decaying vegetation that would readily feed a wildfire.

The pony stopped on the path, her velvety nose quivering and ears erect; a soft whinny escaped her throat.

Rachel felt a stab of unease and pulled up. Bear tracks had been spotted in the general area during the previous week. The animals avoided contact with humans, but they were omnivorous and she would make a tasty meal for a hungry bear. A black bear could move fast enough and was strong enough to bring down a horse, unless the horse was running full out across open land. In the crowded grove of aspen, the two of them wouldn't stand a chance. She loosened the revolver in her belt and eased it out of its holster.

"What is it, girl? Take it easy."

A click of her tongue accompanied by a dig of her booted heels, and the pony moved forward. Cautiously. If Wind Song had smelled bear, she would have balked and refused to move, probably would have thrown her rider and fled in panic.

They entered a clearing in the trees. Shrubs and scrubby pine enclosed the grassy circular opening. The sound of rushing water sang louder here. Wind Song whinnied in anticipation of a refreshing drink and pawed at the pine needles under her hooves. The smoky scent of a campfire drifted toward them.

The pinto had led them unerringly to her mate.

Rachel's heartbeat accelerated. Thank God.

Ever the woodsman, he'd built the fire in a small pit and scraped away the surrounding grass to expose raw dirt. A grate stretched across the coals, and coffee simmered in an enameled pot. His tent was pitched under the shelter of a giant pine tree. He'd obviously used the campsite before.

She slid stiffly out of the saddle letting the reins drop, and Wind Song bent her head to feed on the lush growth. An impatient neigh came from the other side of the clearing. Tethered among a stand of saplings, Dragon ordered his mate to come to him. Wind Song lifted her head, nickered a response and went back to munching.

"Good girl." Rachel patted the pinto's neck and shoved her pistol in its belt holster. "Do your own thing and to heck with what that bossy male wants."

Puma sat cross-legged beside the bright campfire. His back was toward the burning coals to preserve his night vision. Details flickered in the glow of firelight, skin that gleamed like polished copper, thick biceps bare below the sleeves of his tee shirt. Puma didn't feel the cold like she did. One of his strong hands clasped a knee, the other wrapped around a steaming cup. The aroma of coffee mingled with the wild scents of night in the forest. His profile was remote, his eyes shut, even as his chest moved with the rhythm of his breathing.

That capacity for stillness. She'd seen it in him before. It didn't mean he wasn't aware of everything around him.

She waited.

"Why are you here, rookie?"

"To talk. About Sundance. About us." Not altogether a lie. He'd learn soon enough about Hooker's plans. She didn't want to be within a mile of the explosion that would follow.

"How did you find me?"

"I let Wind Song loose on the trail. She seemed to sense where you and Dragon would be."

Puma slit his eyelids and swiveled his head. He shifted and whistled softly. Wind Song hesitated, gave a nicker and loped forward.

"Thanks for keeping her out of trouble, girl," Puma growled. The mare lowered her head and whinnied a greeting, and Puma scratched behind the pony's ear, crooning softly.

"She led me right to you."

"There's a law against stealing a man's horse, Ms. FBI."

"I didn't steal her. Just borrowed."

His eyebrows lifted in amusement. "A matter of opinion, I'd say. Coffee?"

"That would be nice."

Puma came to his feet in one fluid movement, demonstrating the easy grace of his namesake. He strode to the clearing edge, snagged the pack he'd hung on a nearby tree branch and lifted it to the ground. The attached bear bells rattled in a cacophony of discord, reminding Rachel of her previous uneasiness.

"Have you seen sign of bear?" she asked.

"Nothing recent. They're usually higher up in the mountains this time of year. Food is plentiful. They won't bother us."

"And a bear might hesitate to mess with a full-grown puma," she observed dryly. "Especially one that's armed." She pointed to the rifle propped on a rock near the fire.

"Out here it's not the wild animals that worry me. It's civilized man."

"Or woman?"

He laughed softly, without humor, as he approached the fire again, carrying another cup and a small leather flask. "Woman most of all."

He knelt and poured her a cup of coffee, refreshing his own drink and set the empty pot off the fire. "Want a sweetener?"

"Just a little."

He poured a generous dollop from the flask into each cup. They clanked cups and drank. Rachel gave a shudder. The scalding liquid burned all the way down. "My God, that's strong stuff."

"The best Kentucky sour mash available. Be appreciative."

"Not the booze. You could float an egg in this witch's brew you call coffee."

"Can't beat campfire coffee for a kick. It'll put hair on your chest."

"So how come you don't have a single hair on yours?" Oops, mistake. She flushed at his amused, knowing look.

"Courtesy of my Ute ancestors. Want to show me yours? It never got that far last time we were close."

She choked on the swallow of coffee. "Pardon me?"

"You run like a scalded cat when I get within ten feet. Fear obviously hasn't kept you from looking."

She huffed out a breath. "If you parade around half-naked, a girl can look."

He tossed his remaining drink into the fire and set the cup down. "Point taken. Hungry? I have some cans of stew."

"I had a ham sandwich a couple of hours ago. I'm not hungry."

"Then drink up and let's go to bed. I'll stoke the fire."

"Ah, Puma?"

"Uh-huh?"

"I didn't come out here to sleep with you."

"Who mentioned sleep?"

Rachel had stopped lying to herself the minute she rode into the clearing. A flash of heat warred with a stab of annoyance. She meant to have sex with him, but he could damn well work for it and they needed to get a few things straight first.

"Look, Puma, I'm here to do my job. Sex isn't in the equation."

He tossed another log on the fire. It flared into life, bathing him in brilliance. His blue eyes swept over her, stripping her to the bone. His finely cut mouth curved into a slow smile. "Bet me."

"I only bet a sure thing."

"A sure thing landed you in trouble before."

"I won't go back home."

"I won't let you. You could get lost in these mountains. Back to the bet. Loser washes the dishes and takes care of the horses for the two days I plan to be on the trail. I'm here for my own reasons, and you'll have to tag along."

Considering, she narrowed her eyes. "Who cooks?"

"I've tasted your culinary efforts. I'll cook."

"Sooo, if I resist your masculine charms, you cook, do the dishes and take care of the horses? And you won't make a move on me unless I ask for it."

"That's the deal. Want it?"

She blew out a breath. After the weeks of hard labor he'd put her through, this was going to be fun. "Oh, yeah. I want it. We have a lot to talk over before we report to base."

"Later." He chuckled, a low sound of pure machismo.

She worried at her lower lip with her teeth. He was

planning something, something evil, no doubt. And he was standing too close. She backed up a step.

He matched her with a step forward.

"Start something, you automatically lose," she warned.

"That's fair. I lose."

Damn him! She retreated again and he followed. They did a slow lockstep pace around the fire. Wind Song nickered and sidestepped as Rachel bumped up against the pony's withers.

Trapped.

"I—I need to take off Wind Song's tack and get her to the stream for a drink. She needs to be rubbed down."

Puma caught her around the waist and pulled her against his hard body. Very hard body. He nuzzled her throat and lightning streaked between her thighs. He nibbled her ear, whispering a seductive promise that curled her toes. She gasped and her arms went around his neck as she clung to him, molding her sex against his. Maybe it was silly to wait. They could always talk later.

His mouth came down on hers and she was lost, pulled into the vortex, spiraling into glory. Chill became heat. The meadow vanished. She could no longer hear the stream bubbling over rocks, the crackle of the fire. She knew only the melting pleasure of his mouth taking and giving.

He ended the kiss, pulled her shirt aside and bit the sensitive juncture between her neck and shoulder. The sharp nip of a stallion gentling a mare. "I'll take care of the pinto. Undress and I'll introduce you to a family secret, rookie."

How could she be shivering when she was so hot? Damn her own weak body. "You deliberately set me up. You knew I'd follow you."

He brushed her hair from her face and stroked her bottom lip with a calloused thumb. "Hoped is more like it. Unless you want those clothes turned into to rags, strip."

CHAPTER 10

Even as a little kid, Puma had never been afraid of the dark. His night vision was excellent and he was brother to the creatures of shadow, knew their hearts and habits. Born predators enjoyed the opportunity that darkness provided.

The puma often prowled at night.

He watched in bemusement as Rachel lifted one long limb and then the other, wiggling her toes, water sheeting from her calves. The reflection of a half-moon floated on the pool surface, and high above a few stars struggled to pierce the Stygian gloom. In the purpled light you could barely see the scars on her legs.

He cupped his hand in the heated spring water and dribbled some on her shoulders. "Like it?"

"Oh, yes," she sighed, sinking deeper into the water. "It's heaven." The center of the pool plunged to a depth of three feet, but it was shallow at the edge where the water lapped her chin and his chest. The bowl-shaped depression was roughly six-feet in diameter, and allowed them to stretch out comfortably. "How do you know about this place?"

"From my grandfather. It's not unusual to find hot springs in the Rockies. Some have been commercialized, but this one is too remote to attract the tourist crowd." He stroked her abdomen with his flattened palm and enjoyed the way her breath caught.

"It's wonderful. Lindy and Frank have been here, haven't they?"

"Lindy planted the wild sage. Indians burn sage in religious ceremonies." He reached and broke off a piece of the herb growing by the pool, rubbed it between his fingers and let it drift on the surface of the water. The strong scent mingled with the steam rising around them.

She breathed in and sighed. "It's magic."

"The location is passed down through the generations. I keep the area clear of debris and replace any dislodged stones. Left unattended the basin would erode and merge back into the main channel." He continued to stroke, wanting to hear her gasp again, to feel the throb of her desire under his fingers.

Her emerald eyes slanted at him in sultry invitation, her tawny hair spiked around her face, the bubbling water caressed her shoulders. She was sister to the Oreads, the mountain nymphs. He knew he was in trouble, the kind of trouble that would screw up his life forever, and he didn't give a damn. A puma could easily tame a nymph.

She pointed her toes toward the main body of water sluicing down the mountain. "The stream over there runs cold?"

"Always. In the winter it's just a trickle under the ice, but in the spring, snowmelt swells it to full size. When I was a kid, my grandfather would bring me here and let me play in the hot springs, then toss me naked into the freezing water. Talk about getting a kid's attention."

"Good heavens! That's child abuse."

"It was a lesson in endurance that I'm grateful for. Besides, he waded right in with me."

"There's a lot about you I don't know, isn't there? When you said you'd introduce me to a family secret, I thought you meant something else." She touched his cheek with tapered fingers and he wasn't sure who would be tamed that night.

His heart pounded. "Like what?"

"Oh, you know, some kind of exotic sexual move. I was braced for it."

The pounding accelerated. "Don't give up on the idea. We've barely started."

She stretched one of her legs skyward again. "Did you know my legs are longer that yours?"

"On the plus side," he said, pulling her bottom into his lap and settling her against his erection. "I have three to your two."

She wiggled and settled back. "Very impressive."

"Glad you like it." He nipped her shoulder and ran his tongue along the elegant curve of her collarbone. "It's all yours, rookie."

"For tonight."

"Tonight. Tomorrow. For as long as you want. Or until I drop dead of a heart attack."

She chuckled and laid her head against his shoulder, idly swishing the water with her foot. "I wasn't going to do this."

"I know. Sometimes you give in to the inevitable."

"Can we just take it as it happens?"

"Works for me." He tipped her chin and covered her mouth with his. The kiss was hot and wild and totally blew his mind. They'd kissed before, but she'd always held back. This time her response was savage. When he stopped to breathe and recapture his wits, she caught his ears and pulled his face close.

"More," she said fiercely. "Your mouth drives me crazy. Show me what you can do with it. On my breasts. Between my legs." She swung around and straddled his lap.

"Jesus, Rachel!" He'd always been the one to take charge in lovemaking. This time he was struggling to keep up.

She arched her back in invitation and he took a wet, nipple between her teeth, tugging gently until the bud hardened, then suckled fiercely. She cried out and clamped her legs around his hips, riding the hard ridge of his erection. "Yes! Now the other one."

Blindly he searched and suckled again. She shuddered and thrashed wildly in his arms, almost slithering from his grip. If it hadn't been impossible, he would have thought she'd already climaxed. "Rachel, you didn't—"

"Not quite," she groaned, grinding her body against his. "Almost."

There was only one way to handle this.

She howled in protest when he broke her grip and stood, dumping her on her sexy butt. She splashed out in fury. "Why did you do that?"

"You need to cool off. And if we don't move to dry ground, one or both of us is going to drown." He pulled her upright and reached for the blanket he'd left on the creek bank. Stepping from the warm water into the night air was like walking into a refrigerator. He grinned when her teeth started to chatter.

"S-sm-smug b-bastard! I was so close!"

He wrapped her tightly in the blanket, trapping her arms to her sides. It seemed safer that way. "You usually have trouble getting there?"

"Yes! I mean, no! Well, sometimes. Dammit, Ansari, don't you dare laugh. I wanted that orgasm bad."

"Nothing wrong with getting there solo once in a while, but seems like a waste when you have a willing partner."

She made a spluttering sound that could have been acquiescence, but was more likely a raspberry.

"You plan to let me take a hand in the game?"

Another spluttering sound. More subdued and very profane.

He clicked his tongue in disapproval. "Trust me, you'll get there more than once. Do you want me to carry you back to camp?"

"I can manage," she snapped, dropping the blanket and reaching for her footwear. Totally naked except for her boots, she stomped toward their campsite.

He retrieved the blanket and his rifle, switched on the Coleman lantern and followed down the trail, intrigued by the disappearing view of bare female legs and undulating backside. She could be a handful, but my God!

He found her standing near the dying campfire, chugging from the leather flask.

"Whoa, Puss in Boots. Save some for your boy toy."

She handed the flask over, glaring. "So I'm a control freak, even in bed. You want to forfeit the game, that's fine. No hard feelings."

He swallowed the last of the liquor and dropped the flask, reaching for her hand. "C'mere, Puss."

She backed away warily. "What?"

"I don't know about you, but I'm freezing my ass off. Picking up the pace sounds damn fine, but I'd prefer doing it in the tent. Course, if you'd rather I throw you on the ground and have you right here? Hey, works for me."

"You see," she said, continuing to back away. "I knew you'd try to take charge. It doesn't work for me."

"How about neither of us takes charge? Something isn't working, you tell me; I want something, I tell you. Would you get your butt over here before we both freeze?"

"Race you." She sprinted for the tent.

He doused the campfire and followed, made his way inside carrying his rifle and zipped the flap. The lantern provided enough illumination he could see her outline snuggled into the down sleeping bag. "Move over, crazy woman. Half of that air mattress is mine. Please tell me you took your boots off."

"Mmm-huh," she answered. "Promise me we won't be sharing space with a wild animal this time."

"Can't do that. Seems more likely there'll be two." She was giggling as he slipped in beside her, and a sharp kick to the shins told him why. She still had her boots on.

"Serves you right for leaving me hanging, cowboy."

"That's it. Payback time."

It took some doing but he managed to wrench her boots off and toss them. She was very ticklish on the bottoms of her feet. She screeched and kicked and bit his thigh. Not a mosquito bite, either. She was the orneriest, most aggravating female he'd ever bedded. And he'd never been hotter or harder. He rolled her on her back and pinned her with his weight, caught her wrists and spread her legs with his knee.

"Bully," she hissed and bared her teeth, heaving under him.

"Bite me again, Puss, it better be when I'm inside of you."

He stroked her cheekbone with the back of his free hand, traced her swollen mouth with a forefinger. She laved the tip of his finger with her tongue, and if possible, he got even harder.

"I won't come before you do. You can't make me."

He laughed in anticipation and reached inside his pack for a condom. What in the hell had made him think sex with a compliant, soft woman was fun?

His probing fingers told him she was slick and ready for him. Hot for him. He entered her slowly, watching her face and throat flush, loving it when the hiss became a low groan of pleasure. When she rolled her hips and clenched her internal muscles around him, white heat flared in his loins and what little blood still in his brain went south.

She wouldn't lose control—-she wouldn't—-let him—-if only he didn't feel so good inside her—-if he wasn't entering her at just the right angle—-She was doing this to get him out of her system, no other reason. Usually after she slept with a man she lost interest. Who the hell was she kidding? She rarely let it get this far. She never let it get this far. Why this man?

She couldn't control the moans of passion in her throat. Her mind was drugged, her body alive with lust. The mingled scent of sex and sage clogged her nostrils. Who knew sage was an aphrodisiac?

She opened her thighs and met his thrusts, wanting him deeper. God, he couldn't get any deeper. He reamed her to the mattress, each sure stroke streaked lightning through her body. The pulse drummed in her ears, fast and erratic. Let him take over. If he stopped, she would die. She wrapped her legs around his waist and surrendered.

She was losing it. It had never happened like this. The

utter abandonment of herself to another, the rapturous loosening. The first internal shudder rolled inside of her, unstoppable, out of her control. His mouth came down on hers and he never broke rhythm, one of his hands cupped her bottom, the other curled in her hair. The connection was electric, a swelling current flowing from her mouth and tongue to his, from her sex to his, from her toes to the roots of her hair.

He lifted his mouth. "Look at me when you come," he ordered hoarsely, his face inches from hers. "Now."

The orgasm had her, lifting her on waves of pleasure, melting her bones with his heat and their passion. At the peak she clenched her eyes shut and screamed his name.

"Look at me, Rachel!"

She opened her eyes. His laser gaze burned. He stiffened and gave a guttural cry, and she welcomed his life force pumping into her, wanting it with every cell in her body.

CHAPTER 11

—◆—

"**D**oes Ansari know he's staked out as a Judas goat?"

Hooker shrugged. "I wouldn't put it that way. But our intelligence indicates Fillmore is having Ansari stalked. We're watching."

Ash Calloway went into his finger-drumming mode, which meant he was more agitated than his bland expression indicated. "I want Chic Fillmore worse than you do, but the Ansari's a civilian."

"He was Special Forces for three years." Hooker placed an envelope labeled Top Secret on the table. "I've been authorized to give you ten minutes with this."

Ash pulled out the file and raised his eyebrows. "I'm supposed to learn something? Half the data is blacked out."

"Read between the lines."

Five minutes later Ash shoved Ansari's dossier back across the table. "Okay, the man can take care of himself. Nonetheless he's a civvie now, and the New Sons of Liberty are bad news. How are we protecting him?"

"If you knew Fletch Ansari, you'd worry more about our quarry. His Delta buddies don't call him Puma without reason."

"I still say we should pick Fillmore up and sweat him."

"If we move on Fillmore publicly, the entire organization

goes underground. We've been working on this for over a year. I'm not about to blow it. When they go after Ansari, we'll be ready. Our agent is on alert and in place."

"Why not recruit the man officially? Get him to cooperate in the investigation." Ash took a small sip of his beer, made a face and lit a cigarette.

"Ansari can be a loose cannon. His skills lean toward hunt and kill, a warrior's skills, and he has no training as an agent. Which is why we're keeping him in the dark."

"You want Fillmore alive and talking, caught in the act."

"Exactly. Fillmore's our only link to the head of the hydra. I'm keeping this investigation so by the book that even Perry Mason couldn't get Fillmore off."

"I'm with you, but why are we meeting at a local pub, rather than my office? It's Friday and I haven't been home before midnight for a week. My wife was planning on me for dinner tonight. She has a martini waiting with my name on it."

"It's private here. No ears listening in. But no smoking allowed. And I thought you'd quit."

"With you breathing down my neck? When are you going to drop the other shoe?" Ash disposed of the cigarette in his water glass.

"We found your leak. You're not going to like this."

The senior FBI man swore and reached for the cigarette pack again. Hooker admired the steady way he held the lighter. The Zippo snapped shut and Ash blew out a cloud of smoke. "The hell with no smoking rules. They can try to arrest me. Damn, these poison sticks taste as good as sex. Who?"

"We had it narrowed down to four names. Grace Chelsea, Rob Kaman in your computer lab, senior agent James Stanley, and one other."

"Had. But now you know. Is the fourth name mine?"

Hooker nodded. "Sorry, Ash. We knew someone was canoodling the computers, someone with firsthand knowledge of what they were doing and where to go for classified information."

"We wouldn't be having this discussion if you hadn't cleared me. You've had my phones tapped and had me followed?"

"We've been investigating all four suspects."

"Damn!" Ash slapped the table and exploded in a fury of curses.

The waitress came hustling over a worried expression on her face. "Is there a problem? Can I get you guys another drink? Sorry, sir. No smoking, please."

"We're fine," Hooker said blandly, throwing a twenty-dollar bill on the table. "Keep it. My friend is trying to quit smoking. He's a bit testy."

"Oh." She smiled and the twenty disappeared in her pocket. "Well, good luck. Those things will kill you." She disappeared with her hundred percent tip.

Ash dropped the still burning cig into the water glass, where it joined the others. He took a careful sip of his beer. "You've known me for years, Dan. How in hell could you suspect me? I've bled for this country. I want a full inquiry and total clearance from the agency."

"Yes, I've known you for years. How long have you known Chelsea?"

Ash set the beer glass down carefully, like it was made of fine crystal. "Please don't tell me it was Grace. She's been with the Bureau for twenty years, five as my personal secretary. I know the woman. Know her family. Jesus, not another envelope."

"It's all in here. Grace Chelsea has her father in an expensive Alzheimer's clinic. Five grand a month, and the old man's on social security. Her daughter has a learning disability and needs special schooling. These people have deep pockets, Ash, and knew the woman was desperate for money. It's not like she's buying diamonds and driving a Mercedes."

"Grace's husband is a corporate bigwig in a tech firm. He makes plenty. They live in a restored mansion near the university. My wife and I were there for dinner last fall."

"She's about to lose the mansion. The husband dumped

her for a twenty-year-old exotic dancer six months ago. Colorado is a no-fault state. Your secretary makes a good enough salary that the rat husband pays child support, but no alimony. Grace Chelsea's been heard expounding on our legal system. Bitterly."

Ash leaned against the leather seat. "Jesus. That was all bullshit you fed me in my office three weeks ago. You were setting me up. Grace, too."

"She has a direct line from your office to her desk. She listens in on phone calls and private conferences. You told her to take a coffee break while you and I talked? She didn't. The information I gave you was correct as far as it went."

"But if she was listening, you as gave her Ansari on a platter. And maybe your undercover agent. That's harsh. What if Grace cashes out and takes off?"

"With her family responsibilities? Huh-uh. She changed her methods and quit using the payphones near your office. I had her purse and car bugged and four real good people on her. She drove to Boulder immediately after we talked and contacted Fillmore. We have her on tape more than once. We deliberately fed Ansari's location to her through you, and she passed it on. As far as Grace knows, our agent is a man. That's bogus. Our agent is posing as Ansari's girlfriend."

"Your inside agent is a woman! You told me it was a man."

Hooker emitted one of his rusty chuckles. "You assumed so, Ash. Your secretary has no idea she was setup."

"Dammit, Grace is a friend. I can't believe this."

Hooker pointed to the report. "Take a look."

Ash shook his head in disgust. "Dan, I've been in the Bureau for thirty-odd years and I've never worked with a more relentless son of a bitch. Does your female agent know you've set Ansari up as bait?"

"She knows now. We had a heated discussion earlier today. Her orders are to latch on to Ansari like a tick. You think I'm relentless? You should meet Rachel."

* * *

Hooker had ordered her to stay close to Fletcher Ansari, but she doubted her boss had meant this close. Puma's hard body curled spoon fashion around her backside, his right arm flung across her waist, the steady rise and fall of his breathing evidence he still slept. Outside the tent the night creatures had ceased their scurrying noises and retreated to their nests. Darkness ebbed in the dead calm before dawn. Early morning birdcalls signaled the wakening of day.

She was wide-awake. Astonishing, considering she'd had maybe—what? Four hours of sleep? After the first frenzied bout of lovemaking, they'd taken it slow and enjoyed each other for most of the night. Her partner's staying power was remarkable. Even scarier was how fast he'd caught on to what she liked, what she needed. She'd lost track of how many times he'd sent her flying. She might have thought the night an erotic dream if her body wasn't completely sated. She'd be lucky to walk straight for the next week.

She shifted a bit, thinking she'd get up and start some coffee on the alcohol stove. He grumbled a protest, his arm tightened on her waist. She grinned. He hadn't gone unscathed. His back and butt bore the mark of her nails, and where had she picked up this penchant for biting? When he'd come the last time she was pretty sure it was ecstasy, not her teeth clamping his shoulder that had caused him to roar like a wounded bull. Afterward he'd dropped into sleep like a stone in the ocean.

"Where do you think you're going?" his voice whispered in her ear.

"To make coffee and answer nature's call. Then a dip in the pool. You were damned thorough, big guy."

"I'll join you in the pool, but it's mouthwash instead of coffee, rookie. And both of us back between the sheets for another hour. We won't be able to do this once we report in. Not much privacy in the smokejumpers' dorm."

"Puma, sweetie—"

"Sweetie?" He grinned and propped himself on an elbow. "I must be better than I thought."

She cleared her throat. "Sex with you is an excellent thing," she said cautiously.

"Back at you, Puss."

"But no way I'll have another, ah—"

"Orgasm? Climax?" His damn hands were stroking gently between her thighs, a sure way to melt her.

She shivered. "I'm done. Maybe next year."

He laughed and climbed out of the sleeping bag, pulling her after him. "Five minutes in the pool. Then I'm taking you over the moon again. Screaming is optional."

"I. Don't. Scream."

"Bet me?"

Zebedee had been raised in a deserted mining town, sixty miles west of Denver. He never knew his mother, and his father was a drunk who augmented monthly welfare checks by delivering the Denver Post to rural customers. As a boy, Zeb cut school more than he attended, but he knew where to hide, and local authorities finally gave up on collaring him for truancy. When he dropped out at age thirteen, no one noticed.

Zeb considered it amusing that his former hometown and others like it were being overhauled as tourist destinations, complete with Vegas style casinos and legal gambling. He hated the place, the abandoned placer mines and crumbling old houses that were now considered picturesque, the trendy boutiques that offered "handmade" trinkets manufactured in Taiwan.

But Zeb was at home in the mountains.

No one was too surprised when his family home, actually a shabby three-room cabin, burned to the ground. He'd been the only survivor. Poor kid. No mother, and his father a drunk who fell asleep smoking in bed. The fact that Zeb's teenage sister was in bed with the old man wasn't mentioned of course. Not in polite company.

The authorities dumped him into the Denver Social Service system, which was grateful to spit him out at age sixteen. He'd been on the streets ever since. Until he discovered that arson could pay, prostituting himself had kept him alive. He had never done hard drugs. Fire was his path to ecstasy.

Zeb had understood the power and beauty of fire at an early age. Flame whispered in his brain, ran through his blood and warmed his bones. He started fires in abandoned sheds and outhouses, even dead trees, always during a storm, so the flare-ups would be blamed on lightning strikes. Still, it was a revelation how quickly the family home had turned into a raging inferno. He'd nailed the windows shut and barred the door. Too bad his old man had passed out and never knew what happened, but Zeb remembered his sister's screams with relish. He hadn't enjoyed setting a fire quite as much since.

It had been so simple. He tied a bundle of wooden matches around a cigarette, waited until the fornicating pair was done and passed out, and lit the cigarette. The smoldering device became a slow-burning fuse and gave Zeb plenty of time to escape. A nearby broken bottle of Old Rotgut fed the flames.

The floorboards were ancient and rotten, and the cabin was littered with trash, newspapers, ratty overstuffed furniture and cruddy fast-food boxes. His cunt sister never cleaned up around the place. All she cared about was drinking and getting laid. The fire took off in a flash that was almost explosive, boiling through the cabin with the ferocity of a snarling beast.

As part of his foolproof plan, Zeb was found "unconscious" a few yards from the fire, an easily staged event. The cabin was reduced to a pile of burnt timber and ashes. He'd blackened his face and clothing, had slashed at his forehead and arms with a broken bottle. People considered it a miracle he'd escaped.

People were stupid. Zeb was smart. Too smart for any of them.

It was interesting to be back.

Twenty years of wind and weather had done its job, and nothing was left of his former home except the charred stones of the fireplace and a few petrified logs. Even the gravel road had eroded and gone back to nature. It was an ideal place to lay low and store his equipment. He hid his SUV among a copse of spindly pine within a stone's throw of the old place, careful to obliterate all tracks and evidence that someone camped there. Hard to tell who owned the land anymore. Probably the county.

His old man had surely gone straight to hell, but Zeb occasionally wondered if his sister's ghost still hung around. He enjoyed the thought. If she'd been as willing to service him as she was the old man, she might still be alive. Or maybe not. Fire was better than sex anytime.

Daily, he climbed on his Honda cycle and made the trek into town to contact Fillmore. A cell phone didn't work in this part of the mountains and no one cared how you looked when you entered a casino. The food was cheap too. He always dropped a few quarters in the slots, had won a buck or two. It amused him to fanaticize winning a big one and getting his picture in the paper. Fillmore would crap his pants.

Zeb hadn't reported killing the dog to Chic. Caution made him hold back that information. No way was Zeb going near the Ansari place again, not for a long time. The last trip, he'd nearly been caught driving along a back road. Some wiseass in a pickup had honked at him to pull over, and seeing it was Ansari's ranch hand and the guy was big and looked crazy, Zeb picked up speed and got out of there. In retrospect, it might have been hasty to kill the dog.

The need for a fire fix was gnawing his gut. If Fillmore hadn't stayed his hand, Zeb would have torched the Ansari ranch when he had the chance, and just for the hell of it. He'd put in a large investment of time on Fillmore's aborted project. For now the plan was on the backburner. Fillmore had promised him another shot after the big show. He licked his lips. Flames would be dancing soon.

He'd be rich enough to shake the memory of this fucking place forever. He was thinking of a Mexico vacation. A man with money could live high in Mexico. The fantasy made him dizzy with anticipation. Getting paid for setting fires was his idea of heaven.

He unrolled the aerial map of eastern Colorado that Fillmore had obtained for him, and spread it out on a tree stump. The chart was detailed down to mountain streams and back roads, complete with pertinent elevations and mileage distances. Ain't it grand what you can download for the internet? Three major areas were highlighted. Other areas by other methods would be put to flame in other states, but these were Zeb's sole responsibility.

He touched his finger to the first, the Arapahoe National Forest. The New Sons of Liberty kept a private airstrip near Nederland, within an hour's flight to the target area.

Flying low and fast, the Sons' copter would transport Zeb over the target areas, and he would eject dozens of devices filled with homemade napalm, a wicked mixture of liquid soap, acetone and gasoline. The Forest Service used the same formula to light controlled burns, although Zeb knew his mixture burned faster and hotter. The copter would be painted with the USFC logo. The Civil Air Patrol wouldn't figure what was going on until it was too late. The timber was dry as powder this year, and he'd hit the slash piles and areas dotted with dead trees. When the timers went off, the fires would quickly cover several hundred acres, and the smokejumpers would be called in.

His finger moved to the second spot. Vail. A short two-hour drive from his hidey-hole. Zeb's knowledge had come a long way since his crude cigarette-fuse days. He planned to set timed, delayed firebombs in and around the Vail area. Two-dozen fusees, timed to erupt at midnight and all at once, two days after the Arapahoe fire. Not in the forests this time, but near hotels and restaurants. Vail was a popular resort area, crowded year round. It would drive the authorities crazy. They'd have to call up every firefighting unit in the surrounding states and would be fighting major conflagrations on two fronts.

His only regret was he couldn't stick around to see it happen.

He took his bowie knife out of his boot and stabbed it into the map. Target three. The forest area surrounding the Air Force Academy. This would be the Sons last strike in Colorado, and a tricky one. The locale was heavy with security, radar and air patrols. He'd have to go in with a four-wheel drive vehicle, take the backroads and operate with care. He was being paid a lot of money, but had no desire to spend the rest of his life in federal prison.

CHAPTER 12

P uma lit a campfire among a circle of stones, burned the cleansing sacred sage and rubbed it on his forehead and bare chest. The fire flickered an amber glow against the evening sky, and provided a small amount of light and heat. Several twists of hemp smoldered in the center of the coals. When inhaled, the pungent fumes would induce a dreamlike state of euphoria. Rachel sat cross-legged opposite him, her face smeared with the same ash. She'd insisted on taking part in the ceremony to send Sundance on his way.

He wasn't completely happy with the ritual he was undertaking. He was a modern man with modern beliefs, yet a part of him still embraced the mysticism of his ancestors. He didn't expect a vision; he'd broken too many rules. Several hours of vigorous sex the night before, for starters.

He had abstained from food and drink all day. His grandfather would consider him a wimp. Technically Puma should have slept apart from his woman and fasted for four days. Suffering enabled the warrior to transcend earthly limits. Rachel had not fasted and he had insisted she drink water along the trail. If she noticed he wasn't eating or drinking, she said nothing.

"He's in a place a lot like this," she said, gently placing her hand on the cedar box containing Sundance's ashes. "Meadows and mountain streams and rabbits to chase."

Puma looked at her. The woman continued to amaze him. "It's closure, Rachel. The Indian equivalent to the white eyes burial practices. More for our sake than for Sundance."

"I saw him yesterday. He was happy."

"You thought you saw him. It's not the same thing."

"Like I thought I saw the cougar? Twice."

"This is the Front Range. The cougars' home. They were here before we were and hopefully will be here after we're gone. If civilized man doesn't wipe them out, destroying their natural habitat."

"You're more attached to your roots than you admit. Lindy says your grandfather was a shaman among the Utes. That could make you part mystic."

"I'm a mongrel, Rachel. My grandfather was full-blooded Ute, but my grandmother was a Baptist missionary. Sometimes I don't know who I am."

"You took your grandfather's name. That means something."

"My biological father was a rodeo tramp, half white, half Shoshone. He deserted us when I was five. My mother drank herself to death a year later. Why would I want the old man's name? He was nothing but a sperm donor."

"Lindy and Frank are Indian. Your wife, Sadie, was Indian. Don't tell me that means nothing."

Sadie. Her name echoed in the seared depths of his soul where he guarded his wife's memory, a soft cry whispering under his ribs. *It's time. Let me go.* He slammed a barrier against the anguished plea. It was this damn place, this mountain. Every time he returned, memories came back and bit him in the ass.

"How much dirt did you dig out of my personnel file? And what do you know about Sadie? Has Lindy been—? Wait a minute. You've spent a lot of time with Frank since he got back from the hospital."

"Don't be cross with your aunt and uncle. I'm good at getting answers. I know your wife died in a car accident a long time ago. Not anyone's fault, but Frank says you blame yourself. He says your animal totem is the cougar. That your totem brings you luck and warns you of danger."

"Rachel, drop it. Frank talks too much."

She blinked, and he regretted his harsh tone. The fasting hadn't helped, nor the pungent smoke or the age-old ritual. He was anything but mellow and just wanted to get this over with. He pushed away his anger. None of his conflicted belief system was Rachel's fault.

"Rookie, don't try to understand any of this. Or me. It just is, and I am what I am. I have as hard a time accepting the supernatural as I do everlasting love. Don't even ask me why I'm doing this, because I don't know. Probably I should have buried Sundance's ashes on the ranch."

She clamped her jaw. "Of course, I'm an outsider, but at least I keep an open mind. No need to yell at me."

Time to change the subject. He rose, lifted her to her feet and circled her in his arms. "I'm sorry, Rookie. You know I have a mean side."

"You're as immovable as that boulder over there. And as ruthless as your warrior ancestors. You never even consider losing. But I think you believe in certain things. And won't admit it, even to yourself."

"What certain things?"

"Mysticism. Love. And in protecting those you love. You're a tough nut, Fletcher Ansari." She swallowed hard. "But I like being with you. What the hell does that mean?"

It meant he had to kiss her. Something he'd wanted to do all day. They clung together afterward. The kiss had done what the narcotic had failed to do. He was definitely euphoric. After her initial melting response, she stiffened in his arms.

"Do you have the feeling someone is watching?" She nodded behind him.

"Watching?"

"It's just a feeling. Not scary. Sort of benevolent."

He turned and looked. "*Togochin*," he whispered.

His grandfather stood by the edge of the cliff, smoking one of his infernal cigarettes and barely visible in the sputtering light of the fire. The cougar with the broken paw crouched beside him. "A fine woman, Grandson," the old man said, smiling. "Don't let her get away. *Pooneekay Vatsoom Ahdtuih.* I'll see you again."

The vision quivered and evaporated.

"Nothing there," Puma said, closing his eyes. The hemp was getting to him. "But I know what you mean. It's a weird place."

"All right," Rachel said, and continued to stare at him quizzically. "So why did you choose this place if you think it's weird?"

He ached to touch her face, lovelier than Eve's under the smear of ashes.

"This is the mountain my grandfather called sacred. Across the valley from the Sleeping Ute Mountain, where the Great Warrior God Manitou was mortally wounded and lay down to rest. The blood from the God's wound turned into living water for all creatures to drink. My grandfather's ashes lie below, so do my grandmother's and my mother's. Someday my nephews will bring me here."

"Oh." Her lips quivered and her eyes filled with tears. "How lovely."

He laughed. "You're overcome with grief thinking of my ashes?"

"Don't you dare spoil this, Fletcher Ansari. You have a wonderful heritage. What do we do now?"

"I'm a little shaky on the ritual. My grandfather taught me a simple prayer chant, if you'll bear with me."

Puma was right, Rachel thought. It was a strange place, full of shadows and whispers, but uniquely peaceful and a wonderful resting spot for Sundance. She wondered how many other spirits had been laid to rest here and felt a tiny shiver. She didn't believe in flying saucers, but spirits? She didn't know. Many things were unexplainable in modern terms.

She watched Puma remove a small reed flute and a feather from his backpack. An eagle feather, she guessed. He played a few quivery notes on the flute, and dropped it in disgust.

"Never could play that thing," he muttered. "I don't suppose you could?"

She shook her head. "I can strum a guitar a bit. That's the extent of my musical talent."

"We'll make do without."

He raised his arms to the sky, holding the feather aloft. He began to dance. His usually rough voice became soft and musical as he chanted in a strange tongue, ancient words, sad and joyous at once. She was mesmerized.

He held out his hand and she understood she was to join the dance. Time and her surroundings swirled away. She was swept into the life-affirming dance, into Puma's smiling, protective embrace. She swore she could hear Sundance barking, that he was dancing with them.

Behind them the flute began to play.

CHAPTER 13

The three-mile flag flapped in the breeze, within eyeshot now. Unless she was hallucinating, she would make it. Rachel concentrated on staying in rhythm and keeping her stride in sync with Puma's.

He set a brutal pace, so she knew they were within the allotted time. At the two-mile mark they were running a steady seven-minute mile. Twenty runners had started out. Half of them sprinted ahead, some over the finish line. Twenty-two minutes thirty seconds to complete the run, the last task on the PT test. When she crossed the finish line, she'd be done with training and placed on the jump list.

She'd been watching the rookies train the past few days, not envying them. The all-male class of twenty-four had weeded down to nineteen, and they were hard guys, seasoned firefighters. The rookies had another week of instruction ahead, and there were rumblings that two more planned to drop out. The second-year jumpers, the snookies, were riding them almost as hard as the instructors. God, she hoped her cover would hold. She'd gotten through the week from hell, but still had to face an actual forest fire.

Her mentor had been right. The least part of being a smokejumper was bailing out of an airplane. The job required mental toughness as much as physical fitness. Her lungs labored with each gasp of air; the blisters she'd acquired on the five-mile pack out the day before had broken open. She was losing her rhythm. Pain shot from her heels, up her calf muscles and thighs, burning pain that gnawed at her concentration. Her chest was a time bomb ready to explode.

The pain was unimportant. Something to be dealt with later. She ran as if her life depended on it. Her job sure as hell did.

"Sasser," Mercer Adams, the training foreman overseeing the finish line, called out. "20:54."

It took another second for Rachel to realize he meant her. Sasser, the new identity Hooker had set up. She was Myra Sasser for the duration of the job. She bent over gasping, sweat running down her face. Her hair, t-shirt and running pants were soaked. She'd made it, and under time. Not a sterling performance, but respectable. Three weeks of Puma's harsh training had paid off.

"Ansari," the trainer intoned. "20:56. A minute-thirty seconds over last year. Been leading the fat life, kumasabe?"

Puma pulled up to massage his calves, politely suggesting the foreman enjoin his private parts with a goat. Merc grinned. "You're just jealous because my Johnson is bigger."

Puma snorted and the other man's eyes went back to his stopwatch. "Hardesty, 21:59. Beating last years' time by eighteen seconds. You squeaked by another year, Badger Man."

Sasser, Sasser. Rachel repeated it in her head, like a mantra. Myra Sasser, a genuine female smokejumper based in Alaska, a five-year veteran who'd been injured the year before but had kept her red card. The bona fide Myra was currently undergoing physical therapy, soaking in seawater and enjoying the good life in the Bahamas, courtesy of Uncle Sam. Rachel had committed the woman's file to memory, but all it took was one slip to give away the game.

Rachel leaned against the nearest tree, forcing her respiration into deep, slow breaths. It would be easy to dislike Merc's smugness. Easy, except he executed every requirement alongside them, without breaking a sweat and grinning like Ronald McDonald the whole time. He even looked a little like Ronald McDonald. Frowsy red hair, freckles, big feet and all.

"You okay?" Puma knelt beside her to massage her calves. "Any blisters?"

"Fine," she lied. "Thanks for pacing me. I know I held you back. Did you say something to Merc? He's left me pretty much alone all week, and he's hounding everyone else."

"Our foreman's smitten. He'd like to jump your bones, so he's laid off the wisecracks. If he gets mouthy, throw the crap back at him like we all do."

"He wants to——you're kidding! That little wart? Has he been saying that I, that we——?"

"Nothing to me; he knows better. But watch out for him. He's the biggest cocksman on base and proud of it." He pulled off her running shoes and swore. The heels of both socks were gummy with blood. "What the hell! Why didn't you protect your feet?"

"It looks worse than it is."

"I've seen guys washout with blisters. You need an Epson Salts soak, antibiotic salve and gauze wrap. Stay off your feet for the weekend."

"I need to keep training, sore feet or not. Am I officially on the jump list?"

"Yep. The list goes up tonight. We could start getting fire assignments anytime. The season of lightning strikes and careless campers is underway." He pulled off her socks and massaged her instep.

She glanced at the running track to be sure no one was within hearing distance. "Maybe you better stop calling me 'rookie'. Technically I've been a smokejumper for five years." She bit her lip to halt the moan of pleasure. His strong fingers extended the kneading pressure to her toes and she shivered.

"How's this for an idea? I'll get us a weekend pass and we fly into the Springs for some R&R. You've been hard at it for a week. Even FBI agents occasionally take time off."

"You can do that? The base manager said no passes. We need to be here for roll call, and the refresher courses in wildlife management and parachute malfunction." And she needed to be on site to continue her investigation. She'd used every spare minute the past week to prowl the base, to meet personnel and get acquainted with the facilities, to check on the transportation and communication installations.

She wished Hooker had been more specific. "We're looking for a firebug," he'd said. "Statistics show that firefighters are sometimes arsonists."

How in the hell was she supposed to know what a firebug looked like?

"Got a pass for both of us," Puma said. "Rank has its privileges. I told Elkins I'd take my beeper along. It's only an hour's flight." He kissed the sole of her foot and the voluptuous sensation streaked from her toes to her abdomen. Her libido leapt into the red zone. The man should be caged.

"Stop that," she hissed, jerking her foot away. "Someone could be watching."

"We're lovers, remember? Part of your cover. Elkins enjoyed ragging me too much to say 'no' to the pass. The word is I'm flopping on your hook like a snared trout, moose-eyed and hurting bad. The guys love it."

"I'd guess you've been a slippery catch up to now?"

"Something like that. I'll take you to dinner. We'll get a room. How does that sound?"

Oh, God. An overnight with Puma. In a real bed. The dorm setup at base made it impossible for them to have any time alone. *Hurry up tomorrow.*

"Good," she sighed. "We'll skip dinner and order room service. I'll buy."

He laughed softly. "I do love a willing woman. You've got a deal."

He stood, took a look around and landed a brief kiss on her mouth. Brief and hot. The pain of the blisters was replaced with another pain, one just as sharp.

"I'll run back," he said. "You ride in the van. And see to those blisters."

"And stay off my feet."

"Starting tomorrow you'll be off your feet for twenty-four hours, baby cakes. Guaranteed." He grinned a wicked promise.

"Baby cakes? Puh-lease. I prefer 'Rookie'."

"You'll always be 'Rookie' to me." He tugged at her hair and trotted away, heading back to base; the three-mile sprint hadn't slowed him down much. If she didn't know he was right about the blisters, she'd have run alongside him.

Knees mushy and mouth aching, she watched the last of the runners straggle in. The allotted time was up and some of them would have to take the qualifying run again. Failure to make it under the limit meant you were out for the year, no exceptions. She struggled to her feet and limped barefoot for the van. No way could she get her running shoes back on.

Nita Faribee, a PT instructor and part of the booster crew, leaned against the vehicle, ready to carry the exhausted runners back to base. A gold tee shirt stretched across her ample breasts, proclaiming Colorado Smokejumper. Thirty-eight years old, a jumper for ten years, and appropriately cynical, Nita served as unofficial chaperone and nanny to the five other females who bunked in the Smokejumpers' dorm. Marie Higgenlooper and Pam Connell were starting their snookie year as smokejumpers. Kim Williams and Patti Lorca were on the loft staff that rigged the parachutes the jumpers' lives depended on.

The building hadn't been designed to house women.

Sometime in the past, a partition had been thrown up at one end of the barn-like structure to accommodate the unexpected, and largely unwelcome, arrival of woman into the all-male fraternity. The partition was thin enough they could hear the guys snoring at night. Nita saw to it that none of the randy males crossed the threshold. Stocky and thirty pounds over the one-hundred-twenty pounds minimum for jumpers, Nita was as tough as leather. Rachel wasn't sure she liked her, but she sure had a lot of respect for her.

"Looks like a severe case of sore tootsies, Sasser. Take care of your feet, they'll take care of you."

Again it took a minute to click in. Sasser. Forget Rachel Cortez. She was Myra Sasser. "So I was told by the smartass expert who decided to jog back. Like a three-mile flat-out run wasn't enough for him."

"Puma?" Nita cocked an eyebrow. "He's something, all right. Slowest time I ever saw him put in. You have anything to do with that?"

"I probably held him back. He was pacing me."

"Looked to me like he was doing more than that. That's a heartache wearing boots, honey. You heard it here."

"Maybe," Rachel nodded. "Maybe you don't know him as well as you think."

Good answer, Rachel. According to Hooker's manufactured cover, she'd left Alaska and joined the Colorado smokejumpers to be near Puma. It was unusual for a jumper to change bases and a love affair served as an understandable excuse. Of course, Hooker had no idea she and Puma were actual lovers. Her boss would be a tad upset if he learned that.

"It's your heart to break, Sasser," the older woman said, shrugging. "Get in and I'll take you back to base."

"There'll be others who want a ride. I can wait."

"I'll come back for them. You and I need to talk."

Rachel hobbled to the front of the van and climbed in. She'd expected a grilling from someone, was surprised it hadn't come sooner. She was the new kid on the block, and while the other women hadn't been rude, they hadn't been friendly either. It made sense they'd chosen Nita as the Grand Inquisitor.

"So you're on the jump list," Nita began casually. "That's a good feeling."

"Sure is," Rachel agreed. "I was medicaled out midseason last year. If it hadn't been for Puma, I probably couldn't have gotten in shape in time."

"Medicaled, huh? What happened?"

"Landed in loose shale and skidded fifty yards in five seconds. Slammed into a pile of boulders and fractured an ankle. Didn't do much for my pride, either. I looked like a damn rookie."

Nita nodded in sympathy and downshifted. They weren't going back to base by the usual route and had encountered some steep terrain.

"Tough luck. Where'd you meet Puma?"

"Spain, last winter. International skydiving competition. I couldn't compete, but—well, you know how it is."

"Oh, yeah. Gets in your blood. So you two hit it off right away?" She shot Rachel an appraising glance.

Rachel allowed a smirk to flit across her face. "Let's say we're a good fit."

The performance was wasted on Nita, whose blue eyes were back on the road. Not a road exactly, more like a wide trail. Probably a ranger access road.

"Uh-huh. Funny, he's never shown interest in any of the other gals. Couple of them would've been willing to get better acquainted."

Rachel went stiff. "Who? Not Patti. She's in heavy with the loft foreman. Tom—what's his name? Snyder? They're practically engaged. Not Pam. She's married."

Nita chuckled. "Since when does that have anything to do with sex? With a guy as hot as Puma. Did I hit a nerve?"

Rachel closed her eyes and cursed herself. God, she was jealous! Not just jealous, but ready to claw any woman who even looked crossways at Puma. *Get a grip, Rachel. The woman is baiting you.* "How about you, Nita? Are you panting after my boy?"

"Not me, honey. He's a hunk, but my tastes run elsewhere." She hauled a flask from under the front seat, uncapped it and offered it to Rachel.

So that's how the wind blew. She wondered if Howard

Elkins knew he'd left the fox in charge of the henhouse. Rachel took a swig, shuddered and handed the bottle back. The raw spirits burned all the way down. "Sheesh. What is that stuff?"

Nita took two deep swallows, recapped and stowed the bottle back under the seat. "Hundred-proof tequila. The only way to go."

"If you want to rot your innards and melt your teeth. Why don't you tell me what's on your mind, Nita?"

Nita swung the wheel and brought the van to a halt. The gearshift ground in protest as she shifted to park and left the motor running. They perched on a ledge that hung over a sheer hundred-foot drop-off.

"Mind setting the brake?" Rachel asked. "I'm not wearing my parachute."

"Heights bother you?" The woman took a can of snuff from her jeans pocket and held it out, her eyebrows quirked in a question mark.

Rachel shook her head. "No thanks. I didn't join up to be one of the guys. Being a woman is too much fun. And no, heights don't bother me."

Nita took a pinch of snuff and tucked it under her upper lip. "Gave up smoking ten years ago, but I need a nicotine fix now and then."

"Makes sense. Get mouth cancer, die young with nice clean lungs."

Nita grinned, exposing tobacco-smeared teeth. "Hot damn, the beanstalk has fangs. Don't suppose I could interest you in any of my other vices? How about a little two-on-one? You, me, and the sex partner of your choice?"

"How about a little sexual harassment suit?"

"Okay, 'nuff said. I'm backing off." Nita spit a brown stream out of the window and reached for the bottle again.

Rachel's wariness increased. The previous exchange had been a warm-up. Nita was zooming in for the kill. The woman leaned back in the leather seat and took another swig, not offering to share. Since the lip of the flask was smeared with wet tobacco, Rachel was grateful for the favor. The combined scent of alcohol and rancid sweat filled the cab of the van. Rachel rolled down her window and breathed air sweet with the perfume of pine and cedar. *Get to it, Nita.*

"Been wondering," Nita said, after another spit. "You remember Mellie Morganfield?"

Rachel rapidly ran through the computer base in her brain. "Morganfield," she stalled. "Mellie. You mean Mellie Fitzgerald? Morganfield must be her married name. Sure, I remember Mellie. I heard she quit jumping to have a baby."

Nita nodded and seemed to relax. "You heard right. She and I used to have some high times. Hoisted one or two at Rusty's Bar and Grill. Ever been to the Rusty Scupper? Best bar in Fairbanks."

"Can't say I have," Rachel shook her head. She doubted Nita had ever been to Fairbanks or even knew Mellie Morganfield, ex-Alaskan smokejumper. Rachel had been keeping track and despite the woman's swagger, the liquor hadn't gone down over an inch in the bottle. "The jumpers did some barhopping in Fairbanks, but I never heard of the Rusty Scupper. Not one of our usual hangouts."

"Maybe it's not there anymore. Been a few years since I was in Alaska." Nita recapped the bottle. "You know only ten percent of smokejumpers in the country are women? Five of 'em right here at our base. Six now, counting you."

"I'm honored," Rachel said, sincerely meaning it.

"We don't haze each other like the guys do," Nita said, swiveling in the seat and nailing Rachel with a glare. "But I had to check you out for the sisterhood. It's taken years and some amazing women to get where we are. A lot of guys still think we don't belong. Women smokejumpers have too much at stake for one of us to screw up. Understand?"

Rachel shrugged. "My records are on file at command, if you're curious."

"Records aren't always reliable. I've lost track of Mellie since she got married. I think I'll look her up on the association website. Give her a call."

A cold frisson crept up Rachel's spine. She had her cover story down pat, but physically she in no way resembled the woman whose identity she'd taken. *Never assume* you're in the clear, Rachel. You know better.

"Tell her hi and check how the baby's doing," she faked glibly. "Little guy must be a year old by now. What's this about, Nita?"

Nita threw the van in gear and backed up. "I don't know," she said. "Something about you just doesn't smell right. I signed on the jump list next couple of weeks. We'll see how you do."

This was not good. "I, ah, thought you were on the booster crew. They only jump during the height of the season, when we're overloaded with fire activity."

"Feeling the itch to get out there." Nita made a quick turn onto a side branch of the trail and suddenly they were back on the main road. "My name's on the list, right below yours."

Worse and worse. Even Puma had no idea how terrified Rachel was of fire. She counted on adrenalin and nerve getting her through the first forest fire encounters, and Puma covering for her if she bungled. But if Nita was on her back watching every move, things could get complicated.

"You actually think Puma would let me on his team if I wasn't qualified?"

"Puma's a good fire boss. One of the best. Wouldn't be the first guy to think with his dick."

"If you believe he'd cut me slack because we're involved," Rachel took a deep breath. "Then you don't know him at all."

CHAPTER 14

The restaurant was really an overgrown bar with casual, seat yourself dining. Rachel followed Puma to an empty table, and he waved across the room for a waitress. The girl returned the wave with a wide grin and a blown kiss.

Rachel sat down before he had a chance to pull out her chair. "Friend of yours? Isn't she a little young?"

"Sheathe your claws, Rookie. Janie's married to a fellow firefighter. Her husband is on the forest service hotshot crew."

She looked around the room. The majority of its occupants were male, men who looked at home in their bodies and their world. A dozen of them slouched around the bar, hooting at the television and the Rockies game in progress. The place was filling up with a rowdy crowd ready for a Saturday night of fun. Men and women in pairs and groups occupied tables around the room. In New York she would have pegged it a cop's bar.

"Do I sense a preponderance of firefighters? A whiff of excess testosterone?"

"They serve an honest drink here and the burgers are huge. Max and Reggie do okay by us."

"A huge burger," she sighed, rolling her eyes. "I'll have two. And extra fries."

He frowned. "You're supposed to be a cheap date. Could I interest you in a beer? Or are you holding out for champagne before you come across with the good stuff?"

"Short memory, mister. Trot out the food and we'll talk dirty."

"Well, damn, if I'd known it was going to be this easy, we'd have been here days ago. Anything else?"

She scanned the menu and nibbled her lip. "Homemade apple pie. And ice cream."

"You better be good, is all I have to say."

"Ansari, I'm the best." They'd just spent two hours in bed in their motel room. Probably would still be there if hunger hadn't forced them to find a food source.

"No argument." He waved at the waitress again, motioning to their table. The pert young woman gave him a thumb up and went back to taking orders.

"She likes you. Not that I care. Your personal life is your own business."

"You're crazy about me remember? Showing a little jealousy would help the charade along here," Puma said.

"Luckily, I'm a good actress."

"And a good liar, as you once mentioned."

She didn't like his tone or the intent stare. Puma wasn't easily fooled. She was deceiving him, and when he found out he'd been set up, he'd be furious. She had a pang of guilt, quickly smothered. "Goes with the territory. Part of the job description."

"I can accept that. Just don't lie to me." He reached with his thumb and stroked her face, her jaw line, her mouth. When he touched her so gently, she tingled in every pore of her body. She quivered and his hand dropped. "Relax, it's a game. We're playacting."

God, if that were only true. Her visceral reaction to his touch was anything but playacting. She looked around the bar scene and tried to decide why the Plugged Nickel was different. She sniffed. The smell of good food and brew. And the crowd was certainly heavily male. Exceedingly fit alpha males.

"There's a sign on the door that says Firemen Only? I missed it."

"It's a popular hangout. Max and Reggie are ex-firefighters."

"Where did the Plugged Nickel name come from?"

"What our lives are worth if we screw up. Reggie has a strange sense of humor."

She stifled a shudder, not that self-mockery was new to her. Cops had their own graveyard sense of humor. It was a way to cope with the pressure and ugliness of the job. "Nice you can joke about it. When do I meet Max and Reggie?"

"That's Max behind the bar. He's also the unofficial bouncer." Puma saluted across the room at the mustached giant deftly filling drink orders. The bartender saluted back, and continued topping mugs with tap beer and sliding them down the polished bar.

"Yummy. He's gorgeous, and tall enough for me."

"Avert the lustful eyes, Rookie. He and Reggie are partners in more ways than owning a bar together. Max may be the muscle, but Reggie's the brains and keeps the place running smoothly. That's him over there."

The man he pointed out was average height and slender, with a cheerful, open face and ruddy cheeks. He was laughing and talking to a couple seated a few tables away. They seemed to be enjoying themselves. She liked the looks of Reggie immediately. In contrast to his partner's casual plaid lumberman's shirt and jeans, he was duded up in a sport coat and neatly pressed slacks. "I can believe it. He seems so sweet."

He frowned and she bit her lip, thinking of Nita and their conversation the day before. Wrong choice of words. Nita was many things, but sexual preference aside, sweet wasn't one of them. Ditto with Reggie and Max. "Gay firemen. Is that unusual?"

"I don't know. Any man or woman willing to put their body in front of a firestorm has my respect. Their lifestyle isn't my business."

Firestorm.

The vision hit full force. Internal shakes. Sweat beading her upper lip. The room blurred at the flash of memory. Her father plunging into the heart of a raging fire to save her brother. Neither coming out alive. Over twenty years gone by, and the memory was sharp as ever. She closed her eyes and fought the nausea, the dizziness. She'd learned to handle this over the years. She would not be sick.

"Rachel, snap out of it!" Puma knelt before her, shaking her shoulders, his voice urgent with concern.

She willed herself back to reality. Gradually the crimson horror faded and her stomach stopped churning. The visions were getting stronger and more frequent. She had to get past this phobia. She'd be jumping fire soon and Puma might not be around to save her ass. Nita would be watching to see if she could cut it, along with the rest of the crew. Watching if she froze or spazed out. "Sorry. Dizzy for a sec."

He stared at her, not letting loose. "What happened? One minute we were talking, the next you almost slid off the chair, shaking like you had a fever."

"I'm okay. I just need some food."

His gaze intensified. "It's more than that. I thought we agreed no lies between us."

"Guess I'm worn out. Let's eat and leave."

He released her shoulders and stood, his jaw set. "All right. It's been a rough week. The waitress is still busy. I'll go to the bar and order something."

Her stomach flipped at the thought of food. "I was kidding before. One burger is plenty. And fries, no pie."

"How about a beer?"

"No, ice water is fine."

She watched him thread his way through the crowd toward the bar. It took him a while because he stopped often to return good-natured arm jabs and handshakes. The waitress, Janie, gave him a tap on the shoulder, gesturing. Puma listened, hugged her, and glanced around the room as if he was searching for someone. Not like a cop bar after all, she decided. The atmosphere was friendlier, less sedate and more festive than any cop bar she'd been in. It was amazing. These men and women faced death every time the fire bell rang. Hideous death. Cops dealt with danger on a daily basis, but she'd far rather die by a bullet than fire.

A glass was placed in front of her. A bulbous margarita glass, sweat beaded and rimmed with salt, cradled in a hairy paw. "Have a drink, doll face. My treat."

The male looming over her matched the gorilla-size hand. He was probably six-two and weighed in at two-thirty. Muscled, but going to gut. Looked late twenties. Wearing a tight tee shirt, tighter jeans and a day's growth of beard, his blonde hair tied back in a clubbed ponytail. Brown eyes and a prissy, rapacious mouth. Something about him made her wish she'd worn her gun.

"Sorry," she said politely. "I'm with someone."

"Yeah, I saw him leave. No use waiting for a guy after he splits. Don't you like margaritas?"

Keep your smile on, Rachel. And your good manners. The first rule of undercover work was never to draw attention to yourself. "Actually, I don't. My friend is bringing me a drink from the bar. You better leave before he gets back."

Muscle-head chuckled, turned Puma's vacant chair around and straddled it, setting his beer down. He scratched his armpit and flashed white, gleaming teeth. Charming.

"I'm in no hurry, doll face. What ya' say we get acquainted? Could be I'm a better deal than the wimp boyfriend. Woman spends a night with me she wakes up smiling, guaranteed."

So much for good manners. "A woman dumb enough to spend a night with you would wake up with fleas. Probably worse. Take a hike."

"Oh, ho, a feisty one. Nice. Call me Bronco. You got a name besides doll face?"

Men found her size intimidating enough she didn't usually get hit on. At least not this obviously. Maybe it had something to do with the two male to one female ratio in the bar. Muscle-head was probably more stupid than dangerous, but he was a lot bigger than she was, and bent on a conquest.

"If you leave right now, Call-Me-Bronco, I won't have to hurt you."

He whooped and slapped the table. "We're going to have fun, doll face. Don't have much of a rack on you, but damn, that's a sexy mouth. Tits aren't everything. A mouth like that could make a man real happy. You don't like margaritas, what're you drinking?"

Rachel chose her words carefully, and still smiling, verbally insulted Bronco's ancestry back to the primal slime he'd oozed out of. The man flushed and swelled. Even a cretin of Bronco's IQ knew he'd been slammed.

"You need a lesson, bitch," he snarled, leaning into her face. "Starting with a fat lip. And I'm the guy can make it happen."

"Go to hell," Rachel said, suggesting her admirer perform an anatomically impossible feat on himself, one involving his tiny privates. Bronco's eyes crossed while he thought about it, then he grabbed her wrist, his fingers bruising her flesh as he yanked her across the table. She winced and curled her other fist, deciding she would break his nose. Stupidity wasn't illegal but assault was. She'd claim self-defense if it went to court.

A rough growl overhead interrupted her anticipation of the good time ahead with Bronco. "Let her go or lose your hand."

Bronco blinked and squinted up at Puma, releasing Rachel. He snorted, pushed the chair back and stood. "You the wimp-ass boyfriend?"

Puma set down drinks he was carrying. "That'd be me. Shall we step outside and discuss how much I dislike someone manhandling my woman?"

This was trouble. Bronco stood four inches over Puma and outweighed him fifty pounds, but Rachel had no doubt which man would end up in the hospital. "Let me have him, Ansari, please, please. It's been a long time since I've had one this good."

"You want this guy?" Puma gave her a half-smile that could've sliced bone.

"Oh, yes," Rachel sighed. "Can I? It's just too cute the way his knuckles drag the ground."

"Welll——"

She stood and did her best slinky stroll over to Call-Me-Bronco, who shook his head and scowled, obviously disappointed. "You gonna let me have her without a fight, wimp-ass?"

"Ladies' choice," Puma said, shrugging a shoulder. "Take her if you can."

"If you can," Rachel purred.

She reached up and caught Bronco's nose between her thumb and fingers, and gave it a vicious twist. The man bellowed and staggered back. Curses burst from his throat and he lunged to engulf her in a bear hug. Rachel released his nose and her knee slammed up, connecting with his groin. His scream of pain rose to pure soprano. The crunching sound of bone on tender flesh caused every man within hearing to clench his teeth and quail. One of her long legs swept sideways, and Bronco crashed like a felled redwood.

She and Puma stared down at him.

A splatter of applause erupted from the surrounding tables.

"Pitiful," Puma said.

"Sorry, Call-Me-Bronco," Rachael said sweetly. "I suppose this means it's over between us."

"Are you done fooling around?" Puma asked. "We have some burgers and fries coming."

She pouted. "It was just too easy. Can I hit him again?"

"Please don't, missy." Max the bartender bent over the moaning man and lifted an eyelid. Bronco was hyperventilating. "You kill him, the paperwork's a bitch. Know his name?"

"He introduced himself as Bronco," Rachel said. "I'm Myra. Puma's girl."

Puma toed his boot at the beached whale of a man. "If

he's a regular, Max, the level of your clientele is sliding."

"He's only been around the past week. The waitresses call him the Margarita Man. His come-on is to buy the woman a margarita and hustle her, but he's always approached women who're alone before. What did he do to bring this on, Myra?"

"Other than insulting my anatomy? Refused to leave and pawed me." She held up her swollen wrist. The redness was beginning to ebb into purple. Puma's eyes darkened.

"So he deserved what he got." Max heaved the stupefied Bronco to his feet. "C'mon, lover boy. I'll buy you a drink for the road. And don't come in here again."

Puma muttered something in Max's ear. The bartender nodded. With Max's arm firmly around his middle, the two men staggered toward the bar. Whistles of approval accompanied the pair's weaving progress.

"Way to go, lady!"

"Yo, Wonder Woman!"

Puma kicked his chair around and sat at the table, pointing at her empty seat. "Sit. Quite an exhibition. Remind me to never piss you off." She sat and reached for the ice water. An adrenalin rush always made her thirsty. He leaned forward, tapped his fingers on his beer mug and gave her the fisheye. "Low profile, huh?" he asked.

Rachel wanted to slide under the table. Hooker would kill her if he'd witnessed the scene. Her boss hated hot-dogging. "It kinda got away from me. Should we leave?"

"After we eat."

"Don't leave!" Both their eyes snapped toward the voice. "At least not till Debbie shakes your hand."

A young couple approached their table. She was dark-haired, petite and very pregnant, and beamed at Rachel like a star-struck groupie. He was a stocky man with sandy hair, wearing jeans, a Save the Eagles tee shirt and a big grin. Puma stood and the two men gripped forearms.

"Hi, Greg, Debbie," Puma said. "The dangerous female is—ah, meet Myra Sasser. Myra, this is Debbie. And the lucky man is Greg Garfield. Greg's taking a year off from the smokejumping team. Has this pervert been violating you, Debbie? If you need me to polish up my shotgun, let me know."

The brunette giggled and blushed. "You're bad, Fletcher Ansari." She turned to Rachel. "Greg and I got married last fall. Fletcher was Greg's best man. After I pop this kid, will you show me how you did that?"

"Sure. It was just two basic defense moves." Since Rachel would be gone long before the baby was born, it was a safe promise.

"Puma and I met in the 82nd Airborne," Greg said. "Both of us Colorado boys, so we hit it off. Debbie's the only one I know besides his sister and aunt who call him by his given name."

"I like the name Fletcher," Debbie said. "It fits him."

"That was something to see, Myra," Greg said. "Happened so fast we'd have missed it if we hadn't been gawking and wondering who you were. Better sign her up, Puma."

Rachel took over the conversation. "He already has. I'm on the smokejumping team this season."

"Ah-ha!" Greg's eyes gleamed with interest. "Sounds like a good story."

Puma cut him off, thinking it was a break the Garfields were there, because there was some immediate business he needed to attend to. "Why don't you join us? Have you eaten?"

"No, but we don't want to intrude."

"You're not. It'll give Myra someone to talk to while you and I catch up." He gave Rachel a look that promised a lecture when they were alone. She grinned and flexed her arm muscle. He snorted and nipped her ear, whispering. "Enjoy it while you can, Rookie. I'm laying you down."

"Maybe." She gave him a lowered-lashes look and his groin tightened.

Puma manipulated the seating so Rachel and Debbie sat side-by-side with their backs to the bar, while he and Greg had a clear view of the TV screen.

"You have an unusual haircut," Debbie said. "Very punk. You must have had it done in Denver."

"Let me tell you about my haircut," Rachel said, with a frown aimed at Puma. "It was done with manicure scissors."

While the women were getting acquainted, Puma gave Greg's knee a nudge and flicked a glance toward the front of the room. The man tensed, responding with a nod.

"How about a pit stop, boss?" Greg asked casually.

"Wouldn't mind." Both men scraped their chairs back and excused themselves. Debbie waved them off, enthralled with the story—entirely false as far as Puma could tell, that Rachel was telling her.

"The big guy propping up the bar," Puma said, moving fast to the front of the restaurant.

"Thought Max was going to throw him out."

"I mentioned to Max to keep the drinks flowing till I had a word."

Greg shrugged an okay. "How do we do this?"

"We haul him outside. Then you back off."

"He's the size of a Volkswagen. Want a hand?"

Puma gave him a look and Greg grinned. "Sorry."

Fifteen minutes later the two men reentered the bar, Greg shaking his head and Puma slightly disheveled. Puma headed for the men's room to tidy up and Greg bellied up to the bar. Max looked up from polishing drink glasses and raised his eyebrows. "Do I call an ambulance or a hearse?"

"Never saw anything like it," Greg said, ready and anxious to talk. "I need something stronger than beer. Bourbon, rocks."

Max obliged, sliding the drink forward. "On the house. What happened?"

"We get the guy out to the back alley and Puma says to him, 'Let's talk, asshole.' So the incredible bulk's still walking funny from riding Rachel's knee, right? More than a little pissed. Plus he takes a look at Ansari's size and thinks easy pickings, so he throws a punch. Big mistake. Puma cold-cocks him so fast I don't see the move. Then he frisks the guy, even pulls down his socks to check for a knife, and digs a wallet out of his jeans. Name on the driver's license is Billy Smith, for your future reference."

"Smith, huh? Convenient. Doesn't matter. He's not coming in here again."

"I'm damn sure we've seen the last of Mr. Smith. Anyway, the guy starts to come out of it, and Puma puts a hammerlock on his throat. Could've killed him easy and the freak show must've known it, but does he have enough sense to keep his mouth shut? Huh-uh. Puma's straddling Smith with the guy's face pushed in the pavement, and the pea brain says something real vile about Myra. About how he planned to——ah, hell, you don't wanna know."

Max whistled. "Jerk Face must have the IQ of a turnip."

"Yeah." Greg swigged the drink, shuddered and snagged a piece of ice to chew on. "I knew Puma was dangerous, but this was something else."

"Then what?"

"Ansari's grandfather was full-blooded Ute, you know that?"

Max nodded. "Real private people, the Ute, but you don't want to rile them."

"After his wife died, Puma joined up with Delta."

Max whistled. "Special Forces."

"Black ops. Real bad boys."

"He'd be good at it." Max quit polishing glasses and started working on the bar. "Myra seems like a lot of woman. Maybe she's the one."

"Maybe. So Puma breaks every finger on the guy's right hand except the pinkie. Cold-blooded as hell."

Max stopped cleaning the bar and gave a low whistle. "Kee-rist. He breaks——"

"All of 'em. One at a time. Guy's screaming like a monkey and begging after the first finger goes. You ever hear a finger break? Sounds like a twig snapping. Then Puma drags his ass to the back entrance and tips one of your busboys a fifty to haul his carcass to the emergency room." Greg shook his head. "Ansari doesn't even break a sweat."

Max laid down his polishing rag. "One of my busboys? I'm not sure I like that."

"Reggie went along for the ride. Said he wanted the guy out of here and didn't want to involve the cops. Smith didn't either. He was real vocal about not calling the cops. I need a beer to wash down the whiskey, Max."

Max nodded and topped off a beer mug, sliding it toward Greg. "Reggie will know how to handle it."

"Anyhow, the guy's cradling his hand, which by this time is the size of a watermelon, and hollering he'll fix Puma and his bitch good."

Greg shook his head. "Stupid."

Max snorted. "What then? Ansari scalp him?"

"Wouldn't put it past him, given the right circumstances. Naw, Puma says something in the guy's ear. Real soft. The guy snarls something back and jumps in the car. Yells at the busboy. We don't see his taillights for dust."

Max laughed. "Reggie will have some story to tell. Wish I could've been there."

"Yeah. Pea brain won't be assaulting a woman again anytime soon."

The likeness that peered back at him in the mirror was grim, the mouth a straight-line slash. Puma turned on the cold water, rinsed his face and ran wet hands through his hair. Greg thought he'd lost it out there in the alley.

He hadn't.

True, he'd been hot-wired. He'd taken one look at Rachel's bruised wrist and gone into combat mode. No one was going to hurt his woman. Or any woman, on his watch.

Jesus, Togochin, are you happy now? I've done it. Fallen for the woman. Hooked, reeled in, and tied up in a bow.

Puma glanced around the men's room, almost expecting Joseph Red Feather to be lurking among the urinals. Of course his grandfather wasn't there. His ghost hung around the ranch. If it was a ghost and not a hallucination. Puma reached for a paper towel and mopped his face. His mirrored image stared back, only part of the grimness wiped away. Even without his grandfather's spirit to prod him, Puma's instincts told him a storm was brewing and they hadn't seen the last of Billy Smith.

There is danger ahead, and great challenge. For you both.

I hear you, Togochin. Whatever it was about, Smith was involved up to his matted eyebrows. Underneath that phony, redneck exterior lurked a cunning, treacherous man, one who'd had extensive martial arts training. If Smith hadn't been overconfident, Rachel would never have bested him.

Maybe I should have killed him. Saved myself some real trouble in the future.

There'd been something about Billy Smith, an internal fury that burned under the man's skin. A hint of madness. Puma searched carefully for a weapon when he had the man on his belly. Other than a pocketknife, there wasn't one. Which didn't mean the man didn't own a gun, might be carrying one in his vehicle. It was in the news often enough. A weirdo flips out, returns with an automatic and ices everyone in range. Puma sensed the kind of insanity in Smith that would make it possible.

Rachel had made a bitter enemy.

A dangerous enemy.

It was a threat that had to be dealt with.

Puma made the assessment and rendered the man's right hand useless. Careful observation had shown the man was right-handed. Few people were ambidextrous with a gun. Puma was, but he'd spent hundreds of hours on the shooting range to gain the skill.

"I know where you live," had been Smith's hoarsely whispered last words. "Next time you both die."

Puma knew truth when he heard it. And hatred.

Smith, if that was his name, would be back, probably with friends. It was time for a heart-to-heart with Rachel. Whatever dangerous game she and Hooker were playing, she damn well was going to let Puma in on it.

CHAPTER 15

Chic downed two Hydrocodone and poured a straight shot of scotch, cursing the awkwardness of his left hand when a generous amount splashed onto the dresser top. He needed every drop to restore his self-respect. His broken fingers throbbed like hell, his swollen nose resembled Rudolph's and his balls were twice their normal size. He was a walking train wreck, but the fact he'd been bested by a woman hurt more.

He swallowed the liquor in one gulp and waited for the euphoria to lighten his mood. The fire hit his belly and he poured another. It might take two bottles. One to relieve the pain, another to erase the humiliation of being taken down twice in one night.

The Indian prick had some moves, Chic gave him that. It would be a pleasure to kill him and Chic could hardly wait to get his hands on the woman. As of now Zebedee was out of the picture. Chic would nail the ex-Delta himself, after he did a slice and dice job on the bitch he ran with. Make Ansari watch an expert at work. It was a better plan anyway. Four Star would be pleased when his first lieutenant humbled a warrior of Ansari's abilities.

That would send a message to the feebs. Mess with the Sons and die the hard way.

* * *

Puma listened to the feminine sounds of splashing, humming and tooth brushing flow from the bathroom. It had been a long time since he'd shared a bathroom with a woman. It was an ordinary, drab motel room, but he and Rachel made their own magic in the king-size bed. Her scent clung to the pillow under his head, and he pressed his face into the sweet softness. It had seemed simple earlier that afternoon. They would stay together as long as it was good, as long as it was what they both wanted. Increasingly Puma was thinking in terms of a lifetime.

She was on the pill and they'd dispensed with condoms. Sliding uncovered into her silken sheath, Puma thought at times his heart would stop, the pleasure was so intense. Their lovemaking was simply, spectacular.

Angry as he was at being duped, he wanted her.

The promises she'd purred in his ear before she disappeared into the bathroom had gone straight to his groin. Nothing too exotic she whispered. Just down and dirty, mind-blowing sex. Maybe he was angry with the wrong person. Could be Rachel had no idea how devious Hooker was. At least Puma owed her the chance to explain a few things.

She craned her neck around the doorway, foamy toothbrush in hand. "Get naked, noble savage, I've got plans for you."

Damn, he hoped she'd be straight with him.

He shucked his tee shirt and unsnapped his jeans. "Come and get me, Rookie. You haven't seen all my moves yet."

She laughed and disappeared. He heard the sound of gargling and water running. Okay, he'd listen. Depending on what she had to say they were either done, or just beginning.

She waltzed into the room, singing off-key, a bath towel clutched around her naked body. "If you want my bahhhdy, and you think I'm sexy—"

Rod Stewart had nothing to worry about.

Her long legs flashed enticingly below the white

terrycloth, her breasts curved above. For a blind moment he considered taking her first and asking questions later. Maybe get her halfway there and stop. If he timed it right she'd tell him anything. When they made love she was totally his, and they both knew it.

He discarded the idea. Either he could trust her or he couldn't. She'd tell him the truth or lie, and he would know which from looking in her eyes. Whatever was going on, if she leveled with him he'd handle it. But lying he considered unforgivable. Lazily he narrowed his eyes as she let the towel slip and did a slow turn, giving him a glimpse of bare ass.

"Nice," he said, his voice rough. "Do I have to come over there after you?"

"Stay put. I'm just getting warmed up." She grinned and ran her fingers through her damp hair, spiking it, emphasizing the impish look.

"I'm willing. Let's see what you've got." He settled back against the pillows.

"Music," she announced, flicking on the television and accessing the music channel. "You probably noticed my talents don't include singing."

"That was singing?"

A slow, bluesy melody throbbed from the tinny speaker. She moved to the music and worked the towel like a pro, allowing him an occasional peek of skin. Were all females natural masters of seduction? This woman certainly knew how to play him. She pouted and stroked her breasts, hips swaying, smirking when he hissed in a breath. Her fingers slid between her thighs and she moaned as she moved in the rhythm of lovemaking. His good intentions dove south.

"How're you doin'?" she crooned, drifting closer, careful to stay out of arms' reach, her eyes on his zipper. "Wowsa, lookin' good, baby. Wanna dance with me?"

"Oh, yeah, I wanna dance." His arm shot out and she shrieked as he flipped her on her back and she landed underneath him. The knot on the towel gave. She wiggled and her bare breasts rubbed against him.

"I love your naked chest touching me," she sighed. "Let me feel the rest of you."

Her hands smoothed down his back and slipped under the band of his jeans. She squeezed his buttocks, and red dots danced under his eyelids. She tongued the hollow of his throat and when her mouth moved to his, it was over. She had a luscious, generous mouth. He took her offering, using his tongue and teeth, diving deep. Sometimes when they kissed like this, he cupped her buttocks and slipped inside of her without breaking mouth contact. It was the most voluptuous, sensual lovemaking he'd ever indulged in, a total blending of their bodies that went beyond the physical.

Their mouths parted and she shuddered a sigh, the ache between her thighs growing unbearable. One kiss from him and her bones turned to water. She dug her fingers in his back, urging him on. "God, how can I want you so much, so soon? I'm a total floozy. Shuck those pants lover, and get busy. We'll do the fooling around later."

He pinned her arms to her sides. "We have to talk."

"Talk? For God's sake!" Frantic with desire, she tried to jerk her arms away. "Isn't that usually the woman's line? We'll talk later."

Much later. Her hormones were raging.

"Listen to me, Rachel. Does the name Billy Smith mean anything to you?"

"Smith?" she repeated absently, intent on freeing her arms and using her mouth to drive him crazy.

"Billy Smith. The guy you decked tonight at the Plugged Nickel."

Gradually it penetrated that he really did want to talk. How crazy was that? She groaned in frustration. "His name was Billy Smith?"

"That was the name on his driver's license."

"No," she shook her head. "Never heard of him. He said his name was Bronco. Oh, my God. Bronco Billy!" She started to laugh. Couldn't help it. "He didn't look much like Clint Eastwood."

"Not much," Puma agreed, freeing her arms and stroking

her face. Something dark flashed in his eyes. "You never saw him before tonight?"

"I said I hadn't!" She struggled to a sitting position and glared at him. "What's this about, Ansari? Why the third degree?"

"It seems too convenient. The waitress said the man asked her to point me out. How did he know I'd be there? And why did he care?"

"Wait a minute! You just couldn't stay out of it, could you? You and Greg were gone a while. Dammit, you followed him outside?"

Puma shrugged. "We had a short discussion. I learned a few things. Some things you need to clarify."

"Discussion! What does that mean?" Rachel knew her temper was heating up. She gathered the sheet around her breasts. The mood for sex was slipping away.

"It means Rachel, that Billy Smith came looking for me and found you and I want to know why."

"How would I know? What did you do, exactly? This Bronco character wasn't the talkative type. Oh, God. You took him down and searched him?"

"Yeah. You were lucky, Rachel. The man is dangerous, and almost as good as I am. You're sure you never saw him before?"

"Never! When would I?" She froze, finally seeing where this was going. Hooker. Hooker was involved somehow.

Puma cupped her chin. "Up to now you've been telling me the truth. Don't lie to me, Rachel, because I'll know it. What kind of game are you and your boss playing?"

She hadn't lied to him exactly, she just hadn't told him everything. Hooker's orders were explicit. Puma wasn't to know that the Sons were after him. "I don't have a game."

"The hell you don't. Bronco Smith—and we both know the name's a phony—has a tattoo on his right instep, Rachel. An eagle's claw. Ring any bells?"

She shuddered. "The New Sons of Liberty. Their mark of loyalty. Smith must be a member."

"Bingo, Rookie. Now suppose you tell me the rest of it."

"I—I can't. I should call Hooker."

Puma pointed to her secure phone on the night table. "Be my guest. I want a word with your boss, also."

Shaking with dread, Rachel dialed Hooker's pager number, adding her coded ID. She hung up, walked to the closet and pulled out her robe. It was the old terrycloth, the only robe she had with her, but she was grateful for its protection. The day before she'd been wishing she owned a satin seductive number to whet her lover's appetite. She shrugged into the garment and tightened the belt, fully aware of the frost in Puma's stare.

During the weeks of training, she had seen him impatient, bemused, and even irate. But never with this cold, dispassionate anger. She shivered.

"He'll get back to me," she said. "But he has no idea we're together."

"I find that hard to believe. You check in every day. I figure between the two of you I don't have any secrets left."

"You and I are private. And none of Hooker's business."

"Depending on what you have to tell me Rachel, there may be no more private business."

She'd known this day would come. When she'd have to choose. What she hadn't expected was the rush of pain. "We need to keep us separate from the job. You've always known that."

"I'm entitled to some answers. Smith has a real hard-on for me. Why? How did the New Sons find me and do they know you're an FBI agent? If you're blown, we've wasted a lot of time and sweat."

Rachel shook her head. "No one knows I'm FBI except you and Hooker. He's been real careful not to leave a paper trail."

"Your boss is a devious sonovabitch. But he wouldn't put you in the field without giving you full disclosure. So whatever this is about, spill it, Rookie."

Her cell buzzed, offering a reprieve.

Typical of Hooker he started in without formality. "What

are you doing in a motel room in Colorado Springs?" His voice was tight with controlled anger. "I told you to stick to the subject like a burr."

Rachel closed her eyes and prayed. Of course Hooker would have the cell location traced before he called it. And he'd be guarded about what he said over the unsecured line. "I'm sticking."

Five seconds of dead silence. "When I said stay close I didn't mean crawl between the sheets. What's going on?"

"What can I say? Stuff happens."

More silence. "Is he there?"

"He wants to talk to you." Puma moved in and reached for the receiver.

"I'll call you back. Ten minutes." Her boss hung up just as Puma grabbed.

Puma snarled in disbelief at the sound of the disconnect. "Call him back!"

"He'll get in touch. He said ten minutes. Probably double-checking the line is secure."

"Yeah," Puma said softly. "Hooker is a careful man. He doesn't do anything without a reason." He stretched out on the bed, keeping his eyes on her. Rachel sat beside him, clutching her phone. Neither said anything more until it rang.

"I'm here," Rachel answered.

"I'm listening."

"There was a dustup tonight. At a local bar."

"Go on." Hooker's voice was hollow, heavy with censure.

Rachel swallowed. "A man accosted me. I over-reacted."

"You attracted attention? The wrong kind?"

"Possible. He was New Sons."

A sharp intake of breath. "Are you blown?"

"No! Definitely not."

Puma wrenched the phone from her fingers. "Hooker," he growled. "Am I going to have to kill you, or just beat you into bloody mush?"

"Interesting choice. What brought it on?"

"A blond guy. Six-two or three, weighs in at two-fifty.

Big gut and receding hairline. Bushy eyebrows and scrawny ponytail. Interesting tattoo on his right instep. Martial arts expert. Or was, until I broke his fingers. Calls himself Billy Smith. Who is he?"

"Sounds like New Sons," Hooker said cautiously.

"Tell me something I don't know."

"Broke his fingers," Hooker chuckled. "You haven't lost your touch."

"And you're as devious as ever. Fill me in or I'm done and your loyal little agent can pack her bags."

A sighed curse. "Okay. Put her back on."

Puma handed Rachel the phone and stalked into the bathroom. The door closed with a bang. She cleared her throat and braced herself.

"It was Fillmore. If you've blown this," Hooker rasped, "I'll see you assigned to Little Rock, shuffling papers for the rest of your career. Got that?"

"Yessir."

"Fill him in on the Hoover Dam connection, but nothing about the brother's death. And absolutely nothing about the trap we've set. Explain we have a line on the mole."

"But—"

"Listen, Cortez. Chic Fillmore thinks we have a male agent in place at Forest Service headquarters. He knows nothing about you, because he knows only what we want him to know. He thinks you're the girlfriend, nothing else. It sounds like he made a mistake tonight."

"Someone knew we'd be there. And passed it on."

"Yeah." Voices buzzed in the background. "Maybe that's good. It substantiates our theory. Who at headquarters knew the two of you were taking R&R at the Springs?"

"The women I bunk with. Howard Elkins, the base manager. Most of our crew. Whoever they passed it on to, I suppose."

"Well, that sure as hell narrows it down."

"I didn't think it was a secret. Sorry."

"How deep are you in it with Puma, Rachel? You know the rules. Chill the relationship."

Rachel rubbed her temples. A migraine was settling in. "I don't think I'll have to chill it, sir. I think it's been done for me."

"You sound regretful."

"Some. But my priorities are straight."

Hooker hung up, and Rachel listened to the sound of the shower coming from behind the closed bathroom door. Probably not a good plan to climb in there with him. She had an idea the water was running stone cold.

CHAPTER 16

They flew westward, leaving the dawn's early light behind, heading deep into the mountains. Low-level winds buffeted the twin-engine aircraft, tossing the plane like a sailboat on the sea of sky. Rachel took a swallow from the water bottle, willing her stomach to calm down. Puma sat in the pilot's seat, his left hand resting easily on the steering mechanism, his right adjusting knobs on the instrument panel. Wraparound Raybans concealed his eyes and his tight jaw revealed little of his thoughts.

"After we reach altitude this turbulence will smooth out," he said. "It's an hour flight to base. Plenty of time for you to explain what your people are up to."

Your people? That drew a line in the sand. Rachel huddled in the passenger side of the Piper Cheyenne, shivering in the chill air, wondering where to start. She and Puma hadn't said fifty words to each other for the past twelve hours.

She'd been under the covers on her side of the bed when he emerged from the shower. "Take off the silly robe," he growled. "It looks damned uncomfortable and I'm not going to touch you."

He hadn't.

In fact, he'd barely acknowledged her presence. When

necessary, terse words passed between them. What do you want for breakfast? Be packed and ready to leave at seven. Take some Tylenol for that sore wrist.

Worse was the look of disinterest in his eyes. That should have made her task easier, but it didn't. Anger she could cope with, but cold indifference, not so much.

"I've always wanted to learn to fly," she said, stalling the inevitable. "I took a few lessons once. Never soloed."

"That so? Why?" His eyes flicked toward the horizon, then back to the instrument panel. He reached and made an adjustment.

"The job got more intense. Skydiving took over my spare time."

Her thoughts wondered. Maybe someday he could teach me? Stupid thought. As soon as the job was over, she'd be back in D.C. If there'd been a chance for them to maintain a long-term relationship it was gone now. There was no denying that she had deceived him, would continue to deceive him. When he discovered the truth, he'd never forgive.

"But maybe I should learn."

He nodded. "It's a skill you should have, Rachel, if you fly in small planes often. Do you remember your basics?"

"Yes. I can steer well enough. And read the instruments. Never did make a landing without the instructor backing me up."

His mouth twitched into a grin, the first thaw she'd seen since the night before. "I'd say landing is pretty basic. What do you have to tell me, Rookie?"

Back to the subject, it seemed.

"Okay," she said. "You remember after 9/11, the FBI director announced they were forming a new terrorist task force? That better communication and cooperation between federal law enforcement agencies would be the new norm?"

Puma nodded and pulled back the throttle, lifting the plane's altitude and leveled out above the cloud cover. "It was in the news. How is that working out?"

"Hooker runs a high security op. Anyone admitted to the task force is vetted and given top security rating. Leaks are damn near impossible."

"I'm glad to hear that. I can rest easy, knowing Hooker is in charge."

"Sarcasm isn't necessary." She glared at him. Her loyalty to Hooker and the bureau would get her through this. "You wanted to hear it, so listen. Nine months ago, someone broke into our master computer. Not an easy task. Whoever it was breached a dozen firewalls to get there. There was concern."

"I can imagine. A leak in the Denver office?"

"Yes. This was shortly after the Hoover Dam incident. It was assumed someone had turned. Only an insider could have breached our security system."

"I pretty much guessed this, Rachel. Where do I fit in?"

"It was decided not to close the wall. To let whoever it was continue to lurk, feed them unclassified stuff and follow the trail backwards. Find out who was behind it." She paused. "It was traced to the New Sons. Our people listened in."

"Okay. What was leaked that shouldn't have been?"

Damn, trust him to go to the nitty-gritty. It was getting tough now. She chose her words carefully. "Hooker's entire report on the Hoover Dam incident."

He shook his head in disbelief. "That's crazy. They let that out? The Sons have my name? And Jake's?"

"It was a mistake. One we regret. But we got a lot in return. Their plan to burn the national forests. And Jake Randolph is safe enough. Based in DC working for the NIA, he's pretty much untouchable."

Puma gave her a slow, steady stare, his ice-blue eyes stripping her naked. "So Hooker put you on me. My own private watchdog. Just in case someone decided to make it personal. But you needed a story I would buy. One that would get you close to me."

She breathed in relief. This was something she could sell. He'd be furious, but would buy it. "More or less," she nodded. "We discovered the plot to burn the national forests. We needed access to the smokejumping operation. Hooker wanted to keep an eye on you. It all came together in a neat package."

"And part of the package was sleeping with me? I'm impressed. What you fed types won't do for your country."

He slammed off the autopilot and took over the controls. A jerk of the wheel and the plane did a double barrel roll that left Rachel's stomach behind. Her coffee and orange juice breakfast resurfaced. She grabbed for the barf bag and used it, wrenching her guts out. It was humiliating, just as he'd intended. The plane leveled out and her temper rose as her stomach settled.

"Dammit, that was stupid, Ansari! You're lucky I didn't heave all over your pretty leather seats. Do that again and I will."

She was right. He'd let his temper get the best of him. Silently he handed her the water bottle and she took a healthy slug. Damned if he'd apologize. "Barf on my seats and you clean it up. Anything more to tell me?"

She spat in the bag. "No. That's it. Sorry if it bruised your ego. I'm sure you can handle anything that comes along, but Hooker felt responsible. And by the way, sleeping with you was my call."

He knew some of what she was passing on was a lie. Which part? Eventually he'd figure it out.

"There's a half-pint of bourbon in the storage container in front of you. Take a swig and settle your stomach. If that little roll got to you so fast, how the hell do you handle real turbulence?"

"Just fine. Usually I don't go upside down in three seconds. Are we even now?"

"No. There's more. How did Smith find me? Do they know you're federal?"

"I don't see how. We've found the leak. It was Ash Calloway's personal secretary. Ash turned her and is running her. The Sons only learn what we want them to."

"Which included our trip to Colorado Springs? Why?"

"No, no. The Sons know someone is undercover, but think it's a man. Probably they were just checking you out, maybe to see if you're working for us. We don't know. But someone at command post is under the terrorists' thumb and feeding them info. Like where fires are flaring up naturally, lightning strikes and wind direction and speed. Vulnerable areas where a fire would do the most damage."

Something reeked. And it wasn't just the barf bag Rachel carefully sealed and stowed under the seat. Why had Hooker set her up as his watchdog? Hooker knew Puma could take care of himself just fine. He changed the subject, probing for answers.

"Are you close to exposing the mole? I know most of the personnel at base. Maybe I could help."

"I don't think it's one of the jumpers. It's someone with real authority and know-how. Maybe Elkins?"

Puma snorted. "Not possible. He's as dedicated a man as I've ever known. He hates fire. Considers it a personal enemy."

"We're eliminating no one." Her jaw was set in that stubborn angle Puma had come to know so well. "We can't afford to."

Nor could he, Puma thought. Nor could he.

Puma's pager went off when they were twenty minutes out from base. "It's Elkins," he said, reaching for the radio.

Howard Elkins came over the air. "We've got a bad one, Puma," the base manger's voice squawked. "How soon can you get here? Rothmeyer went out with an eight-man crew at ten-hundred yesterday. Jeanette took another six jumpers in four hours ago and they need backup. If you can't get here, I'll appoint another crew boss."

"ETA twelve-fifteen. Where's the jump?"

"Arapahoe National Forest, west of the Divide. A dozen active fires. Radar indicates fifty plus dry lightning strikes in the past two days, so these must be latent flare-ups. Or improperly extinguished campfires. But it's early in the season for fire on this scale and so many all at once."

"Arson?"

"If it is, God help us. I've ordered aerial reconnaissance and computer analysis."

"I'm there. Roger and out." Puma switched off the radio.

Rachel leaned forward, listening intently. "Is this what we've been afraid of?"

"Hard to tell. I'll know more after I jump it."

"I'm going along, regardless of where I stand on the jump list." She braced for an argument. No way was he leaving her behind.

"Yeah," he agreed, surprising her. "I'm not letting you out of my sight until I figure out what you're up to. Besides, with two other crews out, Elkins has reached the bottom of the list. You're on for your first real forest fire, rookie."

If there had been anything left in her stomach, it would have come up.

CHAPTER 17

———◆———

Puma lay on his belly by the open cargo door of the Sherpa J173 and surveyed the rough terrain five-hundred feet below. Tom Snyder, the loft supervisor and their spotter, was stretched out beside him. Snyder, who had the final call on the jump site location, wore earphones and a mike to converse with the pilot, and by his orders the plane made a second sweep over the fire area. The acrid scent of burning conifer and dense plumes of smoke rose from several spots in the landscape. Puma grunted. He'd seen enough.

He crawled out of the wind and into the safety of the plane's interior, tapping Tom on the shoulder to signal time for a discussion. The man nodded and followed, stripped off his earphones and unfolded the aerial incidence map.

"It's pretty much what we expected, Puma, and what the reconnaissance survey indicated. A dozen fires burning simultaneously. Rothmeyer's team has two of the smaller fires under control. Fires marked AF5 and AF6 on the map. They built a helispot here." He indicated the circle on the map. "But it's a good five-miles from your jump site. His team is mopping up and cold trailing the area. Then they'll head back to base."

Puma nodded. After some rest, Rothmeyer's jumpers

would move on to the next hotspot. "Any special instructions for us?"

Tom pointed his finger on the aerial photo. "Nita Faribee's crew needs help. Two of the blazes slammed together and her crew beat the hell back to the safety zone. Looks like we've got eighty-acres of fire moving north at about a mile an hour. Your crew needs to get down there and cut another helispot so we can bring in the hotshots. Your jump site's here." He stabbed at the map again. "That open area on the west flank. We'll send Nita's crew around to the east flank. Both teams will move north, cutting line, and eventually pinch off the head."

"We let the rest burn?"

"Unless the wind shifts and a blowup heads back toward Granby. Infrared detection doesn't indicate any smoldering hotspots, so if we get the big one under control we'll have the situation contained. The Rangers have evacuated the recreation areas and cleared civilians from known campsites."

Puma nodded. It was a good plan. Keep the largest fire under control until the hotshots arrived, then the jumpers could move on to stanch the lesser blazes in the surrounding area. The smokejumpers expertise was to hit a fire hard and fast while it was small, get it under control and move on to the next. "I don't like the looks of the terrain. No roads to speak of and all those gullies and steep cutbacks mean we can't move fast. We need air tankers and helo drops to get the situation under control."

Tom shrugged. "You know how it works. Denver's been notified. If the fire were nearer a settlement, they'd act quicker. Help's on the way but it could take a while."

Puma knew the Fire Coordination Center well. Too often politics and cost were the first considerations before copters and expensive air tankers were sent out. In this rugged terrain, retardant drops meant the difference between controlling the blaze, or having it escalate.

"All right," he said curtly. "You and Elkins keep on them, Tom. We don't want another South Canyon. You might remind them of that." The deadly South Canyon fire was a permanent blot on Colorado's firefighting community, where a mixture of bad weather, human error and shortsighted bureaucracy had culminated in the death of fourteen men and women firefighters. The terrain that lay below looked similar in nature to Puma.

Tom winced. "God, don't even say it. Never again."

"Never again," repeated Puma. "I'll get the team alerted. After you let the streamers out, give me your drift estimate. And it'd be nice not to have to climb trees or wade a stream to get at the supplies this time."

Tom grinned. "You know me, Puma. I'm real careful when I kick out the supply boxes. Guaranteed I'll hit the target."

"Right." Puma snorted in disbelief and turned his attention to the crew. As fire boss, he would jump first.

Rachel took her place in line, behind Puma. There were fourteen smokejumpers. They'd jump in two-man sticks and would rendezvous at the jump site, pick up supplies and attack the fire as Puma directed.

"See ya' down there," she whispered, wishing she could touch him, knowing he wouldn't hear her words over the rush of wind hammering the plane.

But he did. He gave her a quick glance and a half-smile. "Take care, rookie." His words were soft, for her ears only.

He snapped on his facemask and assumed the jump posture at the cargo opening, rocking back and knees slightly bent, each gloved hand grasping the metal frame of the door. Snyder tapped him on the shoulder and Puma pushed away, the static line trailing in his wake. It tightened, and then swung free.

Snyder retrieved the static line, attached it to the cover of her main chute, and a minute later the tap came down on her shoulder. She took a breath, blanked her mind and leapt into the void, assuming the tuck position as she fell. It was a leap of faith she'd taken many times, but this time it was different. This time adrenalin pumped fear into her bloodstream. Fear of facing the inferno that lay beneath her. Fear that she would freeze and disgrace herself. Dense smoke hovered over several sections of mountainous forest. Intermittent flames shot fifty-feet above the smoke.

One thousand one, one thousand two—

At count three, a snap and a jerk. Briefly her legs went over her head before dangling free. At count five, she floated in space. Not much wind drift, as Snyder had said. Sixty, maybe a hundred yards. She was dead on target. Far above the droning plane disappeared into the clouds. The pilot would circle back and drop the next two-man stick.

Puma's chute bloomed below her.

She adjusted her toggles and aimed for the jump spot, a dot of meadow with a ribbon of stream curving west, located a half-mile from the fire. The tiny spot grew in size as she fell; the stream became a gusher surrounded by shale and rocks, one of the thousands of unnamed streams that veined the Rockies. Not a comfortable place to light. She'd practiced water landings, knew how to unfasten the rigging and divest her chute. But water landings weren't fun. Not only did it mean a drenching, a strong current could pull an encumbered jumper down to his death.

She came in too fast, lit in loose shale and skidded out of control, her chute billowing behind her, her right hip taking the shock. The smack of a boulder against her shoulder stopped her and she rolled awkwardly to her knees. The padded Kevlar jumpsuit had saved her from injury against the sharp rocks, but her right thigh ached and she'd bear some bruises.

Any landing you can walk away from is a good one.

Thirty yards away, Puma was gathering up his chute and she began to do the same, squinting overhead. The sky was peppered with jumpers. The plane continued to circle above the landing spot. When they were all safely on the ground, Snyder would direct the pilot to zoom in low and drop supplies. Hardesty, a fifteen-year veteran fondly called "Badger" because of his stippled gray hair, and his stick partner, Bob Jackson, landed flawlessly in some tall meadow grass. The other four jumpers lit near the forest edge, where one of them hung up on a tree on the outskirts of the clearing. Alvarez, from the sounds of the Latin swearwords that blued the air.

Her radio squawked. Puma, calling them together to work out an attack plan and safety zone. The sound of powerful twin engines ripped the air and the Sherpa gunned toward them, its wings narrowly clearing the treetops. Behind her, a supply box thumped to the ground; its parachute trailed across the rocks and dragged the cargo into the stream. Ice ringed the edges of the swollen channel, spring melt not quite complete. Damn cold wading. She could imagine Snyder cackling. The spotter had the rep of scattering supplies from here to hell, and it seemed it was deserved.

Nothing to do but go after it.

She shucked her harness and jumpsuit. Down to her yellow Nomax shirt and green pants, she forded into the stream and freezing water sloshed over her boots. Fortunately the box had hung up on a boulder and stopped its downstream progress. It was loaded with tools and damned heavy. She dragged it by the straps over the shale and into the middle of the clearing.

The others were stripping out of their jump gear and gathering up supply boxes. Ben Alvarez joined them, limping slightly, his torn chute slung over one arm, his facemask askew over a thunderous scowl. Two of the jumpers dropped to their knees and kowtowed in adulation. The chorus of hoots dissing Ben's chute handling technique produced another string of swearwords. Just as well none of them understood Spanish. None of them except Puma, who shook his head and went back to his clipboard.

"Cut the bullshit," Puma said. "Unless we get an afternoon shower to knock the fire back, this one could go into overtime. We need to get on it fast."

"Yes, yes!" the jumpers hollered in unison. "Overtime! We want overtime!"

"The terrain's tricky here, and steep."

"Tricky and steep," shouted the jumpers. "We want tricky and steep!"

Puma shrugged. "Comedians. Have we rounded up all the supplies?"

"A bundle hung up in a tree thirty yards in," Alvarez said sourly. "And thirty-feet above ground. A Fat Boy loaded with food and MREs. Someone'll have to strap on the spurs."

"I'll do it," Rachel heard herself say.

Puma shot up an eyebrow and she knew he was remembering her hug-a-tree fiasco. "Fine, Myra." He said the name casually, as if it belonged to her. "Alvarez, you go along and help out. The rest of you, start unloading tools and make camp. We can use the stream to fill the backpack pumps, but don't drink it without boiling it. Chances are it's loaded with parasites."

He waved the two of them off, pulled out the recon map and began briefing the crew. Rachel grabbed a pair of climbing spurs, checked to be sure her emergency knife was at her belt, and after a minute's hesitation, retrieved her gun and a magazine from her backpack. Technically a jumper could carry nothing smaller than a .357 magnum, and then only with specific permission, but the Glock 23 was a familiar friend she refused to part with. It was compact, easily concealed, and if it were noticed, no one here would turn her in. Nita might. But Nita and her crew were on the other flank of the fire, scratching line. Chances of running into her were slim.

Alvarez picked up a handsaw and trotted toward the forest's edge. A handsaw. She should have thought of that. Four weeks of intensive training, and she knew less than the greenest rookie. She accelerated to catch up. The resiny odor of burning pitch and heavy smoke hung in the air, searing her nostrils and eyelids. But that was good. Hovering smoke meant the wind wasn't blowing much, which would slow the fire's progress.

Alvarez halted beside a sturdy pine. Bits of smashed fruit drink boxes and branches were scattered around the tree trunk. "Some animal has already been here. See something up there, Myra?"

She craned her neck and peered upward. "Nope. Whatever it was is gone."

"Give me the spurs and I'll go up. Those branches are none too sturdy."

"It's fine, Ben. Heights don't bother me, and I weigh less than you do." It wasn't heights, but fire that terrified her. Probably that's why she'd volunteered for a job no one wanted, to get away from the actuality of what she faced. She strapped on climbing spurs, pulled on gloves and hung the saw from her belt. Maybe she wouldn't need it if she could shake the snared pack loose.

"You're sure about this?"

"Positive." Rachel grasped the lower branches of the pine and dug in her spurs. Yellow pollen sifted down on her helmet. Fortunately she'd fortified herself with antihistamines before the plane left the ground. Slowly she scaled her way up, choosing her footholds and handholds carefully. Her gloved fingers rasped against the rough bark.

"Just a few more feet," Alvarez shouted. "Can you shake it loose?"

"Nope, it's lodged. Stand back, Ben. You don't want a can of pineapple landing on your head." She could see what had happened. The supply chute had failed to deploy, causing the Fat Boy to hurtle toward earth at ninety-miles an hour, becoming a virtual missile. She glanced above. The upper part of the tree had slowed the supplies' speed, but the force had ripped out several branches and torn the packaging away on one side before stopping its' descent.

Ben moved out of sight and Rachel lifted the saw from her belt and went to work. The branch was maybe six-inches thick. The wood was green and tough, her perch precarious. Grimly she muscled through the branch, concentrating on her task. Alvarez hollered and she ignored him. Just a few more swipes.

"Myra!" Ben shouted. "I'm coming up."

She glanced below. The man moved like a monkey.

Amazing agility considering he was climbing without spurs. "Ben, hold on. I'm almost done here."

Ten-feet below her Ben stopped and gasped for breath. She could see the top of his helmet and the splash of his yellow jacket as he clung to the gummy branches of the swaying pine.

"Alvarez, have you lost your mind? You'll fall!"

"Bear," he gasped. "A female with cubs. She's right below and climbing. She wants the rest of the food."

Rachel froze and dropped the saw.

Alvarez heaved himself up to where she could have stood on his helmet. The saw fell through the branches and hit the ground. Rachel could hear the bear now, growling and grunting as she scrambled for purchase on the bark of the tree. Bears were better equipped for climbing than humans. This one was moving slowly, probably pudgy from snacking on spring berries and the ample rodent population. The greedy creature knew easy food when she smelled it. The MREs and packets of dried fruit, crackers and other foodstuffs would be a true bruin treat.

"Myra," Alvarez said hoarsely, "Loosen the bundle. She'll back off if she gets the food. She wants to feed her cubs."

"No way! We need this food."

Awkwardly she fumbled for her Glock. A bullet or two whizzing in the marauder's direction might discourage it. She wouldn't actually target the bear. Not if Alvarez was right, and the female had cubs. What was the edict from the Forest Service about shooting bears? Yeah. Shoot to kill only if one is gnawing your leg off. Stupid rule. Probably dictated by someone sitting in a cozy office high-rise. Someone who'd never heard the ferocious snarls of a hungry bear climbing a tree in their direction.

The growls from below intensified and the tree shook wildly. The female was trying to dislodge her prize by shaking the trunk. Alvarez bellowed a warning. "Myra! Food's no good if we're dead!"

She reassessed the situation. Okay, the bear got the food. "Hold still! I'm going to get off a shot!"

"What the hell, you've got a gun?" Alvarez yelled as the tree swayed precariously. "Don't shoot. I'm losing my grip here and you could hit me."

He was right. She couldn't risk it. But how was she going to dislodge the food bundle with the saw lying thirty feet below? No way would her knife chew through that tough wood. Not fast enough to help the situation much. "Hold on! I won't shoot at you. I need to shatter the branch so the bundle will fall."

She took careful aim, closed her eyes and shot at the weakened spot where she'd been working the saw. Splinters flew as the wood exploded and several struck her cheek. Ouch. A rub of her cheek produced a smear of blood. The supplies still hung tightly in the crook it was lodged in.

She shot again. Again. At least the tree had stopped shaking, although the fierce animal sounds from below weren't comforting. Not just bear sounds. She swore she could hear the guttural snarl of an angry mountain cat. Sweat poured down her face, salt stinging the abrasions on her cheek. A bear and cat below them, fighting over their territory? Mountain lions could climb trees just fine.

More animal sounds, along with the distant shouts of men. The report of gunshots had mobilized the crew. Another two shots and the bundle broke free, tumbled through breaking branches and landed with a thump. The tree stopped shaking and the grunting subsided.

"God," Alvarez moaned. "If I knew who thought up that Smokey the Bear crap I'd kill him. Are you okay, Myra?"

She peered below, straining to see what was happening. Pig-like squeals and savage snarls accompanied the sound of a turbulent scuffle. Something whacked hard against the tree trunk. Rachel took a firmer grasp of the branch above her head. "Fine. Maybe we better wait a while before we climb down."

"Yeah. Sounds like World War III down there. That crazy bear is chasing her tail and going nuts. Can you see anything?"

Rachel parted some branches and saw flashes of black fur and a blur of gold rolling on the ground together, snapping, clawing and biting. With an outraged roar, the bear shook free, her muzzle clamped on the food bundle and she dragged it from sight. The tawny mountain cat leapt after her. "Not much, but our guests have left. How do you feel about bear meat for supper?"

"Suits me. I'll start back down."

Rachel followed, scrambling to the ground. Scattered underfoot, a trail of trampled foodstuffs disappeared into a growth of pine. The thief would doubtless return to tidy up. The first of the smokejumpers came storming through the brush, Jackson in the lead.

"What the hell. Who was shooting?"

"Me," Rachel said, patting her holstered gun.

Puma brushed Jackson aside, and grabbed her arm. "Explain yourself."

"Lighten up, boss," Alvarez said. "Mama Bear wanted a piece of us but settled for our grub."

"You gave up the food!" Howls of anger and curses erupted from the crowd of jumpers. Booted feet churned the ground, teeth gnashed, and Rachel was surrounded by angry accusing men. Nothing was more sacred to jumpers than their food, unless it was their time slips.

Puma laughed. "Back off boys, she's got a gun. What are you doing carrying a weapon, Ms. Sasser?"

"It's licensed," she said, laying her hand protectively over her holster. No one was taking the Glock.

"She shot to dislodge the package, boss," Alvarez put in. "Probably saved our ass. That she-bear wasn't taking no for an answer. She came right up the tree after us."

The jumpers griping subsided. Rachel figured most of them had run into bear a time or two. No one argued with a mama bear.

"All right," Puma said briskly. "No harm done. We can radio for more food if we run out. Break it up, we've got a fire to put down."

Still grumbling, the men separated and started back for

the camp area. Rachel waited until they were out of sight.

"Puma look over there," she urged, nodding toward a brushy thicket some thirty feet away. His eyes followed and narrowed.

The cougar was crouched in the dried grass, almost invisible unless you focused. He was licking bloody claws. The big cat yawned and stretched to his feet, shot them a sloe-eyed glance and limped back into the forest.

"He came out of nowhere," Rachel said. "And attacked the bear. Alvarez didn't see him." And that was strange. Alvarez had seen the bear, but not the two animals rolling on the ground together in a furry bundle of fury.

"Well, hell," Puma said in resignation, rubbing his forehead. "Didn't do me much good to break up with you. I don't suppose my grandfather appeared too?"

She frowned, trying to make sense of it. "Of course not. What does that mean?"

"My grandfather's spirit is around somewhere. Never mind. The cougar is my totem. Has been since my vision quest."

Puma was close-mouthed about his heritage and it was time he explained some things. "Puma, I understand about a vision quest, a little. But totem? This can't be the same animal we saw near your ranch. That's over two-hundred miles south of here."

"The totem protects what's mine. That bear must have been damn close to tearing you apart. Nothing less would bring him out."

His casual 'protects what's mine' comment blew all other questions away. "What's yours? Excuse me!"

"Mine," he repeated, stepping into her space. She backed up. He followed. She smacked up against the tree she'd just shimmied. His gloved thumb stroked her chin. A light touch, nothing more. "You're hurt. I'll get the first aid kit."

"It's not important. A scratch from some flying bark." The light strokes continued and she shivered, jerking her head away.

"If anything happens to you—dammit! Why didn't you radio for help?"

"There wasn't time. I handled it."

"Christ, you're independent. I should send you packing before you get into more trouble."

She swallowed, knowing he was capable of doing just that. "I take care of myself. I don't need a man."

He laughed softly, a low sound of masculine self-assurance. "Is that so? I could nail you right here, right now, and you'd love it."

"No," she whispered. Heat spread between her thighs to her belly and breasts, and bloomed in her throat and cheeks.

"Yes." He pulled off his gloves and dropped them; two tugs and hers followed. "You're dying to get your hands on me."

His fingers brushed her hair, danced across her cheeks. His palms cupped her chin, lifted her face and his mouth brushed hers, lightly, teasing, intimate sounds humming in his throat, and settled on the sensitive spot under her jaw. Lightning streaked, her knees buckled and she moaned in acquiescence.

She was weak, so damned weak. His mouth found hers again, not teasing this time. Taking. Her nails dug into the strong muscles of his neck. Her legs wrapped around his thighs and he pressed his hard length into her soft cleft, stroking her to paradise. The sounds and smells of the forest vanished along with coherent thought. Rainbow, rainbow of color and light.

"Nooo!" The protest burst from her throat when he pulled his body away.

Pain darkened his eyes and regret etched his face. "Now's not the time or place, but you're mine. We both know it."

She buried her face in his chest, shaking her head. She couldn't deny it. It was insane, this thing between them, but it was very real. She wanted his sex, but even more she wanted to curl herself around him and just be. Stay there forever. "What about you?" she whispered. "Are you mine?"

"Hell, yes. I couldn't even get it up with another woman."

Emotion gripped her throat. Delight. Longing. Sorrow. "As if I care!"

"You care all right. What would you do if I slept with someone else?"

Strangle her. Beat you with a ball bat. Set you on fire— All things she couldn't say. "Your call," she hissed. "Alvarez is cute," she added spitefully.

"Yeah, pretty much my reaction if the situation were reversed. Only mine would include feeding your sex partner to the totem piece by piece. And Ben knows better. Look at me, Rachel. Let's try for honesty here."

She raised her head and met his eyes. The pupils were dilated with arousal. His mouth was swollen from their kisses, the bronze skin taut across his cheekbones. She breathed in his essence, the scent of pine and musk. A pulse jumped erratically along his jaw. Unable to resist, she reached and stoked the stubble of beard on his chin. "There are a lot of problems."

He nodded. "When this is over, we talk. We work it out."

Work it out? Would he want her after he learned the truth of her mission, and what Hooker had planned? Again, things she couldn't discuss. Again, she had to lie. She backed away. Away from his closeness, his maleness, her aching awareness of their mutual need, and dropped her eyes. "Yes. Then we'll see."

CHAPTER 18

Hooker waited impatiently for the weeping Grace Chelsea to get control of herself, pacing the confines of the interrogation room. He was furious. Rachel Cortez was in the field, and he'd heard zip from her. The other agent he had in place had turned up nothing new. At this point, the Chelsea woman was Hooker's best hope for rooting out the mole.

Intelligence indicated the fires raging in the Arapahoe National Forest were set deliberately. Computer printouts showed a dozen blazes erupting within minutes of each other, all by combustion, not lightning strikes or natural causes. So many fires exploding within such a short timeframe meant arson. Graveled roads and woodland trails crisscrossed the area. An arsonist could travel by four-wheel drive to some of the hotspots, but not all, and not with any speed. Some were remote. Which meant a copter or small airplane drop of incendiary devices. The NTSA, National Transportation Security Administration, was looking into unsanctioned air traffic over the area for the past twenty-four hours.

Too little, too late.

The sniveling woman in front of him knew something, whether she realized it or not. These fires were only a test run. Hooker got that by the intuition he'd developed in his years as an agent. The next blazes would be far more lethal, far more disastrous, and they wouldn't use the same method. Whoever Fillmore had hired to set the fires was an expert. And whoever was bankrolling the operation had unlimited funds, because mounting a blitzkrieg on this scale didn't come cheap.

"You realize what you're facing, Mrs. Chelsea? Conspiracy against your government. Twenty years minimum in the federal penitentiary. With the mindset of judges these days toward terrorism, it could be double that. If someone dies, they'll throw away the key."

"I don't know anything," Grace whispered, dabbing her eyes with a drenched handkerchief. "The stuff I passed on was mostly unclassified. Just junk, really."

"Let's examine what you passed on. The status of our antiterrorist force, pointing out our vulnerabilities. Number and expertise of personnel in the field. Response techniques in place. God knows what else before we were on to you. You've been champagne and caviar for these people, Mrs. Chelsea. Whatever they paid you wasn't near enough."

Grace dabbed at her eyes again. Nice touch, Hooker thought. Save it for the judge.

"I'd like to help," she said. "I know I made a dumb mistake. I didn't realize something this horrible would happen."

The past week all phone calls between Grace Chelsea and any contacts were recorded. Every email Fillmore sent or received was studied carefully. Nothing had predicted a hit on this scale. Somehow the terrorist lieutenant knew they were on to him, and he was playing them. And this woman was in it up to her swollen eyeballs.

"Let me explain the facts of life, Mrs. Chelsea. We've been at this, what? Two hours?" Grace bobbed her head, peering up at him suspiciously. "I'm just getting warmed up. When I get tired, Ash Calloway will take over. And believe me, the SAC is pissed enough you'll want me back. After he wears down, you'll get me again. When we need a break, it will be someone else asking questions. There's one of you, Mrs. Chelsea, and an unlimited supply of us. We're in this room, you and the FBI, for as long as it takes. Ten hours, fifteen, whatever. You need to pee, a female agent goes in with you. Sits on your lap while you do your business."

Grace set her jaw. "I want a lawyer."

"Nice try. Not happening. We've yet to charge you with anything."

"You can't do this to me. I know my rights."

"This is a matter of national security. Since you live in a country that believes in human rights, a country you betrayed, yours won't go away. You'll get your day in court." Hooker leaned over the woman seated at the table, using his height and muscular frame to intimidate. "People like you frost my ass. You jeopardize the freedom and safety of law-abiding citizens, and then scream for your rights? If I had my way you'd be in leg irons at the next terrorist site, given the job of *sorting out body parts.*"

He swore violently and stalked to the door. A female agent was waiting on the other side and snapped to attention the moment the door opened. Hooker nodded his head. "Keep an eye on her," he said curtly. "If she moves, restrain her. The SAC will be in shortly."

The agent stepped inside, leaving the door slightly ajar. She was wearing navy slacks and tailored jacket with a frilly white blouse, a black woman with an impassive face, but there was no mistaking the bulge of the pistol at her belt. She said nothing. Simply took up her post beside the door and watched. Her eyes never wavered.

You'll get your day in court. Oh, God she was in serious trouble. Grace liked to pretend she'd been playing a game. Clandestine phone calls, money shoved under the door, just like in the spy novels. But this man Hooker wasn't playing at anything. She had to be careful. She had to think of Rakib.

How many fifty-year-old women had a young, vigorous lover like Rakib? She hugged the knowledge to herself. Her ex-husband had deserted her for a twenty-year-old chippie, but Rakib found Grace beautiful and desirable. When life's burdens got her down—-her father, whose life was trickling away with Alzheimer's, her twelve-year-old daughter who needed expensive special schooling. When those things threatened to overwhelm, there was always Rakib. Rakib, who gave himself so generously.

He'd wanted so little in return, not even commitment, just her in bed for one wonderful afternoon a week. The Saturdays that once had meant errands and housecleaning, a joyless end to a joyless week, were now filled with sparkle and light. Dare she think it? With love.

She licked dry lips and looked at the impassive woman standing by the door. "Could I have something to drink?"

"I'll bring something as soon as I'm relieved. Coffee?" Her voice was polite but Grace heard the undertone, the contempt.

What had she done to deserve that? "No. Something cold, thank you. A cola."

It had happened slowly. Coffee dates after a chance meeting at a local bookstore. The initial camaraderie grew intense and quickly developed into intimacy. The past three months had been the best in Grace's life. Rakib was a superb lover.

But it was more than sex.

After making love to her, Rakib would light one of his strong Turkish cigarettes and they would talk. About her family, her problems with a skunk ex-husband, about the problems she carried. How the courts had screwed her over. Sometimes they would talk about work. It was another interest they shared. Rakib's life was computers and gossip. My, how that man loved to gossip. He gobbled up every bit of news about the goings on in the Bureau. Sympathized with her low salary compared to the agents, when everyone knew she did the scut work and the place couldn't run without her.

No one could convince Grace that Rakib meant her harm. Her lover was ambitious and wanted to do well at the

Agency, that was all. She'd done a little cribbing on his background check to help him get the job in the computer lab. Rakib's last name was French; no one needed to know he had an Arab mother. What did that have to do with anything, anyhow? And the lie detector technician's report, casting doubt on Rakib's loyalty to the U.S.? It had been no problem to alter the technician's report.

In retrospect perhaps she'd been a bit indiscreet, but no harm was done. After she explained, Ash would understand, but she wouldn't mention Rakib or the generous cash sum he left on her dresser every Saturday night before he returned to his apartment.

She moved restlessly in her chair. She really wanted a drink and she was uncomfortable. Maybe if she could stand and stretch she'd feel better.

"Please stay seated, ma'am," the agent said quietly. "I don't want to restrain you." There was no mistaking the threat and Grace settled back into the hard, plastic chair.

She'd objected to the money at first. But Rakib looked at her with liquid dark eyes, stroked her hair and whispered. "It is nothing, my moonflower. A gift from a friend to a friend. A friend who has more need of it than I do."

He'd given her a number to call because he was worried about her lack of funds. The things she'd told the rough, accented voice on the other end of the line had been unimportant, the lowest classified stuff. A lot of it was available on the Internet. Envelopes stuffed with small bills were periodically left inside her back screen door. True, the money didn't mean the difference between eating or not, but it paid for her daughter's expensive schooling. Her daughter was entitled to that because she was special. Not retarded, Grace was convinced. Special. Proper schooling was necessary to develop her full potential.

Sorting out body parts! Oh, God, how horrible.

Dan Hooker said she'd been passing classified information to a terrorist group that wanted to destroy the United States government. Surely Rakib wasn't involved in anything that awful. She wouldn't even consider it. She dabbed at her eyes again and gave a sniff. The agent's face didn't show a flicker of sympathy.

Rakib, Grace long ago decided, had put her in contact with the Israelis. And Israel, after all, was an ally of the United States. People should share. There shouldn't be all these secrets in the world. Especially among friends. Maybe taking the money was wrong, but her intentions were good.

Ash Calloway walked in and Grace took a relieved breath. She'd known Ash for years and considered him a friend. Probably he and agent Hooker were playing bad cop-good cop. Grace knew all about that from watching TV. Agent Hooker's pale blue eyes were as cold as arctic ice, and he was quite frightening. Ash had long-lashed collie brown eyes that crinkled humorously at the edges. He was soft-spoken and kind. She felt much safer with Ash than with that awful Dan Hooker.

Ash Calloway's hand came down on her shoulder and squeezed gently. He set a can of cola on the table beside her, and she wondered briefly if the room was bugged and he knew she wanted a cold drink. No, of course not. Ash was thoughtful, a real southern gentleman.

"Grace, we have to talk. I need your help."

Good cop, bad cop. She'd been right. Her secrets were safe. Grace sighed. "Oh, Ash, I can't believe this. You know I'd never do those awful things that agent Hooker is accusing me of."

"Why don't you tell me about it?"

Something in his voice made Grace straighten her shoulders and look up. It was Ash who returned her stare, and it wasn't. This man had her boss's face but someone else's eyes. These eyes were as dark and cold as river stone. Terror struck her heart. She'd lost Rakib. The only thing left to do was salvage herself.

"It is I, brother."

"Rakib? Are you well?"

Rakib's heart leapt and warmed at the sound of Musa's

voice, speaking in their native Farsi tongue.

Rakib eased deeper into the niche where the public phone was located in a far corner of the mall. He spoke softly. "My heart longs to see you, Saladin."

"This is not wise. Why do you call?"

Of course that would be Musa's first thought. The two of them had agreed to forgo communication unless the matter was urgent. Still, Rakib was obligated to downplay the danger.

"I humbly apologize for disturbing your evening."

"Again, why do you call? Is there a problem?" Musa's mellow tenor sharpened.

Rakib looked around quickly, conscious that he was in a public place. It was nearing closing time and the mall was almost empty. "It is merely that the woman is no longer of use, and I found it prudent to vacate my hated post at the FBI. I sorrow if this inconveniences you and our cause."

"She no longer enjoys copulation? I thought you more skillful, Rakib."

Rakib winced at Musa's bantering tone. It was his brother at his most dangerous. "My skill is not in question. A foolish and silly woman, her love is strong, but she is inept and allowed herself to be caught. The agent Hooker, the one who is beneath contempt, arrested her this late afternoon."

"Ahh." A long pause and Rakib's heartbeat accelerated.

At age twenty-two, Rakib was sixteen years younger than Musa. The brothers had the same mother and different fathers, hadn't even met each other until two years before, but their souls were united in passion for the mission of Islam. Still, Rakib never forgot how dangerous his brother was. How hot-tempered. And how rich. While Rakib was a pauper, his brother was a billionaire many times from the estate of his French father, a businessman once involved in the lucrative field of arms dealing.

The world considered the Society of Assassins to be extinct since the thirteenth century. Rakib knew better. Musa was the Saladin, the current leader of the arcane sect, and had killed many times. It was understood that Musa would not spare his brother, if Rakib betrayed or disappointed the Society.

"It would be my pleasure to serve you further," Rakib said. "In any capacity," he added cautiously.

"Of course," Musa answered briskly. "You erased the hard drive on your computer and any evidence of our existence? You vacated the apartment and left nothing behind?"

"Nothing. The woman was quick to email me a warning before she was arrested. Thanks be to Allah."

"More thanks to your skill than to Allah," Musa chuckled, his good humor restored. "The information the woman provided was of use. You've done well."

"Your praise is honey to my ears."

"Will she betray you?"

"Not at once." Rakib hesitated. "Probably later. She is weak and this Hooker is a demon. Of course, they will use drugs. Maybe torture."

Musa sighed. "Rakib, you swallow our own propaganda. The FBI does not use torture. Now if it was the CIA—"

"They will find nothing of value. I wiped every fingerprint and cleaned the apartment and my cubicle thoroughly. I swear it on our mother's grave."

"I believe you. She and your father would be proud of you."

"They are with the prophet," muttered Rakib, not altogether sure it was true.

In her later years their mother had become a strict fundamentalist in her interpretation of Islam, and had denounced his Iranian father for neglecting his prayers and turning to the path of secularism. The Imam had ordered him stoned, and for good measure had thrown his mother in the pit with him, because doubtless she'd been corrupted. Women were full of deceit and treachery, and betrayal of a husband was the darkest of sins. It was possible she lusted after another, and chose this way to rid herself of the encumbrance of a husband.

Rakib had been sixteen at the time.

And had witnessed their just punishment.

It was not a good way to die.

Rakib knew he had a lot of penance ahead to absolve the sins of his parents and pave his way to paradise. May Allah purge him from their sins! He had scourged his own body until it bled when he learned of their hypocrisy. He had fasted and gone into seclusion, reciting the Koran steadily for seven days and seven nights. Still, it was not enough. Now he had committed his path to jihad.

"Ease yourself, my brother," Musa said more gently. "You've earned a rest. Make your way to Montana."

"No!" Rakib spoke sharply, without thought. He broke into a sweat as his voice reverberated within the public phone booth. A pedestrian passing by gave him a startled look and scurried away. Praise Allah, no one spoke to Musa in that tone. Not if they wanted to live. Not even Rakib. "Forgive me, Saladin. Of course it will be as you ask."

A sigh. "You hate Montana that much, my beloved? It offers safe refuge."

Rakib relaxed. Beloved. Of course his brother loved him. He should never doubt that. "I sorrow at my weakness. It is difficult there."

"I understand. No one speaks our tongue. Or professes our faith. It is regrettable, but the fools who call themselves the New Sons of Liberty have their uses. For now."

It was much more than that. If Musa could only understand. His brother never visited the compound. "They look at me with loathing and spit when my back is turned. They shave their heads and exude bad odors. If you would allow it, I would kill the one called Fillmore. He is the worst. He threatened to use me like a woman and blasphemed Allah."

A long pause. "I did not know. Fillmore is not in Montana at this time. He is directing our Colorado activities and is useful there. Montana is sanctuary. No one could find you, and those at the base will protect you at my orders. Chic Fillmore failed the Society by bungling the Hoover Dam episode. You may kill him when the time comes."

Pleasure bloomed in Rakib's chest. "The method of my choosing?"

"Of course. He will be my gift to you."

"I shall cut off his ears, nose and lips."

"Superb."

"He will die with his severed male member in his mouth."

"I look forward to the day."

Tears trickled down Rakib's cheeks. "Saladin," he whispered huskily. "All will be as you decree."

Ah, how he wished he could be more for his half-brother. That he could ease his burdens, could take him to bed and kiss and stroke him until the harsh lines of his face would ease, until his body would arch with pleasure. Had the prophet himself not blessed such unions as the purest of sexual encounters? But the one time he had dared to touch his brother's whipcord body in the way of lovers, Musa reacted like lightning and Rakib nursed a broken arm for weeks. Neither of them spoke of it again, and Rakib ached with unrequited carnal love.

"Go with Allah's blessing, my brother." Musa's voice was laced with affection, but there was no mistaking the underlying command. "I will contact Fillmore myself, and inform him of our change of plans."

A sharp click and Rakib held a buzzing receiver. He hung up and reached for the yellow pages to find the number of the local cab company. A false ID and plenty of cash would get him on the first flight out of Denver. The small valise he carried contained fresh clothing, some toiletries and nothing more. Nothing to alert the authorities to hold him at the gate.

At the other end of the line, Musa replaced the elaborate gold and ivory rococo telephone, leaned back in the French Directoire chair and stared thoughtfully into space. Under his strict instructions, the obscenely expensive decorator had interspersed the room's priceless antiques with modern paintings. The bold colors of a Frank Stella abstraction graced the far wall; a bronze Louise Nevelson assemblage dominated the Renaissance mantle. The result was a striking montage of the very old and the brashly contemporary that Musa Shaykl Khater found amusing. Musa was comfortable here, in what was only one of the Society's costly dwellings scattered throughout the world, but abandoning it would cause no emotional anguish.

Musa's real home was the elaborate villa south of Paris, the Aubrette family home, where Pierre Aubrette had allowed his love of his wife's sybaritic Persian heritage free rein. The ancestral home was graced with paintings and great art from the ages, and costly furnishings upholstered with Aubusson tapestries, chinoiserie lacquered chests and Meissen porcelain. The exquisite appointments, the lovely garden and formal 16th century Moorish architecture were a salute to the Spanish duchess rumored to have contributed to the Aubrette bloodline. How Musa missed home.

Being born an Aubrette was something to cherish, something to take pride in. Sleeping in the bed where one was conceived? Comfort beyond price. The view from the Seattle pied-à-terre was superb. On a clear day one could see the tip of Mount Rainier floating above the clouds. Musa seldom noticed. There was too much work to be done, holding together what Pierre Aubrette had entrusted his only heir to expand and nurture.

His brother was immature and a zealot, but faithful, and would do anything for the brother he adored. Too much adored, Musa thought ruefully. The duties of the Saladin were heavy. A homosexual relationship would shatter the machismo, and endanger the myth. Enough disgrace had been suffered with the Hoover Dam failure. The Society of Assassins expected results, or a new Saladin would be elected.

Another strike at the underbelly of the United States was overdue. It had been too long since 9/11. More recent terrorist incidents, such as the Boston Marathon, Musa likened to the buzzing of a pesky insect. A city in flames would soothe the swollen vanity and pride of even the bloodthirsty Assassins. The decision made, Musa reached for the phone. Time to contact Fillmore. Time to unleash the dogs of war.

CHAPTER 19

F lames crept toward the laboring smokejumpers. Sluggish flames biding their time, like a baleful, crouching dragon. Rachel hefted her shovel, blanked her mind and got on with the task at hand. Puma had placed her at the anchor point of the west flank, a short distance from a burned-over area and a convenient safety zone if the fire took a turnaround. Presently the fire was fifty-yards to her right, a smoldering mass that made her heart pound with apprehension.

Ben Alvarez was chopping hand-line thirty yards ahead, casting occasional glances her way. More of Puma's work. Her lover couldn't birddog her himself, he had too many responsibilities, so he'd set Alvarez to the task and the man was taking the responsibility seriously. Rachel hadn't made a fuss. You didn't argue with the fire boss, but it aggravated her. Women weren't cut any slack as smokejumpers, and both men damn well knew it. Puma was being obnoxiously protective and Ben, it seemed, had adopted her.

Her job was to throw dirt over the fire-line, as Ben laboriously chopped it out with his Pulaski. She shoveled furiously, determined to match his pace. The jumpers were working their way to the head of the flames, building line with a steady rhythm. In the distance she could hear the sputtering whirr of an electric saw taking down trees too big to chop out with an axe. When a firefighter caught up to the man in front of him, he'd shout "bump" and everyone would move forward. It was backbreaking, grueling work.

Who was she kidding? She'd never catch up with them.

She stopped and pulled off her helmet and gloves, wiping the dripping perspiration from her forehead. Her shovel-worn hands came away black. She reached for her water bottle. When the wind whipped up, and it did frequently, cinder and ash eddied around her, clogging her nostrils and eyes. Her throat felt like she'd swallowed sand. She poured water over her head, relishing the temporary coolness, and took a swallow from the flask. The liquid was lukewarm and tasted of grit.

Where in hell's the glamour, she thought. The glory? She wanted a bath, and hunger gnawed at her stomach. They'd been on the job for four hours without a break. Puma was a hard taskmaster, but things got done. In another hour, maybe two, the team should be ahead of the fire. They'd head east and meet up with other crew, and this particular blaze would be under control.

She replaced her helmet and gloves, stretched and bowed her back, rubbing at the nagging pain. No glamour, no glory, just an aching back, blistered palms and sore throat. Worse, she had no idea if this fire was caused by arson or nature. She had whispered the question to Puma and he'd shrugged before answering. "Doesn't matter at this point. Our job is to put it out. They'll send in the experts to decide how it started."

It mattered to Rachel. She'd thought of little else since she'd learned of the strange configuration of the fires. She'd been at jump base for a week, and had little information to show for it. Elkins was her main suspect. As base manager he had his fingers on the pulse of the operation. He knew the forest areas, areas where slash piles and debris would nourish the spread of fire. He had access to radar and computer data. Data that could be altered, or misinterpreted. He was the one who made the decisions on where the men and base resources would be allotted.

Or did the rot go higher?

The Forest Service had a complex system in place to combat fires. Sometimes the network broke down under its own bureaucracy. Where were the aerial drops of retardant that would insure this fire were was controlled? Long past due, according to the grumbling she heard down the fire line. It was something for Hooker to look into.

There'd been no time to contact Hooker. The minute she and Puma landed at base, they sprinted for the jump shack where the other smokejumpers were already suited up. After a quick trip to the bathroom, with her jumpsuit half-fastened, boots flapping and facemask in hand, Rachel ran for the tarmac while the Sherpa revved its engines like a cranky rhinoceros. Snyder and Puma yelled for her to hurry and rough hands pulled her into the belly of the beast, just as it taxied into takeoff. She endured some ragging about barely making it, but ignored the complaints. A fully-zipped and buckled jumpsuit was the devil to get out of, and she'd be darned if she'd pee in a bucket in front of a bunch of randy male smokejumpers.

In the frantic hurry, she'd left her cell phone behind, not that it mattered. In this mountainous terrain, the signal would bounce from cliff to cliff and dissipate. Hooker was probably trying to contact her. She needed to talk to her boss about the nature of the fires. From what Elkins had said, they were of suspicious origin. Later, when the situation was under control, she'd get the answer to some questions.

She bent to work again, ignoring the ache in her back.

"A little slow with that shovel, aren't you, Sasser?"

Rachel paused and looked up. *Nita.* Her crew was supposedly working the east flank. "Cut me a break. I've been at this for four hours."

Nita snorted derision and Rachel bit her cheek. Stupid thing to say. Nita's crew had been on the ground for ten hours, and her appearance showed it. She carried a Pulaski that was caked with sludge, and had a portable sprayer strapped to her shoulders. Her Nomax shirt was more black than yellow, and the only features discernible in the grime of her face were bloodshot blue eyes. The blue eyes that were shooting icicles at Rachel.

"Why don't I do that?" Nita asked. She set down the Pulaski and swept off her helmet, her face split in a wolfish grin.

"Do what?" Rachel asked, uneasiness growing.

"Cut you a break. You'll never bump Alvarez, so let's have some girl talk."

Girl talk? In the midst of a raging fire? Hardly. "What's up? Something important enough to leave your crew?"

"We'll get to it. I'll bet you're hungry." Nita reached in her jacket pocket, produced a beef stick and handed it to Rachel. "You need to keep your energy up."

"I'm starving," Rachel admitted, dropped the shovel and reached for the spicy treat. It was a bit linty, but who cared? "Where did you get this?" She took a bite and sighed. How could a dried-up piece of meat taste like ambrosia?

"You learn things when you've been on the job as long as I have. Always pack an emergency food stash, just in case." She produced another stick from her pocket and chewed thoughtfully, watching Rachel.

Rachel finished off the beef and reached for her water bottle. Almost empty. She drained the last of it. Maybe noshing on salty meat hadn't been a good idea, although God knew she'd sweat out all the salt in her system by now. Silently Nita produced a full water bottle from one of her copious pockets and handed it over.

"I can't take your water. Puma will call a break soon, and I'll refill mine."

"Take it. I've got another. Ansari won't call a break until he's breached the head and met up with my crew. If you need water you should stop to refill. Letting yourself get dehydrated is stupid."

"Yeah." Rachel flushed. Nita always put her on the defensive. "I've been drinking plenty." She took another swig to prove it and handed the bottle back. "Thanks for the water. And for the food. I'm recharged."

Nita raised her eyebrows and stowed the bottle. "You look beat and you're a piss poor firefighter, lady. What in the hell was Ansari thinking, taking you on?"

Oh, God. The beef stick knotted in Rachel's stomach. She gave the woman a cool smile. "I'll get back to work. If Puma's unhappy, he'll let me know."

Nita snorted. She had a terrific snort. "Isn't a man alive who can think straight with a stiff dick. But Puma's too smart and too good to let sex interfere with his work. You're either hell in bed, or you've got something on him. Which is it?"

Rachel really wanted to slug her. Which wouldn't solve anything. Nita was on a fishing expedition, trying to rile her, and Rachel refused to fall for it. She clenched her jaw, dug her shovel into the raw dirt and tossed a load of clods toward Nita's boots. "Think what you want. I'm busy. Don't you have a crew to boss?"

Nita reached, grabbed Rachel's shovel and wrenched it forcefully from her hands. "My crew is doing fine. It's you I'm worried about."

"Why? What the hell is this about?" Okay, you want to play rough? I can do that. Piece of cake to retrieve the shovel and bean the odious woman with it. Maybe not a good idea, though. Hardly low profile.

"Who are you?" Nita demanded. "You're not Myra Sasser. Does Puma know you're a phony? I want some answers."

Oh, my God. Did the woman know the truth or was she guessing? Rachel went from irritated to full alert. She kept her tone cool. "I don't know what you mean."

"Listen up, lady. I talked to my old pal, Mellie Morganfield two days ago. According to Mel, Myra Sasser is twenty-six years old, five-foot-five, with curly blonde hair and dimples. Not exactly what I see looking at you. Care to explain?"

Damn the bad luck. Rachel had been sure Nita wouldn't follow through on her threat to check her out through the network. Or that if she did, it wouldn't be this soon. "Look, your friend made a mistake."

"Hell, she did. She jumped with Myra for two years at Missoula, until Myra made a bum landing and shattered her ankle. No way she'd be back jumping so soon."

She let out a string of swear words worthy of any male jumper and slung Rachel's shovel ten feet into the brush. "You don't talk to me, we go see Ansari. Now."

"All right," Rachel acquiesced. Time for damage control. How little could she tell Nita and still convince her to keep her mouth shut about Rachel's true identity? "Look, I can't tell you the whole story. Not now. Maybe someday. If you'd trust me."

"Trust!" Nita exploded. "Smokejumping's a tight male fraternity. Do you know how long and hard the sisterhood has fought for acceptance? Over thirty years we've been at this, and we're only ten-percent of them. Some still want us gone. If we're not as good as the men—damn it if we're not better, it could happen." She made a sound of disgust and reached for her radio.

Rachel grabbed her wrist. "Don't. Not over an open line. Please."

"Do you think I'm stupid? That I'm going to let you put my people in danger?" Nita said, her free hand tugging at Rachel's grip. "I'm sending you back to base. We'll sort it out later. And don't think I won't file charges." Fury clogged her voice.

Rachel had no choice. A fast wrist chop and Nita's radio was on the ground. Rachel's thumb flew to the shorter woman's throat and pressed on her carotid. "Chill down. I squeeze any harder you pass out, Jeanette. Understand?"

Nita made a strangled sound, falling to her knees.

"No radio. And you better listen. I'm not the enemy here."

More strangled sounds. A slight nod.

Rachel eased the pressure and backed off. Nita rubbed her throat and gagged. In the distance Ben Alvarez gave a shout, asking them if they were okay.

"We don't want him in on this. Stand up and give him a wave," Rachel ordered.

The woman struggled to her feet, not taking her eyes off of Rachel. She waved an A-OK signal at Alvarez and kneaded at her throat again. "I wanted a reaction, but I wasn't expecting that one," she said. "You might've killed me."

"If I'd wanted to."

"God, you're fast! Who are you? How did you do that?"

Rachel grinned. "Like you said. I'm a piss poor firefighter. But it happens I'm a damn good at martial arts. Truce?"

"Temporary. What's your game?"

"I'm on the—ah, state arsonist squad. Undercover. A lot of fires have been deliberately set. We need to put a stop to it."

"Arsonist squad? That's a new one." Nita shook her head. "Why should I believe you? Does Puma—hell, of course he does. It explains why he let you on his team."

"Don't blame Ansari. He tried to mold me into a smokejumper. Considering he only had three weeks to get it done, he did a good job."

Nita looked skeptical. "You're hiding something. I'll have to check this out with Ansari."

"Just don't use the radio."

"I'll take a hike up the line, and find your lover."

"He's not going to like what you say. He went to a lot of trouble to put me here."

"Yeah, you may not be a smokejumper, but you can shovel dirt with the best of them. He taught you that much. Maybe he can convince me you should stay. We'll see."

Scant hope, but Rachel latched on to it. She needed a few more days to continue her investigation. "I'd just as soon you forgot this conversation. Didn't pass it on."

"I won't say anything until I talk to Puma." Nita searched in the brush and came up with Rachel's shovel. "Better get back to work. That fire's gaining ground."

Rachel swiveled her head and saw what she meant. The wind had picked up and swirls of black smoke were headed their way. "Oh, God. That looks bad."

"Just a flare-up in a tree stump, but we need to get on it before it spreads." Nita gave a shrill whistle and motioned at Alvarez, snugged her helmet back on and started for the blaze, her portable pump sprayer at the ready. Pissers, the firefighters called them. Alvarez jogged their way, carrying his Pulaski, hollering at Nita to wait up.

Rachel stood welded to the spot in the trail, every instinct telling her to beat feet and get the hell out of there. She yelled a warning, "Nita, get back! It's moving fast!"

Her voice came out a crow squawk. Nita gave a hand wave and kept on going.

"Radio Puma. I may need some backup," she yelled. She picked up her stride to a fast trot, halted at the outskirts of the flare-up and aimed a stream of water into its heart.

Steam and dense smoke rose around her.

Alvarez paused beside Rachel. "You okay? I need to help Nita out."

There was a coughing sound, like a silenced pistol.

The earth belched.

A firestorm boiled from beneath the ground like pus bursting from a ruptured carbuncle. In a scant breath, a spinning vortex of hot gases shot smoke, debris and flame fifty-feet into the air. Burning coals landed at Rachel's feet and the grass sizzled into flame. She watched in horror as it licked up her pants leg. She couldn't move.

"Jesus!" Alvarez tackled her to the ground, tumbling her away from the flames, beating at her clothing with his gloved hands. "What the hell happened?" He grabbed his radio, keeping Rachel pinned under his body. "Mayday! We have a situation on the west flank. One man down. Request backup, now!"

A blur of memory. Nausea, dizziness. The vision. The smell of ashes and burning wood, asphalt and cotton. Her nightgown was on fire. Terrified, she beat at the flames with her bare hands.

A weight held her back. "Daddy?" she whimpered, struggling and kicking against the weight. "Don't go in there."

Couldn't he see the flames were too hot? She rocked to her knees, moaning. The heat. She had to ignore the heat and help her father. She crawled toward the fire. Curses sounded in her ears. A hard hand grabbed her by the collar and dragged her across the ground, dumped her on a bed of choking ashes. It was cooler here away from the flames. Her nightgown was very dirty.

"Stay here. There's nothing you can do." A man's voice. But not Daddy. She clawed at the ground, sobbing, determined to get back into the house. Her father was in there, and her brother. Where was her mother? No one was helping. She had to do something. Anything.

Some primal instinct had told Puma to leave the head of the fire where he was hosing down the creeping flames and go in search of Rachel. She was in as safe a place as he could put her, working the tail where the fire had mostly burned out, but the uneasiness that hit him couldn't be ignored, and he handed the hose to Jackson and told him to take over.

He'd been fifty-yards down the trail when the blow-up shook the ground. It rumbled beneath his feet like a small earthquake, a fireball shot upward and incandescence lit the sky. The nearby grass, leaves, dead pine needles ignited in a flash. On the run, he grabbed his radio and shouted an all-out alert. A blow-up could increase the intensity of a fire to the point where direct control was impossible. He needed all his men there now.

Alvarez's Mayday call interrupted his warning.

"Alvarez! This is Ansari. What's happening?"

"Looks like a smoldering stump blew, boss. Jeanette is down, maybe dead. I'm headed that way."

Sweet Jesus, where was Rachel? "Myra! Where's Myra?"

"Here with me. In the black area."

"Alvarez! Stay back until we get the hoses here! There could be another explosion."

A powerful updraft swooped near the perimeter,

producing a violent whirl of ash and a wave of intense heat. Alvarez cursed, and the connection broke. Puma took off in a flat-out run.

He couldn't see for the smoke.

The cougar came running alongside him, and shot ahead with a burst of speed.

For one shocked moment he marveled at that, then he raced behind the golden blur, knowing the cat would lead him to Rachel.

Rachel was on her knees in the black area, crawling toward the fire. He caught her shoulders. "Stay here. There's nothing you can do."

"Daddy," she moaned, breaking from his grip. "Scotty. Please come back."

What the hell? Jesus, she'd regressed to the fire that killed her father and brother. This wasn't Rachel. This was a ten-year-old child. "Rachel" Puma said, catching her again and shaking her. "For God's sake, snap out of it."

It did no good to shake her and she obviously didn't hear his pleas. She was hysterical, but he'd have to deal with her later. The fire was raging. Jeanette could be dead, Alvarez was in trouble, and his men needed every hand to prevent further tragedy. Grimly he grabbed her by the hair, doubled his fist and clipped her on the jaw. She crumpled in his arms.

He bent and stretched her on her side, arranging her palms to cradle her cheek. Her profile was pale and still as a cameo. He took a fleeting second to kiss her brow. She'd have a headache when she woke up, but she'd be safe here in the burned-over swatch of upland. As safe as he could keep her right now.

A low growl caught his attention.

The totem sat on his haunches, a few yards away. He snarled a low warning. Puma rubbed his eyes. The image of the gold cat wavered and vanished. With a last look at Rachel, Puma sprinted for the area where the crew was struggling to put down the flare-up, knowing she was safe. With the big cougar on guard, anyone who touched her would be torn apart.

CHAPTER 20

Rachel jolted out of unconsciousness. Her head throbbed fiercely and her jaw hurt. Gradually she became aware of the shouts of the firefighters, could smell hot tar and the acrid scent of charred wood. The taste of ashes was in her mouth. She lifted scorched eyelids to a scene from Hell.

The entire forest was on fire.

The bony skeletons of trees were backlit in blood, trees in a fiery death throe. Flames shot fifty, a hundred feet in the air, fire so intense it created its own wind. Eddies of ash whirled around her head; the violent convection blasted her face with the heat of an inferno, peppering her face with grit. The only sky visible was a murky gray-brown.

She heard them before she saw them.

Planes, the earthshaking sound of air tankers incoming. The first tanker zoomed in low and released its contents on the flank of the fire. Three-thousand gallons of water, clay and fertilizer. Pink rain. The smokejumpers' first line of defense in a forest fire. Desperately needed help that had arrived almost too late. In the wake of the deluge, steam rose from the blaze. A rosy mist floated her way, raising the humidity and cooling her face. She shuddered. She'd blacked out. Why couldn't she remember what happened?

Puma. Where is he?

She scrambled to her knees and croaked his name. A streak of amber shot by and headed for the heart of the fire. She squinted to adjust her blurred eyesight. Surely that had been the cougar. Puma's cougar. She blinked again. Saw nothing. Was she going crazy? Or losing her eyesight?

Another tanker roared overhead and dumped its load of retardant. Further away this time, toward the head of the fire. The Incident Management Team had finally responded to Puma's request. Perhaps other measures would be put in place now. From the looks of the out-of-control inferno in front of her, reinforcements were desperately needed. If the tankers had shown up a few hours earlier, perhaps Nita would still be alive.

When she caught up with the crew, Puma said little. Merely handed her a shovel. None of the smokejumpers acknowledged her reappearance. Maybe they hadn't noticed she was gone. But Alvarez knew of her disgraceful performance. And Puma. Three hours later, the forest service hotshots arrived by helo and the inferno given over to their control. The weary smokejumpers climbed onboard the chopper to return to base. It was no longer their fire.

Rachel huddled in the slick leather seat, cradled her head in her hands and fought despair. The copter blades beat steadily, a monotonous, mesmerizing sound. How could she have lost it like that? Her memory continued to be vague after the blowup and a burst of smoldering embers landed at her feet. Little memory of anything until she woke, face down in the charred meadow.

She knew her heavy boots and Alvarez's quick action had saved her from disaster, and her scorched trousers were a hideous reminder. Not only of what fire could do, but of her own cowardliness. The grief around her was palpable. Smokejumpers were a close community. When one of their own died, they lost a member of the family.

Nita.

Could Rachel have done anything to save the woman? Unless her memory returned she'd never know. She and

Nita had been arguing. The recollection flooded back. Nita had found out the truth. That Rachel was bogus. Puma sat directly across, his hard hat in his lap, so close their knees were touching. She whispered his name. He turned tired eyes in her direction, blue flint glittering in a mask of black soot. He gave a slight shake of his head. "Not now," he said. "Later."

"Now," she said urgently. "No one's listening. I need to know some things."

He looked around. A dozen jumpers were dozing in their seats; the heavy thumping of copter blades was loud enough to prevent the pilot from overhearing. He leaned and spoke softly. "And I need to know some things. Why didn't you tell me you were so traumatized by fire?"

She struggled with the words and shrugged her shoulders. "I assumed I could handle it. I was wrong."

Wearily he rubbed his unshaven jaw. "I can't let you jump fire again."

"Yes, you can. I was okay when I rejoined the fire line wasn't I? I handled my job when I got my head back."

He nodded reluctantly. "Yeah. But we lost a good man. One of the best."

"Was that my fault? Could I have done something?"

"What do you remember?"

"Nita knew I wasn't a bona fide smokejumper, and I was trying to convince her not to blow my cover. The wind rose while we were talking. There was a flare-up. Nita took off to put out the blaze. I don't remember the rest. I should have helped, gone with her."

He reached and put his hand on her knee. "Stop kicking yourself. The explosion was manmade and had nothing to do with you. If you'd been with Nita, you would've been killed too."

"Manmade?"

"Yeah." He reached into the pocket of his jacket. "When we pulled Nita from the fire she was beyond help. But I found this." He laid a twisted, blackened piece of metal in her hand.

She turned it over. "It looks like maybe a timing switch?"

"It is. Attached to an incendiary, probably napalm. The timer failed and the device lay dormant. Shit waiting to happen. The fire hit the combustible material and it blew."

"Arson," she said, catching her breath. Proof of what she and Hooker were looking for. "You retrieved the timer before it was consumed, or we might never have proven it."

"We need to have it analyzed."

"Hooker will send it to Langley. Find out the source. Trace the elements. Maybe the bastards finally made a mistake."

"A big one," he said bleakly, clamping his jaw. "It's fucking personal now. Someone's going to pay with the skin off their balls."

Rachel had never seen him look more dangerous. She knew what he was capable of, and the prospect of his operating solo alarmed her. "Hooker's good at what he does. You need to trust us to do our job."

"Not this time. Hooker's not an arson expert. I have friends in the ATF who are. They'll search their database and come up with the names of arsonists who work with these components and are for hire. Then I go hunting."

"Look, it's terrible about Nita. But there's a way to handle these things. Now that we have concrete proof, Hooker will get in touch with the ATF Arson Response Team in Quantico. They'll bring in accelerant detection dogs and technical specialists. Our agencies have a joint program to handle arson incidents."

Puma retrieved the piece of twisted metal from her grip. "I found this embedded in Nita's face. It could just as easily have been you. I won't be shut out of this investigation. You can tell your boss I work with him on this, or without him. Ask me which I prefer."

There was no need to ask. She knew.

Dan Hooker leaned across the table, verging into Grace's space. The man absolutely terrified her. She glanced mutely at Ash Calloway, who stood pressed against the wall of the interrogation room, his face closed and remote. There would be no help from her boss. His posture and silence told her how deeply he felt her betrayal.

"The game has changed, Mrs. Chelsea," Hooker said. He had a low, soft voice and the hooded eyes of a cobra. "A woman firefighter was killed. In a fire we believe was set by your cohorts. That adds the charge of murder to espionage. You'll never see daylight again. Any more people die, and they'll strap you to a gurney and wheel you into the federal execution chamber."

Someone had died. A woman firefighter. Grace knew how that would turn public opinion. Rakib never said anything about setting fires. Or about insurrection against the United States. "Ash," she whimpered. "My daughter. What will happen? For God's sake, help me! I swear I don't know anything about this."

"You're lying, Grace." The SAC's dark eyes didn't flicker. The normal laugh lines around his mouth had deepened into slashes of strain. "We broke into your computer. We know you sent Rick Percy an alert right before we arrested you. Further, you forged his credentials to get him hired. His real name is Rakib Kahlel. He's an al-Qaida agent and part of a cell of local terrorists."

"No, no! Rick's father was French. He's very loyal!"

Ash shook his head. "Unfortunately his loyalty doesn't lie with us. They may let you see your daughter occasionally," he said. "After the trial. After the sentencing. Your ex-husband will be given custody, and considering the seriousness of the crimes he may decide you shouldn't see your daughter at all. Nothing I can do. Unless you cooperate and help us, you'll go down with Rakib and his buddies."

Did she see some regret there? She seized on the hope.

"Rick and I were lovers, I've admitted that! He needed a job and I did him a favor, but the position wasn't high-level security. He entered data in the computer and answered the phone. Just clerical work. He had no access to classified info."

"He was good with computers, Grace. Very good. Far better than we realized. We have no idea the damage he's done. But we will, I swear we will."

"You can search his hard-drive. I can do it! I can sort out what's important!"

"He wiped his hard-drive within minutes after he got your email. It's as empty as my head. Damn it, what were you thinking?"

"Rick was kind," she said shakily, wiping moisture from her eyes. "I trusted him. I loved him." She'd been royally deceived. Had Rakib ever loved her?

"Rakib," Hooker interjected smoothly. "His name's Rakib. Which incidentally is how you addressed him in your emails. Scorching reading, by the way."

"He told me to call him Rakib while we were making love. It's a beautiful name. And those emails were private! Not on the office account, my personal email."

Hooker slapped the table. Grace jumped. "To hell with this! You don't have any privacy where the government is concerned, Mrs. Chelsea. Not now, or ever again. You lost that privilege when you decided to betray your country for a roll in the hay. I hope to hell he was worth it. Your daughter. Your job. Your freedom. Maybe your life?"

Grace trembled in despair. She'd made a mistake. Surely not that bad a one. Surely she could salvage something. "I've told you all I know. We met three months ago at the Tattered Cover. We had coffee. Talked books. I never knew any of his friends. He had no family. He was as alone as I was."

Hooker swore and turned his back. She'd get no help there. Ash sighed. "He used you. It's an old story. Young man, older woman newly divorced and vulnerable."

"But we met by accident! I didn't tell anyone I was going to the bookstore."

Ash gave Hooker a brief frown and turned his attention back to Grace. "You were followed. Probably had been for weeks. Maybe there were others here that were approached. I'm making inquiries on that. But when they bagged you, it was perfect."

Again, she glimpsed the pain her deception had caused him. "Why? I'm not important. Just a secretary."

"My personal secretary. One who had access to classified information. And someone who could get him inside. We know you falsified his records and lie detector test."

Tears rolled down her cheeks. She had no control over them. "He had the most beautiful eyes," she whispered. "He said he loved me. He made love like an angel."

"Good God, Mrs. Chelsea," Hooker snarled. "You're forty-two years old, and you sound like a teenager. And terminally stupid."

"I never passed on anything top secret! Just routine stuff."

Ash held up his palm. "Hold it, Dan. Lighten up. Grace is as bright as a new penny. She was misled by a master, but she's going to help us. Right, Grace?"

She nodded vigorously. "Yes! But what can I do? I told you about Rakib and his friends. How they sometimes left money at my backdoor. But I never met any of them. I don't even know where Rakib lives."

"His address was on his job application," Hooker said. "His place is clean. Not a speck of dirt or dust. Not a scrap of paper or a crust of bread. Place looks like no one ever lived there. That's interesting, don't you think, Mrs. Chelsea? Beautiful eyes, makes love like an angel and cleans up after himself? Truly a paragon."

"Back off, Dan," Ash said. "Did he ever drop a name? Mention a place where he liked to shop? Did you ever go out anywhere?"

"No," she shook her head. "He thought it best we keep it secret. Because of the divorce. Because we worked together at the field office. It seemed to make sense. God, I was stupid, wasn't I?"

"First sensible thing I've heard today." Hooker sneered at her again.

She really hated the man. Hated his low, whispery voice and cold eyes. She hated all men. Except maybe Ash. She locked her jaw. "I won't say another word with him in the room, Ash. Make him go away."

Ash raised an eyebrow. "Can't do that. He's my superior. And the way things look, he could have my ass fired. In this office, the buck stops with me and I let this happen."

Hooker stalked to the door and threw it open. "We're wasting time and I need some air. See she's locked up, Ash, and throw away the key. We'll find another source."

Her tormenter left with a slam of the door and once again, Grace wondered about the Good Cop, Bad Cop scenario. No, Dan Hooker might operate that way, but her boss wouldn't. "Ash, I can't think of anything to help. Please believe me."

"I do." He took her hand and patted it gently. "But let's go over it again. Anything you can remember. Maybe Dan's right. I'll have a female agent take you to confinement and we'll talk later. After you've rested."

Confinement. She quailed at the thought. She had to think of something. How many times had she and Rakib had been together? Seven times. Seven Saturday afternoons. Her ex-husband had their daughter every other weekend, and it had been an ideal time for a romantic rendezvous. She fixed supper or ordered in. They drank wine. Listened to music. Sometimes watched a little television. And made love for hours.

"He liked Mozart," she said, grasping at anything to keep Ash interested. Anything to prevent being taken back to that sterile, windowless cell. "And old movies. Star Wars was his favorite."

He nodded. "Okay. We'll canvas the neighborhood music and video stores."

This was good. This was helping her remember. "He liked Thai food. Spicy food. And he drank wine, Ash. I thought true Muslims didn't drink."

Ash frowned. "That might not be important. He was putting on a show for you, remember? Fundamentalists are forbidden to shave or to use alcohol, and must pray five times daily. But terrorists make their own rules. Where did you buy the Thai food?"

"I bought a recipe book when I found out what he liked

and cooked his favorites." She wrinkled her brow and thought. Something about food.

"Go on," Ash patted her hand again.

"Maybe it's not important."

"Everything's important at this point."

"The money was sometimes in a plain brown bag."

Ash shrugged. "With no logo. No indication of where it came from. We've gone through that several times, Grace."

"Yes. But once there was a grocery receipt stuck inside the bag. Like the bag had been recycled from a grocery purchase. And the bag was greasy. Pungent smelling. Like sauce or something had leaked inside."

Ash leaned forward. "Do you remember where the grocery receipt came from?"

"No," Grace shook her head.

"Okay," Ash sighed and stood. "Let's call it quits for a while. I'll see you later."

"But I saved the receipt."

Ash sat back down. "You saved it."

"Yes. I always save my receipts. You know, to keep track of my budget so my ex-husband can't claim I'm wasting the child support. You can't imagine how vindictive that man is. Wants to cheat his daughter and spend every cent on that chippie."

"The receipt, Grace."

"In a manila envelope, in one of my kitchen drawers. Didn't you say that Hooker person and his team searched my house?" she asked tartly. "Maybe he's not as good as you think he is? Maybe he's the one who should be fired?"

But Ash was already out the door.

CHAPTER 21

The cabin Zeb rented was cheap because it was primitive and isolated, located three miles of backroad from Vail. He'd picked up the key from the rental service, used phony ID and paid a week in advance. In cash. The gum-chewing bimbo behind the desk barely glanced at him. Too busy doing her nails and jabbering on the phone. Nice for her. If she'd paid attention, he'd have to torch the office after the job. With her in it. Maybe he would anyway. One more fire wouldn't be noticed with the holocaust he planned. And it had been a long time since he'd burned a woman.

The cabin was short on amenities, but gave Zeb what he needed: solitude and a place to work undisturbed. In a few hours he would be ready. In the meantime, there was a job to finish. He stripped the stiff plastic sheathing from a length of copper wire and replaced it with fine surgical tape. Common electrical supplies were too clumsy for his delicate work. With the reconstructed wiring complete, he clamped it to the tiny battery. Hearing aid battery packs were jumbled on the floor. The batteries were powerful enough to trigger the timing devices, and their diminutive size made his creations unique.

This was the last one. Twelve firebombs were arranged

along the low bar that separated the living area from the monastic kitchenette. He'd decided on shoeboxes to house the mechanisms. Hidden in trash bins or near other sources of fuel, packed with cakes of napalm and totally innocuous to look at, the deadly devices would lie in wait. When the timer triggered, the powerful accelerant would explode, producing heat with the intensity of rocket fuel. The greedy flames would suck in oxygen and spread quickly.

Heat, fuel, and oxygen. The basic components of fire.

He stood, stretched and strolled toward the kitchenette, thinking about a hot shower and something to eat. Long hours hunched over the sensitive equipment had seized up his muscles, and he'd been concentrating too hard to notice hunger or the lack of heat in the cabin. His eyes burned from squinting at his exacting task, his only light that of two battery-powered lanterns.

Zeb was proud of his trade. He kept a low profile, but those in the business knew of his expertise, and knew there was no one better at constructing incendiaries. He was expensive and worth every penny. No need for Fillmore, or whoever he was fronting for, to know Zeb would do it for a lot less. Come tomorrow he'd be on a mind-blowing high no amount of dope could touch. On the other hand, the money was fine.

The cabin was four walls of peeled logs, built as a hunting and fishing cabin and furnished with a pair of lumpy bunk beds for sleeping accommodations, and not much else. A wobbly chrome and plastic table with four chairs, a tattered sofa and matching lounge chair. Both uncomfortable as hell. The worn carpeting might once have been blue, but was now a filthy gray. Zeb had pulled shut the burlap curtains that hung limply at the two front windows. The last thing he needed was a peeping tom watching through the rattling window glass.

Any fresh food was stored in a wooden box structure that was built in the cabin wall. The mountain stream that flowed beside the cabin served as nature's refrigerator, and kept his drinks and perishables chilled. He popped a cola tab and drank deeply. With the fastidious electronic work done, he could afford to put some caffeine in his system. Zeb didn't eat, didn't drink anything except water while working. Caffeine caused his hands to shake and booze was out to the question. And food made him sluggish.

Plenty of time to party after the job was done.

There was no electricity, but he'd brought a battery-powered radio with him. The news was full of the fires that were raging in the Arapahoe National Forest. The smokejumpers had been called in, and the Forest Service was blaming it on lightning strikes. He chuckled. Zeb, aka, Mr. Lightning.

It was further proof that someone with deep pockets was bankrolling the project. Forest Service personnel weren't incompetent. Plenty of people there could detect arson from radar readouts. Zeb figured someone had been paid off, someone with enough clout to make the lightning story stick. Probably to avoid any public panic. It wouldn't do to discourage tourist traffic. Too much money being made.

He shucked his flannel shirt, dropped it on the floor and shivered in the chill. The rattling propane wall heater was World War II vintage and pumped out scant warmth. The best heat source was the fireplace in the corner of the one-room dwelling, but the fire had long ago burned to embers. His fingers were so stiff that he'd halted his task several times to warm them under the hot water faucet. Stiff fingers could lead to a slip. Thank God the cabin had a propane-fueled water heater. Instructions on how to light it were tacked inside the backdoor.

Zeb knelt and stuffed kindling in the fireplace. When the fire flared he added some split logs, and the smell of burning wood filled the air. He took a deep breath. Reminded him of his boyhood. During the winter season, the only time he'd been warm was when he gathered fuel to build a fire in the fireplace. Pa was usually too hooched up to notice the cold, and when his sister bothered to come home she warmed herself up on Pa.

He slathered some peanut butter on a slice of bread,

added a few slices of bologna, and taking his drink with him, ambled toward the bathroom. Guess he should count himself lucky the place had a septic tank system and flush toilet. Piped inflow from the nearby mountain stream furnished the cabin's running water. Ingenious system, really.

He'd shower until the hot water ran out, build another sandwich and sleep for a few hours. Come daylight he'd pack up the SUV and head for Vail. Explore the town like any other tourist. Maybe buy a few souvenirs. Have a nice meal in a nice restaurant. He toyed with the idea of renting a motel room with a comfortable bed and central heating. Discarded the idea. It was tough to rent a motel without leaving a paper trail.

Which reminded him he needed to clean up the cabin before he left. He'd bury his garbage and wipe down any prints. Leave nothing traceable behind.

Fillmore's orders had been explicit. The holocaust would be set off the following night. It would be a thing of beauty. A dozen fires raging simultaneously. Even the combined fire departments from the surrounding communities wouldn't be able to handle it. Shops, hotels, restaurants and houses within a two-mile stretch would surrender to the fire's voracious appetite. Finally, a burning worth his talents. He doubted he could sleep much with his adrenalin running so high.

CHAPTER 22

Howard Elkins laid the fragment of twisted metal on his desk and shook his head. "It might be a timing device, Puma," he said. "Or it could be part of a camera that some hiker dropped. There's not enough left of this piece of junk to be sure."

Puma and Rachel had brought their suspicions to the base manager as soon as their copter had landed. But Elkins had accepted headquarters' interpretation that lightning strikes were the source of the fires, and when he made up his mind, a Sherman tank couldn't budge him. Howard was a good man but a plodder, not one to take the initiative, and when faced with a puzzling situation he fell back on the rulebook.

Puma reached across his boss's desk and retrieved the device. "This proves arson, Howard. We need to get it to the FBI. They'll analyze the components."

Howard's pudgy face went stubborn. "We'll handle this internally. I doubt the situation is what you claim."

Puma stifled his irritation. If the evidence was sent to Denver for analysis, it could be weeks before action was taken. It bugged Puma that he didn't know more about the device. He'd been the demolition expert on their Delta squad, but this is something new. "Howard, I know an explosive device when I see one. Our arsonist is no amateur. The FBI will search their database. Maybe they've run across something like it before."

"Protocol is to send evidence to the Fire Coordination Center in Denver," Howard snapped. "It's up to them to do something about it. I've no plans to involve the FBI."

"If it's arson, the feds should be informed," Puma said, trying for diplomacy and stalling for time. Because Rachel had called Hooker, and Howard's kingdom was about to be invaded.

Howard snorted. "Why should they?"

Rachel stirred. "I'll take over, Puma."

"You're sure?"

"What choice do I have? Unless you've reconsidered."

Let her stay on his crew and continue to poke around? After she'd almost been killed in the explosion that took Nita out? No way. Puma shook his head. "Not a chance. My part in the charade is over. Yours, too."

Rachel breathed deeply and faced the base manager. She had to establish control over the situation fast. "This is a federal matter, Howard. I've contacted the FBI."

Elkins seemed to notice her for the first time. "Excuse me?" he sneered, lifting an eyebrow. "It's my fire and my decision, Ms. Sasser. In fact, why are you even here?"

"Myra was close by when Jeanette was killed," Puma said. "It's a wonder the blowup didn't get her, too."

Howard sighed. "Terrible thing about Jeanette. She was a fine firefighter. But let's not jump to conclusions." He paused and squinted his eyes at Rachel. "What do you mean you've been in touch with the FBI? Who gave you that authority?"

"The United States government," Rachel answered, her voice hard. "I need a full report of everyone on duty here for the past two days. From the top down to the dispatchers. Someone is at fault here. Maybe several someones."

Howard spluttered and reddened. He jabbed an angry finger at Rachel. "I report directly to O'Shea, the Incident Commander, and I'll do nothing of the sort! Of all the asinine, idiotic demands. Who do you think you're talking to?"

"She has the right to investigate, Howard," Puma cut in. "She reports directly to an FBI task force."

Howard went from scarlet to white. "Task force? What task force? Who are you, Myra Sasser?"

She sidestepped Puma's blocking body. The base supervisor needed to understand who was in charge. "I'm with an FBI team that investigates terrorist activities. Anti-government militants are operating in this area, and it's our job to investigate. Your cooperation will be noted and appreciated."

"I'll settle this!" Howard grabbed the phone and punched in a number. Probably the Forest Service main office.

Rachel laid her fingers on the telephone release button. "Give it a rest, Howard. You can save yourself grief if you talk to the FBI when they get here. Do you want the newspapers to get a hold of a story that exposes your incompetence?"

That was harsh. Puma worried his boss may be working up to a heart attack. Howard was forty pounds overweight and prone to hypertension, and his authority was being undermined in a serious way. "Hear her out, Howard," he urged. "Chill the incompetence charge, Ms. Sasser. We're not sure what happened yet."

"I call it incompetence. Or outright negligence. The system didn't respond like it should, Puma. The fire was too much for smokejumpers to handle alone, and you knew that upfront. That's why you requested help. And Jeanette told me she'd radioed for retardant drops hours before the planes arrived."

She was right. And it wasn't the first time it had happened.

Howard slammed his fist on his desk. "That's enough! I'm in charge here! I don't care who the hell you are."

Rachel leaned into the man's face. Puma knew the signs and could sympathize. She was on a roll, and relentless. Howard was about to be cut off at the knees.

"Why wasn't an Incident Two fire declared from the beginning?" she demanded, her voice dropping to a hiss. "Where was the hotshot crew, the retardant drops? By the time help came we'd lost Jeanette and the fire was out of control. And Puma had asked Tom to send backup right after we jumped the fire."

Howard nervously worked a finger to loosen his tie. "No one questions my competence. We do the best we can, but there's a lot involved you don't understand. Politics. Funds. And we did ask for help. It takes time to process these requests."

"Puma?" Rachel turned to him. "You're the expert. Does it usually take eighteen hours for help to arrive?"

Puma shook his head. "No. But in Howard's defense, he operates in a bureaucracy. If he says the request went out in a timely fashion, I believe him."

"I'll need to interview the staff and get to the bottom of this." She addressed Puma, but her eyes were on Howard.

Howard exchanged a suffering glance with Puma and sighed. "If Puma says you're who you claim, I'll go along with it. For now, Ms. Sasser."

"Actually, it's Cortez. Rachel Cortez. Who has the authority to see your request was stalled?"

"We radioed an alert to the Rocky Mountain Coordination Center. I assume it went up the chain of command and incident objectives were drafted. There would be a division assignment list drawn up, a communication plan, medical and safety plans. And assessments of available personnel."

"Whoa! Is it always that complicated?" Rachel shot a puzzled glance at Puma.

He shrugged. "Howard's right, Rachel. There's protocol to follow. Sometimes it's a wonder we get the job done."

"Ye Gods. I thought the FBI got bogged down in red tape. I'll need a list of everyone involved, Howard. I'll conduct interviews until my boss gets here to take over."

"The boss is here, Rachel." A smooth voice came from the doorway. "Why don't you fill me in and we'll go from there?"

The three turned in unison.

Hooker strode into the room, dressed in a vested suit and precisely knotted tie. Rachel, who'd watched his workouts in the gym, knew that hard muscle lay under the smooth exterior. And a heart of stone. She winced, remembering her own grubby appearance. The next few minutes would decide whether her FBI career was derailed or stayed on track. Her boss's manner was amiable, but Rachel sensed the chill behind the words. A chill directed at her. How long had he been standing there, and what had he overheard?

"I'm interested to know what happened to Myra Sasser, Rachel." Hooker folded his arms and addressed Rachel as if they were the only two in the room.

Right to the point, as usual. She fell back on good manners to cover her distress. "Howard, this is Dan Hooker, special agent in charge of the terrorist task force. Dan, Howard is the—"

"I'm aware of Mr. Elkins position." Typically, Hooker brushed aside the formalities. "We appreciate your cooperation, sir. Has Rachel given you the facts we have so far?"

"I just became aware of Ms. Sasser's, ah, Ms. Cortez's— Dammit, agent Hooker! I want to object to the way things have proceeded. Why wasn't I told that you had an agent in place?"

"I apologize for the oversight." Hooker turned to the agents trailing in his wake. "Agents James Stanley and Zelda Carmichael from the Denver office are here to assist me. James, Zelda, why don't you see Mr. Elkins to another office and fill him in? I need to talk to Rachel alone."

Shaking his head in bewilderment, Howard trotted out of the office, the FBI agents closing in behind him. It always amazed Rachel how everyone snapped to when Hooker gave an order.

"Go with them, Ansari." Hooker's friendly pose had disappeared.

Rachel figured she was in for the Mother of all Dressing

Downs. She deserved it and knew it. Chances were good she'd be on a flight to New York within hours. She was blown, and the fault was hers. Her frozen act at the fire scene had exposed her own incompetence.

"I'll stay." Puma's tone was as frosty as Hooker's.

Almost everyone snapped to when Hooker gave an order.

The two men exchanged black looks and Rachel was reminded of a pair of pit bulls pawing the ground to establish the dominant male. Next thing they'd be charging. Much as she might enjoy that, it wasn't the direction to go.

She cleared her throat. "I had to break cover with Howard Elkins, Dan. There was no choice."

The FBI man turned his attention toward her. "Explain that. As far as I know, your job here wasn't finished."

Rachel swallowed. She'd have to admit that she'd frozen under fire and Puma didn't consider her fit to continue on his unit. "You said get out if the situation went sour. Puma cut me from the jump squad. Which means I'm useless here."

"And he cut you because—?"

"Because your damn cover story didn't hold, that's why," Puma snapped. "One of the smokejumpers checked her out. I warned you we were a tight community. Her cover was blown because you didn't set it up right."

He wasn't going to give her away. Rachel struggled with her feelings. She owed Dan the truth, but damn, it was just a slight stretch of the truth. She shut her mouth and waited.

So did Hooker. He could do that. Simply outwait an adversary. The silence stretched and finally her boss scowled at Puma. "That's it? No fault of hers?"

"In a word, no."

"You're sleeping with her. Why should I believe you?"

"I don't lie for anyone about my job. Not even someone I'm sleeping with."

Someone I'm sleeping with? That made her role clear enough. She was a warm body to have sex with. Fine. She could handle that. "Nice, Ansari."

"Work out your problems on your own time," Hooker

interjected, again all business. "Where is the piece of evidence you found, Rachel?"

"On Elkins' desk," she said, giving Puma a We'll Settle This Later glare.

Hooker walked to the desk and picked up the twisted metal. "What is it?"

"Puma says it's a part of an incendiary device."

Hooker looked at Puma. "Ever seen anything like it?"

"No. But it's a signature. Whoever constructed it has an unusual technique. Readily identified, I'd think."

"We'll send it to Quantico for analysis." Hooker replaced the object on the desk. "If we run into one of these again, can you disarm it?"

"Probably. All firebombs have the same basic components. A detonator and an incendiary mixture. Separate the detonator from the chemicals and nothing happens."

Rachel doubted it was as simple as Puma made it sound.

Hooker raised a mocking eyebrow. "I bow to your expertise. Let's go, Rachel. Stanley and Carmichael will take over here. You've got twenty minutes to change and I'll brief you while we're in flight."

Relief made her giddy. She wasn't off the case, and Hooker still needed her. "Go where?"

"Vail. The scene of the next planned arson attack."

Rachel shook her head. "I'm out of the loop, Dan. Why Vail, and what's up?"

"We were tipped that a mom and pop grocery store in Denver was a terrorist front. SWAT took the place down and we cracked their computer. The information was solid. For now the target is Vail; the Air Force Academy is next."

"Good God," Rachel said softly.

"The conspiracy goes beyond what we suspected. The picture's still murky, but it seems the New Sons are being used as a cover for a mid-eastern terrorist cell."

"Al Qaida?" Rachel asked, shaking her head at the concept. "The New Sons consider themselves true-blue Americans. Some of them are ex-servicemen. They're misguided crazies, but they'd never align with a radical Muslim group."

"The same crazies almost blew up the Hoover Dam," Puma interjected dryly. "I was there."

Rachel frowned at Hooker, looking for further explanation. "It doesn't fit the New Sons profile. The eagle claw tattooed on the instep, the flag-waving rhetoric, their hatred of everyone who isn't Aryan male."

"I didn't say the New Sons were willing allies, but they're being used. The storeowner and his wife are illegals from Iran. So were the three men living above the store. Hardcore extremists who put up a fight. The ones still alive have been detained for questioning."

"The Arapaho Forest operation was planned with military precision, Dan," Puma said. "The devices had to be dropped by copter or plane, and from the fire pattern I'd guess at least a dozen of them were planted. Someone with large bucks is involved."

"We're working on that," Hooker said, his jaw set. "Trying to trace the money, among other things. I'm going to need a full report, Rachel. From what you say, it's likely the conspiracy has connections at command post."

"I think so. Elkins is drawing up a list of names for me. I'm not convinced he's clean, but Puma vouches for him. Stanley and Carmichael need to follow up."

"They know what to do." Hooker looked at his watch. "You're relieved here."

"Hold it." Puma held up his palm. "You played me, Dan. Far as I can tell, you're still playing me."

"We told you what you needed to know. Take your gripes up with me later."

"I plan to. For now I'm going along."

"Yeah. Thought you might."

"One question. Am I official?"

"You're official. You've been on the books as a consultant from the beginning. A stipend to be paid on completion of the job. But you won't get rich on it."

Puma nodded. "I want a weapon."

"I'll have one issued. Right now, I want both of you take a look at these." Hooker reached into his inside breast pocket and pulled out a sheaf of photographs. He fanned them across Howard's desk.

Rachel stepped forward to look. She pointed. "That's—"

"Billy Smith," Puma interjected, staring at the photograph. "Our friend from the Plugged Nickel fiasco. Who is he, Dan?"

"We're not sure," Hooker answered. His eyes sent Rachael a warning. "New Sons, is all we know. Recognize any others?"

He was telling her to keep her mouth shut, that he wasn't ready to tell Puma the whole story, to expose Billy Smith as Chic Fillmore, and the history behind his vendetta against Puma. Rachel reminded herself never to believe anything Hooker said unless she had ironclad proof.

Puma shook his head. "None I recognize. Rachel?"

"I don't think so. Is it important, Dan?"

Hooker pointed. "Grace Chelsea, Calloway's personal secretary and the mole in the Denver office. One of them."

"There's more than one?" Rachel bit back an expletive.

Hooker tapped the photo of a sleek, handsome young man, slimly built, with black hair and dark liquid eyes. "Chelsea's lover. She set him up in our computer lab."

Rachel checked the photograph again and shook her head. "Not familiar. He's very good-looking. I'd remember."

"Puma? Ever see this guy?"

"No. Good-looking, huh? I'd say more like a snake."

Rachel sniffed.

Hooker nodded. "I agree. A dangerous snake. I need a few minutes with Howard Elkins, Rachel. Get cleaned up. Both of you reek of smoke and worse. You want to tag along, Ansari, be ready."

"Count on it." Puma took Rachel's arm and led her out of the room. "I'll walk you to your quarters, Ms. Cortez."

The trail wound past clumps of alpine clover and through a stand of stately lodgepole pine. Ahead of their tromping boots, a ground squirrel skittered by and disappeared into his burrow, a pine nut clenched in his jaw. Bees buzzed lazily among the bobbing heads of Columbine. The air was sweet and fresh, untainted with the pall of smoke, but Rachel's mind was haunted with the scene they had left behind, their copter taking off into a sky ablaze in scarlet, and the heavy odor of Jeanette's burned flesh. Hooker was right. They stank of it. The stench could be washed away. She didn't think it would be easy to erase the memory.

She endured Puma's hand under her arm until they were past the administration building and out of sight. She yanked away. "I can manage, thank you. And don't touch me. It'll be a snowy day in hell before we sleep together again."

"Pissed about that Someone I'm Sleeping With crack, are you? Your boss brought it up." His long strides matched hers as she stormed toward her quarters.

Pissed didn't cover it. She stopped and glared. "Go away. I'm done with you."

He grinned and rocked back on his heels. She flushed. Cocky bastard. If he dared crook his finger at her—

He did. "C'mere."

She managed to keep her feet planted in place. "No, thank you," she said, gritting her teeth. "I'm not even tempted."

He shrugged and started for her. "Hell, I'm not proud. Meet me halfway."

She shoved as his fingers grasped her shoulders. "Back off, jerk."

"Nice to be asked," he muttered, and settled his mouth on hers.

He hadn't kissed her for days. All right, thirty-six hours. It just seemed like days. She came up for breath. "You've no right to be mad at me. I was following orders."

"What about now? Still keeping Hooker's secrets?"

Of course she was. She knew what her job was worth. She lowered her eyes and didn't answer. Let him think what he would.

He sighed and stroked her hair, smiling ruefully. "Never mind. I know where I fit in your list of priorities, but that explosion scared the hell out of me. I underwent a fast attitude adjustment."

She swallowed. It was getting harder to keep her feelings for him separate from her loyalty to the Bureau. "Me, too. Rachel Cortez, the tough FBI agent freaked."

"I know, sweetheart. There's no shame in it." He gathered her up and kissed her again. A lingering, sweet mating of tongue and soul. Afterward he held her against his chest, and it felt good. Right and perfect.

"I swear to God, rookie, I can keep you safe if you'll let me. But you have to trust me. Tell me what's going on."

She did trust him. With everything except the Bureau's classified information. She clung tighter. "I've missed you. Can we shower together?"

"Later. Your boss has plans."

"We have twenty minutes."

"Hell, twenty years won't be enough."

Her heartbeat accelerated. "When this is over, I'll be gone. All we have is now."

"Think so?" He bent and took her mouth again, making a good job of it.

She sunk into the sensation. Melting heat. Brandied honey. There was no reality except Puma. His hard body pressed against hers. The ache built between her thighs. His hand cupped her bottom and pressed her female cleft against his erection. She gasped when he broke the kiss and clung to him, her legs wrapped around his thighs. "Twenty minutes is better than nothing," she said, rubbing against him.

"Woman, you're killing me. We'll finish this later."

"Now," she whispered against the beating drum in his throat. "We only have now."

"What about your job with the task force? Because that's what it would cost you if we miss the flight to Vail." His voice was rough, anguished.

A chill washed over her libido, restoring sanity. He was

right. Hooker wouldn't stand for divided loyalty and the job wasn't finished. She slid away, shaking with the effort. The chill deepened into pain. It was like the flesh had been ripped from her body. Why did love have to hurt like this? When had love happened? Over the past weeks, or when she'd seen him outlined against the moonlight that first night, had first bumped into his raw masculinity?

He caught her again and held her, his strong hands clamped around her waist.

"Don't ask me to choose," she whispered.

"If I laid you down right here, took you, shouted to the world that you were my woman, you wouldn't fight me."

Would she? She wasn't sure. "Is that what you want? To take away my choice?"

He released his hands and stepped back, a rueful frown on his face. "You know better. Stay hungry, because when this is over you're mine, Rachel Cortez."

A flash of heat seared her bones. True. For however long it lasted, she was his.

CHAPTER 23

The Vail Town Council Chambers was a medium-sized room, with an elevated dais at the far end, flanked by the United States and Colorado flags. The city council members were grouped around a semi-circular table on the platform, slumped in lush leather armchairs that swiveled, a name plaque and microphone placed in front of each. Four rows of public seating, totally empty, faced the raised podium. Rachel positioned herself inside the closed door, following orders not to let anyone in or out. Hooker stood in front of the council, holding a clipboard with his notes. He'd finished speaking and waited their reaction.

Rachel watched their faces. None of the council liked what they'd heard.

In the far corner of the room, Puma leaned against the wall, his alert eyes contradicting the indolent posture. The Vail police chief waited nearby. Armed agents patrolled the halls and exterior of the Municipal Building, their job to halt unauthorized entries, and though the council members didn't know it yet, to prevent anyone leaving without Hooker's specific okay. Rachel, Puma, and all of the agents except Hooker wore windbreaker jackets with FBI lettered prominently on the front and back.

"Are you sure about this, agent Hooker? Before the

Boston Marathon attack, we wouldn't have bought into this crap. But Boston's a huge metropolitan area. Now you're saying our peaceful little town is being targeted?"

Mayor Sal Langtree shifted in his chair and stared at Dan Hooker. The police chief had pried the mayor away from his evening television, and His Honor's manner bordered on belligerence. He wore an unbuttoned sport coat over a rumpled shirt, collar askew; his hair uncombed.

"Boston was a tragic wakeup event, mayor," Dan agreed. "But please recall that more recently we've had attacks in Orlando, Ohio, and California. I won't go into intelligence details, but hard evidence points to the Vail area as the next terrorist target. May I outline our strategy if an incident occurs?" In his expensive suit, freshly shaved and his hair impeccable, Hooker was the quintessential FBI agent, confident and in command. It wasn't his usual style, but when he wanted to, Hooker could spread the manure with anybody.

After the mayor gave a go-ahead nod, Hooker continued. "We appreciate the council gathering on such short notice. The Bureau is operating jointly with the ATF, and the Vail Fire Department has implemented its emergency contingency plan. Your men are already on the streets, working with our personnel to locate the explosive devices. We've been assured of the police departments' cooperation, and Chief Wohjinoski has put his force on full alert."

Hooker indicated the police chief who gave a sober wave of acknowledgement. Hooker paused and wearily rubbed his eyes.

"People," he said quietly. "I'm sure of my facts. We expect the firebomb activity will be centered in Vail Village and nearby Lionshead, but there is a possible five-mile strip to cover, much of it heavily populated with tourists. Your fire chief has informed local fire departments along the I70 corridor of an emergency situation. We have three hours to prevent a disaster. There's a plan in place, but we need your help."

The seven members of the city council were in closed session, the public uninvited. Using his authority as the town's highest-ranking elected official, Langtree had called an emergency meeting, and his disheveled appearance was mirrored by that of the six other council members. Their eyes darted spasmodically from Rachel to Puma, to the chief and back to Hooker, dismay on their faces, as well as disbelief. These were responsible citizens, but none of them was prepared for the shocking news Hooker had given them.

Rachel knew exactly what they were thinking. Terrorists operating in their peaceful town? Impossible!

The lone woman on the council—the name printed on plaque in front of her read Donna Higgenlooper—cleared her throat and asked the question the mayor should have. "Okay, you've scared the hell out of us. What do you want us to do?"

At least one council member had a grasp of the situation.

Hooker turned his FBI face toward the woman and gave a brief smile. "We've fifty agents combing the area for explosive devices, along with dogs trained in accelerant detection. We don't want widespread panic. If the council makes a public announcement that a disaster drill is being conducted, it would cover our activity. We need your discretion as to the present situation."

"Let me get this straight," the mayor said. "We're nowhere near any government or defense facility, have no vital infrastructure to protect. Nothing that would make a terrorist statement. We're a hundred miles from Denver and we're a resort area. Families visit here for fun and relaxation, for God's sake. Why hit on us?"

"We can't be certain. In the past, prominent terrorist attacks focused on high-profile targets. The World Trade Center. The Pentagon. The Federal building in Oklahoma City. Lately they've branched out to local sites. A Florida nightclub, a Christmas gathering in California. But what better terrorist statement than to destroy an entire town in the heartland of our country? None of us would feel safe again."

"Remember, Sal, we have a senator who lives in the area," Mrs. Higgenlooper said. Her voice shook. "And he often has important guests."

"The senator is not in residence at this time," Hooker said. "Nor any other high-ranking federal official. That has been determined."

Rachel was sure the Secret Service had hustled the senator and his family to safety as soon as the Bureau had informed them of the situation. The FBI, the ATF, Homeland Security, even the CIA were on red alert until the firebombs were located.

Donna Higgenlooper stood and gathered up her purse. "There's only one route in and out of Vail. If it comes to evacuation, there's no way I70 can handle the outflow. They'll be bumper-to-bumper traffic and major accidents. Vote my proxy, Sal. I'm going home to my family."

Hooker motioned to Rachel and she shifted enough to block the doorway. Puma lost the slouch and ambled casually in her direction.

"I'm sorry, Mrs. Higgenlooper, we can't allow that," Hooker said. "We're asking the mayor to go on television to announce the ongoing disaster drill. This building is being searched as we speak. In the meantime, I have a copy of a declaration I want you all to hear. As per your bylaws, passing the emergency ordinance requires a unanimous vote by the council members. Food and drink will be provided and an agent will escort anyone who needs to use the facilities. Until the danger is past, you'll remain here."

Rachel knew her boss was a firm believer that the only way to keep a secret was tell no one. Chances were excellent that despite avowed intentions, that once out of FBI custody the council members would heat up the phone lines, warning friends and relatives of an impending disaster.

Shocked murmurs ran around the council table. Several shot to their feet, as if to rush the door. Higgenlooper clutched her purse to her chest and looked ready to claw someone. "I'm a single mother. I have two teenaged kids at home!"

"Please sit down!" Hooker raised his voice, something Rachel rarely heard him do. The sharp command startled the members back into their seats. Including Higgenlooper. "The best thing for your families is to eradicate the danger. We know what we're doing."

"The hell with it! This isn't Communist China!" Mrs. Higgenlooper leaned forward and slapped the table in defiance. "We'll vote and leave whether you like it or not. Right, Sal?"

"Now, Donna," the mayor said soothingly. "When we took this job we swore to serve the town with integrity. Seems we're being tested as to whether we mean that. Understand we all have families who'll worry if we don't get home soon, Agent Hooker."

"You'll be allowed one phone call, but no mention of this can leak out. I sincerely apologize, but this is the way it must be. It would do no good to leave the area, Mrs. Higgenlooper. The State Patrol is blockading all traffic in and out of Vail for the next twenty-four hours. We want to catch those responsible, and the fact that there is limited access to your community works in our favor."

A babble of angry voices erupted from the council members. The mayor banged his gavel so vigorously on the table that the mallet split. He swore, dropped it on the table and resorted to shouting. "People! Let's have order! We have a job to do and the sooner we get to it, the sooner we can go home. Isn't that right, Agent Hooker? We can leave as soon as we draft a resolution and publicly announce the drill?"

"Of course," Hooker agreed, his voice smooth with the lie. "Just a few technicalities. If we get right to it, the announcement could be made immediately. My people and yours are already patrolling the streets."

"What technicalities?" Donna Higgenlooper asked, sitting ramrod straight in her chair, her eyes dark with fury. Smart lady. The mayor might buy Hooker's evasive promise, but this woman didn't.

Hooker beckoned at Rachel. "I wonder, Mrs.

Higgenlooper," he said. "As a local, you're familiar with landmarks and roads?"

The councilwoman gave a snort of agreement.

"Would you mind consulting with one of my agents? Agent Cortez will take you to a conference room to study some maps and ask you to point out any vulnerable targets."

Maps? Conference room? Rachel wondered where in the hell she would find those. All she knew was it was her job to hustle the disruptive element from the room. Donna Higgenlooper was a slightly-built woman who looked fit. An interesting face. Deep-set dark eyes, close-cropped hair lightly streaked with gray. Tanned skin and freckled arms, an outdoor lover. She wore a tee-top with an ankle-length peasant skirt, heavy Doc Martin shoes, and gold hoop earrings. Probably mid-forties, with a mind of her own and an offbeat fashion sense.

"Please, would you come with me, Mrs. Higgenlooper?" Rachel asked, stepping forward, keeping her voice light and pleasant.

The woman huddled into a compact ball and glared up at Rachel. "Do you have kids, Agent Cortez?"

Rachel was startled into an answer. "No."

"Then you wouldn't understand. Don't think you can lock me away. Do what you do, but I'm going home to my kids. Touch me and I'll scream bloody murder."

Was she supposed to physically haul the woman from her chair? Instead, Rachel dropped to her knees, bringing herself to the other's eye level and spoke quietly, urgently. "Donna, let's both do our jobs here. We need your help, you need ours. If we work together we can get this done, and you can go home."

The woman's chin wobbled and Rachel saw the terror behind the belligerence. "You're not going to lock me up?"

Rachel shook her head. "Of course not."

"My kids? How will I get them out if the worst happens?"

"If it becomes necessary, we have an evacuation plan.

Why don't we go get a cup of coffee and look at those maps?"

"A plan?"

"It's something we've been trained to do. You've read how the east coast evacuates when a hurricane is predicted? We have a similar plan. The State Patrol will clear the highway and direct traffic, and all federal and local agencies will assist." Rachel hoped she was right about that. Dan Hooker hadn't mentioned evacuation, but it only made sense that an emergency plan was in place.

The woman held Rachel's eyes for a long moment, and finally nodded. "The county surveyor's office has maps. Really detailed maps. It's just down the hall."

"Excellent. You lead the way."

Rachel held her hand out. The woman took it and rose, heading for the door. After a quick glance at Hooker, Rachel followed. Her boss's face had cracked into a barely perceptible smile. Puma stood aside letting them pass. Rachel opened the door and at her soft request, the two agents in the outside hall stood aside also.

"Nice work," Puma muttered in Rachel's ear as she brushed past. "I'll be out of here in five. Hooker's got it under control, and I want to get on the streets."

Rachel did too, but it appeared that wasn't to be her assignment. She shot him a "Take Care of Yourself" look, and followed Councilwoman Higgenlooper down the hall.

He was out there. Puma could smell him.

Someone with crafty fingers, a keen mind and a black heart.

Rachel gave Puma a half-hearted smile, as she and Councilwoman Higgenlooper disappeared around the corner, headed for the County Surveyor's office. It was the one thing that Puma had asked Hooker to do, to see to it that Rachel was kept out of the line of fire, that she'd be nowhere near the possibility of an exploding firebomb. Puma knew his woman. Rachel was chafing that she wasn't in the action, wasn't out on the street looking for an arsonist and a killer.

But Puma couldn't go through it again. Couldn't see her come apart; see the memories and terror engulf her at the sight of fire. He hadn't explained why, had just taken Hooker aside and made the request. The FBI man's face had tightened as he listened, and for a heartbeat Puma thought he would refuse. Finally, Hooker nodded and muttered, "This makes us even."

Whatever that meant. Probably The FBI agent thought it had something to do with the sexual relationship, and Rachel would pay for it later. Puma regretted that, but it wasn't his main concern. He wanted her safe and out of the way while he went hunting.

The council meeting was on the first floor, its location making it accessible to the public. He proceeded down the long hall, his footsteps echoing against the high ceiling. Two policemen were guarding the front door. Young, both of them. One tall and lean, clean-cut and blonde, the all-American boy type. One shorter, muscular, with shaggy dark hair and matching five-o'clock shadow. Maybe some Apache blood, Puma thought. He'd be the harder of the two to take down. From the once-over the 'Pache gave him, Puma figured the man had similar thoughts. Aware of the gun snugged at his belt, Puma kept his hands in sight.

"Sorry, sir," Tall-and-lean said, as Puma approached. "No one goes in or out without FBI clearance."

Silently Puma flashed the picture ID he wore on a cord around his neck. Hooker had provided him with the ID and the weapon. The weapon was second-rate, a single-shot revolver, but accurate and reliable, better than nothing. The blonde cop looked at the photo and consulted his clipboard.

"It's okay, Darin," 'Pache said. "He's on the list."

"I see it. Unlock the door, Capote. You can pass, sir."

Capote. Not Apache, then. At least part Ute. Capote was a well-known name among the tribes. Vail had been the summer residence of the Ute Indians long before the arrival of the white man. Made sense that some of them would have settled in the area. A flash of understanding leapt between Puma and the dark-haired policeman.

"Frank Capote," the man said, offering his hand.

"Fletch Ansari," Puma answered softly, taking the hand. "Some call me Puma."

"Puma. Wish I could go along."

"I could use you. You know the town?"

"Should. Lived here all my life."

Capote produced a ring of keys and unlatched the glass double doors. A gush of chilled night air entered the building, floral-scented with a hint of damp pavement.

There'd been a brief evening shower, and flower boxes and plantings lined every walkway in the town. Streetlights glowed like a string of fireflies dancing in the gloom.

Where to start?

Blonde Darin's radio squawked. He gave a gruff greeting and listened, holding up his palm to stop Puma's progress. Switched off and looked puzzled. "They want you in the men's room, second floor. ASAP."

Puma didn't ask why, because it couldn't be good. Hooker interfering with Puma's plans? Maybe. "The quickest way up?"

With a glance at his partner, Frank Capote nodded. "I'll show you. Stairs are faster than the elevator."

Puma took the stairs two at a time, leaving the policeman to get back to his post. Head of the stairs, turn right, Frank had said. Three, maybe four doors down. On the second floor, there was no need to search. The door stood wide open, a cadre of FBI personnel clustered nearby.

"Here!" one of them shouted, motioning urgently.

Inside Hooker and another man bent over a metal trashcan, the lid up, and clumps of paper towels scattered on the tile floor. Puma knew instantly. "You found one."

Hooker looked up, the other man too. Hooker had discarded the suit coat and was wearing the same type of windbreaker jacket all the FBI personnel wore. The other man wore a bulky padded suit and heavy gloves. Bomb squad.

The bomb squad guy nodded. "Hooker says maybe

you've seen a similar device. It's packed in a shoebox. Sound familiar?"

Puma shook his head. "No. But anything's possible. He wouldn't carry a firebomb around without disguising it. Have you touched it? Any wires in sight?"

"Still scoping it out. No wires. I'm going to lift it out now. You should leave, Agent Hooker."

Hooker backed up. "I'll stay out of the way, but I'm not leaving."

Sometimes a device was rigged so that it blew if it was moved. Hooker would know that. If he chose to stay, Puma figured it was the other man's decision. Ironic the incendiary would be found in a building that Puma had thought a safe shelter for Rachel. At least she was a full floor down in a rock solid concrete building. Puma put everything out of his mind as the bomb squad guy lifted the shoebox and set it on the floor.

"Taped shut," the man grunted. He bent over a toolbox and removed a razor-cutting tool. "Only one way to find out what to expect."

"Wait!" Puma reached for the cutter. "Let me do it."

"You don't have on gloves. Or a protective suit."

"Yeah. I'd bet he didn't either."

"Good point," the man said, stripping off his gloves. "Damn things get in the way anyhow."

"I'll cut the tape. You lift the lid."

They both crouched on the floor and Puma slit the tape carefully. "Standard packing tape," he noted. "You can buy it anywhere."

"Off-brand shoes. Probably came from a discount store. Guy bought the shoes and threw them away. Kept the box."

"Be my guess," Puma agreed. "Untraceable."

The man's hands hovered over the box, ready to remove the lid. They exchanged glances. "Sam Templeton," the bomb squad guy said.

"Nice to meet you, Sam." Puma gave his name and grinned, knowing why the guy took the time. If they were going to die together, it would be on a first name basis.

Sam lifted the lid. Swore.

Puma whistled. "Impressive. The man knows what he's doing."

"Ingenious," Sam agreed.

Behind them Hooker growled. "What the hell are you two talking about? Can you disarm the bastard?"

Puma settled back on his heels. "Nope."

Hooker swung his attention to the other man. "Sam? You're the expert."

"Maybe, Dan. But I won't try. He's hardwired it so if I cut anything it'll blow. Damn, he must be dexterous to get the wires that short. Look, Puma, he's constructed every piece of this by hand. Even the wire. Used 312 batteries. That's homemade napalm, formed into jelly. Nasty stuff."

"Yeah," Puma nodded. "That's how he kept the device so small. When do you think it's set for?"

"Hard to tell. Not like the movies, with a convenient countdown timer attached. Could be five minutes or five hours."

"Five minutes?" Hooker demanded hoarsely.

"No way to know." Sam got to his feet. "Some kind of putty packed around the timer. If I pull it off, the whole thing could blow."

"What do you suggest?"

"Sorry, I know you'd like to analyze the components, but I have to move it to a safe place and explode it. Notice the small amount of incendiary, Puma? Strange, don't you think? Considering where we found it. Wouldn't do much damage here."

Puma had been thinking the same thing. The john was a small, self-contained room. Two urinals, one metal-doored stall. Tile floors and wall. No window. His eyes swept the area. No combustible material except the discarded paper towels from the trashcan. He glanced up at the ceiling. Smoke detectors and an automatic sprinkler system. The fire would be out two minutes after it started. Any experienced arsonist would know that. A guy unlucky enough to be taking a piss at the time it went off would be a goner, but no one outside the room would be in danger. "Diversion, you think?"

Sam nodded, carefully replacing the lid on the shoebox. "Maybe. I'll put this in the hotbox and we'll wheel it to the truck. The fire chief located a gully a few miles from town. Mostly rock and a little scrub. They'll have equipment onsite to contain the damage when it blows."

Hooker grunted agreement and left, calling over his shoulder. "Save what you can for evidence. And if they're all like this, you're in for a busy night, Sam. He won't be nice enough to leave the rest of them in such a convenient place."

"More fun," Sam said, grimacing. "Let me know when you locate any others."

Puma and Hooker watched while Sam placed the shoebox in a mesh sling and lowered it into the hotbox, a massive, wheeled contraption built to contain the impact of an explosion. Constructed of lead-lined steel, Kevlar padded, it wouldn't stop a nuclear weapon, but it would be sufficient to render the shoebox device harmless in the event of an accidental blast. If the detonator blew, it would be contained and deprived of oxygen, and the accelerant would fizzle and die. Sam had donned his gloves again, and drawn a heavy, protective shield over his face. He locked down the cover on the hotbox and lashed a Kevlar blanket over it. Despite his calm exterior, the bomb squad expert treated the device with the utmost respect.

Hooker began talking quietly into his radio, alerting his people what to look for. A shoebox. Taped shut. Probably would be stashed near sources of ready fuel. Restaurant kitchens, hotel lobbies, wooden structures. Don't touch the device if found, his people were warned. Let the bomb squad handle it.

"I wish we knew how many of these bastard devices we're looking for," he said as he shut off the radio.

Puma looked up and down the hall, his instincts on alert. That had been too easy. "Has the rest of the building been searched?"

"Room by room. That's all we found."

Puma nodded. "Let's do it again. Where would we find a shoebox?"

CHAPTER 24

Puma's shaman sixth-sense woke as soon as he opened the heavy door to the basement area of the city administration building. Rachel had shucked Councilwoman Higgenlooper's company and joined him in the search. At least this way he could keep an eye on her. The unpleasant odor of leaking sewage assaulted their nostrils as they descended the stairs. Discarded furniture and barrels of paper waiting to be recycled occupied one side of the room. Nothing else to look at except an oversize water heater, gas furnace and dusty pipes. Since it was summer, the furnace was shut down.

"Phew," Rachel said. "Someone should look into the plumbing. I thought the arson dog and his handler checked down here."

"Hours ago, but they didn't know what to look for. Now we do. Watch that last step. It's dark as Hades down here." Puma aimed his flashlight on the floor, illuminating their way.

"There's got to be a light source," Rachel said. "Maybe the pull chain by the furnace."

"Don't." Puma put out a hand to stop her reach. "Use your flashlight."

She retrieved her flashlight from her duty belt and switched it on. "Why?"

"I don't know. But it's something strange. Just don't touch anything."

He sensed the firebug had been there. Wasn't there now, but had been. It stood to reason that something foul had been left behind. Slowly they circled the basement, their flashlights bouncing from wall to wall, floor to ceiling, glancing over the discarded piles of building refuse.

"Anything could be hidden in this junk," Rachel said. "We need the dogs."

"The handler said he and his partner searched thoroughly. Found nothing."

"There's a storage closet," Rachel said, aiming her highest beam at a wooden door labeled Maintenance. "Standing open a crack. Our guys must've left it unlocked."

Scrub buckets and wet mops, brooms, an industrial-sized vacuum cleaner, along with a pegboard hung with a variety of tools, occupied the right side of the long narrow space. Inside, the stale air was heavy with the scent of furniture polish, ammonia and disinfectant. Strong enough it made his nose itch. A jacket and cap hung on the back of the door. Had to be an employee's stuff, so the night maintenance man was around.

Rachel swept the light along the walls. "There's the light switch, behind the door. We could see a lot better if we turned it on."

Puma aimed his flashlight toward the ceiling. "Don't touch it. My sense of smell isn't as good as the dogs, but flammables are stored here. My nose hairs are quivering."

"Look at this." Rachel hefted a metal can from a lower shelf and held it up. "This must be what you smell."

The can was labeled: Multi-Purpose Solvent. CAUTION! DO NOT INGEST. CONTAINS NAPHTHA. HIGHLY FLAMMABLE.

Puma grunted agreement. "That could be it." He whistled as his flashlight beam continued to explore the shelves. "No smoke detector or sprinklers. Bare wood beams overhead. And check this out. Another shoebox."

Rachel gasped. "My God! They're all kinds of

combustibles stored here. If that box is what it looks like, the blaze would be out of control in a flash."

The shoebox was shoved on the top shelf, sharing space with stacks of toilet paper, paper towels, plastic bags and an assortment of janitorial supplies. All typical paraphernalia for a building of this size and function. Innocuous. Virtually invisible.

"Got him," Puma agreed with satisfaction.

"Until we disarm that mother, I'm not sure who has who."

"Yeah, I'll get to it, but something I need to check first." Something was very wrong. What was it? Something so dangerous it was a bad taste in his mouth.

"I don't understand why the other agents didn't find this," Rachel said. "Hooker has his best guys out searching. None of them are amateurs."

"It's up on a high shelf and looks like it belongs there. The smell would have confused the dog, and the handler would've put the odors down to the cleaning substances. They missed it." He continued to prowl the long, narrow space, stepping carefully, every sense alert.

Rachel shivered, catching his mood. "Hooker will chew them a new one. Let's get that thing down and out of here."

"We're not sure what it is yet. Hold this and aim it toward the ceiling. Use yours, too." Puma handed her his flashlight and retrieved a six-foot ladder that leaned against the far wall.

"We don't need a ladder, Shortie. I can reach the top shelf without it."

"Very funny," he said, positioning the ladder in the center of the closet. "Stay where you are and don't even think of touching the light switch, the shoebox or anything else. And I'd appreciate a little less mouth."

"You're just mad because I'm taller than you are when I have my boots on. At least an inch."

"We'll discuss my inches later, Rookie. Hold the lights steady."

He climbed cautiously until his nose almost touched the

overhead light fixture, which consisted of a bare bulb screwed into a porcelain socket. Jesus! His breath stopped and his scalp crawled. He'd heard of this type of nasty booby trap, but had never actually seen it. When he caught up with the fucker who did this, hell wouldn't offer sanctuary.

"Rachel," he said softly. "See if you can find a clean rag. Nothing oily or dirty."

"There're some rags here in a box. Looks like old, torn-up sheets. They're clean."

"Good." Puma reached and grabbed the soft material. "Now, go get Hooker."

"I'll radio him to send help."

"There's no time. I want you out of here, Rachel."

"I don't know what this is about, but I'm not leaving you. And someone has to hold the light." Her voice shook.

He knew that tone. She wasn't going to budge. Useless to argue, and she'd read it right. Without light, the task would be twice as dangerous. "Stand by the doorway and direct the beams toward the ceiling. Keep it steady."

If the damn thing blew, his body would take the brunt. Because there was nothing to be done about it, he disengaged his mind from the danger. The task was simple. Wrap the glass bulb with the cloth. Unscrew it slowly. Gently. One spark and he'd be shaking hands with either God or the Devil.

He twisted. The bulb squeaked and moved slightly, not smoothly or easily. The fixture was old and corroded. The smell of accelerant was stronger now. He could feel the sweat run down his neck and armpits. Could hear Rachel's rapid breathing. His hands shook but he didn't dare let go of the bulb. It might crash to the floor and explode. Every hair on his body stood at attention. Every second increased the danger.

He took a steadying breath. A half-turn. Another half-turn. Agonizingly slow work, but a harsh scrape of metal against metal could generate a spark, and obliteration.

One more should do it. He muttered a prayer to the spirit

of his grandfather. "I could use a little help, Togochin."

The bulb came out, wrapped snugly in the cloth. A glass orb of death, harmless now. Puma took a moment to calm his heartbeat. He looked down to find Rachel standing directly below, the flashlights held steady, one in each hand, her face drawn and white, ghostly in the dimness.

"Okay?" she whispered.

"Okay," he answered and skinned down the ladder, holding the disengaged bulb with care. It could still be dangerous. "You're not much good at following orders."

"What is that—that thing?"

"A little present from our friendly pyromaniac. He drilled a hole in the bulb, used a hypodermic and filled it with gasoline. Sealed the hole with putty. Probably the same putty he uses in his shoebox contraptions."

"So when someone turned on the light switch?"

Puma shrugged. "Bam."

"My God! He didn't care who he killed. That's diabolical."

"And ballsy. The technique isn't without danger for the guy who sets it up. We're dealing with a hardcore pro." And something else. What had he missed?

"Hooker will want to run it for prints."

"I guarantee the only prints will be mine. We need to drain the gasoline."

Rachel stepped to the backend of the closet. "There's a utility sink here. You can dump the nasty stuff and rinse it down with water."

Sink. Water. Of course.

"Good girl," he said, turned on the faucet and removed the putty plug. The heavy scent of gasoline wafted in the air as the contents dribbled down the drain. Damn. The arson dog should have found this. They were trained to detect even the smallest amount of combustibles. "We need to get that shoebox out of here right away. Any idea where Sam Templeton is?"

"Taking care of the package found earlier. Be a while before he gets back."

"What about your other bomb squad guys? Templeton can't be the only one you've got working this."

"Busy. They're checking the hospital and the big hotels. Looks like it's you and me, Ansari. Are you thinking what I'm thinking?"

"That this guy got very lucky, or someone did some reconnoitering for him beforehand? The arsonist had to come in with his neat little booby trap already prepared. And the timing's screwy. You're right. Our agents should have spotted this. And if they'd looked in the closet, turned on the light—"

"Bam." Rachel said, her voice heavy with irony. And fury. "The terrorists have inside help. Someone who can come and go without raising suspicion scouted the building in advance. That's how the arsonist knew about this closet. And the altered light bulb had to be put in place later."

"After our agents checked down here." Puma finished her sentence. "Where's Hooker?"

"He's set up a command post in one of the courtrooms on the second floor. Joint effort with the local fire and police departments. Coordinating the search."

"Get on the radio and fill him in. We need a bomb squad guy ASAP. And the building needs to be searched again, thoroughly. If we get lucky, maybe the arsonist is still around."

Rachel spoke rapidly into her radio, and raised her eyebrows at the squawking sound at the other end. "I'll pass it on," she said, and turned to Puma. "They've located another firebomb at the hospital admissions area. And one in the Aspen Hotel lobby."

The hospital! And a hotel packed with tourists. Mentally Puma swore a violent oath, and added to the score yet to be settled. Sundance. Nita. Thousands of acres of forestland destroyed. Shoeboxes of death.

Rachel laid a hand on his arm. "Puma, no one's available for a while. Hooker wants to know if you can disarm it."

He made a rapid assessment. If this device had the same components as the other, he didn't have the necessary equipment to handle it. It would have to be a low-tech solution to the problem. A sink full of water. "Tell him okay, and to get some personnel down here. I don't care where he hauls them in from."

Rachel passed on the word, 10-4ed and hung up. "What should we do?"

"I'll hold the light while you plug the sink and fill it with water. Then stand back with the flashlight while I retrieve the shoebox. I mean it, Rachel. Stay out of the way."

She shrugged her disinterest in his wishes, and moved past him toward the sink. It was a large, deep basin made of stainless steel. High faucets. Made so the janitor could fill buckets and wash out mops. About the best setup Puma could have hoped for at the moment. He waited until Rachel was back by the doorway and handed her their flashlights. The beams stayed strong, thank God.

The ubiquitous box once held the same brand of running shoe as the box they'd found upstairs. Taped tight. He wouldn't risk opening it until it was in the sink and waterlogged. In seconds, he had the device submerged in the water. He wiped his sweat-drenched forehead on the sleeve of his shirt. His gut unclenched.

"Think that will do it?" Rachel was at his side again, inches away from the deadly explosive.

He really wanted to shake her. "Dammit, woman."

"Shut up." She poked a finger in his chest. "I'm not any woman here. I'm FBI."

"How could I forget?"

"Backup's on the way. Maybe fifteen minutes. We need to find the body. That must be what we smelled when we first got here."

He nodded. She was aggravating as hell, but damn, she was smart. He should have caught it immediately when they came down the steps. God knew he'd smelled death often enough. "Who do you figure it is?"

"Maintenance person. Has to be. We shut the building down at seventeen-hundred. Only authorized personnel with proper ID get in or out. Someone was in here earlier and rigged the light fixture, killed the janitor, stole the ID and split."

"Had to be," Puma agreed. "Otherwise he would have turned the closet light on to pick up his stuff, and would've bought the farm."

With the overhead lighting judged safe, the brightly-lit basement area soon crawled with feds, systematically tearing the place apart. They found the janitor's body stuffed in one of the recycling barrels, buried under used copy paper. A bloody smile gaped jaggedly across the man's throat.

"We'll take it from here," Hooker said, addressing Puma and Rachel. "Get on with your job. There's an arsonist dog and his handler standing by upstairs. Local guy, knows his way around the area."

Puma looked at Rachel. "Okay, FBI. I'm going out on the street. Care to join me?"

"Try and stop me."

Damned if he wanted to. There was no one he trusted more at his back.

CHAPTER 25

Zebedee patted his contented stomach. He'd deserved a good meal after a week of living on baloney sandwiches, and Sweet Basil restaurant had lived up to its reputation for great food. The last two firebombs lay hidden in his knapsack, slung out of sight under his table. He'd deposit them before he left town. One in the alley behind the posh eatery, the other in an abandoned shop he'd spotted during his recon. The glass storefront was papered over, a "For Lease" sign in the window. He'd enter the shop in the back, disable the smoke alarm, and the fire would burn unchecked until it spread to the adjoining buildings.

He'd left himself a two-hour window to hit I70 and put the pedal to the metal. Two hours would take him to the outskirts of Denver. He'd be well out of reach by the time his deadly little packages began to pop.

He signaled for the waiter. Time for one more beer. His only regret was he couldn't linger to watch the fun, but Chic Fillmore had ordered him to do the job and vacate the area. Fillmore was paranoid. One of those militia types who saw bogies behind every bush and tree. But the man's ridiculous militia group was paying Zeb enough money he could afford to follow orders. There'd be other fires.

The waiter appeared by his table. "Yessir? Anything else?"

"Ricky", his nametag identified him. College kid, working the summer tourist crowd. Good-looking, sporting the shadow of a beard the babes liked these days. Zeb knew the type. Carried his brain in his dick. Rick the dick. Oozing phony friendliness. Probably made enough in tips to live high all season. Zeb had hated his kind all his life.

"I'll have another short one," Zeb ordered, enjoying the power of knowing the kid had to make nice. "Be quick about it. And bring the check." He'd leave the guy fifteen percent. Adequate, so he wouldn't be pissed enough to remember what Zeb looked like, and not too much, which would have the same effect.

"One draw beer, coming up." The waiter grinned his tip-earning grin. "You going to be around for a while? Vail's a boss vacation spot. If you come back tomorrow, ask for Ricky."

"Sure thing, Ricky," Zeb lied breezily. "Great food. I'll probably see you tomorrow. Be here a few days, getting in some fly-fishing. I hear it's good around here."

"The best. The rivers and streams are full of trout. Hey, when you get back outside, check out the feds. They're all over the downtown area. Some excitement for Vail. Nothing much ever happens here."

Zeb's grin froze.

"Feds?" he asked, his voice thick with apprehension. "Why? What's going on?"

"The mayor just came on local television. Special announcement. The feds and the Vail PD are conducting an emergency defense drill. Bomb-sniffing dogs, fire department and medical personnel on active alert, the whole bit. Not that Vail would be a place terrorists would target, but hey! Like the mayor says, it pays to be prepared."

Coincidence? Not likely. Zeb rose from his seat. "I need to use the john. And where's your public payphone?"

"Same hall as the restrooms," Rick answered. "I'll get

you that beer and the check. It's been a pleasure—"

Zeb was already halfway across the bistro, heading for the blue neon sign that read "Restrooms."

He paused as he passed the front door. Maybe a little reconnoitering was a good idea. Could be the waiter didn't know what he was talking about. Zeb stepped into the vestibule and peered out the glassed-in front. Streetlights blossomed against the night's inky darkness. Tourists strolled by, looking into shop windows, laughing and chatting. He relaxed. The stupid kid had it wrong. Everything looked normal.

Then he saw the dog.

Zeb knew an arsonist dog when he saw one. He feared a dog more than any cop. A cop could be fooled. A dog couldn't. The dog tugged impatiently in the handler's grip; the guy's jacket read VPD. Vail Police Department. Bad news. Worse news followed. A man and a woman, both wearing FBI jackets, and another Vail policeman trailed in their wake. So the waiter had it right.

Zeb eased back into the shadows as the four passed directly in front of his view. Christ! Ansari. He'd spent two days hanging his ass over a cliff, binoculars trained on that one's ranch house. The long-legged bimbo with him was the same babe Zeb had spotted living there. Damn, she was FBI! Fillmore's easy money didn't look so easy anymore.

He dialed the cell phone number with shaky fingers. "Z here," he rasped. "Emergency. Five minutes." He recited the phone number he was calling from and hung up. If the phone didn't ring within the allotted time, to hell with what the militiaman and his fellow creeps wanted. Saving his own skin was something Zeb was an expert on.

He checked his watch. A few more minutes and Zeb was out of there.

The phone rang. He picked up the receiver.

"Z," he said softly.

"This better be good." Fillmore answered, sounding annoyed.

"Where are you?"

"The Springs. What's up?"

Zeb's glance darted around the hallway. No one in sight, but he kept his voice a muted hiss. "I'm getting out. The place is crawling with feds. What the hell happened to your inside source? You're supposed to have advanced notice of crap like this."

"What do you mean, crawling with feds?"

"They're calling it a drill, but I'm taking no chances. And if they pick me up, swear to God you'll pay."

"Okay, okay," Fillmore snapped. "What about the packages?"

"An even dozen, primed and in place," Zeb lied. "I'll pick up my fee at the drop-off. What about the third target?"

"Put it on hold for now. I'll leave the fee and your instructions at the drop-off. Get out fast, and we'll reconnect at the Denver base. Don't call me again."

"Wait!" Zeb said hurriedly, before Fillmore could hang up. "I spotted that Injun asshole prowling around, the one you've got a hard-on for."

"Ansari! You're sure?"

"After I wasted two days spying on his place? Damn right I'm sure. Swear to God he's sniffing the air like a Goddamn wolfhound. The bitch with him is FBI. What did you set me up for Fillmore?"

"No names! I couldn't get to a land phone!" Fillmore all but shouted.

"Fuck it. You better fix this fast."

"Okay. I know how to smoke the Indian out. Hit his family, and he'll go running home. Be careful. If he's working with the FBI, it's real bad news."

"Careful's my middle name," Zeb said, breaking the connection.

Two giggling broads shouldered their way past him, on the way to the women's john. One of them gave him a curious look. Damn, he was getting as paranoid as Fillmore, but too many people in the restaurant knew what he looked like. He'd pay his bill and scrap the plans for the last two firebombs. Leave the knapsack shoved under his table. Clear this fucking town fast.

Rachel watched the arson dog sniff at the flowerboxes in front of the restaurant. Boxes dripping with colorful blossoms were everywhere, the air heavy with their sweet scent. She'd never seen anything like the way flowers loved the climate in Vail. Flowers decorated every shop and restaurant; beds of blooms were planted beside the curbs, baskets hung from balconies. Any other time she would have stopped to admire and enjoy. Not tonight. The lush vegetation furnished too many places to conceal an innocuous-looking shoebox.

Puma prowled restlessly by her side, forcefully reminding her of his namesake. To date, the searchers had located seven firebombs. God knew how many others were out there.

The dog jerked at his leash, anxious to move on. "Nothing here," the handler announced. "Darby would have picked up on it. Where to now, Frank?"

Frank Capote paused. "Let's split up and check the alley behind the restaurant. Sweet Basil's one of the town's most popular places to eat. It's an obvious target. People will be hanging out here until midnight."

"Good plan," Puma agreed. "Rachel and I'll sweep one side, you guys the other. We'll meet at the end."

"Roger that." The handler whistled at his dog, and he moved toward the alley.

The restaurant door swung open. A crowd of laughing customers departed, shouting good-natured jibes at each other. They stared at Rachel and her partners. Curious faces, but not alarmed.

"Let's go," Rachel said. "We're attracting attention."

"I'll meet you there. Give me a minute." Puma lifted his gaze to the steady stream of people passing them by.

"What is it?" Rachel asked.

"Something."

A shout from the restaurant doorway spun them both on

their heels. A waiter stood at the doorway, holding a knapsack. She and Puma moved simultaneously.

The waiter jumped at their speedy approach. "Hey, you see a guy leave here just now? Short and scrawny. Had a mustache and shoulder-length hair. Wearing a red plaid shirt. He left this behind."

"The knapsack," Puma said tersely. "What's in it?"

"Dunno. Guy threw a fifty on the table and split in a hurry. That's a thirty percent tip. Thought the least I could do was try to catch up with him. Hey!"

Puma snagged the knapsack from the kid's fingers. Unzipped it fast. Swore. Two shoeboxes inside.

"Look, that belongs to a customer. Give it back or I call my manager."

Rachel stepped in front of the waiter, who glared at her with open hostility. "FBI," she said tersely, holding up her badge. "How long ago did this man leave?"

The waiter shrugged. "Maybe five minutes. Maybe ten. Can't say for sure, but he left a full beer behind. What's going on?"

"Go back inside," Rachel said, keeping her voice calm, her heart racing with tension. "Stay by the door. No one can leave until we give the all clear. Understood?"

"Hey, I get it. This is part of that drill the mayor announced. Was that guy some kind of phony terrorist? A plant?"

"That's right," Rachel said. "Want to help us out?"

"Sure," the kid said, nodding eagerly. "What do I tell people who want to leave?"

"Offer them a free drink," Rachel suggested, giving him a wink. "On the mayor."

"My manager will have a zit fit. I love it." The kid grinned and disappeared inside the restaurant.

Puma used his radio and snapped off an all-call for any bomb squad member available. Rachel radioed Hooker with the suspect's description. Capote, the dog and his handler appeared from the alley, breaking speed records. The dog approached the knapsack at Puma's feet, sniffed and sat, quivering from nose to tail.

"The nearest water? A stream? Anything." Puma threw the question at Frank. "Away from these tourists."

The Vail cop understood immediately. "There's a fountain a block from here. Runs until midnight. We'll clear the people out."

He took off, barking in his radio, calling for backup. They followed, Puma carrying the knapsack as carefully as a newborn babe. The fountain spumed arcs of water into the night air; a circle of spotlights turned the spray into silver shards. Puma sank both boxes in the brimming basin. Rachel's muscles relaxed. Until the bomb squad arrived, it was the best they could do.

The dog handler and Frank Capote herded the spectators away from the scene. Two more VPD jackets appeared and began to string yellow crime scene tape around the fountain perimeter. The nearby pedestrians gawked and shouted questions, but none tried to breech the tape.

"I'll stay and watch the package," Rachel said. "You guys keep on with the search. There may be more."

Puma gave her a look that said forget it.

Her radio hummed. "Cortez," Hooker said. "Is the problem taken care of?"

"Under control. We're in the town square. Two packages, soaking in the fountain."

"That leaves three unaccounted for. We put out the suspect's description. We'll find him. Let me talk to Puma."

"He's busy. Can I pass it on?"

"Leave the cops on the scene, and you and Puma get back here. We've got a situation."

CHAPTER 26

Zeb made his way out of the town center, walking with steady purpose. Vail Village was strictly foot traffic. No motorized vehicles allowed except in an emergency, and he'd parked his wheels in one of the city lots. Groups of laughing, chattering tourists passed him, jostling for space on the pathway. He was just part of the crowd.

Oh, oh. Not so good.

Ahead, emergency lights were blinking with red-eyed ferocity. A fire truck. Maybe a roadblock? He slowed his pace but kept on walking. Another group of pedestrians passed, and he joined the tail end, keeping pace. They were too self-involved to notice. The crowd's pace slowed by the fire truck that was parked slantwise across the street. After a glance, the firemen waved them through. Zeb could breathe again.

He pushed around his fellow hikers and crossed the footbridge that spanned Gore Creek, his recent dinner a lump in his gut, expecting a spotlight to drill his back at any second. The tiered parking lot was thinning out as people drove away. A couple coming up behind him shouted noisy farewells to their friends, and headed for their vehicle. Zeb stayed behind until their taillights disappeared down the off-ramp.

Everything from Hummers to BMWs to inexpensive family sedans was parked between the painted lines. Glancing around to be sure he was alone, he shucked the plaid lumberman's shirt and stuffed it into one of the plastic garbage bags he kept in his SUV, along with the false mustache and blond wig he'd worn while going about business. He scratched at his close-shaved scalp, relieved to have the sweaty wig gone.

Dressed in knee-length walking shorts and a plain black tee shirt, he climbed into the SUV and scuffed into a pair of ratty sneakers. All of his equipment, some of which he would miss sorely, would have to go. It took him a few more minutes to unload everything. When he was done two garbage bags were full and his car was clean. He used a battery-powered hand vac to suck up the residue on the carpet, and ditched the vacuum.

The only refuse left in the car was a half-empty cup of cold coffee sitting in the cup holder, and a crumpled hamburger wrapper in the trash bucket. Genius touch, he thought. A too-clean car might rouse suspicions, and a dog sniffing at a hamburger wrapper was normal enough. He stuffed the bags into a nearby garbage bin. He'd used up precious time, but it was stupid to take chances, and he was for damn sure on his own now.

He eased down the off-ramp, driving slowly, his eyes alert behind wire-rimmed spectacles. In addition to the phony eyeglasses, blue contact lenses camouflaged myopic brown eyes. What was best about the disguise was it wasn't a disguise at all. With the exception of eye color, it was who he was.

None of his clients, not even Fillmore had seen Zeb without his stringy blond wig and false mustache. He had nice clothes, but never wore them when he was working. Zeb's clients considered him a skuzzy lowlife, and that was fine. No one had any idea he owned a modest condo in the Cherry Creek area of Denver. His neighbors thought he was a salesman who traveled a lot and kept to himself.

He swung onto South Frontage Road and headed for I70. An ambulance passed him, its seesaw siren screaming.

Emergency drill, my ass. Zeb knew when he was being hunted. He debated whether to turn onto one of the roads that crisscrossed the main highway and led to nature trails and campgrounds. He could stick to the back trails until he stumbled onto a lone camper, take the guy out and extract his supplies. Properly equipped, Zeb could hide in the woods for the rest of the summer. Or he could return to the isolated cabin he'd rented. If he didn't light a fire, no one would suspect the dump was occupied by anything more dangerous than a field mouse. Good alternate plans, but I70 was his best bet for a quick and safe escape.

He braked sharply. More flashing lights. *Roadblock.* State Troopers were checking each car. Several vehicles were stopped ahead of him, and one immediately pulled up behind him. His hands shook on the steering wheel. He could smell his own odor, strong and ferret-like, his scent glands working overtime.

The line of cars inched forward a car length. There were four ahead of him. He could abandon the SUV and make a run for it. Stupid idea. They'd have him in seconds. He'd have to bluff his way through the roadblock. His mind raced. Had he dumped everything that could incriminate him? The only weapon he carried was the switchblade knife stowed under the front seat. The same knife he'd used to slice the janitor's throat.

Fillmore's orders: "Get rid of the old geezer. When he figures out why we hired him to scout the place, he'll blab to the cops."

Not that Zeb wouldn't have done it anyway. The janitor had a good look at him, and Zeb didn't like loose ends. Thinking ahead, he'd prepared the explosive light bulb, a primitive but efficient deathtrap, and Zeb would be long gone before the blast went off. Unfortunately the old guy had spotted Zeb climbing back down the ladder, grabbed him and pulled the wig askew. Zeb took care of the immediate problem of the janitor, and pressed for time, had left the tampered light bulb in place. Anyone who got nosy would be cancelled, along with the evidence.

Cops didn't like knives.

He had to get rid of it.

He'd washed the blood from his shirt and hands and knife in the janitor's sink, but forensics could detect even a trace of blood. He daren't toss it out the window. Too much chance he'd be seen. Casually he opened the vehicle door and stepped out, leaving the motor running, the knife wrapped loosely in a handkerchief and clasped to his right side.

"Hey!" Zeb shouted at the troopers. "What's holding us up?" Behind the concealment of the door, he let the knife slip to the ground and kicked it under the car.

Two troopers broke from the front of the line and started his way. The lead officer touched his hat in deference, but his face was impatient. "Get back in the car, please, sir. You'll have to wait your turn."

"For what? I can't sit here all night."

"Just a routine traffic stop. We'll move along as fast as possible."

"I'll bet you're looking for drugs," Jeb said, putting petulance in his voice. "No drugs here, boys. Search away."

"We have your permission to search your vehicle, sir?" Both men gave him an eye sweep. Their hard stare told him what they were thinking. His cargo shorts, tight tee shirt and sockless tennis shoes couldn't hide much. Certainly not a weapon.

Zeb grinned cockily. "Hell, yes. Just get to it, will you?"

"Would you pull over to the side and vacate your vehicle, sir? We need to see your license and registration." The head trooper was doing the talking. The other one just stood there, looking tough and stupid. Grumbling, Zeb returned to the driver's seat and gunned the engine, an irate citizen who wanted to be on his way. The troopers stepped back, their faces impassive, but each had a hand resting lightly on their weapon.

As soon as Zeb pulled out, the jeep Cherokee next in line drove into the vacated space, the knife invisible under the blocky van. Even if the cops found it later, they'd never know where it had come from.

Good work, Zeb. Cops're so damn dumb.

All he had to do was remain cool and things would be fine. Zeb stepped out of his SUV and silently handed the first policeman his driver's license. It was a phony provided by Fillmore. So was the car registration.

Trooper Two took the registration and started back to the patrol car. To call the number in. Didn't matter. The car had been purchased legally and was registered to the name on the phony license. Time to make some conversation with Trooper One.

"Busy night," Zeb said.

A grunt and a nod.

Behind them, one of the cars in line gave an impatient beep. "Guess I'm not the only one in a hurry," Zeb ventured.

The cop gave a bare nod. "Everyone's in a hurry. Mind telling me where you're headed, sir?"

Zeb's mind raced. If he said Denver, the cop might ask follow-up questions. He might remember later. "I've rented a condo for the week," he answered. "Getting in a little R&R and some fly fishing."

Too late he remembered he'd told the waiter in the restaurant the same story. Fuck.

"Good fishing this time of year," the cop said neutrally. "Where're you renting?"

Always stick to as much of the truth as possible when telling a lie. "Couple miles down Bighorn Road," Zeb answered swiftly. More like six miles. And nowhere near Bighorn Road. "Cheapo accommodations, but good enough. I kinda enjoy roughing it. You know, get away from the wife and kids. Don't have to shave or shower unless I feel like it. Eat some good grub for a change."

The cop twisted his mouth into a parody of a smile. "Sounds like a fine vacation. Here comes my partner."

The man's partner handed back Zeb's license and registration. "You're good to go, sir, after we search the vehicle."

Another officer stepped into the headlights, a Doberman

police dog on a leash. God, he hated dogs. This one stopped dead at the trainer's command, his ears laid back, fur standing up on his neck, a low whine directed at Zeb. The handler spoke sharply and opened the car door. The dog leaped in, sniffed at Zeb's duffle bag and fishing gear.

Trooper Two handed Trooper One a sheet of paper. "Just came in, Jerry. The FBI worked up a composite."

Zeb forced his body to stay loose. His eyes darted to the paper as it was exchanged from one cop to the other. He caught a glimpse of a sketch. A longhaired man with a mustache, wearing a plaid shirt. Bulbous nose and thick brows. Sweat trickled down his face. The damn waiter! The FBI had made him, and the kid had worked with a police artist to come up with an identity sketch. Thank God he'd taken time to change his appearance. Other than the nose, the man in the sketch didn't resemble Zeb much. He pulled off his wire-rims and wiped his face and balding head with his handkerchief. "How much longer, officers?"

"Vehicle's clean, boys," the trainer announced.

The head cop took a look at the sketch and then at Zeb. Nodded. "You may go, sir. Have a nice vacation and we're sorry for the delay."

"Hey, you're doing your job," Zeb said, giving the guy a mock salute. "As a citizen, I appreciate that."

The cop winced and stepped away. "You'll need to reverse your vehicle, sir. Bighorn is the first turn to the right."

The trooper would watch to be sure Zeb took the turn. The choice had been made for him. He'd have to go back to the cabin.

Rachel entered the second floor courtroom that Hooker had set aside for a command center, Puma close on her heels. Her boss looked rumpled, no jacket or tie, shirttail untucked. He and the police chief stood beside an enlarged map that had been tacked to a wall. An aerial view of Vail. Red pushpins dotted the map. She counted nine. The already located firebombs.

"How can you be sure there're only three packages unaccounted for?" she asked, approaching the two men.

Hooker gave her a quick glance. "We've had a breakthrough," he said. "You and Puma come with me. There's something you both need to hear."

He spoke a quiet word to his agents, asked them to keep him posted of any developments, picked up a small recording device and motioned to Puma and Rachel to follow him out the room. Rachel had a creepy feeling. It was unusual for Hooker to act so strangely. He seemed—Rachel searched for the word—harassed? Troubled? Not his usual in-command self at all. Why leave the room? Why the hand recorder?

Hooker led them to the end of the hall corridor, pushed open a door and snapped on the light. It was a small conference room furnished with a ten-foot table, surrounded by folding chairs. A water cooler, whiteboard at the far end, overhead projector on a stand. No windows. Harsh fluorescent lights. Nothing comfortable about the space.

Without comment, Puma reversed one of the chairs and straddled it, his complete attention on Hooker. Rachel elected to sit in the conventional manner. She wiped sweaty palms on her jeans, a knot growing in her stomach.

"The news is good and bad," Hooker said and gestured at the recorder. "We've had a listening device and a trace on both of Chic Fillmore's cell phones for weeks."

"This is the guy Rachel and I ran into at the bar?" Puma asked. "The one in the photo?"

"Yes. The current New Sons leader. Fillmore takes a call, listens to a coded message, hangs up fast and finds a land phone to return it. We've been unable to pinpoint his location. Tonight he took a chance and answered an urgent call from his cohort, our firebug. Fillmore's call was traced to the Springs."

"You discovered his identity?" Rachel exclaimed.

"Not exactly," Hooker answered, frowning at the interruption. "But no question the contact was from the man behind the shoebox devices, and it came from the Sweet Basil restaurant. Where the man is now is anybody's guess. We've mounted a full search." He ran his fingers through the brown stubble of his hair.

"Whatever this is about, Dan," Puma said. "Let's have it."

"Yeah," Hooker said, returning the other man's steady gaze. "The thing is, I owe you an apology, Puma. I made a misjudgment. I promise you, I'm doing my best to fix it. Dammit to hell, I will fix it."

The vise in Rachel's stomach tightened. Hooker never swore. "Dan," she whispered. "What have you done?"

"The thing is," Puma said softly, "I'd guess you're part of it, rookie. It's late to play the innocent."

Rachel bit back the irritation. She'd just been doing her job. "What happened?"

"Listen to the recording, please," Hooker interrupted. "We'll discuss this later." He switched on the recorder.

"I'll smoke the Indian out—hit his family—he'll go running home—he's working with the FBI—bad news—ten packages in place—"

Puma was on his feet and headed for the door before the last of the tape ran down. Rachel froze to her chair. Oh, God, Puma's family! She'd not considered they might be pulled into Hooker's web.

"Hold up, Ansari!" Hooker rapped out the order. "Let us do our job. I know it sounds bad, but we're handling it."

Puma turned. His eyes blazed, and Rachel had never seen him look more dangerous. "You FBI asshole. This is my family you've involved in your games. I volunteered for this duty and can take care of myself, but my aunt and uncle are old and defenseless. Their only protection from these psychopaths is my ranch hand, and Sully is barely out of high school."

"Agents are on the way to your place as we speak."

"I wouldn't trust your agents to protect a Barbie doll!" Puma stepped closer. "Have you contacted my home? At least warned them to get out?"

Hooker winced. "We called. No answer. We'll keep trying, Puma, but they likely aren't on the premises. I've sent agents to check."

"I want transportation out of here. And fast. Think of it as a way to save your worthless hide. I swear to God, if anything happens to them, there isn't a hole deep enough for you to hide in."

"Transportation is arranged. One of our cars will take you to the county airport. Our helicopter is waiting."

"How long have you had the tape?"

Hooker gestured helplessly. "Maybe half-an-hour."

"And I'd guess it was made, when? An hour ago? Two?"

"No more than an hour. Puma, I swear I had no idea this would happen. We've had no indication he'd try anything like this."

Rachel felt sick. She'd never told Dan about the dog. If Dan had known Sundance was poisoned, maybe he'd have given Puma warning.

"An hour ago," Puma echoed. "And Fillmore is in Colorado Springs, less than an hour's drive to my ranch. How long have you known this, and why would he attack helpless old people? Why is he after me?" Puma exploded into a string of curses.

Rachel spoke. "Tell him, Dan. If you won't I will."

Puma turned his attention on her, his gaze black and fathomless, empty. "Too late. I wouldn't believe a word Hooker's flunky said."

He despised her. She couldn't blame him. She'd been secretive too long. "Fillmore hates you because you killed his brother."

"What the hell does that mean? What brother?"

Hooker stood silent and Rachel plunged on. At this point she no longer cared about the consequences. "His brother was in the pickup that you shot up last year. The one that the terrorists were driving during the Hoover Dam terrorist threat. Fillmore was one of the co-conspirators, and the FBI has been using you for bait to draw him out of hiding."

"Bait? With my aunt and uncle? Damn you all to hell."

She shrugged helplessly. What could she say?

He looked at her with absolute contempt and turned his attention back to Hooker. "Is the car waiting?"

Hooker nodded.

Rachel stepped forward. "I'm going along. I'll tell you everything I know."

"No!" Both men spoke at once.

Hooker's face was haunted. Rachel's fear deepened. Her boss thought the LeChats were already dead. Rachel jabbed her finger at him. She was likely reassigned to Fargo, North Dakota, anyway. "I go along, or we don't give Ansari transportation. He'd never get there in time."

Puma snarled a vile malediction. If he hadn't hated her before, he surely did now.

Hooker nodded. "It's best she goes along, Puma. We'll give you all the assistance we can. That's my word on it."

Puma pulled the revolver from his belt. "You can have this piece of crap back. I want a semi-automatic rifle. Night vision goggles for both of us. And a 10mm. FBI issue. Yours will do fine."

Again, Hooker nodded, removed his shoulder holster and Glock from under his arm and handed it over. Rachel couldn't believe it. Her boss could be fired over that action alone.

"You've got it," Hooker said. "I'll see the rifle and goggles are aboard the copter. And ammunition. Anything else?"

"A copter isn't fast enough. Get me a light plane. Two parachutes. Ever do a night jump, Cortez?"

"No." She shook her head. "But I can do it."

"Good. A plane landing would be heard, and I plan to go in quietly." He jerked his head toward the door. "I'm out of here. You coming or not?"

She was. Her head cleared. It seemed they were going to war. In this, she wouldn't fail him.

CHAPTER 27

Hooker sat slumped over his laptop, the bustle around him merely an annoying hum in the background. Once again, he flicked through his files on Code Devilfish. Someone, someone with access to limitless funds, was running the New Sons, using the militants to their own end.

There were too many inconsistencies with the usual nutcase militia profile. The vast amount of money being spent on bribes, for one thing. The New Sons didn't have that kind of money. Nor did they have the organizational skill required to mount last year's attempted attack on Hoover Dam. That one had been a near thing. The recent arson incidents? Not militia style at all. Again, very organized and extremely difficult to stop.

Fillmore was a flunky. The arsonist was hired help. Who was behind this? Rumors of a secret Arabic society with 13th century roots had reached the Bureau over a year before. Not al-Qaida. This was no ragtag group of wild-eyed loonies. There were no inflammatory propaganda speeches on television, no suicide bombers eager to visit Allah and earn their seventy-two virgins, no shouting crowds thronging the streets and mobbing embassies. No YouTube postings of beheadings.

These people were subtle. They wielded blackmail and

bribery more effectively than a sword. Hooker was convinced the motivation behind the group was economic. Control the money supply and you control the world. Keep the United States government busy protecting its interests at home, and it would be forced to back off from meddling in Middle East affairs.

Hooker prided himself on staying cool under pressure, but he was frustrated. He was nowhere near chopping off the head of the Devilfish whose tentacles had even reached into the Bureau. He wanted to slam his fist into something. They had to find the threads and follow the trail backward. The firebug and Fillmore were their only leads.

Over a hundred men and women on the job, and still their quarry had vanished. The FBI Swat team, bomb squad and a dozen agents were working with local cops. The Vail police chief was coordinating the efforts of the State Patrol, the local police, fire, and sheriff departments. Where had the man gotten too? If he slipped through the roadblocks, he'd disappear for good.

Hooker glanced at his watch. Two hours since Rachel and Puma had left. By now they would be landing near Puma's ranch. He shook off a stab of apprehension. But he hadn't gotten where he was by second-guessing himself. Ansari was a warrior, one of the best. If Fillmore was anywhere near the ranch, Puma would find him. Rachel was a good agent, cool and competent. Hooker hoped his confidence in her wasn't misplaced. She had orders to bring Fillmore back alive, and Puma might have other ideas.

Rachel would have backup. Ash Calloway had dispatched agents from the Denver office. Matter-of-factly, Hooker accepted the fact that his career was on the line. Forty years old and all his adult life he'd worked at the Bureau. Not a good age to start over. If the operation blew up in his face, if he couldn't justify his methods, he'd be asked to resign. Without pension or severance pay. Probably Ash as well, and Rachel would surely be axed. Even worse, Puma's family could be harmed, an outcome that he hadn't foreseen and it haunted him.

"Agent Hooker?"

"Yeah?" He turned to face the Vail police chief. The man was obviously bursting with some news.

"A break," the chief said, grinning. "We found the knife."

"The knife that killed the janitor?"

"Looks like. Forensics matched the blood type. We need to do further DNA tests."

"Any prints?"

"That's the best part. The weapon's been run over dozens of times. Looks like it was tossed from a vehicle. But they found a partial. We're running it through the national crime data base."

"If that means the perp got by your roadblock, I don't find anything good about that scenario, chief."

"There was one guy the troopers didn't like the smell of. Guess he was a real smartass. But his car was clean, nothing but fishing gear and some clothing. He didn't resemble the sketch we've been circulating. Bald. No mustache and wore glasses. His license and registration checked out, so they let him through. You can't hold a guy because you don't like his attitude."

Hooker bit back a curse. He should have had his own people running the roadblock, but they were already spread too thin. "Did this man drop the knife?"

The grin became even wider. "He did. I told you the troopers didn't like the guy's looks? One of them lifted some latents off of the driver's license. The prints match."

"God in heaven! And they let him get away?"

"Take it up with the troopers. You don't feel any worse than they do."

Hooker reached for his jacket, rapidly adjusting his plans. "I want an all-out search mounted for this man. Maybe there're two of them working as a team. Get the sketch artist to work with those troopers."

"There's more. My men found this." The chief hefted a bulging plastic bag. "And another like it, stuffed in the trash bin in one of the parking lots. I figured you'd want to send it on to Denver. Your forensics lab is top drawer, and ours isn't. There's a box of what looks like tools and equipment suitable to rig a firebomb. And someone dumped clothing and a set of boots. Long-sleeved plaid shirt, medium. Size-eight hiking boots."

Hooker's pulse hammered. It was plodding investigative work that usually broke a case. "Drop the other shoe, chief."

"A blonde wig and false mustache." The chief couldn't keep the glee out of his voice. Obviously the chance to one-up the FBI was too rich not to crow over. "That means the sketch you guys worked up ain't worth Shinola."

Fuck it. This case continued to be one step forward and two steps back. "We're looking for one man then. I assume the troopers got the license tag. Did they get a good look at the bald guy? Enough to work up another sketch?"

"Not just a look. They got him on tape. All troopers' vehicles are fitted with video cameras." The chief pulled a USB flash drive from his pocket. "Want to run it?"

Zeb drove the last mile with extreme care, watching his back, his headlights switched off. He was pretty sure the cabin lay beyond the next turn in the trail. A trip that should have taken half an hour had been never-ending. Just because the State Patrol let him pass, didn't mean he was home free. It could be days before the roadblock was lifted, and once his shoebox mechanisms started popping, the hunt would be intensified. It annoyed him he couldn't be there to see the burning he considered his masterpiece.

He'd made it. He drove into the rough clearing and parked. After tonight, even this hole wouldn't be safe. He'd pack out in the morning. Dump the SUV in a gully where it wouldn't be found for a while, maybe ever. There were a few supplies stowed in the cabin kitchen, canned goods, flour and coffee. He'd steal a couple of blankets. With his fishing gear and a compass, he could hide in the mountains for weeks. He'd learned to live in the woods when he was a kid, and some things you don't forget.

Zeb climbed out, reached for his duffle bag and slung it over his shoulder. His body ached from the effort of staying alert. He needed some shuteye the worst way. Even sacking out on one of the lumpy bunk beds sounded good.

A twig snapped. Behind him.

Zeb went stiff. Listened. Nothing. Just a night creature. The air was strange, heavy with fog. Almost viscous. No stars. The quarter moon had disappeared behind a dark cloud. He risked turning on his flashlight. Pine needles crunched under his feet, their sharp odor seeping into his nostrils. The cabin squatted a few yards ahead of him, just as he remembered it, derelict and deserted. In the days he had stayed there, Zeb hadn't seen another human being. Tonight the place seemed sinister. Dark as a nightmare.

He shivered, his skin gone clammy. Someone had walked over his grave, as his old man would've said. Now where had that come from? His old man—what a loser. *Get a grip, Zeb.* You got away clean. Nothing wrong with you a hot shower and some sleep won't take care of. Yeah, a hot shower sounded good.

He didn't dare risk a fire. The smoky scent of burning wood would drift for miles. But he could light the propane water heater. Thank God something in the dump worked. He hadn't bothered to lock the place up when he left. Nothing in there worth stealing.

He shoved open the door, the harsh screech of rusty hinges paining his ears, like the sound of a fingernail scraping a chalkboard. Damn, he was jumpy. He dropped his duffle bag by the door and flicked the flashlight beam over the dingy room. The fog had drifted into the cabin. One of the burlap curtains was slightly ajar, ruffling in the night breeze. He must've left a window open; no wonder the place was damp and cold. He shut the window with a bang, anxious to get to that hot shower. The light of the moon streamed through the dirty glass panes. The night chill had seeped into his bones.

He shivered again, and made his way to the alcove that housed the water heater. It was a small tank, maybe thirty gallons, so it would heat up fast after he lit the pilot. He snapped on his flashlight and reached for his box of matches. Wait. He stopped in puzzlement. The gas valve for the heater was twisted to the open position, but he knew he'd shut it off before he left. He knelt to look, his light beamed toward the boiler burner. The rotten egg odor of escaping gas stung his nostrils. *What the hell?*

An ominous sound pricked his ears, like the clicking of claws on a hard surface. Was that a snarl? Every hair on Zeb's body lifted. Jesus, some animal searching for food had crawled in through the open window. He swung the flashlight toward the sound. A big cat squatted on the kitchen counter looking down at him; its eyes glowed red in the flash beam, a rumble of warning vibrated his throat. Zeb had come across a mountain lion or two in the past, but this was the biggest he'd ever seen, not twelve feet away and crouched to attack. The animal bared his teeth.

Zeb screamed. The flashlight clattered to the floor. Winked out, stranding him in moonlit dark with the killer cat. *His matches!* Cougars were afraid of fire. He fumbled the matchbox open with shaking hands. No need to panic. He'd been the master of fire all his life. Fire would save him.

Another snarl from the beast. Closer, this time. The fetid odor of feral breath.

Jeb's terror betrayed him. The box slipped from his fingers, its contents spilling helter-skelter onto the floor. *Get it together, Zeb! You know what to do.* Stealthily, he retrieved several of the wooden sticks. These weren't safety matches. These were strike anywhere matches, and one of the arsonist's favorite accessories, a tool of the trade that was always in his pocket. *Okay, fur ball. Take some of this.*

Zeb flicked one of the matches with his thumbnail and tossed the burning stick toward the crouching menace. And two more. Another. He didn't care if the shit-box cabin burned to the ground. All he needed was a brief distraction, and time enough to escape to his SUV. The wooden matches ignited with a flash of phosphorus and sulfur and dropped to the ground, caught the tattered carpet.

Too late, Zeb remembered the rotten egg odor escaping the water tank, and what it meant. The flames spread and leapt toward the leaking gas line. No stopping it now. *Run!* Zeb caught a glimpse of tawny fur streaking in his direction before the firestorm exploded, engulfing the cabin in blinding fury. Powerful jaws clamped his throat; the metallic taste of his own blood gushed into his mouth.

Burning. There would be a burning.

CHAPTER 28

━━━◆━━━

They dove from the plane strapped together, Puma's hard chest pressed against her back, his arms and legs wrapped around her body. The air was cold, a deep, biting cold. Humiliation kept her warm. His insistence they jump tandem meant he still thought of her as a rookie. They landed in a high pasture overlooking the ranch grounds. With the stars buried behind black clouds it was difficult to acclimate visually, even with the aid of night goggles. They might have floated into the end of the world.

Puma stuffed their collapsed parachute under some brush, along with his jump gear. "Leave everything behind except your weapon, radio and flashlight. We need to travel light and fast. It's about a quarter-mile hike."

She stripped off her gear down to her black FBI jacket and black sweat pants, and added it to the pile. They both wore bulletproof vests under their jackets.

"Turn your jacket inside out so the monogram doesn't show," he said. "No need to advertise."

He pulled off his own jacket, and for the first time she saw the knife. Sheathed in a leather scabbard, it hung on a cord at the back of his neck. Not a combat knife, but a slender blade balanced for throwing. Razor-sharp. He tucked it behind his shirt collar, where it lay completely hidden and slipped the jacket back on.

She reached to touch the hidden scabbard. "This isn't standard issue."

"No." His teeth flashed white in a grimace that wasn't exactly a smile. "A throwback to my ancestry. Belonged to my grandfather. It's come in handy at times." She withdrew her hand quickly. In combat, he meant. Where he was a trained killing machine. Rachel had been in some dicey situations, but had never fired her weapon at anyone, had never killed. She wondered if she could. It was a question everyone in the Bureau had to answer eventually. In a life or death situation, could you kill? "Are you sure Fillmore will show?"

"You know more about the man than I do. What do you think?" He settled Hooker's nylon shoulder holster over the jacket.

He wasn't being caustic. He really wanted her opinion. She ran her memory over the dossier she'd read on the militant. "My impression is he's more tenacious than bright. He hates you. I'd guess he'll show."

"Alone?"

She wasn't sure. She chose her words carefully. "Probably. From what we know, his dead brother was his only immediate family. His heritage is backwoods Ozarkian, and big on 'an eye for an eye'. He's set himself up as the brother's avenger."

"Nice to know, Cortez. Since the Bureau involved me in Fillmore's vendetta, and there was an oversight in informing me of it."

Now that was caustic. "I've apologized. I'm here, and Hooker is sending backup."

"We move in quietly and communicate with hand signals," Puma said, ignoring her protest. "Stay close to me. Since no one's answering the phone, my family must be gone. I hope to God they are. We'll circle the grounds after we recon the houses. If we get separated, use your radio. If we spot Fillmore, you hang back and cover me. If he's not here, we hunker down and wait."

Rachel hesitated. "Puma, I have to be there when you take him."

"No. Hang back, cover me, and I'll bring you in when it's over. It's not what you're best at, but in a combat situation, you follow orders."

The problem is, whose orders?

"And I will." *Maybe.* "But we want this man alive, Puma."

"So do I. More than you do. Let's move out."

He cradled his rifle and took off in a slow trot, instantly all-military. Dispassionate. Cool and deadly. And very, very alert. If she were on the wrong end of that purposeful intent, she'd be panicked as hell. She slid her pistol from her holster, checked that there was a round in the chamber, returned it to her belt and followed.

Nearing the house, they went down on their bellies, moving from one clump of scrubby growth to another. The wet grass quickly soaked through her sweats. The wind was raw and the air dense with night fog. Puma led the way, crawling military style on his knees and elbows, his M40 held level in front of his body. He moved soundlessly. Worming on her stomach behind him, Rachel followed his wake.

The fog lifted as they approached the edge of the ranch grounds, and pale moonlight broke through the low clouds. Their night goggles bathed the surroundings in a hue of green. The bungalow lay a hundred yards beyond, outlined in brooding silence. No lights shone, not even the yard light. Sully's trailer was dark. Since it was past midnight, none of that was alarming, but there was a strange car parked in the driveway. A black sedan, a Chrysler. The door on the passenger side was ajar; the interior dimly lit.

Something was very wrong. Had Fillmore gotten there ahead of them? If so, where were Frank and Lindy? And Sully?

She crawled to Puma's side and tapped him on the shoulder. He clamped a hand over her mouth. "Shh." His voice was a soft hiss against her ear. "Someone's hiding in the scrub just ahead."

She froze. Not only did he move like a cat, he had the ears of one. Puma lay aside his weapon and crawled away. She went to her knees and listened, her pistol out, her nerves fried in the electric silence. A thud. Cursing. Thrashing in the brush. Rachel shot to her feet, weapon at the ready, and leapt toward the ongoing fray. Two male figures were rolling on the rough ground. Puma and who else? Fillmore? An impossible shot. She crouched in the classic shooting stance, her left hand steadying her right.

"You! Stand down or you're dead!" she shouted. "I've got your back, Puma."

Puma rolled to the top, his weight pinning his opponent to the ground. He was furious and ready to kill. No one threatened his home, his family. It hadn't been much of a fight. The man wasn't Fillmore; he was slight and thin. Muscled, but not the blocky build of the man Puma had taken down during the parking lot altercation a few weeks back. He vised one hand over the man's throat, poised and fisted the other. "I've got him. Make one move, you bastard, and I'll snap your neck."

"Puma?" The voice came out cracked and rasping under Puma's unrelenting grip. "Jesus, boss, ease up."

"Sully?" Shocked, Puma let go and came to his knees. "What the hell?"

Rolling away, Sully took labored, shuddering breaths. A part of Puma's brain registered their surroundings, saw a flat depression in the grass, a twenty-two rifle lying nearby. His ranch hand had been hunkered down in the area for some time. Puma fumbled for his water bottle and extended it.

The younger man took a swig and found his breath. "Jesus, man, you near choked me to death."

"Sorry. What are you doing here, Sully? Where are Frank and Lindy?"

"In Pueblo, visiting your sister, Leona, and her two kids. They took off yesterday and won't be back for a couple days. Left me in charge of the livestock. Frank told Devlin's guys to take a break." Sully gave another strangling cough.

Thank the gods. He wasn't too late. Puma rocked back on his heels, his night vision glasses sweeping the ranch yard. "That's good news. What's going on? What about that car parked next to the house?"

"It's been real bad, Puma. I don't know where to begin."

"The car," Puma prodded patiently. The kid was obviously scared to death. "Whose is it? Why is it here?"

The heavy goggles were beginning to steam up. He yanked them off, pinched the bridge of his nose and wiped his brow. Despite the night chill, he was sweating.

"I think they were cops."

"Were?" Rachel holstered her weapon and knelt beside the two men. She grabbed Sully by the shoulders and shook his slight frame. "What do you mean were?"

"Is that you, Rachel? You guys look like giant bugs, wearing those weird glasses. Where'd you come from anyway?"

Rachel pulled off her glasses, breathing hard. She grabbed the kid again. "What happened to the people in the sedan?"

Sully swallowed, his Adam's apple bobbing. "This guy. I think he shot them."

Rachel shook harder. "You think! What guy!"

Puma pulled her hands from the kid's shaking shoulders. "Rachel, give him a chance. What happened, Sully?"

"I was asleep in the trailer, but not sound asleep, ya' know? I'd watched the Late Show on TV, and with Frank and Lindy gone—"

"Dammit, Sully! Get on with it." Dread was tightening in Rachel's stomach.

"I heard a car drive around the side of the barn. I thought Frank had come back, so I got up and looked out my window. He stood in the shadows, but I could see it was a stranger, and he was scoping out the house. A big guy. He was carrying a weapon. I pulled on my jeans and boots to go check him out. It was kinda creepy." His voice cracked as he glanced apologetically at Puma and Rachel.

"Why didn't you call Devlin on your extension phone? Or the sheriff?"

"I tried. There was no dial tone. And my cell needs charging."

Crap. The line had been cut. This just kept getting better. Puma's mind raced, considering possibilities. "What'd the guy look like?"

"Big shoulders. Six feet or better. I couldn't see his face, but he wore black leather pants and jacket."

"Fillmore," breathed Rachel.

"I didn't know what to do," Sully said. "So I crept inside the barn and climbed to the hayloft and looked out the big crack in the loft door. You know, where the boards are split and you can see the front of the house?"

Puma growled impatiently.

"Please, Sully," Rachel interjected, her voice desperate.

The young man shifted nervously. He swallowed. "Another car drove in. This one parked in front of your house. Two people got out. A man and a woman. They stood there a minute, talking, and then headed for the front door."

"You could see them from the barn loft? And the other intruder?" Puma asked.

"Pretty well. The big yard light was on. You know, the one set to go on at dusk and off at dawn?"

Puma nodded, and Sully swallowed again. "The big guy hid behind Lindy's butterfly bush. I could see his shadow move." He dropped his head, trembling. "He shot them. They both went down. The guy didn't move, but the woman crawled back to the car. She got the door open and climbed inside, but—", Sully's voice faltered.

"He cut her down," Puma said wearily. "At that range she never had a chance."

Sully nodded. "He walked over and shot them again, the gun set on rapid-fire. Left them in shreds. Then he laughed like he was loony and kind of danced around. Neither of them has moved since." Sully's lips quivered. "I never saw anything like it. I pissed my pants. I should've done something, but I was too scared."

Fucking hell, Puma was too late after all. Fury boiled in his gut. Icy fury.

Tears ran down the young man's face. "Jesus, Puma. He laughed! He killed those people and laughed!"

"Sully. Look, kid—" It could just as easily been Frank and Lindy lying dead on his doorstep, or Sully. Or God help him, Rachel. *You're a dead man,* Fillmore, you spawn of evil. I'll gut you like a trout. I'll cut out your black heart.

Rachel jumped to her feet, a Valkyrie ready to storm the enemy fortress. "They had to be the agents Hooker sent. I'm going after the asshole that did it."

Puma pulled her back down. "Yes, you will. And so will I. But we're going to do this the smart way. Is he holed up in the house, Sully?"

"I think so. He shot out the yard light afterwards, and I couldn't see exactly where he went. It was too dark."

"How did you get a hold of Frank's twenty-two?"

"Frank saw a big rat last week, so he left the twenty-two and a box of shells in the tack room in case the thieving critter came back. After the light went out, I waited a few minutes, took the gun and snuck out the back of the barn. Thought I'd—hell, don't know what I thought."

Puma put his arm around the shaking teenager, whose macho self-image had gone down the toilet that night. Sully was no match for Fillmore, and thank God he hadn't tried anything stupid, like going after the man with the twenty-two, a popgun compared the automatic weapon Fillmore was toting. "It's okay, Sully. But you should have gone for help. The man's a stone killer. He's no one you should mess with on your own."

The kid wiped moist eyes with his cuff. "But now you're here, we'll get him. Right, Puma?"

"Rachel and I will handle it. I want you to cut across the fields and get to John Denzell's place. Have him call the sheriff. And the FBI. Tell them what happened. If you hustle, you can make it in thirty minutes. Wait there. Don't you or John think of coming back here without help." He reached down, retrieved the twenty-two and handed it to Sully. "Take this. And be careful. There could be more than one of them."

Sully took the weapon. "I can help. I've shot plenty of rabbits with a twenty-two. I'm a pretty good shot, Puma."

And a nineteen-year-old boy. One who'd seen enough violence that night to last his lifetime. "No go, kid. I need someone to rouse the law."

"Don't you have your cell? Does Rachel?"

Puma shook his head. "We left them behind. All we have are our radios, and the range maxes out at two miles. You have to go for help."

The kid hesitated, his face giving him away. His loyalties were torn, but he really wanted to get the hell out of Dodge. "If you're sure."

"Go," Puma said gently. "Follow orders."

Sully took the pint-sized rifle and started off at a stumbling run. Two steps away, he tripped and fell flat on his face. Rachel heard the whoosh of air that left the teenager's chest, followed by the crack of the twenty-two. The sharp sound startled a hooting protest from an owl nested in a nearby tree, and the bird took flight toward the barn, its gliding wingspan outlined against the moonlight.

Sully came to his knees, gasping for breath. "Jesus, Puma. I'm sorry!"

Puma reached for the kid's jacket collar, and jerked him to his feet. Too harshly, Rachel thought.

"Get out of here, Sully," he hissed.

"Yeah." Sully hurriedly reached for the discharged gun. "I'm gone. And I'm real sorry, boss. Good thing that shot went wild."

Rachel watched Sully depart, more cautiously this time, and gave a shuddering sigh. "You think Fillmore heard the shot?"

"Anyone within a mile heard it. We've lost our edge. Stay three-feet behind me on my left flank, rookie. Have your gun ready and be careful."

She stiffened. "I'm always careful with my weapon. What now?"

"We'll circle the house and decide on the best entry. I go in and you cover me; you follow in five minutes. Remember, he'll be waiting."

CHAPTER 29

They skirted the split-log bungalow, staying in the shadows, and stopped behind the flowering shrub that Lindy referred to as her butterfly bush. The scene was a nightmare viewed through infrared lenses. The two downed agents lay bathed in green light, their bodies slumped into grotesque shapes. If she hadn't heard Sully's story, Rachel would have thought they were mannequins posing for a slasher movie. Their pooled blood reflected a green so dark it appeared black.

No sound or movement from the house.

She whispered into Puma's ear. "It's quiet."

"Too quiet."

"Maybe he left?"

Puma shook his head. "The night creatures tell a different story."

Night creatures? Then she got it. There were none of the normal night sounds. No crickets chirping. No feral rustlings in the brush. No owls calling. The animals knew a dangerous predator was abroad and had gone to ground.

"Wait here," he spoke softly. "I saw something move near the barn. I'll send two clicks on the radio when it's safe to proceed. One click means stay put."

She swiveled her head. She saw it. The wavering gleam

of a flashlight. It appeared for a second and was gone. From the confines of the barn, Dragon's whinny rang in the air, answered by alarmed nickering and hoofs shuffling, as his mares milled around the adjoining corral.

Puma slipped into the night. Rachel crouched behind the shelter of the juniper bushes, her weapon drawn. Time stretched into infinity. She cadence counted the time elapsed. Six minutes gone and no signal. Maybe she'd move forward a bit, to the thicket of scrub spruce that stood between Sully's trailer and the house. She shoved her gun back in its belt holster and stood. A moment later a shadow appeared beside her, and cold steel pressure dented the back of her neck. She went rigid.

"Going somewhere, doll face?"

Oh, God. She'd heard nothing. Not the rustle of clothing or the sound of footsteps. And where was Puma? "Chic Fillmore," she said. "Otherwise known as Bronco. So you brought a friend along."

"Got it in one," he chuckled. "My buddy's keeping your wimp-ass lover busy." He jerked her gun from her belt holster and tossed it away. "Turn around."

She faced the militant. An automatic rifle hung over his shoulder and a .357 magnum pointed at her chin, a Smith & Wesson revolver, heavy-duty enough to blow a hole in the side of a house. He wore night vision apparatus. Military issue. It explained how he had spotted her furtive movements. "You killed two FBI agents," she said. "Whatever happens to me, you and your buddy are dog meat."

He chuckled. "So if they find one more body, won't matter much, will it? Hell, let's make it two more. They can only pop me the needle once."

She bit her tongue. Goading him was stupid. Keep him talking. Puma will come. Sully went for help. "Look, if you cooperate, give us what we need to know—"

"Right," he snorted. "Shuck the goggles and drop them."

She complied, blinking. Green sparks swirled under her eyelids. Temporarily, she'd lost her sight and he had the weapon. He seized her by the hair, and once more the gun pressed at her throat. "How do you contact him?" he asked softly. "What's the signal? Don't lie, bitch. He'll come running if I shoot you."

She clenched her jaw. She'd never had a gun at her throat, and it was terrifying. She could use the radio, send a signal to Puma. She indicated her duty belt with a finger.

"Radio," she whispered. "One click means it's 'Go'. Two it's 'Hold off'."

He backhanded her. She fell to her knees and fought the urge to vomit.

"Liar." He wrenched her radio from its leather holder and clicked it on. "Ansari," he snarled. "It's over. Drop your weapon. Come into the yard, hands on your head or the bitch loses an ear and that's for starters. You know the drill."

He aimed and pulled the trigger. One shot. The blast was deafening.

Rachel screamed, her hand to her ear. No blood. Just the smell of singed hair.

"Oops," Fillmore cackled. "Next one I'll aim better."

"I'm on my way." Puma's voice came over the radio. Calm. Unruffled. Tears ran down Rachel's face. Still on her knees, she lurched at the militant's legs. The revolver crashed into the side of her head.

She came to gradually, face-down on the floor. Her skull felt like it had been used to kick the winning field goal. Her hands were lashed at the wrists, bound with the same cord that Lindy used to stake plants in her garden. She opened one eye cautiously. Lindy's kitchen. The lights were on. She could smell stale coffee.

"Roll over, doll face. I know you're awake." Rough hands jerked her upright. She looked into Fillmore's nasty grin and spat at him. He swore and yanked her to her feet, tossing her into one of the kitchen chairs. Her head banged against the wall. She closed her eyes and breathed deeply. Steady Rachel. Don't be stupid. Play for time.

"Fucking cunt," he said, wiping spittle from his face. He reached with one hand and squeezed her breast. Hard.

Bile rose in her throat. "He'll kill you."

"Ansari won't be killin' anybody. He'd be dead, if my partner hadn't butted in."

Rachel tried to think over the vertigo. How could she have miscalculated so badly? She'd been sure that Fillmore would come alone, that his cowboy mentality would dictate his actions. "The sheriff is on the way, and the FBI. I assume your partner is the smart one, given you have the brains of a gnat."

"Sticks and stones," he grinned. "I'm not the one trussed up like a turkey."

"Where is Ansari?"

Please, God. Puma was like the elements. The wind. The earth. Indestructible. The idiot grin widened, and she knew it was bad.

"My partner's havin' a discussion with him in the front room, but it seems the breed is sufferin' from a memory problem. Now that you're awake, maybe he'll be more talkative." Fillmore gave a sharp whistle. "Hey! She's come to!"

Sounds of a heavy blow, followed by angry curses. Moments later Puma appeared in the kitchen door, stumbling, prodded from behind by an automatic rifle. His arms were tightly bound and face bloodied. His captor struck viciously with the gun barrel and shoved. Puma fell heavily and didn't move.

"If he knows anything, Fillmore, he's not telling. Personally I don't think we have the time to break him."

Rachel froze, her eyes riveted on the man hidden in the shadows. Hope for rescue died. "Sully?" she whispered. "My God, are you part of this?"

Sully gave a mocking salute. "Hey, Rachel. How's it hanging?"

"I don't understand."

Chic Fillmore gave a whoop and slapped the counter. "Look at her face, boy. She hadn't a clue. Neither did her pet Injun."

"Don't call me boy." Sully's voice was soft, but it lifted the hair on Rachel's scalp. "Secure Ansari's legs while he's out. The man is dangerous in ways you can't imagine."

Fillmore shrugged. "Man's a pussy. Let us take him because of the bitch."

Sully sighed. "Forgotten those broken fingers? Tie his legs up and lash his wrists to the sink drainpipe."

Fillmore reddened and convulsively clenched his jaw. The fingers of his right hand were bound together with adhesive tape, the pinkie finger bent at an odd angle. He was holding his gun in his left hand. Puma had done that? The parking lot altercation? He'd been evasive about what happened.

"Whatever," Chic said sullenly. "No dice getting the FBI honcho's cell number from him, huh?"

"I'm beginning to think he doesn't know it. But Rachel does, don't you, sweet stuff?" Sully knelt in front of Rachel, the rifle casually across his knees. He reached and patted her on the cheek. "We need to contact your boss, Ms. Cortez. Directly. Not go through ten flunkies to get his ear."

She blinked and shook her head. He smiled at her with a sweet, angelic Sully look. She blinked again, hoping it was a mirage, knowing it wasn't. She licked her lips. "You mean Hooker? Who are you?"

"Right now I'm your friend, Rachel, standing between you and Chic here, and you can't imagine the games he wants to play with you." He patted her cheek again. "We have a message for your boss. What is his cell number?"

"I don't know. I only have the main office number."

"Tch." He clicked his tongue. "Wrong answer." He stood, the smile still in place. "Throw some water on Ansari, Fillmore," he said. "And pull off her sweatpants."

Five minutes later Rachel and Puma were propped side-by-side against the kitchen sink. Puma was bound knee to ankle, his wrists anchored to the drainpipe. Rachel's hands were securely tied to the pipe also, but her bare legs were unfettered. She knew what that meant, and from the fury in Puma's face, so did he.

Fillmore frowned down at her. "Would you look at that? Ugliest damn legs I ever saw on a woman. Puts a man off of fuckin' her."

"From his expression, Ansari doesn't agree," Sully said thoughtfully. "I see why she always wears long pants."

"Go to hell, both of you," she hissed, and kicked Sully in the shins, bruising her bare foot. She knew struggling was futile. There were two of them and eventually they would do whatever they pleased to her body. But she'd fight them, kick and bite until her strength was gone.

A low growl came from Puma's throat, followed by a string of muttered vowels. Unintelligible, but menacing. Both men stepped back, Sully looking amused, Fillmore slightly alarmed.

"I believe we've been cursed, Fillmore." Sully said, laughing. His boot lashed out and struck Puma in the ribs. "Shut up, Ansari. To paraphrase the movie lingo, I'm your worst nightmare."

Rachel couldn't believe the transformation. Sully, the shy, all-American boy, morphed into a snarling killer. She'd thought his bleached, spiked hair signified an effort to be with it, but she could see it now for a disguise. In profile the nose was hawkish, the black eyelashes and brows jarred with the shaggy blonde hair. He might have some Native American blood, and he was a lot older than nineteen. And he was educated. Not everyone used 'paraphrase' in a sentence. Whatever his background, he had to be one of the world's great actors.

Puma took the blow, showing no reaction. "You're a bad TV script, Sully. Or is that your name? I had you checked out before I hired you. Raised on a Nebraska farm, both parents dead, a juvie record of petty theft but nothing too serious. Will the real Brent Sullivan please step forward?"

"Sullivan?" Sully snorted in disdain. "A loser, and he doesn't need the name anymore where he is, fertilizing a Nebraska cornfield. Before Fillmore starts on your woman, you want to reconsider giving me that info?"

"Give him the number, Rachel. Now. Before this goes any further."

"Why do you need it?"

Sully looked amused. "You think I spent three months shoveling shit because I want you and the breed? You're bit players, sweet stuff. Both of you. It's Dan Hooker we're after. The man's causing us problems. So, you call him, set up a meet, and we'll take it from there."

"You use us to set Hooker up," Puma said matter-of-factly. "When he arrives, you'll kill us. Then torture Dan Hooker for what he knows."

"That's pretty much the deal," Fillmore interjected, chuckling.

"If that's true," Rachel said. "Why tell you anything?"

"Back off, Rachel," Puma said. "Give him the number."

Sully squatted in front of her. "See, Rachel, your lover understands the situation. We will get the number. How we get it is up to you." He swiveled and snapped at Fillmore. "Your cigarette lighter. We'll start with the bottoms of her feet."

"Rachel, for God's sake!" Puma sounded desperate. "Hooker can take care of himself."

She shuddered when Fillmore pulled his lighter from his pocket and snapped it on. Blue flame leapt from the silver cylinder. Talk. Stall. Those were their only options, because if he touched that flame to her bare foot, she'd tell him anything. "You're wasting your time," she said. "I don't know his private number. I can call the field office number and leave a message. He'll get back to me, but it might take a while."

"I get to do this part," Fillmore said, flicking the lighter off and on. "I kinda' hope it takes a while."

Sully shook his head. "We don't have time for this. Give me your gun."

Looking disappointed, Fillmore pocketed the lighter and handed over his magnum. "You shoot her, we won't learn anything. Careful, there's one in the chamber."

Sully expertly checked the weapon and aimed it at Puma.

"I'm not going to shoot her. I have another target in mind."

"Hey, don't forget, I'm in charge here! You promised I could do him. Som'bitch killed my brother."

Sully shrugged, lifted the gun and put three rounds squarely into Fillmore's forehead. The militant's head jerked backward and his body tumbled in a heap. He laid there, muscles twitching, his sightless eyes staring at the ceiling, his mouth a weeping red blossom of shock.

Rachel screamed.

Sully rolled the body over with a kick, bent and felt for a pulse. "Moron," he muttered contemptuously. "Just a little present from Frenchie."

Beside her, Puma laughed softly, not looking surprised. He lifted an eyebrow. "Frenchie? Moving up in the food chain, Sully?"

"That's the idea," the other man nodded. "Just following orders to take out the trash. Frenchie calls the shots. Fillmore made the mistake of forgetting that." His face and eyes were empty of emotion.

"Whose?" whispered Rachel. "Whose orders? The one they call 'Four Star'? Do you know him?" This was what she had set out to do, to find the man behind the New Sons. The man bankrolling their terrorist activities.

"Four Star. Frenchie. Whatever." Sully shrugged. "Don't know him personally. He's a voice on the phone. Got a French accent. The man's set us up on a thousand acres of prime Montana wilderness, and he sends us money to get the job done. Lots of money. Good ole U.S. currency." He turned the gun on Puma. "Now, Ms. Cortez, the phone number, or guess who's next?"

She didn't have to guess. The demonstration had been adequate. She gave him the number, her lips stiff, her mouth dry. "That's his voice mail. You'll have to leave a message."

"Not me. You'll do the talking."

"I thought the phone and your cell were out of order," Rachel said.

"I lied. Tell your boss that Ansari has the place here

secured, and that you've got a possible location on Fillmore you want him to check out." He dialed, handed her his cell and held out a paper. "Repeat this message. I'm guessing he'll bust ass to get there. Tell him you'll meet him."

"Hooker's too smart. He'll bring backup."

"Not your worry, and it won't matter if he does. There are some real bad dudes waiting for him. I'd take you along, but it's too much trouble." He cocked the heavy revolver and pressed it to Puma's temple. "Do it. Make it sound good."

If she twitched a muscle, the gun would discharge. She recited the message, kept all emotion from her voice and omitted her ID number. Hopefully that would be enough to set off alarms at her boss's end.

"Okay." Sully clicked off, looking pleased. "Some last minute business, and I'm out of here."

He opened the backdoor and retrieved a gasoline can from the steps. From the way he hefted it, it was full. She and Puma watched silently while the ranch hand splashed gasoline around the perimeter of the kitchen, dousing the liquid on the walls and cupboards. He left the room trailing gasoline, and they could hear him opening windows throughout the house. The knot in Rachel's stomach tightened beyond terror. They were going to die in the most horrible way. The way her father and brother had died. The way Nita had died. A low moan escaped her throat.

"Shh," Puma crooned. His eyes were intent on the militant's actions. She knew the look. Puma would never stop planning and scheming, not until the flames engulfed their final screams.

Sully dropped the empty can, and dug the lighter out of the dead man's pocket. He paused and looked at Puma thoughtfully. "You know, Ansari, it might be a good idea to cap your ass first."

Puma didn't answer, merely stared at the other man, his eyes and face expressionless. The air shimmered with hatred. Sully's gun hand wavered as the two men crossed wills. Then the militant's eyes dropped, he tossed the gun onto Fillmore's body and moved toward the door. "Hell with it; I'll give you time to kiss goodbye. This place is built of seasoned cedar and dry as a bone. Won't be enough left of the three of you to fill a bucket."

He paused at the doorway, gave a mock salute, and touched the lighter to the pool of gas soaking the threshold. A peal of laughter echoed his disappearing footsteps, was drowned out by the full-throttled whine of his motorcycle. And more than that, she swore she heard the screams of a wild animal.

"Puma! Did you hear—?"

"Yeah. About time he showed up. Sully's in for a surprise if he thinks he's home free. That big cat can run forty or fifty miles an hour. Let's concentrate on our problem."

A ring of fire crept around the room, accompanied by the sound of her sobs. How much time did they have before the blaze reached them? Five minutes? Less? Already it curled up the walls, and smoke billowed in the air. The orange sheet of flames crackled and spread hungrily.

"Rachel," Puma said urgently. "Can you reach behind my back? They didn't find my knife."

Yes! The slim blade he kept in the sheath under his collar.

She wiggled and twisted sideways. "No," she gasped. "I'm tied too tightly."

"All right." He gritted his teeth. "We need to yank at the pipe. I'll count one, two, and we yank together on two. Okay?"

"Okay," she said. Their bindings were tough and unyielding. The pipe was soldered to the wall, but it was all they had.

"One," he said. "Two!" They yanked together. The pipe didn't budge. The cord cut cruelly at her wrists. Neither fiber nor pipe gave a millimeter.

"Again," he said. Counted and yanked. "Again!"

The flames had leapt into the living room. She could hear the greedy roar as the fire met fresh fuel and air. The fire rose to the ceiling beams. The smoke thickened. Her lungs burned. The heat grew to the unbearable. Each time they yanked, the cord cut deeper. Blood streamed down her wrists and hands. "It's not working!" Rachel cried.

"Rachel, this is up to you. My hands are too big. I can't slip the cords."

She looked at his wrists. The bindings had sawed into his flesh. His forearms were bloody to the elbow. Several blood vessels had been cut. And still he rhythmically yanked at each cadence count. One, two, pull. The pipe gave slightly. If he could ignore the pain, so could she.

With the next pull, the cord slipped slightly. Her own blood was acting as a lubricant. Her fingers and arms were numb. She yanked again, methodically slicing her own flesh to ribbons. The cord slipped a bit more.

The fire reached Fillmore's dead body. His clothes caught. Then his hair. The smell of burning flesh mingled with the acrid vapor of smoke. "Puma!"

"Rachel, sweetheart, don't look! You have to do this."

She knew what she had to do. She gave one last fierce pull and slipped her bonds, her thumbs dislocated. The pain was agonizing. She fumbled at his collar and clumsily drew the knife from it leather sheath. She dropped the knife, her fingers numb.

"Good girl," he urged. "Try again."

The fire licked at Puma's boots, only inches from her bare legs. She sobbed and went to her knees, retrieved the knife and sawed at the tough binding at his wrists. It gave, and he seized the knife, quickly slashing through the restraints around his ankle and knees. The fire was almost on them now. The room was engulfed, both exits blocked. The smoke was dense as mud.

"Up into the sink," he urged. "Out the window."

She hoisted herself up. He landed right behind her; his heavy boots kicked and shattered the window frame. She jumped, fell hard and landed in a patch of juniper. The needles gouged her bare flesh, but broke her fall. Puma crashed beside her. He grabbed her hand and they ran. Behind them part of the roof caved in with an explosive boom. A fireball of heat and burning pitch roared toward the night sky.

CHAPTER 30

Smoke clogged the air and charred bits of debris rained from the sky. From the shelter of the barn, they watched while the flames that could have been their funeral pyre leapt toward the night sky. Rachel's breath came in gasps. "That was the most awful—"

"I know." He held her close. "But it's over." He smoothed her hair from her smoke-smeared face. "We got out because of you. Because you didn't panic."

"For years, I've been terrified of being caught in a fire again. It happened, and I didn't freeze."

"You were great." He kissed her. Not a passionate "Let's get it on" kiss, but a loving "I'm glad we're alive" kiss.

She leaned against the refuge of his body. "Your house is gone. I'm sorry. I know your grandfather built it brick by board."

"Joseph's main concern would be that we survived."

Did a chuckle emanate from the shadows in the back of the horse stalls? She swiveled her head, saw only dust motes hanging in the air, and blinked herself back to reality. Dragon was kicking frantically at the boards of his stall, whinnying the clarion call of a medieval trumpet. "You better see to the stallion. He's going to hurt himself."

"He can smell the smoke, and wants to go to his mares."

She sat on a hay bale while Puma tended to his high-strung horse. Dragon exited the stall jerking his head and fighting the halter, ululating his alarm, while Puma rumbled soft, soothing sounds. He trotted the stallion out of the barn, through the rail fence corral and out the gate that led to the pasture. The mares and colts milled in confusion, agitated by the roar of the flames. Freed from the leather lead, Dragon rose on his hind legs, gave a shrill whinny, and the herd thundered toward the broad expanse of meadow.

Rachel watched Puma silhouetted against the horizon, as the first pink wisps of dawn crept over the rise, the man rooted to the earth as firmly as an oak tree. She could never ask him to leave and she couldn't stay. She loved him, would never stop loving him, but he belonged here and it wasn't her world. Layer-by-layer, she would build a shell around the pain, until it was bearable, until it was something she could live with.

Puma visually tracked Dragon's path, as the stallion led the herd toward the sanctity of the high meadow. When laggards stopped to graze, Dragon circled and gave them a nip on the shoulder or rump to move them along. Puma's lips curved in amusement at the stallion's bullying. That was what a man did, wasn't it? Kept his family safe, whatever it took?

He walked back toward Rachel, deep in thought. After Sadie died, he'd determined to never remarry. It wasn't just the guilt he felt after the accident that killed her, it was the knowledge that he never wanted that responsibility again. Then Rachel came into his life. Rachel, with her spirit and courage, her loyalty and strength. And passion. God, she exuded passion.

He'd been content with his life the way it was. He had his sister, his nephews, Lindy and Frank to love, and they loved him back. That, and his work was enough. When his grandfather died, Puma could no longer ignore the heritage that conflicted him, a heritage he lived with but didn't particularly embrace. Strangely, much of the confliction was gone. He was who he was. Perhaps his conversations with his grandfather's spirit had been an illusion, but they had led Puma to see that contentment was not the same thing as happiness.

And Rachel made him happy.

She was still sitting on the hay bale, her eyes closed, a distant coolness haloing her taut body. Puma felt a twinge of apprehension. She loved him, he knew she did. But Rachel had her own demons to fight, and he didn't know how to help her. Ruefully he wished his life were as simple as Dragon's. A nip on the shoulder might get Rachel hot, but a tumble in bed wouldn't deflect her from the path she'd chosen.

She opened her eyes and he took hold of her brutalized hands. "That was gutsy, dislocating your thumbs like that. It must hurt like hell. We'll go to Frank's place. Clean and bandage your wounds. We need rest and food."

"You're worse off. Those cuts on your wrists go deep. I'm okay." She rubbed her arms, her wince denying her words. "I need to contact Hooker ASAP."

"Frank or Lindy might have left their cell behind. If not, I'll hike back to where we stowed our gear."

"No need. Sully lied. I checked the land line here in the barn, and it's operational. The sheriff and fire department are en route. The fire department already had an alarm out. Someone spotted the smoke and phoned it in. One of your neighbors."

"Figures. The possibility of a wildfire scares the hell out of everyone around here."

"I can't believe Sully's part in this. If the FBI puts out an all points, maybe it isn't too late to stop him. If he's going after Hooker, we need to warn him."

"Forget about Sully. He didn't get far."

She glanced at him with disbelief. "That rat took off on his motorcycle. He's halfway to Denver. How am I supposed to forget that? A crazy killer on the loose."

"Remember how my access road dead ends at the highway?"

"There's a steep drop-off on the other side of the guardrail," she said, nodding. "Where're you going with this?"

"How fast do you reckon Sully was driving? With the big cat chasing him?"

"Sixty per, at least."

"At that speed, it took him three, four minutes to reach the crossing. And his brakes weren't worth shit. He would've smashed right through the guardrail. If he's alive, he won't be in good shape."

She gaped at him. "You jimmied his brakes?"

"Uh-huh. Before I let them disarm me."

"You let them?"

"Not that I had a choice."

She swallowed. "If you knew Sully was involved, why didn't you tell me?"

"I wasn't sure. Sully wasn't much of a hand, but he wasn't clumsy. His rifle shouldn't have fired when he fell. The safety was on. Looked deliberate, like a signal."

"So when you were prowling around the barn, you cut his brake line."

"Figured if I was wrong, I'd owe him a repair job. And if I was right, he wouldn't get far. Sully always did drive that cycle too fast."

He grinned as she clamped her jaw shut, shook off his arm and stomped toward the LeChat's bungalow. It was unusual for Rachel to have nothing to say.

CHAPTER 31

Two hours later, Rachel sat at Lindy's kitchen table, her emotions a tangled mess. There was the memory of the cold steel of Fillmore's gun pressed against her throat, of the odor of the man's burning flesh, of Sully's nasty smirk as he left them to the same fate. There was the overwhelming relief that the ordeal was over, that she and Puma had survived. And there was anxiety. Her lover had put his anger at her duplicity aside, but it still simmered, and she was in for the mother of all dressing-downs. Her mood was a strange combination of exhaustion, guilt, and elation.

They had showered, tended to each other's wounds. She wore one of Lindy's robes, and Puma had found one of Franks' plaid shirts and a pair of worn jeans that stayed put when the belt was cinched. Currently he was at Lindy's stove, scrambling eggs, after refusing her offer to help. His air of calm was an illusion. Underneath the cool facade there simmered one angry jungle cat.

Hooker and his team were on the way. The local sheriff had secured the crime scene, and stood guard over the murdered FBI agents. His deputies had found Sully's body at the bottom of the ravine across from Puma's property line, a few yards from his wrecked motorcycle, his neck broken, claw marks on his body. Nearby she could hear the shouts of the fireman as they doused the last of the dying embers, ensuring they didn't flare up and spread.

For the first time in weeks there was nothing to do, nothing to worry about. It was a strange feeling.. Hooker had let her know that her role in the investigation was over. Not the investigation, just her part in it. She had no idea where she was headed next.

Puma plunked a platter of sausage and scrambled eggs in front of her. "Eat something. You must be starving."

She stared at the food, stomach churning. She wasn't sure she could lift the fork. He sat across from her and attacked his own plate of food. She swallowed a sip of coffee. "It looks good," she said. "I didn't know you could cook outside of a campfire."

"Enough so I won't starve to death. I'm not in Lindy's league."

"Me, either," she admitted and picked up her fork. "Mostly I defrost and microwave. Guess you should know that about me." She took a bite. It was good, and she was hungry after all. Neither spoke again until their appetites were satisfied.

He pushed his plate away and gave her a steady stare. "We're due to talk, but maybe it should wait until after we get some rest. We're both beat."

"I want it over with. You don't like Hooker or trust him. You're furious with me for not telling you what was really going on. I get that."

"That covers part of it." His eyes blazed. "And there's this. If you and your hotshot boss had let me in on the scheme, I would have volunteered to be your bait. Gladly. After I got Frank and Lindy out of the picture. An old man and old woman, Rachel. Total innocents and sitting ducks for Fillmore's viciousness. Just pawns in the game you and your fed boss are playing. That's no kind of life to live. I want you to resign and get out."

She rose from the table, her legs unsteady. "You've no right to make that call. If my job bothers you that much,

Hooker will be here soon and I'll leave. There's no need for us to see each other after today."

He touched her cheek, but she pulled away. "There's all the need in the world. When people love each other, they forgive. They work things out. Leave the Bureau. Come live with me."

She stepped back. "That's it? Chuck eight years of my life?" She paused when his words caught up with her. "You love me?" she whispered. "When did that happen?"

"I don't know. I didn't plan on it, but it happened. When did it hit you?"

"I never said—"

"Am I wrong?"

If there was one thing Rachel had learned, it was never lie to herself. But there were too many obstacles. "Whatever it is, it isn't love. It can't be."

He scraped back his chair and stood. "Because it won't be easy? Because there're thorns in the rose garden?"

She shook her head, fighting tears. "Because it's impossible."

"What about this?"

He pulled her close and she went limp against him. She'd been in torment, needing his touch for days, had been afraid it would never happen again. He traced the outline of her mouth with his fingertip, his touch delicate. She licked her lips, her mouth aching. His tongue went to the hollow of her throat and slid to the crease above her collarbone. Raw need spurted through her belly.

He kissed her mouth softly, thoroughly, a tingle down to her toes kiss. She wrapped her arms around his neck and held on. The kiss deepened and she was lost. She sank into the texture, the taste of him, wanting more of his heat, needing it.

"Stay with me," he whispered, when he broke the kiss. "It's right. You know it is."

One last time, she promised herself. At least I'll have that. A memory when the loneliness became too much. Because life without him would be forever lonely. His hands slid down to her hips. He wanted her as badly as she ached for him. His hand slipped under the robe and cupped her bottom, lifting her and rubbing his erection against her sweet spot. She cried out at the stab of pleasure. "Tonight," she said, shaking with lust. "I'll stay tonight. Take me to bed, before I die!"

"Just tonight?"

"I can't stay. You know that. But we can have this." She reached for his kiss. The hunger to have him inside of her raged out of control.

"No," he said, let her slide down his body and stepped away. "That's not enough." He ran his fingers though her hair, his mouth set in a thin line. "I'm going to bed. Alone. If you change your mind, you know where to find me."

Despite the warmth of the kitchen, the cold of winter closed over her heart.

CHAPTER 32

Five months later

The sharp scent of pine permeated the last warm breath of the season. Golden aspen leaves rustled in the autumn wind like sheaves of ripe wheat. Rachel walked up the brick path toward the trailer where Puma lived. This was the craziest thing she'd done in her life, but she was desperate and out of options. When your man wouldn't accept your calls or answer your texts, when no amount of groveling would soften his unreasonable attitude—well, she hoped Hooker knew what he was talking about.

She pulled the boonie cap Puma had given her low on her forehead. It gave her courage, and maybe he would see it as a symbol of the first time they had made love.

The ashes from the fire had been bulldozed away, and trees planted over the foundation of Puma's former home. The roofed framework of his new house rose against the darkening sky, set slightly back from the old location. It was going to be larger, and a two-story. She supposed with the fire season done, he'd be working on it fulltime. Lindy and Frank would have retired to their place by this time of night. Puma would be alone. She knew he was home because his pickup was parked in the driveway, and a flicker of light shone from the trailer windows. The metal door stood ajar. She knocked.

"It's open," Puma's husky voice came from inside. "C'mon in, Tim."

"Ahh, it's me." The words came out a shaky squeak. "Could you help here? I've got my hands full of pizza."

"What the hell?"

The door swung wide and Puma stood there, unshaven, bare-chested and barefoot, his hair too long and shaggy. Much like the first time she'd seen him, except his eyes were set in deep hollows and he looked awful. He looked wonderful. Her naked legs trembled under the Nomex jacket and her bare feet rattled in her logger boots.

She hiccupped. "Ah, hi."

He nodded acknowledgment and his scowl deepened. "What are you doing here? I thought you were in DC, saving our country from evil. Didn't Hooker offer you the job?"

"If you'd answered my phone calls, you'd know he did. Can I come in?"

"No."

Well, that was plain enough. She thrust the pizza at him. "Here, take this. I'm following Hooker's orders."

He widened his stance and blocked the doorway. "Don't you always?"

She bit her tongue. The words had come out wrong. She and Hooker were on Puma's short list of People Never to Trust Again, and if anything she'd made him colder and angrier. "Okay, I'm not following Hooker's orders, just his suggestion. If you'll let me come in?"

"If this is a peace offering, tell the man, thanks, apology accepted and we're square. Good enough?"

"That's it? You're going to brush me off? Not give me a chance to explain why I'm here?" She felt her cheeks warm with the beginning of temper, and she'd promised herself she'd stay calm. Talk to him reasonably.

He dropped the pizza on the miniscule table inside the trailer door. "Some things don't need explaining. You got what you were after. A federal commendation and a big promotion. Thanks for the pizza. Don't slam the door on your way out."

He turned without a backward glance. But he'd read her texts or he wouldn't know about the promotion.

"Puma! Dammit, you'll listen if I have to follow you to hell. After that, if you don't want me around, I'll leave."

He swung on his heel and snarled. "And yet, you're still here. What's it going to take, rookie, for you to get the picture? You made your choice. We're done, finished."

She took a deep breath and slowly unsnapped the top buckle of her Nomex jacket. "I didn't take the job, you jerk. I came to tell you that."

He narrowed his eyes. "You're kidding. It's what you wanted more than air."

"No. What I want more than air is you." She undid another buckle. "I transferred to the Denver office. Happens it's only an hour drive from here. A snap, after fighting DC traffic the past months."

"What? No!"

"Oh, yes. I have a week off and then I report. The SAC agreed to give me time to unpack. FYI, everything I own is stowed in my SUV. Parked in your driveway."

"Huh?"

She sighed and undid another buckle.

He swallowed. "Ah, Rachel?"

"Yeah, baby?" She said softly, feeling the vibes. She almost had him. She undid the last buckle and the curve of her breasts appeared, followed by her bare navel. Even a blockhead like Fletcher Ansari should be getting the message.

"You're naked under there," he said, his voice hoarse.

"Uh-huh. Since you've stonewalled me for months, I asked Hooker for advice. How can I get a bonehead, mulish male's attention? Know what he said?"

Puma made a strangled sound she took as interest.

"He said, 'Show up naked. Take food.' So here I am."

She unfastened the last buckle and spread her long legs.

The bulky jacket sagged open, barely hanging on her shoulders. Underneath she had on a tiny black G-string. She'd rouged her nipples. She could feel them tighten and her breasts plump under his burning gaze. "Remember me?"

"Holy mother." He seemed to be choking and the bulge in the front of his jeans was nicely prominent.

"Sometimes Hooker has good ideas. Want a little of this, big guy?" She dropped the jacket to the floor, smiled and crooked her finger.

She heard a gurgling noise behind her, and whirled in shock. A young male was standing in the doorway, his jaw dropped to his Adam's apple, his brown eyes large and round as platters. She shrieked and grabbed the jacket from the floor, using it to cover her naked body.

Puma stepped in front of her, blocking the view. She wanted to laugh, but it came out a sob. "Oh, damn. This is beyond embarrassing."

"Rachel, this is my nephew, Tim," Puma growled. "He's staying with Frank and Lindy. Going to college in the Springs, and helping us out on the ranch. Tim, this is Rachel, the love of my life. You didn't see her naked, did you?"

Tim swallowed. His Adam's apple bobbed. "Ah, no, Unk. Sure didn't. She's wearing a yellow raincoat, far as I can see."

"Good. Then I won't have to explain your early death to my sister." Puma scooped the pizza box from the table one-handed and tossed it to Tim. "Take the provisions down to Frank and Lindy. Have a party on us."

Tim stood frozen, his eyes still glued on Rachel. She cowered under the coat, biting inside her cheeks to keep the laughter from bubbling out.

"Party?" Tim asked, the same stupefied expression on his face. "Ah, can I borrow the pickup, Unk?"

Puma handed over the truck keys. "Tim, I'm losing patience. Take the pickup and the pizza. Look up one of your girlfriends. The usual curfew. Be here in time for morning chores."

"Yeah, okay." Tim shambled toward the door, backwards. Slowly. Obviously reluctant to leave. Sweat beaded on his forehead.

"Out!" Puma growled. "Or I shove the pizza up your ass."

"Ah, yeah. See ya', Unk. Rachel, nice to meet ya'." He bobbed his head and took flight. The screen door screeched on its hinges and slammed behind him.

Puma shut and locked the heavy metal door, leaned against the wall, his nostrils flared, a feral gleam in his blue eyes. "Now, rookie," he purred. "Message received. Where were we?"

"Have you been as miserable as I have?"

"Worse. Abysmal, terminal funk. Can't get a rush jumping out of an airplane. Food tastes like sawdust and I sleep lousy."

"You could've taken my calls. Answered my texts."

"Yeah." He shrugged and sighed. "I was pissed. You left me, remember?"

"Okay," she said, nodding. "I was pissed, too. You didn't give me much choice. You're so damn bossy with that "my way or the highway" ultimatum. But at least I tried to talk to you."

"Point taken. I was giving it another week. Then I was hopping a plane and dragging you here by the hair. Since I'm building the house for you, the least you can do is kiss the owies when I hit my thumb with a hammer. Are you letting your hair grow?"

She ruffled at her shaggy locks, which had reached the I Can't Stand It stage. "You like it long. So I thought I'd let it grow back."

"I don't care what you do with your hair, rookie," he said softly. "I don't care if you're bald." He gave her that hot, dark look that made her toes curl. He opened his arms.

She jumped and he caught her, staggering slightly. "Bed," she said, biting his neck. "And fast."

Luckily it was only a few strides to the cubicle that served as his bedroom, and she was already naked. He stripped off his jeans in two blinks, and she was flat on her back underneath him. "We talk later," he gasped, parting her thighs and ripping off the lacy G-string. "Now, we need this."

A tear slid down the side of her cheek. She had missed him so terribly; if she died at that moment it wouldn't matter. She tried to tell him how much she loved him, but it came out a throaty croak. The tension of the past weeks ebbed away and she surrendered to the bliss of their lovemaking.

When she opened her eyes, a sliver of moonlight peered under the curtain of his bedroom window. She lay sprawled on top of him, totally content. "Hey, sleepyhead," he whispered, as his hand stroked her bare bottom. "I thought you'd never wake up."

"Mmm. Don't bother me." She wiggled against the smooth warmth of his chest, settling in for another nap. "This is the first sleep I've had in months."

"Really?" His hand continued to stroke. "Why's that?"

She yawned. "That damned cougar. Every night, I drift off and he sits on my chest and licks my face. I swear, I wake up with his slobber running down my chin. I'm sure it's a crazy dream. But it's freaking scary."

He laughed softly and nibbled her neck. "I haven't seen him lately. I wondered where he'd gone. I'd guess he's checking no one else is in bed with my woman."

The stroking and nibbling was getting to her, pulling her out of the lassitude of sleep. "Lech. It's the middle of the night."

"Tough. I'm not done yet," he said, and rolled her under him. She suddenly was wide-awake. He most assuredly wasn't done yet.

This time their lovemaking was a joyful melding of souls, neither of them in a hurry to end it. Dawn was streaming into the window when they went over the rainbow one last time. She came back to earth languidly, never more content in her life.

"Nice," she sighed, enjoying his pleasure as much as her own.

He flipped on his back, gasping for breath. "My God in heaven. Oh, my God."

She bit his earlobe. *Got him.* "See what you've been missing?"

"Smart ass. You hit high-C over high-C with that last one. Tell me you didn't."

"I did," she admitted. "You melted my toenails."

"Now that you've had your way with me, are you sure about us?" he asked softly, stroking her face with the back of his fingers.

"Never more. You?"

"Rookie, you couldn't get rid of me with a buffalo gun. We went crazy last night. You could be pregnant."

"Guess you'll have to marry me. Because if I'm not now, I want to be soon. When can you finish the house?"

"Sooner than I planned, it seems. What will the Bureau think of a pregnant agent?"

"The Bureau has found political correctness. I'll get maternity leave. By the way, Hooker says if you don't marry me, he'll have to shoot you. He wants to be best man."

Puma laughed. Not just a chuckle. He roared.

*Turn the page for an
excerpt from*

DUET

I'm Your Man Series
Book Four

Blaine Kistler

Part One: Bad Girl

May swallowed the last of her martini, and signaled the woman behind the bar. "Another clear, Hoppy. Three olives this time."

Hoppy removed May's special vodka from the fridge, and using a fresh, chilled glass, poured her another. Speared three fat green olives. No vermouth. Then slid the brimming martini toward the woman she considered her best customer. She sure as hell was the best tipper. Anytime May patronized Essence, Hoppy went home with two pristine Jacksons in her pocket. Paid in advance.

It was May's favorite bar. Besides pouring a great martini, May trusted Hoppy not to serve another customer from the Ciroc Ultra-Premium stashed under the counter. With money no problem, it was May's booze of choice. Straight up, the first-class vodka had a fresh, clean taste. And never a hangover. At twenty bucks a shot, none of the other customers would be interested anyway. It was Hoppy and May's secret that the contents of the pricey bottle had long ago been consumed, and now contained only mineral water.

"Better cash it in, girlfriend. Those olives'll get you every time."

Keeping up the pretense, May shook her head. "Not a problem. I'll leave the ragtop parked and call Uber."

"Here's a thought. Loan me the Mustang and I'll drive you home myself. And stay for breakfast."

They fist-bumped, snickering at the inside joke, and Hoppy went on to her next customer. Both of them knew May would suffer a colonoscopy before she'd loan anyone her classy black convertible. And Hoppy had a steady girlfriend.

May chewed on olive number five, savoring the saltiness. God, she missed drinking. Six months without a cigarette and a proper drink. The only vice she had left was sex, and that was currently off the table. She'd given up the cigarettes to shut down Carolyn's nagging. Surprisingly that had proved a good thing. For the first time in years, May could climb stairs without gasping for breath. One time when Mom knew best, it seemed.

But temporarily swearing off booze and sex? That was May's personal atonement for Billy. If she'd been a better mother, Billy would still be alive. Only God knew when the burden of his death would become bearable. If ever.

She should be at a meeting tonight, but wasn't in the mood. While Carolyn attended al-anon and prayed for May's soul, May brooded at the local pub. So far the praying hadn't helped. May's soul refused to be saved. And what the hell good had an innocent soul done her son? Tonight boredom had overcome the guilt. So instead of showing up at AA, May had parked herself on the corner barstool at Essence, looking for some action.

She'd missed the saloon's atmosphere as much as she missed the booze---the polished oak table tops, the knock-off Tiffany hanging lamps, the fake ferns. All tacky elements in daylight, but magic when the sun went down. She glanced around the neighborhood hangout, soaking up the ambiance. These were her people. This was where lost souls came to find themselves.

"Drowning your sorrows tonight, May?"

Startled, May turned to the man who had taken the empty bar stool next to hers. Damn, the last thing she needed was another hustler. He looked vaguely familiar. On second thought, not possible. Standing at six plus feet, probably one-eighty pounds of ripped testosterone. Cropped brown hair, pale blue eyes, opaque with secrets. Wearing pressed khakis and an open-throated black golf shirt. Too neat and classy for this place. Mid-thirties, she figured. Clean-shaven, unlike ninety percent of the current scruffy crop of male barflies. This guy she would've remembered. He was male to the max. Her scalp tingled a warning.

"You've lost me. Do I know you?"

He shrugged and tipped his bottle of Sam Adams toward her in a silent toast. "Not yet. I'm hoping that will change. Dan Harper, pretty May."

"Go away. It's creepy that you know my name and I don't know you." She rebuffed him with reluctance. Six months ago she'd have been straddling his lap. If any guy could break her chastity vow, this one might.

He set the bottle down. "Huh-uh. Not so much creepy as costly. Twenty bucks, actually."

Ahh, Hoppy, of course.

May glared at her friendly neighborhood bartender and extended her middle finger. Hoppy returned the gesture and mouthed *You're welcome.*

"Sorry you're out the twenty. I'm not interested in company."

"Okay. So why are you here at the local pickup bar?"

Good question. The truth was that abstinence aside, May enjoyed flirting and stirring up male lust. Sex was out for now, so the fun came in leading the suckers on, then dumping them. It was a daring game she played when she was bored, edgy and depressed. Tonight she was wearing her best slut outfit: tight and short black leather skirt, clingy white tee-top that dipped to sinful cleavage, and four-inch red sling pumps. Score.

She smirked at Dan the hustler. "What does it look like? Having a quiet drink. Alone."

"Yeah. About that," He snared her martini glass and took a sip. "Pricey bottled water. What's up with the charade?"

May froze in shock. No way Hoppy would've given her secret away. "Hey, what—"

"Let's say I'm observant. Your third double martini in less than an hour, and you're not the slightest bit tipsy? Pretty good act though. So far you've shot down two guys who snapped at the bait. Got a reason for the 'come and get me boys' act? You and the bartender got something going? I'd bet my next paycheck you're as hetero as I am."

This could be an interesting night after all. May did love a challenge. Her fingers lazily ruffled her short, dark curls, and she gave him the sassy trash smile. "I'm briefly on the wagon. A Ciroc martini is better than sex any day. Take my word on it."

"Your opinion. I'd say it depends on who you're having sex with. You'd do me fine. Looking for trouble, May?"

"Sorry, you're not what I'm looking for. What part of Not Interested didn't you get? I've got Ciroc, I don't need you."

"What you need is a spanking and a thorough fuck. Didn't your mother teach you it's dangerous to goad a grown man, May?"

The evening definitely was looking up. "Ooo, interesting line. Does it usually work?"

"Not a line. Just my opinion. Want to fool around some more? Or shall we get to it? Your play, your teenage game."

Okay, now she was flummoxed. The scalp tingling increased. He'd caught her out, and the charade wasn't fun anymore. Her voice came out a croak "Just go away."

He slid the beer bottle aside and propped an elbow on the bar. His cold eyes narrowed, his tone became soft. "Let's say I was interested in sabotaging an airplane. Hypothetically. For whatever reason. How would you suggest going about it, pretty May?"

Oh, shit, she'd been blind-sided. Who was this guy? A cop? Maybe. Or maybe something worse. What she'd feared for months was happening. *Keep your cool, May baby. And get out of here. This guy isn't going to play nice.*

She swung her purse over her shoulder and stood on shaky legs. "Sorry. Gotta go."

"Was it something I said?'

May didn't bother to answer. And she didn't look back.

Dan Harper, aka Dan Hooker, watched as May bolted across the dimly-lit barroom, out the door and into the humid Florida night. He was surprised. It was an interesting beginning, but disconcerting. And demonstrated that while he knew a lot about her, he knew nothing.

He hadn't expected her to panic, and it never paid to underestimate your prey. Some of the men in her past had made that unfortunate mistake. His detective buddy, Bry McNair, had passed on photocopies of May's official police records, along with the opinion that not only was May manipulative, she was far more intelligent than most people realized. Bry had parted with the file reluctantly, and Dan figured there was some past history involved.

No question May was smart. It had taken six months to find her. And that was with covert help from some of his ex-buddies at the Bureau. Since Dan was on an official FBI leave of absence, formal help was out of the question. May had escaped arrest with enough cash to buy a new identity and start her life over, but it was harder to leave old vices and habits behind. He'd been sure when he found her, she'd be holding up a barstool somewhere.

In the end it hadn't been the Bureau's considerable expertise that had exposed May's whereabouts. It had been Carolyn Diedrichsen who'd led him here. Carolyn, a Grandmother who couldn't let her grandson's life be forgotten, a grieving Grandmother who had arranged for fresh flowers to be placed monthly on Billy Diedrichsen's grave.

Dan had yet to discover what May was fully capable of. But along with the sexy package, the lush mouth and body that gave a man wet dreams, he knew she was deadly dangerous. And he believed she was an ice-blooded murderer.

⬥

DUET

Summer, 2018

THE
I'M YOUR MAN
SERIES

ABOUT BLAINE KISTLER

After a twenty-year career of teaching the language Arts, I'm pursuing my dream of writing stories. I write the kind of relationship stories I find intriguing and passionate. Hopefully my readers will enjoy the *I'm Your Man* series, because stories are meaningful only if they have an audience.

The most important thing in my life is family. I grew up the oldest of six girls, and while we live widely separated, our love keeps us close in heart. After writing, I enjoy reading, swimming and cooking. I love flowers and animals of all kinds. Flowers give us beauty and animals give undemanding love, asking in return only that we are kindly caretakers.

As my characters are on a journey of discovery, so too am I.

You can contact me through my website

www.blainekistler.com